WHEN
SECRETS
STRIKE

Center Point
Large Print

Also by Marta Perry and available from
Center Point Large Print:

Search in the Dark
Abandon the Dark
The Rescued
The Rebel
Where Secrets Sleep

**This Large Print Book carries the
Seal of Approval of N.A.V.H.**

WHEN SECRETS STRIKE

—House of Secrets—

Marta Perry

CENTER POINT LARGE PRINT
THORNDIKE, MAINE

The text of this Large Print edition is unabridged.
In other aspects, this book may vary
from the original edition.
Printed in the United States of America
on permanent paper.
Set in 16-point Times New Roman type.

ISBN: 978-1-64358-228-3

Library of Congress Cataloging-in-Publication Data

Names: Perry, Marta, author.
Title: When secrets strike / Marta Perry.
Description: Large Print edition. | Thorndike, Maine :
    Center Point Large Print, 2019.
Identifiers: LCCN 2019013660 | ISBN 9781643582283 (hardcover :
    alk. paper)
Subjects: LCSH: Large type books. | Amish—Fiction. |
    GSAFD: Mystery fiction | Christian fiction.
Classification: LCC PS3616.E7933 W49 2019 | DDC 813/.6—dc23 LC
record available at https://lccn.loc.gov/2019013660

Dear Reader,

I'm so glad you decided to read my latest Amish suspense series. I always intended to make Sarah, the Amish quilt shop owner, the protagonist of this story. But as I began the planning, I became aware again of the difficulties involved in having Amish characters in a suspense novel. The Amish believe that faith means following Jesus's teachings, including the one about turning the other cheek. They will not return violence for violence, and of course suspense often does involve attacks, danger and threats. Obviously my Amish characters could not be police officers or use violence in any way against another person. As I wrote, though, I found that this seeming handicap brought an interesting facet to my characters, as they had to struggle against the temptation of anger and violence in the face of attack.

If you've read *Where Secrets Sleep*, I hope you enjoy revisiting familiar places, browsing in the quilt shop and catching up with what's happening in the lives of people you met there.

Please let me know how you feel about my story. I'd be happy to send you a signed bookmark and my brochure of Pennsylvania Dutch recipes. You can email me at marta@martaperry.com, visit me at facebook.com/martaperrybooks or at martaperry.com

Blessings,

Marta Perry

This story is dedicated to my husband, who always believes in me, with much love.

In nature there are neither rewards nor punishment. There are only consequences.
—Amish proverb

CHAPTER ONE

BE CAREFUL OUT THERE. Sarah Bitler smiled, thinking of her mother's familiar goodbye as Sarah had climbed into her buggy this morning. Mammi always said the same thing when any of her family left her sight. She'd really rather they stay safely on the farm, even Sarah, who was nearing thirty and had long since been accepted as a maidal, an old maid, by their Pennsylvania Amish community.

What was there to be careful of on this peaceful back road that wound between Amish and Englisch farms on its way to the town of Laurel Ridge? The route took a bit longer to reach her quilt shop than if Sarah had gone by the main road, but was worth it to keep her mother from worrying.

"Mamm is being a little silly, ain't so, Molly?" She could talk to her buggy horse out here without fear of being overheard. "There's not even a storm cloud in the sky today."

Molly flickered her ears in response to Sarah's voice and then broke stride. The mare tossed her head, snorting.

"What are you—"

Sarah stopped, seeing a few seconds later what Molly had sensed immediately. Smoke, snaking

9

its way up between the trees ahead of her.

"Someone burning trash, that's all." But doubt threaded her words. There was too much smoke for that, surely. Hard on the thought she saw the sparks shooting upward, landing among the trees. Her heart thudded in her chest.

Fire. The one thing that farmers feared most, especially in a dry summer like this one. She slapped the lines, sending the mare surging ahead. She'd have to see for herself what was burning.

Around the next curve in the winding road, the source was visible. Flames licked the back wall of a barn, and smoke billowed upward, fanned by the summer breeze. An unused barn, thank the gut Lord, part of the property belonging to an elderly widow who lived in town. No animals were in danger, at least, but if the fire spread—

Sarah froze for an instant, undecided. Race to the nearest phone to call for help? Or check first in case someone needed help?

A glimpse of the small cottage near the barn decided her. The cottage wasn't empty—Mrs. Everly let Gus Hill live there in exchange for keeping an eye on the property. Sarah had to be sure he wasn't in danger.

Turning an unwilling Molly onto the lane, Sarah touched her with the buggy whip, and they bucketed up to the cottage. Sarah jumped down from the buggy seat and raced to the door, her breath coming quickly. If Gus was there, surely he'd have smelled the fire by now. Unless he'd somehow provided himself with a bottle, in which case he could well be passed out and unaware of the danger.

"Gus! Gus Hill! Are you in there?" Sarah pounded on the door, glancing toward the flames that licked at the barn roof. "Gus!" She twisted the knob, and the door swung open.

A quick glance around the two littered rooms told her that wherever Gus was, he wasn't here. But the barn—

She ran back outside. The fire ate greedily at one corner of the roof, sending a shower of sparks toward the trees. He surely wasn't in there. He couldn't be. She should hurry to the nearest phone. But she couldn't, not without being certain.

Her breath catching, Sarah raced to the barn. The heat radiating from it was terrifying, but she had to look—had to be certain Gus wasn't in there. She grabbed the hem of her apron and held it over her mouth and nose. Eyes watering, she peered through the open doorway.

Empty—not even any old hay bales to feed the fire. And no crumpled body lying unconscious, either.

A timber crashed, flaming, to the barn floor, sending a trail of fire heading toward her. Sarah spun, fleeing to the buggy, not needing to use the whip to persuade Molly into a gallop. They jolted back down the lane, back around the bend. The Stoltzfus farm, that would be closest, and they had a phone shanty near their barn.

Molly raced up the Stoltzfuses' lane, heading straight for their barn as if it were her own. Sarah halted the mare at the phone shanty, stumbled down and grabbed the receiver, hitting 911. By the time she'd gasped out the information to the emergency dispatcher, Ben Stoltzfus was running toward her from the barn, followed by three of his sons, while his wife, Miriam, hurried from the house, wiping her hands on a dish towel.

"Was ist letz, Sarah? What's wrong?" Ben grasped her arm.

A fit of coughing seized her, and she could only point.

"Ach, how did we not smell it? Fire—the old Everly barn, ja?"

Sarah nodded, catching her breath. "I spotted it when I was passing. The sparks . . ." She didn't need to explain the danger to Ben. He was already turning to his sons.

"Buckets and shovels into the wagon, quick. We must keep the fire from spreading until the fire truck gets here."

Wide-eyed, the boys ran to obey. Ben raced for the paddock and his buggy horse.

Miriam had reached Sarah by then and wrapped

her arm around her. "You're all right? Komm, let me see. You didn't burn yourself?"

"No, no, I'm fine." A cough interrupted the words. "Just need a drink of water, I think."

"For sure. Into the house, now." Miriam glanced to the oldest of her daughters. "Emma, go and call the neighbors. Tell them the Everly barn is burning. Quick!"

Ten-year-old Emma paled, but she bolted to the phone shanty.

Suddenly weak in the knees, Sarah was grateful for Miriam's arm around her as they headed for the farmhouse. Miriam, like any Amish mammi, clucked and comforted and scolded all at once as she gently shoved Sarah onto a kitchen chair and then set a glass of water in front of her.

"You rest a minute. I'll start coffee. Lucky I have a couple of jugs of lemonade I can take over, too. The firefighters will need a drink."

Sarah nodded, accepting Miriam's automatic assumption that they would provide what was needed. It was what neighbors did.

"Maybe take drinking water, as well. I don't know what the water source is over there."

"Ja, that's true." Miriam bustled around, putting one daughter in charge of the baby and enlisting the other two in carrying jugs and cups to Sarah's buggy.

"I looked for Gus Hill." Sarah cleared her

13

throat and took another gulp of water. "No sign of him."

"He's never one to hang around if there's trouble," Miriam said darkly. "I don't know what Julia Everly pays him for looking after the place for her, but he's not worth it, that's certain sure."

Reluctant as she was to speak ill of anyone, Sarah had to admit that Miriam was most likely right. Gus was a fixture in the township, well known for his talent for getting by on the least possible effort.

By the time the buggy was loaded, Ben and the boys had already taken off in the wagon. The wail of a siren pierced the air. The fire truck roared by, followed by the usual cars and trucks carrying extra volunteers. Most of the able-bodied men in the area belonged to the volunteer fire company, both Amish and Englisch. Like Aaron King.

Sarah shoved the name to the back of her mind as she and Miriam drove Sarah's buggy in the wake of the volunteers. She had no right to be more concerned for Aaron than for any other of her Amish brethren. Now if she could only convince herself of that fact . . .

By the time they reached the Everly property, the barn was fully engulfed. Figures in yellow protective gear swarmed around it, but Sarah could see they were more intent on keeping the fire from spreading than on trying to save the structure. It was too late for that.

Molly whinnied, shaking her head nervously, so Sarah led her a short distance away and tethered her to a tree. Miriam had shoved a folding table into the buggy, behind the seat. They pulled it out and began setting thermoses and jugs on it.

Scanning the firefighters, all so alike in their gear, Sarah couldn't deny she was searching for Aaron. She caught a glimpse of a chestnut-colored beard, and her breath went out in an involuntary sigh of relief. He was there, of course, and he was safe. That slighter figure next to him was probably his teenage brother, Jonah. Aaron would be keeping a close eye on the boy.

The barn roof collapsed with a roar and a shower of embers, and for a few minutes the scene reminded Sarah of an angry beehive as the volunteers fought to extinguish the flying sparks.

Miriam caught her hand, and Sarah realized the woman was watching her husband. Ben leaned on his shovel, coughing, but a moment later he'd straightened and was back at work.

Finally the barn was nothing more than a sullen black heap, still sending smoke and fumes into the air. In twos and threes the firefighters began drifting over to the table, and Sarah and Miriam were suddenly busy pouring out drinks.

"Sarah?" The sound of her name had her turning.

Mac Whiting, Laurel Ridge's police chief, stood behind her, pulling a notebook from his pocket. He looked very official in his blue uniform with a weapon at his hip, and only the fact that she'd known him since childhood kept her from retreating into the usual Amish reticence when confronted with Englisch officials.

"Some coffee, Mac?"

He shook his head. "Save it for the guys who did all the work." He snapped his pen. "I understand you called in the fire."

"I was on my way to town. To the shop," she added, although Mac would know that well enough. "I saw the smoke before I came around the bend, and then I saw the flames. In the back, the fire was, then," she said, pointing.

"So you went over to Ben and Miriam's to call?" He jotted the information down, though what good it would do anyone, she didn't know.

"Ja. But I checked first to see if Gus was here. I pounded on the cottage door. No answer, but I was afraid he was asleep, maybe."

Mac grinned. "That's a diplomatic way of putting it. I take it you didn't see him."

"The door wasn't locked, so I checked inside, but the cottage was empty. Then I feared he might be in the barn." Sarah seemed to feel the heat on her face again. "I looked, but no—"

"You never go near a burning building!" Aaron King was suddenly at her side, looking as if he'd like to shake her. "Ach, Sarah, whatever were you thinking?"

His obvious concern warmed Sarah's heart despite the fact that he was looking at her as if she were an erring child.

"I was thinking same as you would have," she said, her voice tart. "If someone was lying there in danger, I couldn't just go away. And don't go telling me I shouldn't have, because I had to."

Aaron's hand closed around her wrist for an instant, and her breath caught. Then he let go, shaking his head, his brown eyes crinkling a bit at the corners. "You always were a stubborn one, Sarah Bitler. Quiet, but stubborn."

Too quiet, she couldn't help thinking. If she'd given him even a hint of what she felt, all those years ago, would it have made a difference?

"It's just as well she looked, or we'd have thought there was a body in there." Mac sounded practical. "We might have known Gus wouldn't be anywhere around when there was trouble."

That seemed to be the unanimous opinion of Gus.

"Julia Everly is going to be so upset." Sarah pictured the tart-tongued elderly woman. "She never would let go of this property, because her husband used to love coming out here. And now that she's laid herself up with a broken leg, she'll really be fretting."

"You mean she'll be calling me every five minutes to find out what progress I'm making," Mac said.

Sarah looked at him blankly. "Calling you? Why?"

"I'm the local fire marshal, remember? I'm supposed to have answers."

"Ja, but what could you do?" she asked. "The firefighters did their best. At least they kept the blaze from spreading. As dry as it's been, it's lucky the woods didn't catch."

"It's not about that." Mac frowned. "Look around you, Sarah. There's not a cloud in the sky. No lightning to set it off. Nothing combustible stored in the barn. No electricity, even. So how did the barn catch fire to begin with?"

Arson. She felt Aaron stiffen next to her. The word didn't have to be said aloud to chill the blood.

SARAH FINALLY MADE it to town by early afternoon. Instead of heading straight for the quilt shop, she drove the buggy down a quiet residential street. Her business partner, Allison Standish, would have things in hand at the shop, and Sarah felt compelled to visit Julia Everly. The elderly woman would certain sure be upset by the fire.

After tying the mare to a convenient porch railing at the modern ranch-style house, Sarah walked to the front door, mentally rehearsing soothing words. Julia was normally the feistiest of eightysomething women, but being confined

18

to a chair by a heavy cast on her leg had taken some of the starch out of her. Sarah had stopped by the previous week, bringing an apple crumb pie her mamm had made, and had found Julia surprisingly subdued.

The door opened almost before Sarah had touched the doorbell. "Oh. It's you, Sarah." Donna Edwards, a distant cousin of Julia's who made sporadic efforts to look after her, gave the impression that a welcoming smile was too much effort. "I was just trying to get my cousin to take a little nap in her chair. I don't think company is a good idea right now."

"I don't want to disturb her, but I thought she'd want to see me." If anything, Sarah would think Julia needed more company, not less.

Donna looked at her blankly, her thin face registering nothing other than a rather peevish attitude, apparently toward being interrupted. She reminded Sarah irresistibly of one of her mother's irascible hens.

"I was the one who discovered the fire," Sarah explained patiently. "I understood someone notified her, but—"

"Yes, of course." Donna's expression relaxed, and she fingered the glass beads that dangled over one of the frilly blouses she always wore. "You must think I'm half-asleep. Chief Whiting came by to let Julia know a while ago. I just didn't realize you were the one who'd found the fire."

19

Sarah nodded. "I spotted it on my way in to work this morning." She had a feeling she'd get tired of saying those words.

Donna glanced back over her shoulder toward the archway into the living room. "I'm sure she'll be glad to see you, but maybe later would be better. I don't want her upset any further."

Donna's air of authority was mildly annoying. Still, Sarah supposed she meant it for the best. "Well, just let her know I stopped by, and—"

"Donna? Who are you talking to? Why don't they come in? You can't expect me to get up and fight with this walker every time the doorbell rings." The voice came from the living room in a subdued bellow.

Sarah grinned. That sounded much more like Julia. "It's Sarah Bitler," she called.

"Well, come in. Why are you standing on the doorstep?"

Donna shrugged, rolling her eyes as she stepped back. "Try not to let her get upset," she muttered. "I thought I'd never get her settled down after that policeman left."

Nodding, Sarah went past her into the comfortable living room. Julia, unlike most of Laurel Ridge's wealthier residents, didn't live in one of the town's classic Victorian houses. After her husband's death she'd sold the place she'd always referred to as a mausoleum, and bought this small, convenient one-story rancher.

The living room was designed for comfort, rather than fashion, with a pair of recliners on either side of a fireplace, a welcoming love seat and built-in bookshelves that were filled primarily with bright paperbacks. A large-screen television sat at an angle to face one of the recliners, and as Sarah entered, Julia reached out to mute the game show she was watching.

"What's going on? Don't tell me Donna is trying to protect me again. I thought she knew better." Julia's round, wrinkled face was bright-eyed and sometimes a little malicious. Just now she darted an annoyed look toward the hallway.

Donna, shoulders stiff, obviously heard the words, as she was meant to. She marched toward the kitchen.

"You shouldn't tease her," Sarah said, avoiding the heavy cast on Julia's leg as she bent to hug her. "She's trying to take care of you."

"I hate to be taken care of." The older woman's tone was so sharp, Sarah knew helplessness was the real cause of her annoyance.

"Give your leg time to heal. You'll soon be able to handle things yourself."

She hoped that was true, anyway. At Julia's age, a badly broken leg could mean the end of independent living, and as far as Sarah knew, Donna was the only relative Julia had. In a typical Amish family, there'd be plenty of people to tend an elderly relative and it was taken for granted, but not so among the Englisch.

"Never mind telling me soothing things," Julia barked. "Sit down here and talk. I heard you're the one who spotted the fire."

Sarah nodded, pulling over a straight chair to sit on. Julia's short gray hair was ruffled, as if she'd been running her hands through it, and she glared at the cast as if it offended her. Obviously the only thing to do was to tell her the story.

"I saw the smoke when I was coming into town this morning. I supposed it might have been Gus burning trash, but as soon as I came around the bend, I saw the flames at the back corner of the barn."

Julia's jaw was clenched. "Mac Whiting said the barn was a total loss."

"I'm afraid so." Guilt pricked Sarah. "Maybe if I'd gone straight for a phone when I saw the smoke, the fire company would have been able to save it, but—"

"Nonsense." The word was sharp, and Julia gripped her hand for a moment. "Mac said you went looking for Gus first. Naturally." Her gaze searched Sarah's face. "He says they're satisfied Gus wasn't caught in the blaze."

"That's certain sure," she said quickly. "I looked, and the others did, as well. He wasn't there."

"I suppose he's staying out of sight, afraid I'll blame him." Julia snorted, her fears allayed. "Silly old fool."

Since Julia was probably a good twenty years older than her handyman, or whatever Gus claimed to be, the description didn't seem to fit very well. And Sarah had never thought of Gus as silly. He managed to eke out a living doing nothing much at all, and he had a weakness for drink, but he had a certain amount of shrewdness, as well.

"I know what you're thinking," Julia said unexpectedly. "You wonder why I bother with the lazy layabout."

Since that was just about what she'd been thinking, Sarah couldn't deny it. "It's not my business."

"Oh, he doesn't fool me any." Julia's eyes crinkled, increasing her resemblance to a mischievous monkey. "I know what he is. But my husband was never happier than when he was pottering around that piece of property, hunting and fishing with Gus. I'm not sentimental, but I just can't bring myself to get rid of the place, no matter how many offers I get."

"Have people been wanting to buy?" That surprised Sarah. She wouldn't have thought the property was that much in demand. It had been a farm once, but the fields were overgrown now.

"Had a call not long ago, but I wasn't interested

in selling the place." Julia brooded for a moment. "I suppose it'll be worth less now that the barn is gone. Maybe I ought to get rid of it before anything else happens." Her hands worked on the chair arms, as if she'd like to propel herself right out of it.

Concerned at her agitation, Sarah clasped her hand. "You don't need to decide anything right away. And I'm sure Gus will turn up soon."

Julia nodded, but she still looked upset. Hadn't Sarah agreed with Donna that she wouldn't upset her? She sought for some subject that would divert Julia's thoughts from a decision she clearly didn't want to make.

"By the way, did you hear about the quilt display we're putting together for the shop? It's Allison's idea. We're setting up a showing of some antique quilts. Allison thinks it will draw in customers from out of town."

Julia grunted something that sounded like agreement. "Probably will. Your partner's got a good head on her shoulders when it comes to business. But she'll never know as much about quilts as you do," she added, as if Sarah might be jealous.

"Ach, I was born knowing about quilting, I think, given the way my mamm and grossmammi love it. And with Allison being so smart about things like the internet shopping, we make a fine team, ain't so?"

"I guess you do," Julia said. "Good thing, too. A woman's got to be able to take care of herself in today's world. Even an Amish woman."

"Especially a single one," she said firmly. There was no point in pretending it didn't make a difference whether a woman was married or not. It did in a community like the Amish that was centered on family.

Julia's gaze seemed to search Sarah's face for a moment. She gave a short nod, as if satisfied with what she read there. "You know, I might have a few quilts to go in your display. Come to think of it, it's about time I got them out and did something with them. Donna!" She shouted the name loudly, and Sarah jumped.

Donna appeared in the doorway so quickly that Sarah wondered if she'd stayed within earshot. "What is it?"

"You remember those family quilts I showed you a few years ago? I'm going to lend them to Sarah for a display. Box them up for her, will you?"

"Box them up?" Donna's voice rose. "That was ages ago. I have no idea where those quilts are. I thought you got rid of them years ago."

"Of course I didn't." Julia sounded testy, and her eyes were dulled, as if she was tiring. "They're in one of those trunks in the attic. I can find them easily."

"You can't go climbing those attic steps with

25

your leg in a cast. You shouldn't do it anyway, not at your age."

It was inevitable that Julia would flare up at that. "My age has nothing to do with it. I'm twice as active as you are, except for this stupid cast."

"You don't need to . . ." Sarah began, but neither of them listened to her.

"I won't hunt through a bunch of old trunks for something that isn't there," Donna declared. "Sarah doesn't want them, anyway."

Sarah opened her mouth and closed it again, unable to think of anything that would resolve the sudden hostilities. As far as she could tell, this was what always happened when Donna got one of her periodic urges to take care of her elderly relative. They couldn't tolerate each other for long. The truth was that they were both stubborn and opinionated, and that inevitably led to a clash whenever they'd been together for a time.

"Sarah will find them for me. Won't you, Sarah?" Julia sent a triumphant look at her cousin and patted Sarah's hand.

"Ja, yes, of course," she said. "But not today," she added firmly. "I must get to the shop. I'll come another time and find them for you. We don't need them right away, in any event."

She rose quickly, before she could get more involved than she already was. "I'll see you soon."

"All right, all right." It was said in a grumbling

tone, but Julia sank back in the chair, closing her eyes briefly. Donna, with a speaking glance at her, accompanied Sarah to the door and opened it.

"Thanks for putting her off," she murmured with a glance back toward the living room. "I shouldn't have argued with her, but really, she gets to me. After all, here I am giving up my time to help her, and does she appreciate it? No."

"I'm sure she does, really." Sarah stepped outside, the heat of the July day hitting her.

"Well, I'm the only family she has, so I guess it's my duty." Donna assumed the air of a martyr. "Don't worry about those old quilts, now. She's so forgetful lately she probably won't even remember talking to you about them."

Forgetful? That assessment didn't match with Sarah's impression of Julia, but she certain sure wasn't getting into a discussion of Julia's mental state with Donna. Instead she gave the woman a quick smile and hurried to her buggy, relieved to get away.

AFTER SETTLING THE mare in the small stable behind Blackburn House, where her shop was located, Sarah rounded the massive Italianate Victorian mansion to the front door. She always found it hard to imagine that the building had once been a private home. Who could possibly need such an imposing residence? Amish families, even those with eight or ten children, were content with simple farmhouses.

Well, Blackburn House had long since been turned into shops and offices, and she was fortunate to have her quilt store in what had once been a fashionable parlor. Doubly fortunate, because her business partner was Allison Standish, the owner of the building.

Once she was inside the double front doors with their elaborate fanlight, Sarah could glance up at the marble hallway that stretched practically the depth of the building. The quilt shop was on the right, with a small workroom behind it, while to the left was the showroom for Whiting and Whiting Cabinetry, with its office. Toward the back, the bookstore and storage rooms took up the rest of the downstairs space. The cabinetry showroom appeared to be empty at the moment, which probably meant Nick Whiting was in the workshop behind the building.

The bell over the door jingled as Sarah walked into her shop, and Allison slid a bolt of fabric into place and hurried toward her. "Here you are at last. Nick said you probably inhaled some smoke when you were trying to find Gus Hill. We were worried about you."

Nick, besides being a partner with his father in the cabinetry shop, was the brother of the police chief, to say nothing of being a very special person in Allison's eyes. Most of the community expected to hear momentarily that they were engaged.

"Nick worries too much, if he said that. I'm fine. I stopped over to see Julia Everly. Did Nick tell you the fire was on property she owns?"

Allison nodded, her dark red hair swinging against her cheeks. "Is Julia all right? I haven't seen her in a few days."

Julia had been a close friend of Allison's grandmother, and Allison seemed to feel a special bond with the older woman on that account.

"I think so. Worried about whether or not she should sell the property, but I managed to distract her." Sarah's thoughts flickered to Julia's quilts, which might or might not be suitable for display.

"Everybody's worried about the fire, as far as I can tell." Allison glanced at the two customers who were browsing through the racks of fabric in the back of the store, and lowered her voice. "I didn't quite see what Nick and his dad were so upset about. Apparently the barn was empty."

"That's just it." Probably Allison, having spent all her life in the city until she'd come to Laurel Ridge in the spring, had little idea how country people felt about barn burnings. "There was nothing in that barn that could have started an accidental fire."

"You mean they think it was deliberate?" Allison shivered a little. "That's frightening." She had had a close encounter with a fire herself

29

not so long ago. She wouldn't have forgotten.

Sarah nodded. "There's nothing worse in a farming community than the idea that there's a firebug loose. It happened once when I was a child, and I remember it so well—Daad staying up at night, keeping watch, never knowing what might happen, afraid to leave the animals in the barn." It chilled her just to think of it.

"Still, there's no reason to believe this is more than an isolated incident."

Allison was obviously trying to look on the bright side, and she was probably right. They might well discover some innocent reason for the fire.

Sarah began to speak, but the words froze in her throat. From the firehouse down the street came an ominous sound as the siren began to wail its alarm. There was another fire.

CHAPTER TWO

AARON WALKED ALONG the edge of the corn-field between his parents' farm and the Bitler place. Or maybe *trudged* was a better word, he thought wryly. Fighting two fires in one day in addition to his usual work had taken something out of him.

He brushed his hand along the stalks of corn, registering the texture of the leaves. Too dry. If they didn't get a decent rain soon, they wouldn't have the winter feed they needed. He didn't want to think about the temptation the dry fields might be to a firebug.

But he had to think about it. Isolated farms couldn't rely on the fire department to get there quickly. He'd talk to Eli Bitler first off. They could set up a plan for looking out for each other's property. As word of the fires spread through the county, other neighbors were most likely doing the same thing.

Aaron had nearly reached the property line when he saw Eli striding toward the house from the barn. Eli was younger than Aaron's daad—probably not yet fifty, hale and vigorous. He wasn't one to stand back and see a problem without wanting to do something about it.

"Aaron." Eli raised a hand in greeting, but his

usual quick smile was missing. "You boys had a long day today, with the fire at the Everly place this morning and another one at Morrison's this afternoon. How bad was it?"

Aaron shrugged. "Just a small equipment shed at Tom Morrison's, and he was able to get his mower and garden tractor out before we arrived with the truck. Good thing, too." Tension seized the back of his neck at the memory. "Our equipment started giving us trouble right away. We were lucky to keep the fire under control."

Eli studied his face for a long moment. "That's bad news. All the will in the world won't help fight a fire if your gear isn't in shape."

"It's old, that's all." They turned, walking toward the farmhouse together. "We can't afford new, a small volunteer company like ours. The chief nearly had to call in the surrounding fire companies for help today."

The worry rode Aaron like a weight on his shoulders. The surrounding townships had small volunteer companies like theirs. Two fires in one day would be a strain on any of them.

"You want to come in?" Eli jerked his head toward the kitchen door. "Hannah's got some coffee in the pot and a fresh-baked peach pie."

Aaron's smile flickered. It would be a rare day when Hannah Bitler didn't have something baked fresh, the way those boys of theirs ate. "Denke, but it may be best we talk out here where the others won't hear. The fact is, there was no gut reason for either of those fires to start."

Eli nodded slowly. "I figured that was in your mind. It's certain sure been in mine since our Sarah came back with the story of the barn on the Everly property burning. No reason, and two fires so close together in one day has to mean someone started them, I'd think."

Eli looked toward his own barn. His oldest boy, Jonah Michael, usually known as Jonny, seemed to be teaching little Noah how to drive the pony cart, while Thomas sat on the paddock fence to watch.

"I remember the last time it happened. Years ago, it was, but they never caught the guy." Aaron had been just a boy then, but he'd taken turns with Daad standing watch, starting at every sound in the dark.

"There's more able-bodied men around here now, at least," Eli said, sounding determined to put the best face possible on bad news. "You and your brother and your daad, plus me and the Whitings." He nodded toward the next farm beyond the Bitler place, where Nick Whiting lived with his parents and Nick's small son. "I'm thinking we'll leave the dogs loose at night from now on. They'll give an alarm fast enough."

"If they're not off chasing a deer." Eli must have more faith in his dogs than Aaron did.

"Jonah and I will take turns walking around a couple of times a night. Maybe get Nick Whiting to switch off with us."

"You can count on me, too." Eli glanced down the lane at the sound of buggy wheels. "Here comes Sarah. If we're not careful, we'll have her wanting to join us." His eyes twinkled. "I hear you scolded her for getting too close to that burning barn this morning."

Aaron grinned. "She put me in my place pretty fast. Sarah might be quiet, but she's got a mind of her own."

The buggy drew up next to the porch, and Sarah's gaze went from him to her father. "What are the two of you conspiring about?" she asked. "You look like you're sharing secrets."

"Just talking about the fires," Eli said quickly. "Your brother will put the mare away for you," he added as Thomas came running up, obviously eager to be trusted with the job.

"Right. Denke, Thomas." She hopped down lightly before anyone could move to offer her a hand, making Aaron smile again.

Sarah was still as slim and active as she'd been when she was a young girl. He had a sudden vivid image of her chasing after him in some game they'd been playing, her braids coming loose and trailing out behind her. Her fair hair was smoothed back from a center part now, fastened in a thick bun under her snowy-white prayer covering. No one outside family or a spouse would see it loose again, and he found himself wondering how it would look.

"What are folks in town saying about the fires?" Eli caught his daughter's hand when she would have gone past them to the porch.

Sarah's normally serene expression sobered. "Same as you two have been saying, I'd guess. That there's a firebug loose. That maybe it's the same person it was the last time, since the police never caught him. Poor Mac is looking harassed already, I think. Nick told us he's reported it to the regional fire marshal. Why should anyone blame Mac for the fact that they didn't catch the arsonist before? He was just a boy then."

"Some folks are only happy when they have someone to blame for their troubles," Eli said.

Aaron's thoughts had headed a different direction. "It doesn't seem likely it's the same person. That must have been—what? Close to twenty years ago."

Sarah shrugged. "I know, but that's what some people are saying." She focused on him, her blue eyes filled with concern. "Are you all right? I heard you had trouble with your gear today."

Her caring touched him. "Nothing serious." Though he had to admit it could have been, if he'd been any closer to the fire when his mask

35

failed. "Some of our equipment is nearly as old as I am."

"That's terrible. Didn't we make enough at the spring sale to buy new equipment?"

The community spring festival in town raised money each year for the volunteer fire company, and Sarah, one of the hardest workers, would feel responsible.

"Ja, well, the money was put to gut use, but the trouble is that there's too much needs replacing. We'll have to rely on the neighboring companies for help in future emergencies, that's certain sure."

"You shouldn't have to take risks." Sarah's smooth forehead wrinkled. "We need to do something."

"There's nothing you can do."

"There's always something." Her sweet oval face was troubled. "There must be."

Sarah had a big heart—he'd always known that. She was a gut friend. He'd never been able to understand why she and Mary Ann hadn't been closer. They'd been neighborly, but never really friendly.

Still, women were unaccountable. As usual, thinking of his late wife made him feel vaguely uncomfortable and more than a little guilty. Logic said he hadn't failed Mary Ann, but his conscience seemed to declare otherwise.

Seeing that Sarah still looked troubled, he

managed a smile. "Don't worry so much. We won't take any needless risks. We all look out for one another."

His words did bring a responding smile to her face. "Don't bother telling me you're cautious. You all get so excited when the siren goes off that you don't think about a thing except getting to the fire, and you might as well admit it."

"Maybe there's a little truth to that," he said, relieved to see her expression relax. Sarah knew him too well for him to deny it. When you'd been friends with someone since childhood, there wasn't much you didn't know about the person.

That was probably why he enjoyed being around Sarah. Any other single Amish woman would be wondering why he hadn't remarried before this, with his wife gone for over two years. Maybe even flirting a little. And since he couldn't look at anybody in a romantic way since Mary Ann's death, they always made him uncomfortable.

But Sarah was different. He could be at ease with her because she didn't have any such notions. She was a friend, a good friend, and that friendship was all they needed from each other.

SARAH MOVED ALONG the rack of quilting fabrics in the shop the next day, sorting and straightening. Several women had come in earlier to choose fabrics for new projects, and that had entailed pulling out dozens of bolts to compare. They'd gone away happy, though, purchases under their arms, and that was what counted.

The shop was quiet now, with Allison having gone upstairs to her office. In fact, all of Blackburn House seemed still after yesterday's alarms. Too quiet? Sarah had begun to feel as if she were holding her breath, waiting for the siren to wail again.

Thank the Lord there'd been nothing more last night or today. Perhaps yesterday's fires had been simply a coincidence. She pulled out a bolt of cotton and restored it to its proper place among the green prints, running her hand along the smooth surface. Still, two unexplained blazes within hours of each other seemed to stretch chance a bit too far.

It was odd, surely, that both incidents had happened during the day. She'd think that an arsonist would be more likely to set about his misdeeds after dark, when there was less chance of being seen. She'd intended to mention that to Daad yesterday to see what he thought, but Aaron had been there when she got home, driving every other idea from her brain, it seemed.

Foolishness, that was what it was. Most people would consider her a sensible woman, but on that one subject, she was ferhoodled. Nowadays young girls, even Amish ones, seemed to fall in and out of love a half dozen times before settling down. Why couldn't she have done the same?

Sarah paused, cradling a bolt of material in her arms, a memory slipping to the surface of her mind for reasons of its own. She'd been the only girl in their small group of childhood playmates—Nick and Mac Whiting on one side of her house, Aaron on the other. During the school year they'd been separated, of course, with her and Aaron going to the Amish school, while Nick and Mac went to the Englisch one, but in the summers, she'd tagged along after the boys wherever they went.

Mac, lively and heedless, had usually been the one to dare the others into some foolish act—such as racing across the field where the bad-tempered bull was kept. No one would say no to a dare, even when they should have.

"If we all run at the same time, that stupid bull won't know which one to chase," Mac had insisted, and even at eight or nine Sarah had thought there was a fallacy somewhere in that argument. But she'd gone, running with the boys, hearing the bull snort with displeasure.

The pasture was uneven beneath her feet, and fear seemed to make her clumsy. She tripped, stumbled, and by the time she regained her balance, the boys were well ahead of her and the bull so close she could almost feel his hot breath. She wasn't going to make it—the boys had already reached the fence, but she'd never get there in time—

Then Aaron was running back toward her. He grabbed her hand, yanking her along—not toward the fence, but to the old apple tree in the pasture. The bull was almost on them when he'd boosted her up into the branches.

"Climb! Go!"

She scrambled up and then turned back, convinced she'd see Aaron flattened on the ground. But he grabbed a limb, swinging himself up and out of range just as the bull thundered past, and she'd never been so relieved before or since.

Funny. She still dreamed of that sometimes, hearing the bull thudding behind her, getting closer and closer. Sometimes in the dream Aaron reached her in time. Sometimes he didn't. She wasn't sure what that meant, if anything.

In any event, she feared she'd fallen in love with Aaron that day, and her stubborn heart refused to fall back out again, even when he'd married someone else.

The bell on the door jingled, so Sarah looked toward it, smiling in welcome. The smile faded when she saw Gus Hill slouched in the doorway. In his tattered overalls and stained T-shirt, he didn't look much like the typical quilt shop customer. As always, his faded baseball cap was pulled low on his forehead, and graying hair hung shaggy around his ears.

"Good morning, Gus. How can I help you?" Julia might have sent him along with a message, Sarah supposed.

His sidelong glance skittered along the rows of fabric, then focused on her. "Miz Everly said as how I oughta come by and thank you. Said you looked around for me when you spotted that fire yesterday."

So that was the reason behind his visit. If Julia directed Gus to do a thing, he did seem to do it, however much he might skimp in other ways.

"I was concerned for you," Sarah said. "I thought you might be asleep and not realize something was wrong."

Gus took a step closer, planting a probably grimy hand on a bolt of pale yellow cotton. She tried not to think of the marks he might be leaving. "If I'd a been there, I'd a smelt it for sure."

Sarah nodded, but she wondered. If Gus had been drinking, as Mac supposed, would he have been alert enough to notice? Folks said Gus was shrewd in his own way.

"Well, I was relieved to see you weren't in danger." And she'd also be relieved if he'd stop handling the fabric, but she could hardly say so.

Apparently feeling he'd satisfied his obligation, Gus started to turn away. Then he swung back, frowning. "Here—you didn't go in my house, did you? Nobody's got a right to go in my house without I say so." His voice rasped, and he glared at her.

A tiny shiver slid along her skin, making the fine hairs lift. "I just looked in to be sure you weren't there, that's all."

Maybe he was afraid she'd report to Julia on the state of the cottage. Julia probably hadn't been out there in months, if not years.

"Yeah, well, see you don't. Man's got a right to privacy in his own home, ain't he?" His tone returned to its usual complaining grumble, and Sarah told herself she must have imagined that note of menace.

"It's lucky you weren't home when the fire started. You might have been hurt trying to fight it on your own." She'd like to ease him toward the exit, but wasn't quite sure how to manage it. "You were out early, weren't you?"

Anger flared in his face, so quickly it startled her. "No business of yours if I was, you hear?" Gus took a step toward her, oddly menacing.

Sarah was suddenly aware of how isolated they were. No one else was in the shop, and the old building seemed to echo with the sound of his words.

Don't be ferhoodled, she lectured herself. Gus might be a bit disreputable, but he certain sure wasn't dangerous.

She straightened. Best to ignore his last remark,

she decided. "Thank you for coming by. I'll be sure to tell Julia about seeing you."

For a moment Gus stood there, close enough that she could smell the rank odor of his clothes. Then the bell on the door jingled, and he jerked around. In another instant he shambled out of the shop, brushing by Aaron King without a word.

Aaron frowned after him before crossing the space to her. "What was Gus Hill doing in here?" He studied her face, his brown eyes seeming to darken. "Was he bothering you?"

"No, no." Gus was harmless enough, despite his manner. "He came by because Julia told him he should thank me, but I could have done without the visit." She pulled the bolt of yellow cotton from the rack. Sure enough, there was a streak of dirt almost the width of the fabric.

Aaron grasped the bolt, preventing her from walking away. "I glanced in the window when I walked past. You didn't look right. That's why I came in."

"I'm fine." She would not be moved by the protectiveness in Aaron's manner. It didn't mean anything. "I was just cringing at his touching this material." She gestured toward the bolt, hoping she sounded natural. "Look at it. I'll have to cut off the end."

Without responding, Aaron took the bolt and carried it to the cutting table for her. She could feel his gaze on her while she moved behind the

43

table and picked up the scissors. Before she could cut, he put his hand lightly on hers, making her pulse jump.

"We're friends, Sarah. You'd tell me if something's troubling you, ain't so?"

"There's nothing. I'm fine." It took a conscious effort to draw her hand away from his. "What brings you to Blackburn House this morning? You're not shopping for quilting fabric any more than Gus was, that's certain sure."

She said the words lightly and was surprised by the way his brows drew down and his lips tightened.

"Aaron?" she questioned. "Was ist letz? What's wrong?"

His broad shoulders moved in a shrug. "Nothing's wrong. I came by to check on something with Harvey Preston, that's all."

Preston was the real estate agent who had an office on the second floor, and she couldn't help a natural curiosity about Aaron's business with him. "From your expression, you weren't happy with his answer, ain't so?" She smiled up at him. "We're friends, remember? You can tell me if something's troubling you." She repeated his words back to him.

Aaron started to shake his head and then broke off, his lips moving in an answering smile. "Guess I can't say it's not your concern, ain't so? You remember that I talked to Matthew

Gibson before he took off for Florida last fall?"

"You offered to buy his place if he was thinking of selling." Gibson's property was across the road from that of Aaron's family. It would make a nice addition to the farm, probably doubling the size.

"He hadn't made up his mind then, but he promised me that I'd have the first chance at it when he was ready to sell." Aaron's clear gaze clouded. "Well, I just found out that Preston was handling the sale for him, and the place is already sold without a thing being said to me."

"Aaron, I'm so sorry." She almost reached out to touch him before realizing that might not be the best of ideas. "It's hard to believe Matt Gibson would do that to you after giving you his assurance."

"Ja." Aaron ground out the word, his strong jaw tight under the chestnut beard. "It was his business, but I certain sure never thought he'd go back on his promise like that. Still, he's old and he's been sick. Maybe he just forgot about it."

"Is it really too late?"

"Preston says the papers are already signed. He apologized, but said Matt never mentioned a word about giving me first refusal. The place went to somebody from out of state." He shrugged again, managing a smile. "Well, it's God's will, ja?"

It was the normal Amish response when life didn't go according to their plans. It was God's will. "Maybe you'll find a place for sale that's even better."

"Nothing else is likely to be for sale along our road." He didn't sound optimistic. "Daad's place isn't big enough to support all of us, but with Gibson's land we'd have been okay, and my mamm and sister could keep watching my girls."

"I know," Sarah said gently. Aaron's two little girls, Anna and Lena, were the center of his life since Mary Ann's death, and of course Esther King was delighted to take care of them. It would be difficult for all of them if Aaron had to move farther from his folks to make a living.

"Well, there's no point in crying over spilled milk, I guess." The finality in his tone made it clear the subject was closed. Aaron glanced at the soiled fabric she had crumpled in her hand. "Are you going to try and salvage that piece?"

She could wash it and add it to the box of remnants she kept for people who needed just a small amount of one color. But the dirty streak on the pale color seemed to remind her of the discomfort she'd felt at being alone in the shop with Gus.

"Not worth it," she said, and tossed it into the trash. There was an end to it. She'd never felt uncomfortable being alone in the shop before, and she wouldn't start now. The shop was her creation and her haven, and it occurred to her that if she hadn't lost Aaron, she'd never have had the shop.

"Gut. I'll put this back for you." He started to pick up the bolt, but then stopped and grinned, looking for a moment like the boy he'd once been. "If you think my hands are clean enough." He held them out, palms up, as if for inspection.

She couldn't help looking. They were good, strong hands—hands that could do a hard day's work and yet be gentle enough to soothe a troubled child. For an instant she imagined them touching her, imagined having the right to hold them close against her—

Sarah yanked her mind away from such dangerous thoughts, hoping the warmth in her cheeks didn't mean she was blushing.

"You'll do," she said briskly. "Mind you put it back in the right place."

"Bossy," he said with a smile, and moved away.

By the time he'd completed that small task, Sarah had her breathing under control again. Aaron headed for the door, and she followed him with a question.

"Is there any news about the fire marshal getting involved yet?" As a volunteer, Aaron would probably know as quickly as anyone.

"Nothing I've heard. Since there wasn't any significant damage, it's not likely the state police marshal would get involved." Aaron stood frowning, his hand on the doorknob. "I have a bad feeling about these fires, though."

She nodded. "My daad must have gone out six times to check the barn last night. He's trying not to let the younger ones see that he's upset, but . . ." She let that trail off, knowing Aaron would understand.

"Anybody old enough to remember the last time we had a firebug has to feel that way." He rested his hand on the door frame.

"It's strange, isn't it, that the fires were during the day?" she said. "From the little I remember, all the ones before started at night."

"Maybe it means the firebug is getting bolder," Aaron said.

"You think it's the same person, then?"

He frowned, looking older for an instant. "I didn't at first, but I'm starting to wonder. Still, it's funny he'd be quiet all these years and then start up again."

"Unless something happened to set him off." She shivered. "That's what troubles me the most—the thought that there's somebody who's not right in the head getting pleasure out of seeing people's property burn."

"Ach, we shouldn't be talking about it." He seized her hands in a warm, strong grip. "We'll be giving ourselves nightmares, that's what'll happen."

"Better to be prepared than pretend it's not happening. And I told Daadi that I'll be doing some of those nighttime trips of his to have a look around, so don't you bother telling me anything different."

Aaron's fingers tightened at that, but finally he shrugged and released her. "I guess if your daad can't talk you out of it, there's no use my trying. Just be sure you call for help if you see anything, and don't rush in on your own." His gaze held hers, even though they no longer touched. "Promise me that, please, Sarah."

She could try telling him that her welfare wasn't his concern, but that would be a waste of breath, wouldn't it? "All right. I promise."

Aaron gave a short nod, brushed her fingers lightly with his and went out. Sarah stood for a moment, watching his tall, sturdy figure silhouetted by the light pouring through the glass panes in the door, and then turned back to the shop.

This was the life she'd chosen, she reminded herself. She had to be satisfied with it.

CHAPTER THREE

MOVING QUIETLY, AARON bent over the twin bed in which Anna slept. At eight, she seemed to be growing out of her clothes practically daily, so Mamm said, but when she was sleeping, with her small face relaxed, her lips a little curved, she was still the baby he'd marveled over when the midwife had put his firstborn in his arms. Her flaxen hair lay in neat braids on the pillow, and one hand curled against her cheek.

Aaron dropped a kiss on her forehead and moved to the other bed. Lena, six, slept as intensely as she did everything, a little wrinkle between her brows as if she concentrated in her dreams. Her hair, as light as her sister's, spread in wild abandon, having long since lost the ties that were supposed to keep it in braids at night.

Funny that neither of the girls resembled him or Mary Ann. They were much more like his sister Becky in looks. Smoothing the rumpled sheet over Lena's shoulders, he kissed her, as well. She turned a little, as if she felt his touch in her sleep, and then settled.

His heart always seemed to expand when he saw his precious girls sleeping. They were so vulnerable, so utterly dependent on him for their present and their future. He would do anything to assure that future.

The thought reminded him of the day's disappointment, and he was frowning as he tiptoed out into the hall, easing the door closed behind him. If he'd been able to buy the Gibson place, he wouldn't have to worry so much about providing for his kinder. Matt Gibson's action had been as surprising as it was upsetting. Aaron would never have expected the man to let him down this way.

He started down the stairs, running his hand along the banister worn smooth by generations of his family. He loved being back here in the house where he was raised, instead of the small house Mary Ann had wanted to rent on the other side of town. This was certainly the best place for his girls, with Mamm and Becky to look after them. The addition of the Gibson place to Daad's farm would have allowed that situation to continue. Now—well, now Aaron wasn't sure what to do next.

He'd probably vented a bit too much to Sarah, but it didn't matter. He hadn't wanted to let his parents see how upset he was, because they shouldn't have to worry about him.

But Sarah was safe. He could say anything to her and know it would go no further. Sarah was, as she'd always been, loyal and honest all the way through. She'd never told on him and the other boys when they were kids, even to save herself from trouble. He hadn't realized how close they'd been until adolescence seemed to push them apart with his sudden awareness of her as a female, not just a friend.

Mamm, Daad and Becky had gathered in the kitchen as they often did in the evening. He paused, rubbing the tension at the back of his neck and trying to erase his frown before he joined them.

As usual, Mamm was piecing together a patch for one of her intricate quilts. Becky, at seventeen nearly as skilled with a needle as Mamm, had material for a dress laid out on the table. Daad sat with a last cup of coffee, the Amish newspaper on his lap.

"They're both asleep, ain't so?" Mamm smiled at Aaron, her soft brown eyes crinkling behind her wire-rimmed glasses. "You don't find Anna and Lena awake and looking out the window at the stars, like you used to do."

"Sound asleep," he agreed. He considered a cup of coffee and decided against it. It didn't seem to bother Daad to drink it this late, but Aaron would be staring at the stars again if he had any. "Jonah is out, is he?"

Mamm nodded, sending a slightly worried glance toward his father. Sure enough, Daad rustled the paper with a bit of irritation.

"I don't see why the boy has to stay out so late on a weeknight," he muttered. "We'll have to yank him out of bed when it's time for the morning milking."

"Ach, Jonah isn't that bad," Aaron said peaceably. "He might be half-asleep, but the cows don't mind."

Daad didn't seem satisfied. "Wish I knew what he was up to. He's not near as responsible as you were when you were going through your rumspringa."

"Funny." Aaron grinned, catching his mother's eye to exchange a knowing look. "I don't recall you saying so at the time."

"Just leave Jonah to have his fun." Becky glanced up from her cutting, the scissors in her hand. "He's not up to any mischief, ain't so, Aaron?"

"That's right," Aaron agreed, although he knew Becky would gladly cover up for Jonah if need be. The two younger ones were so close in age that they'd formed a special bond, always looking out for each other. Much as Aaron tried to bridge it, the age gap between him and his brother was just too big for Jonah to confide in him.

Daad grunted, giving the paper a shake. "Hope you're right, that's all." He let the newspaper flop down again to look at Aaron. "You know, I was thinking about Matthew Gibson going and selling his place without a word to you. Seems to me you should write to him. Just ask him what happened."

Aaron shook his head. "It wouldn't do any good now. The matter's settled, from what Preston told me."

"Well, I'd still write." Daad's graying beard seemed to bristle. "Must be some explanation."

Maybe, but he didn't feel like ruffling any feathers over it. Matt Gibson had the right to do as he pleased with his property.

Daad looked as if he intended to press the matter, but before he could say anything else, an unexpected sound crackled through the quiet kitchen, startling them. Scarlet-faced, Becky dived for the drawer of the china closet and unearthed her cell phone.

"Sorry, Daadi. I forgot to switch it off." She turned with the phone in her hand. It was jingling a tune that was certain sure not typical for an Amish household.

Aaron fought to control his twitching lips. "Maybe you ought to see who it is," he suggested. Daad had tried to hold out against the use of cell phones, but as Mammi had pointed out, all the rumspringa teens had them, and Jonah and Becky must learn to be responsible with temptations if they were to live Amish.

Daad had given in, with the stipulation that the phones be turned off in the house. Now he frowned at Becky as she checked the screen. She looked up, puzzled. "It's from Nick Whiting. Why would he be calling me?"

Aaron's nerves jumped. "Check it. It might be important."

Becky glanced at their father, got a nod in response and clicked the phone. She held it to her ear, and Aaron saw her face lose its usual rosy color. She murmured something, clicked off and turned to him.

"Barn fire," she said, voice shaking. "At the Stoltzfus place. He says he'll be here for you in a minute."

Aaron didn't wait for more. He bolted toward the back closet where his gear was kept, grabbed it and plunged outside. By the time he reached the driveway, Nick's pickup truck came roaring toward him, its beams piercing the dark.

Scrambling in, he braced a hand on the dash as Nick made a fast U-turn and headed back out the drive.

"How bad is it?"

"Don't know, I just heard it's the barn." Nick's expression was grim in the reflected glow from the dashboard. "If they didn't get the animals out . . ."

He didn't bother to finish. He didn't need to. They swung onto the blacktop road, and Aaron could see it now—the red glow in the eastern sky that heralded a blaze, and someone's livelihood going up in smoke.

"No lightning tonight," he commented. "And Ben's one of the most careful men I know when it comes to safety."

Nick nodded. "Maybe this will get the state police fire marshal moving in our direction at last. Another fire can't be a coincidence."

"All three fires in the same area, too." *Our area.* "What's going on?"

There wasn't any answer to that, and they raced down the road without speaking, hearing the wail of the siren in the distance.

SARAH FELT HEAVY-EYED when she walked toward the shop the next morning. No one out their way had gotten much sleep the previous night, with vehicles racing along the road, and the scream of the sirens as additional fire trucks arrived from the adjoining township. When she thought of the loss to Ben and Miriam, her heart was even heavier than her eyelids.

The first person she saw at Blackburn House was Mac, leaning against the door frame of the shop. Waiting for her? She'd already told him everything she knew about the fire she'd discovered.

"Morning, Sarah." He straightened at her approach, giving her the mischievous smile she remembered from childhood. "Sorry to be your first customer, especially when I'm not even going to buy anything."

"I'd faint if you did. Or maybe I'd think you were sick." She put her key in the lock and entered the shop, turning on lights as she went.

Everything was just as she and Allison had left it the previous afternoon. How would she feel if, like Ben Stoltzfus, she'd lost something as crucial to her business as his barn was to him? Ben would put a good front on, she supposed, but gazing at the ashes of his fine big barn must be devastating.

"You look about like I feel this morning." Mac shoved his uniform cap back and tried to stifle a yawn. "Long night for everybody."

"At least you're getting paid for it." Nick came into the shop with Allison in time to hear his brother. "We volunteers do it because we're civic-minded."

Mac snorted. "If you think my salary covers all the extra hours, Mr. Mayor, you're dreaming."

Sarah smiled, knowing how Mac loved to tease his brother about his role as mayor of Laurel Ridge. "You boys behave, or I'll tell your mother."

For an instant Allison looked left out, not having shared a childhood with them, but then Nick put his arm casually around her waist, and her eyes lit with her love for him.

Nick focused on his brother. "Did you find anything at the fire scene this morning?"

"Are you asking me to tell official secrets?"

"No, I'm asking you to let us in on anything that half the town will know or guess before the day is out," Nick retorted.

"True enough," Mac said. "And what they don't know, they'll make up, especially when the PSP fire marshal arrives."

"PSP?" Allison questioned.

"Pennsylvania State Police," Nick said. "So they've agreed to investigate?"

Mac nodded. "The financial cost of last night's fire, combined with the fact that it was third in a string of fires, convinced them. And the truth is, they have more expertise in investigating fires like this than anyone in the county."

"Arson fires." Sarah said the words they were all thinking.

"The one at Stoltzfus's barn for sure." Mac's forehead wrinkled and he rubbed it, looking tired. "I'm no expert, but I found enough to convince me. I can't prove anything one way or the other about the first two, but . . ."

"But three fires in a space of a few days can't be coincidence," Nick said. Sarah looked at him more closely, realizing that one side of his face was reddened.

"Nick, were you hurt last night? You look as if you were burned."

"He was, but he won't give in and go to the doctor." Allison's arm tightened around him.

"The doc would just tell me to use burn salve, and I can do that without advice." The way Nick looked at Allison took away any hint of sharpness in the words.

For just an instant, Sarah felt a sharp pang of something she feared was envy. If anyone looked at her that way . . . She slammed the emotion down before it could catch hold.

"He's just being macho," Mac said. "He and Aaron King were the big heroes last night."

Sarah's breath caught. "What . . . what did they do?"

"Nothing." Nick sent a glare of annoyance at his brother. "Aaron and I were first on scene, that's all."

"And the two of you rushed into the barn to try and save the animals," Mac added.

"That was doing our job, not being heroic. Besides, Ben was trying to go in without any protective gear. I dragged him back out while Aaron opened as many stalls as he could get to." Nick's face turned bleak. "It was bad, hearing the animals we couldn't reach. The loft started to collapse, and for a minute I was afraid I was going to lose Aaron. But he got out just in time."

Sarah put a hand on the nearest table to steady herself, her heart beating so loudly she could hear it in her ears. Allison glanced at her and moved closer.

"Aaron's all right, then?" Allison said, obviously seeing more in Sarah's face than either of the men did.

"Burned his arm, that's all." Nick shook his head. "He wouldn't have, if we had some decent protective gear. We're using stuff we bought secondhand way too many years ago."

He's all right, Sarah repeated to herself. And he certain sure wouldn't want anyone fussing over him. Besides, she didn't have the right.

"That's terrible." Allison's tone was sharp. "You're going out risking your lives for the community. The least Laurel Ridge can do is provide the equipment you need to stay safe."

Nick shrugged, obviously used to the situation. "Laurel Ridge is a small town, and this isn't an affluent area. The fire company got a nice amount from the spring festival, but between repairs to the truck and replacing some equipment, it doesn't stretch very far."

Mac interrupted the argument that was obviously hovering on Allison's tongue. "Listen, I have to get moving, and I still haven't told Sarah why I came over this morning. Too many distractions." He looked meaningfully at his brother.

"Right, okay. You need to talk to Sarah. We'll be quiet." Nick touched Allison's arm lightly.

"What is it?" Sarah felt a flicker of concern.

"Nothing scary." Mac smiled. "I expect the fire marshal to show up this afternoon. You're one of the people he'll want to interview, so I thought I'd give you a head's-up in case I'm not with him."

Sarah clasped her hands together. "Why does he want to see me? I can't tell him anything." And despite dealing with Englischers daily in the shop, she wasn't comfortable with the thought of this unknown official. She'd conquered her shyness a long time ago with her own people, but outsiders were different.

"That's how they work. He'll talk to everyone I interviewed about the fires. Nothing to worry about. Just answer his questions the best you can, okay?"

She nodded, feeling tension in her neck as she did. "If you say so."

"Good. I'll come with him if I can, but he may want to interview people without me." Apparently having fulfilled his purpose, Mac headed for the door. "I have to get back to work. I'll see you later."

The door closed behind him.

"Now can I talk?" Allison's words rushed out. "We really have to think of something we can do. Both for that poor family and for the firefighters."

"You don't need to worry about the Stoltzfus family," Sarah said. "Everyone is rallying around to help—lending equipment and replacing that first cutting of hay they lost. The men are already planning a barn raising." Seeing that Allison looked doubtful, she smiled. "Really. We've done this before, you know. I'm not saying it isn't a blow for Ben and Miriam, but you'll be surprised at how quickly the barn will be replaced."

"She's right," Nick added. "The Amish take care of their neighbors. It's a lesson the rest of us could learn."

"There's still the problem of the fire company equipment." Allison wore a crusading expression. "Maybe some sort of fund-raiser would work."

Nick shrugged. "Maybe, but we just had the spring festival a couple of months ago. I'm not sure people would respond." Seeing that Allison didn't think much of his reaction, he added, "We ought to bounce some ideas around. I have to get back to work now, but I'll think about it."

"Do that." Allison shot him a determined look. "I'll talk to your mother. I'm sure she'll agree that protective gear for the firefighters is crucial."

Sarah hid a smile. Allison had gone straight for the bull's-eye. Ellen Whiting wouldn't be easily deterred if she thought her sons were in danger.

With a quick kiss for Allison, Nick left, heading down the hallway and to the detached workshop of Whiting and Whiting Cabinetry.

Chuckling, Sarah turned her attention to a

box of fabric they hadn't finished unpacking yesterday.

"What are you laughing about?" Allison joined her. "I'm right. We have to do something."

"I know." Sarah pulled out a bolt of cotton print in fall colors—orange, russet, gold and red. It might be July, but women who sewed would soon be looking ahead to the next season. "I'm just amused at how fast you figured out the Whiting family. Go to Jim for wise advice, but go to Ellen if you want something done."

"It wasn't hard." Allison pulled out another bolt, and they worked in silence for a few minutes.

Sarah felt her partner's gaze and knew she was going to speak. And guessed, too, the subject.

"You're not worrying about Aaron, are you?" Allison was predictable. "I'm sure if the burn had been serious, the EMTs would have taken him to the hospital whether he wanted to go or not."

"I . . . Was I very obvious? Did Nick or Mac notice?"

"I don't think so." Allison made a face. "When did you ever find a man who noticed emotional responses without being hit in the head by them?"

She had to smile at that. "I guess you're right. It just startled me, that's all."

Allison's gaze remained fixed on her face. "I don't want to pry. I know you cared for him but he married someone else. If you'd like to talk about what happened between you and Aaron . . ."

Sarah shrugged. Pulling out another bolt of fabric, she held it against her, hands smoothing the chintz. "Nothing happened. Not really."

She didn't talk about Aaron, though it was certain sure that her family had long since guessed. But she and Allison had formed a solid bond in the few months they'd known each other, and the longing to speak about the thing she held so tightly in her heart was strong.

Allison waited.

"You know Aaron and I have been friends since we were kinder." She smoothed her hand down the surface of the fabric again. "Friendship turned into love on my part. But not on his."

"He seems to feel close to you," Allison said. "Didn't he ever give you any sign that he felt something warmer than friendship?"

Her fingers tightened on the bolt, and she avoided Allison's eyes. "Once, maybe. When we were teens. He took me home from a singing, and I thought maybe that meant he was getting interested. But he never said anything. And then Mary Ann—"

"Mary Ann?" Allison queried. "Oh, right, the girl Aaron married."

Sarah nodded. "She was so pretty and popular. Everyone wanted to be around her."

"You mean all the boys," Allison said.

"Well, you can understand it. She made a

point of talking to me. She said that she really liked Aaron, and since he and I were such good friends, maybe I could give him a hint."

"And you did?" There was so much outrage in Allison's voice that Sarah stared at her. "Oh, Sarah. Why didn't you let her know what you wanted? Or better yet, let Aaron know?"

"I couldn't."

Allison didn't understand, but then, Allison hadn't been brought up Amish. And she didn't have a shy bone in her body, as far as Sarah could tell.

"It would have been impossible." Sarah took a breath, trying to ease the tension that came with remembering. "So I told Aaron that Mary Ann was interested, and . . . well, it went just as Mary Ann wanted."

Allison was silent for a few minutes, but Sarah could almost feel the thoughts teeming in her friend's mind. They emptied the box and broke it down before she spoke.

"Aaron's free now," she pointed out. "Maybe it's not too late. He's still around. Still your friend."

Sarah shook her head, busying herself with picking up the flattened box. "Exactly," she said finally. "I'm a friend. He's not likely to see me any differently now."

"You have to give him a hint. A strong hint." Allison leaned toward her, voice eager.

"Remember what I said about men and emotions? Just start him thinking, and let nature take its course."

"I can't." She put out a hand to stop Allison before she could bubble out with a list of suggestions. "Really, I can't imagine doing it. I'm not outgoing and confident like you."

Allison seemed to make an effort to restrain herself. "You should be. Confident, I mean. Look at all you've accomplished." She waved a hand to encompass the shop and its contents—the fabrics, quilts, wall hangings, all products of women's industry. "You might have been too shy to say what you wanted at sixteen or seventeen, but you're a grown woman now, an accomplished businesswoman."

Sarah's heart was so heavy she put her hand over it, as if that would ease the weight. It shouldn't still hurt after all this time.

"It's true that I'd never have imagined myself actually making a success of my own business. And I've learned a lot along the way. But that hasn't changed who I am inside." She patted her chest. "In here, I'm still the same person." She managed a smile. "Maybe it comes of being taught all my life to be humble. Whatever the reason, there are things I know I can never do, and telling Aaron how I feel about him is impossible."

Allison pressed her lips together briefly,

holding back with an obvious effort. "I won't argue. But I do believe you're capable of a lot more than you've ever thought."

Sarah just shook her head. Allison meant well. But Sarah knew herself. To speak out—to claim what she wanted—the very thought made her stomach twist. She would have to be content with being Aaron's friend, because she'd never have anything more.

THE STOREROOM AT the rear of Blackburn House was theoretically for the use of all the residents, but in actual fact, only the quilt shop and bookstore staff made much use of it. Sarah stacked a box on one of the metal shelves, making sure the contents were marked on the side facing front. She'd hate to become like the former bookstore owner, who'd had such a scrambled method of storing things that he'd never known what he had.

The poor man was gone now, and Emily, the new owner, was far more organized, if a bit dithery when things upset her. Sarah and Allison had become used to calming Emily down whenever business threatened to over-whelm her.

Sarah made a quick survey of their storage section, just to be sure nothing had been neglected. It wasn't too early to start thinking about Christmas fabrics, as the crafters in Laurel

Ridge would soon start working on Christmas gifts and items for the various bazaars and craft shows.

Satisfied that all was in order, she stepped out of the storage room, keys in her hand, her thoughts still occupied with possible orders, and nearly bumped into Harvey Preston, who had the real estate agency on the second floor.

"Sarah! Just the person I was hoping to see." His round, jovial face lit with a smile. Harvey, she'd always thought, had the perfect personality to sell real estate—outgoing, optimistic and soothing to the stressed nerves of sellers and buyers.

"How are you, Harvey?" She gestured toward the door. "Were you going in?"

"No, no. I don't have occasion to store much in there, with practically all my work done online these days." He waited while she locked the door. "I noticed you when I was coming down the stairs, and wanted to have a word."

"Of course." She couldn't help the curiosity in her tone. She and Harvey were fellow tenants, of course, but other than that they had little in common. "How can I help you?"

"I know you're a neighbor of Aaron King. A friend, too." He shook his head, his normally cheerful face sobering. "I suppose he told you about this business of the Gibson farm."

She nodded, not sure what, if anything, she

should say. But Harvey didn't seem to expect a comment.

"It's very distressing." He fell into step with her as she headed toward the shop. "I didn't know what to say to Aaron when he told me about the understanding he had with Matthew Gibson. I really knew nothing at all about it. If only Gibson had told me . . ." He let the words trail off, shrugging.

"It is a shame. And very unlike Matthew, to go back on his word to anyone." The man she remembered had always been the soul of honor— the kind of neighbor anyone would want.

"True, so true." Harvey nodded. "But on the other hand, his health hasn't been all that good lately, according to the conversation we had about the property. In fact, that's why he entrusted the sale to me, not even making the trip back to clear the house. Depend on it, he forgot all about his conversation with Aaron."

"I'm sure that's what happened," Sarah agreed politely. If Harvey had been taken by surprise by Aaron's visit, it was natural enough that he wouldn't have thought everything through. The situation had clearly been bothering him. "The King family certainly doesn't blame you for what happened."

"Are you sure?" His brows drew down, and he looked as woeful as someone with his round, cheerful face could. "I feel terrible about it, but there's simply nothing I can do. I wouldn't want to be on bad terms with anyone over it, especially not with any of my Amish neighbors."

Enlightenment dawned, and Sarah smiled. Harvey's real estate agency did a great deal of business in the area, and the Amish were the primary buyers and sellers of farmland. Naturally he wouldn't want to get a bad reputation with them.

"I don't think you need to worry about it." She stopped at the door of her shop. "I'm sure it's just as you say, and—"

Allison opened the door behind her. "Sarah, you'd better come in. The state police fire marshal is here to see you."

Harvey looked startled, as well he might, and Sarah's stomach seemed to do a somersault. She took a steadying breath. Mac must not have come with the man, or Allison would have said. Apparently Sarah would have to deal with the investigator on her own.

CHAPTER FOUR

"SARAH, THIS IS Norman Fielding, the investigator Mac sent over to talk to you." Allison gave her a reassuring look as she made the introduction. "I'll just get back to work while you talk."

The fire marshal turned out to be a diminutive man, barely her height, with the kind of wiry build that suggested he'd go on forever. Sarah guessed him to be about her father's age, with a thin, noncommittal face and a way of looking suspiciously over the top of his wire-rimmed glasses as he took down her name and address.

"Now, then, Ms . . . um, Miss Bitler, I understand you were first on the scene at the initial fire." In his clipped tones the fact sounded almost like an accusation.

"Yes, that's right. I saw the smoke when I was driving into town that morning." As often as she'd been over it, she'd begun to feel as if she could tell the story in her sleep.

"That's what I was told." He darted a glance around the shop. Allison was at the counter a few feet away, occupied with the quilt files but within easy earshot, and several women browsed through the racks. "Maybe you'd rather we talked in private," he suggested.

Allison flicked a frowning look in her direction.

"This is fine," Sarah said, trying to appear more at ease than she felt. "My partner knows all about what happened that day."

She thought Fielding seemed dissatisfied, but he didn't raise any objection. Sarah took a couple steps closer to the counter, which forced him to do the same. As Allison had pointed out a short time ago, she had gained a lot of confidence in dealing with the Englisch from running the shop. Still, her stomach seemed to churn at the idea of being questioned by this stranger and having everything she said put down in his report.

"Were you on your usual route to town?" He looked at her over the frame of his glasses. "You were coming here, I suppose?"

"Yes, that's right. And it's the way I normally come."

His eyes narrowed. "I've had a look at the area. That back road wouldn't be the most direct route from your home to the store."

Allison stirred, as if about to speak, but she didn't.

"I drive a horse and carriage back and forth. There's less automobile traffic on the road I take."

Fielding gave a rather disparaging look at her plain navy dress and apron. "That's an Amish thing, is it?"

Sarah nodded.

Allison took a step closer, and Sarah frowned

at her. Nothing would be gained by challenging the man's apparent ignorance of Amish customs. That is, assuming it was ignorance and not prejudice.

Fielding had moved on. "Now, about the smoke you saw. Can you describe it?"

Sarah blinked. How did one describe smoke? "It was just smoke. I thought it might be from someone burning trash, but it seemed too thick for that."

"What color? Brown? Gray? Black?" He snapped the questions at her.

Determined not to let him fluster her, Sarah took her time, trying to picture in her mind the moment when she'd first seen smoke rising above the trees.

"It was dark," she said finally. "Dark gray or maybe black."

"What is the significance of the smoke color?" Allison's curiosity had apparently gotten the better of her.

Fielding eyed her for a moment before deciding to answer. "Wood burns brown or lighter gray. Black signifies the presence of gasoline or some other accelerant."

"But . . ." Sarah frowned, visualizing the scene. "There wouldn't have been any gasoline stored in an unused barn. Anyone would know better than that."

At least, she'd think so. Gus Hill drove a

rattletrap old pickup that looked as if it were held together with binder twine, but surely he wouldn't do something so foolish as to store gas in the barn.

Fielding made a noise that might have been agreement. "Did you approach the barn once you got there?"

"I checked the cottage first, looking for the caretaker, but it was empty. Then I went to the barn. I had to be sure the caretaker wasn't inside, you see."

Unlike Aaron, Fielding didn't criticize that decision. "How could you see inside? Did you open the door?"

"No, I didn't have to. The door was standing wide open."

He nodded, and she understood now what he was thinking. Why hadn't she seen it before?

"The doors are usually closed. I've passed that barn a hundred times and never seen them standing open before."

"Why? I mean, what's the point of the doors being open?" Allison didn't bother to disguise her interest.

"Someone might have left them open to allow the air to get at the fire," Sarah said. "That would feed the flames."

"You seem to know a lot about it." Fielding peered at her again.

Maybe she'd better not volunteer opinions so

quickly, with the investigator writing down her words.

"Anyone who burns trash knows that much," she pointed out.

He made another note on his pad. "Could you tell where the flames were concentrated when you first got there?"

Sarah tried to put herself back in the jolting buggy, urging the frightened mare up the lane. The image rose in her mind.

"The two back corners," she said without hesitation. "At first I thought it was just one, but then I saw the other burning, too. I remember that's how it appeared at first, and then after I'd checked the cottage and looked again, the whole back was in flames."

"Moving fast?" He tilted his head to one side, his eyes intent, looking like a robin that spied a juicy worm.

Sarah shivered. "It seemed so to me. When I looked in the front to see if anyone was there, the flames seemed to race toward me across the floor in kind of a narrow path."

Fielding made a satisfied sound and jotted a few more words in his notebook. Then he snapped it shut decisively. "Good. That's all for now, but I might want to talk to you again."

Sarah couldn't imagine what else there was to say, but she nodded. "I'm usually here during the day and home in the evening."

"Don't take any trips without letting the police know," he said shortly, then headed for the door like a man in a hurry.

Allison waited until the door had closed behind him before she spoke. "Condescending jerk," she muttered. "I'd have told him a thing or two about his attitude, but I knew you didn't want me to."

Sarah shrugged. "He probably hasn't been around the Amish much."

"That's no excuse for rudeness," Allison snapped. "You are a witness, not a suspect."

"He probably thinks everyone is a suspect." She frowned, uneasy. "I hope he doesn't stir up trouble."

"What was all that about, anyway? You seemed to understand the importance of where the fire was when you first saw it, but I didn't." Allison pushed a wing of coppery hair behind her ear.

"When I drove up the lane, the smoke was coming from the two back corners." Sarah visualized the scene again. "I didn't even realize that until he asked me the question. Don't you see? An accidental fire wouldn't start in two different places at the same time."

"So that means someone started it." Allison considered the idea for a moment. "Well, we've suspected it all along, so I'm not exactly shocked."

"It means more than that," Sarah said, her voice dragging as she saw the implications. "It means that the fire had been started a short time before I saw the smoke. So when I reached the barn, the arsonist couldn't have been far away."

"You didn't see anyone? No, of course not, or you'd have said." Allison answered her own question.

"Not a glimpse."

Sarah had a sudden image in her mind of a faceless figure lurking in the woods, watching her run toward the barn, and her stomach turned over. He'd been there, whoever he was. He could have seen her, and she'd never known it.

"CAN WE GET any treat we want?" Lena tilted her head to one side and gazed up at Aaron as they entered the sunny interior of the coffee shop across the street from Blackburn House late in the afternoon. "A doughnut would make my arm feel better."

Anna gave her little sister a skeptical look. "Shots don't hurt after they're over," she pointed out.

"Lena was a brave girl when the doctor gave her the shots," Aaron said peacefully. "And you were very patient to wait. So you each get a treat, so long as you promise to eat your supper when you get home."

"I promise, Daadi," Anna said quickly, and Lena nodded vigorously.

Ella, the cheerful Amish widow who ran

77

the restaurant, came to the counter as they approached. "My, look at these two big girls. What brings you to town today?"

"I got my shots so I can go to school this year," Lena announced. "And we get to have a treat."

"That is a special event," Ella said. "It deserves a special treat. What will you have?"

While the girls pondered, pressing their faces against the glass case to debate the merits of crullers and peanut butter doughnuts, Ella glanced at him. Her perpetually flushed face was concerned.

"Have you heard? The man from the state police is in Laurel Ridge to look into the fires. And none too soon, I'd say. The damage—"

Aaron shook his head, glancing at the girls. They'd had enough trauma in their young lives with losing their mother. He didn't want them losing sleep fearing a fire.

Ella, stricken, snapped her lips closed and seemed to be trying to think of something else to say. He saw that Anna was watching her, apprehension lurking in her blue eyes.

"Anna and Lena. How nice to see you today." The door closed behind Sarah, and she advanced on his daughters, smiling. "What are you doing in town?"

Lena, distracted, began to repeat the story of her injections. She even insisted on pushing her sleeve up so Sarah could see her bandage.

"You'll be all ready for school, won't you? And you're so lucky." She reached out a hand to draw Anna closer. "Because your sister is going into third grade already, and she knows everything there is to know about first grade. She can tell you all about it, ain't so, Anna?"

Anna brightened, clasping Sarah's hand. "Ja, that's right."

Aaron watched, smiling a little. What a shame it was that Sarah had never married. She'd certain sure have made a good mother, seeming to understand his kinder by instinct. He'd never pictured Sarah, of all people, being a maidal. But when he thought about who she might have married, the question stymied him. Was there anyone he'd have thought good enough for his friend?

Still chatting to them about school, Sarah got the girls settled at a table, and Ella brought them their doughnuts.

"Ach, I'm sorry," the widow said softly, when both women came back to the counter. "I wasn't thinking, that's for sure. You don't want the little ones worrying about somebody starting fires."

"No harm done," Aaron said. "Sarah distracted them." He smiled at her. "What brings you to Ella's? A late lunch?"

Sarah shook her head. "Ella has promised me a quilt her great-aunt made—for our display. So I came to pick it up and save her a trip."

"I have it here for you." Ella dived behind the counter and emerged with a quilt wrapped loosely in paper. "It ought to have the binding mended or even replaced, but I'm too busy in the shop to find the time."

"It's lovely," Sarah said, turning back the paper to reveal a Log Cabin design, its deep colors faded to a mellow tone. "We're happy to have it to show." She held it so he could see.

But Aaron wasn't especially interested in quilts, at least not at the moment. "I heard the state police fire marshal talked to you already."

She nodded, a shadow coming over her face. He saw her glance at his arm, obviously knowing he'd been burned, but his sleeve covered it. "I guess he's going to talk to everyone who was at the fires. He seemed convinced, I thought, that the one I saw had been deliberately started."

"I'm not surprised. We'd figured it out already. I just hope he can find the person who's doing it before it gets any worse."

Sarah clutched the quilt against her, as if for comfort. "It's terrible, wondering who it could be."

Aaron wanted to reassure her, to say that nothing bad would happen. But how could he? None of them knew that for sure.

"We're keeping watch," he said, fearing it wasn't enough. If someone was out there looking for a chance to set a fire, he'd find one.

The bell on the door jingled as a customer entered, and he recognized that cousin of Mrs. Everly's. She hurried to the counter, and he stepped politely out of her way as she nodded at Sarah and set an oversize purse on the counter.

"A loaf of cinnamon raisin bread for my cousin," she said to Ella. "She says she's hungry for it."

"Right away." Ella beamed, happy to have her baking expertise noticed.

"How is Julia today, Donna?" Sarah asked.

"Not as good as she thinks." The woman shook her head, pressing her thin lips together. "Like this cinnamon loaf. By the time I take it to her, she'll have forgotten she asked for it. I'm telling you, she gets more and more confused every day. I don't know what I'm going to do with her."

Sarah's gentle face seemed to tighten. "I didn't find her confused when I visited her," she said.

"Yes, but you're not there every day, like I am," the woman said quickly. "You don't know. And much as I hate to say it, having visitors just makes her worse. Anything out of the ordinary is upsetting. All I can do is keep her as quiet as possible. People should be more understanding."

"Julia always enjoys chatting when I come by." Sarah said the words carefully, keeping her tone mild.

But Aaron knew his Sarah well enough to

recognize the annoyance lurking in her eyes, and it surprised him. Obviously her caring extended well beyond her own family.

That shouldn't be a surprise, he told himself. Sarah was a woman now, and those qualities of kindness and caring she'd shown as a child had grown with her.

"Yes, well . . . I think I know my cousin best." Seizing the loaf of bread from Ella, the woman flounced off.

Sarah looked after her, worry lines forming between her brows. "Julia didn't seem nearly that bad the last time I talked to her. If Donna is right . . ." She let that trail off and shook her head. "Maybe Allison and I should drop in on Julia. She's wonderful fond of Allison because of her friendship with Allison's grandmother."

"Don't look so worried. Maybe the woman is exaggerating." Aaron brushed Sarah's hand with his, wishing he knew how to remove the stress from her face. "You don't have to take care of the whole world, you know."

Her lips seemed to tremble for an instant, and then she pressed them together. "If someone needs help, I can't pretend it's not my concern," she said.

No, he supposed she couldn't. It wasn't in Sarah's nature to ignore her responsibility to a neighbor, no matter who that neighbor happened to be. And he wouldn't want to change one thing about her. His little playmate had grown into an admirable woman, and that fact battled with a startling need to protect her from discomfort.

SARAH FOUND HER thoughts returning to Julia Everly that evening. Washing dishes while Grossmammi dried and Mamm put things away, she felt more than usually thankful for family. Grossmammi would never have to think of growing old alone. She'd live and die surrounded by those who loved her, unlike Julia Everly.

Julia had friends, of course, acquired over a long life, but her tart tongue had sometimes isolated her. And Donna Edwards, a several-times-removed cousin, was apparently her only family.

Mamm flicked the dish towel at her. "What has our Sarah so silent tonight?"

"Ach, I was just listening to the two of you." Mamm and Grossmammi had been chatting away as they always did, and no one listening to the love flowing between them would think Grossmammi was Mamm's mother-in-law, rather than her mother.

"You listen to us every day of your life," Grossmammi said. "You are fretting. Is it about the fires?" She lowered her voice on the last word, as if hating to say it aloud.

"No, well, not at the moment, anyway. I was thinking about Julia Everly. I ran into Donna today, and she says that Julia's memory is failing her. I thought Julia was fine when I talked to her, but Donna seemed convinced."

Grossmammi listened to her account of Donna's words, her gray head tilted to one side like a tiny snowbird. Never more than an inch or two over five feet, she'd shrunk in recent years. But her eyes still held their sparkle, and her fingers had never lost their cunning with a needle.

"It does sometimes happen that a person might perk up for a visitor but show more loss to the one who cares for them every day," she said when Sarah had finished. "Your grossdaadi was like that, remember?"

Sarah nodded. "But we were all around, so it was as if he had company all the time, ain't so?"

Grossmammi chuckled. "That's certain sure. And he loved it." Her smile faded a bit. "Julia doesn't have any kin except for Donna, so I've heard."

"Donna said Julia would be better off if people didn't drop in to see her, but that seems so wrong to me. Julia enjoys visitors. I'd think she'd be better off with more, not fewer."

Mamm opened her mouth as if to say something and then frowned, shaking her head a little. "If her doctor thinks that . . ."

Her words trailed off as she glanced toward the window over the sink. "Someone's coming. That's Allison's car, ja?"

Sarah put the last pot in the drainer and dried her hands. "I hope nothing's wrong. She didn't mention stopping in tonight."

"I'll put the kettle on." Grossmammi hustled to the stove. "Allison always likes a cup of my mint tea. She says it's soothing."

In another moment Allison was coming in the back door, too much at home in the cozy kitchen to need to knock when she spotted them through the window. Greeted with hugs, she was soon ensconced at the long maple table with a steaming cup of mint tea, while Mamm tried to persuade her to have just a sliver of blackberry pie.

"A tiny, tiny piece," Allison agreed, laughing. "I know what your slivers look like."

"There's nothing wrong, is there?" Sarah poured tea for her grandmother, as well, before sitting down.

"No, but I had an idea. You know, about needing to raise more money for the fire company." Allison's green eyes lit with enthusiasm. "We have to do something. I talked to Ellen, and she agrees with me."

"We heard about Aaron getting burned," Mamm said. "That's bad. The boys should have what they need to do the job, ain't so?"

"That's what I think." Allison sparkled, obviously sensing an ally. "Nick says they really need a new truck, as well. Their pumper is on its last legs, so they've been saving up to buy a good used one."

"I don't think there's anything—" Sarah began, but Allison interrupted her.

"Oh, I know we can't do everything at once, but it seems to me if we get the ball rolling, more people will understand the need and become involved."

Mamm nodded. "That makes gut sense. Sometimes folks just have to be pushed a little."

Sarah eyed Allison cautiously, wondering what notion she had come up with. It was sometimes a bit unnerving to have such a go-ahead Englisch partner. Allison never seemed to see obstacles, only opportunities.

"What were you thinking we might do?"

"Well, we're already planning the antique quilt display for the shop, and I've been working on some ways of publicizing it. What if we expanded the idea? Got hold of a bigger place to have it, and turned it into a quilt festival? I just read an article about one out in Ohio that brought visitors in from all over, and made a lot of money besides. You know how quilters are—they can't get enough. A display of antique quilts, combined with a sale of quilts and quilted products, demonstrations, maybe even some workshops on different techniques . . . I think with the right publicity, we could make much more money for the fire company."

Before Sarah could catch her breath at this grand expansion of their original idea, she realized that both her mother and grandmother were nodding eagerly. Was she the only person who saw any flaws in that plan?

"But . . . that's a very big job. It will take ages to plan and put together—"

"Not that much if we all work together." Allison waved away her objection. "It's all in the organization. I've worked on big design expos several times, and the crucial thing is to decide on a date and a place and start getting the promotion out." She studied Sarah's expression for a moment and smiled. "Trust me. I do know enough not to dream too big. But even a small one- or two-day event will draw in quilters ready to spend money."

Mammi nodded. "Look at the Englisch who come to the quilters' group and class at the shop. They wouldn't hesitate to travel—why, some of them will drive half a day just to visit a big fabric store or see a quilting demonstration."

"You girls aren't going to leave us out," Grossmammi declared. "What can we do?"

After another half hour of talking, Allison had several lists drawn up, and Sarah's head was spinning. It was a fine idea, and she didn't doubt her partner's ability to plan it out. What did set her stomach churning was the thought of what Allison might decide Sarah should do. Her friend seemed to think Sarah was as brave as she was.

"Goodness, look at the time," Mammi said, standing. "The boys should be getting to bed."

Allison gathered her lists together. "I shouldn't have kept you talking so long, but your input was invaluable. I'll start working out the plans tonight, and with a little luck and a lot of cooperation, we should be able to put this on by the end of the summer." She looked at Sarah and her lips twitched just a little. "It's going to be fine. Don't worry."

"I wouldn't dream of it," Sarah said with mock solemnity. "I'll get a flashlight and walk out with you."

The air was still when they stepped outside into the dark, and the sky was spangled with stars. Not a single cloud marred the view.

"If only it would rain," Sarah said softly. "Everything is so dry."

"I know." Allison fumbled in the pocket of her bag for her car keys, and they jingled, the sound carrying in the still night. "But maybe knowing the state police are investigating will scare the firebug into hiding."

"Maybe." Sarah wished she could believe that, but somehow she thought he wouldn't be so easily deterred. "But it seems to me anyone who sets fires for fun isn't right in the head."

Allison gave her hand a quick squeeze and then

slid into the car. "I know. That is the scary aspect of it. Good night. Take care."

Sarah stood where she was while Allison turned around, and then watched the taillights until the car disappeared onto the road at the end of the lane.

It was so quiet, the darkness so intense, that it was a relief to see the lights from the Whiting place. Jim had put a pole lamp in back, bathing the area between the house and the first of the outbuildings with its glow. But his barn, like theirs, was dark.

She took a few steps, holding the flashlight loosely in her hand, but not bothering to switch it on. As her eyes grew used to the dark she could make out the lines of each of Daad's buildings—chicken house, brooder coop, corncrib, barn, a couple sheds. All of them wooden, all of them vulnerable. As long as she was outside, she might as well take a walk around now to be sure all was secure.

Sarah glanced to her left. Across the fields in that direction lay the King farm, and she could just make out the glimmer of the twin silos. Aaron or his daad could be out right now, doing the same thing she was. Nobody would be sleeping well until the firebug was caught.

Taking a firm grip on her courage, Sarah advanced toward the chicken house, switching on the flashlight but keeping the beam lowered. No point in stirring up the chickens when they were in their roosts for the night. In the instant after she'd turned it on, she heard a sound—quick, low, unidentifiable. Her fingers tightened on the flashlight.

Don't be ferhoodled, she lectured herself. *You wanted to help patrol. You're not going to back out now because you imagine things, are you?*

She listened, but the sound wasn't repeated. It had probably been one of the hens, disturbed by the unexpected light. She advanced on the henhouse, keeping the beam of her flashlight low, but aiming it into the dense shadows around the building. Nothing. Besides, if any stranger were that close, the hens would certain sure be making a racket.

Sarah moved slowly around the other out-buildings, checking each one. Daad had taken to padlocking any that could be easily locked, making her search easier. All was serene, the dry grass rustling under her feet.

Just the barn now, and her steps quickened. She'd been tempted to leave Molly out in the field tonight, but hadn't liked to give in to the fear. Still, she'd be glad to double-check to assure herself that the mare was safe.

A sudden sound from the side of the barn made her freeze, and her heart was suddenly pounding so hard she could feel it in her chest. Biting her lip, she raised the torch, remembering in the same instant the promise she'd made to Aaron.

If you hear something, don't try to deal with it yourself.

But she wasn't sure. And she couldn't go running for Daad when it might be nothing but a bird or a bat.

"Is someone there?" Somehow the sound of her own voice was reassuring. "Hello?" She aimed the light, saw something move in the shadows, and drew a breath to yell.

"Sarah? It's just me." Jonah King stepped into the circle of light. "You're not going to scream, ain't so?"

She managed a chuckle. "No, but I came close. What are you doing here, Jonah?" Aaron's teenage brother was physically very like Aaron had been at that age, but he had a quick, changeable personality that meant you were never quite sure when he might take offense at something you said. Aaron had always been the same as he was now—steady, calm and dependable.

"I'm taking my turn to patrol." Sure enough, Jonah sounded a bit prickly. "Daad acts like I can't be counted on to do it right."

"I'm sure he doesn't think that," she said, hoping to dampen the teen's irritation. Jonah was at the age to be at odds with his daad, she supposed. It was hard to imagine her little brothers hitting that point, but no doubt they would. "I'm glad you're here," she added. "That means I don't have to go in the barn alone."

His slight figure seemed to straighten. "Sure, I'll go with you. Aaron says you shouldn't be out patrolling, anyway."

"He does, does he?" She already knew that, but felt a surge of annoyance that Aaron had spoken to young Jonah about it. "It's just as much my concern as anyone's. Besides, I want to make sure Molly is okay."

Jonah swung the door open. "You wait here while I take a quick look," he said, a note of importance in his tone.

Sarah bit back the response that sprang to her lips. Let Jonah have his moment of masculine strength—he could probably use it if he was on the outs with his daad.

"Denke, Jonah." She waited while he stepped inside, shining his own flashlight around the barn before gesturing to her to come in.

"Everything looks okay," he said. "I'll just check the loft."

While he clambered up the ladder, she moved to Molly's stall, crooning to her softly. The mare came to have her muzzle rubbed, whickering.

"That's my good girl," Sarah murmured.

Jonah scrambled down a few rungs and then jumped the rest of the way, too impatient to take every step. "All clear," he said. "I'll wait and close up for you."

"I'm ready now."

She gave Molly a final pat. Jonah seemed intent on showing how competent he was, so she let him close the barn door and double-check the latch.

Daad wouldn't think of putting a padlock on the barn. In the event something did happen, a minute or two spent opening it could be crucial in getting the animals out. She shivered despite the warmth of the night when she thought of the cows that had been trapped in Ben's barn.

"Thanks again," she said, once they were outside.

Jonah nodded, switching off his light. "No problem." With a long, easy stride, he headed off toward the lane.

Sarah watched until the darkness swallowed him up, uneasiness stirring. If Jonah was heading for home, why was he going that way? It would be much shorter to go across the fields. Shaking her head, she went back into the house.

CHAPTER FIVE

AARON MADE A brief stop at the harness shop to pick up a piece of mended harness the next morning, and then headed for Nick's workshop. He wanted to know what progress the arson investigator was making, and his friend always seemed to hear everything in town.

Aaron pulled into the drive that ran along Blackburn House to the rear, sparing a brief glance toward the windows of Sarah's shop. The lights were on, but he couldn't see her. Not that it mattered. He'd tell Sarah a lot of things, but not the worry that currently occupied his mind.

It was probably nothing. Almost certainly nothing. So why did it continue to nibble at the edges of his thoughts like a mouse getting into the grain?

Aaron took his time about tying the gelding to the hitching rail, trying to clear his mind. Then he walked toward the door into the clapboard building that housed the workshops of Whiting and Whiting Cabinetry.

He'd expected Nick and his father to be there. He hadn't expected to find Sarah and Allison, as well. They were standing by a workbench, deep in conversation with the two men.

Nodding to the women, he managed a smile. "The shop is running itself, is it?"

Sarah's dimple showed. "Mamm is helping us out this morning."

"What brings you in today, Aaron? Got some work for us?" Jim—lean, weathered and what Nick would be in twenty years or so—smiled to show he was joking.

"Just wondering if there was anything new from the arson investigator. I thought Mac would know, and—"

"And Mac would tell us," Nick finished for him. "I suppose if there was something that had to be kept secret, Mac would manage, but we're too used to talking about anything and everything over the supper table."

"He doesn't tell us anything sensitive," Jim corrected.

Nick smiled at his father, as if knowing Jim would always stand up for either of his sons. "Anyway, he says the investigator is being very closemouthed about what he's doing, but doesn't think he's found out anything."

"At least there wasn't a fire last night," Sarah said. "Allison wondered whether having someone from the state police here would scare him into stopping."

"Either that, or it might make him even more daring, I'd think," Aaron suggested.

Jim nodded. "Encourage him to mock authority,

you mean. That fits with what I've read about firebugs. They're usually male, often young and rebellious."

Aaron's hands clenched at his sides, and he forced them to relax.

"It would almost be worse if it did work out that way," Nick said. "If the fires just stopped, like the last time, then we'd never know who it was, and we'd always wonder."

"Ja." Aaron's throat seemed tight, and he cleared it. "The barn raising isn't set for sure yet, but they're talking about a week from Saturday, if we can get the site cleared and ready by then."

"Good." Jim slapped his shoulder. "Count on us to help, okay?"

"Ben and Miriam will appreciate it," Sarah said. She gave her partner a worried glance. "There's so much to do that—"

"We're not going to postpone the quilt festival, if that's what you're going to say," Allison said promptly. "Did you hear about our plans, Aaron?"

"Ja. The fire company appreciates it. We'll help any way we can, that's certain sure."

"What we need first is a place to hold the festival that will accommodate a lot of visitors, as well as plenty of space to display quilts." Allison pulled a small notebook from her bag. "I've started a list of possibilities."

"You'll need display racks. Nick and I can knock some up." Jim turned away when the phone began to ring, waving his hand at Nick as if inviting him to take over.

Nick nodded. "We can do that easily. We don't have any big jobs on hand at the moment. Aaron, would you have time to help us?"

"Sure thing. My mamm and sister will do anything they can as far as the quilts are concerned."

"That would be sehr kind of them," Sarah said. "Everyone knows Esther is one of the best quilters in the community, and Becky is wonderful gut, as well."

Allison jotted down notes. "I'll take care of the publicity, of course, and check into any permits we need. Sarah, if you'll have a look at the different venues I have listed, you can sort out the ones that are possible. All right?"

He noticed that Allison had already jotted down Sarah's name, taking her acceptance for granted. But reluctance was written in Sarah's eyes, at least for him to see. And he knew why. She was always hesitant about taking on something outside her experience, especially if it might bring her into negotiating with the Englisch.

"I'll give you a hand with that, Sarah," he said on impulse. "I can check out how easy or hard it would be to set up the display racks at each place, ja? We'll do it together."

He shouldn't volunteer for too much, busy as

he already was, but if it would make things easier for Sarah, he couldn't resist.

"There, you see, Sarah?" Allison exclaimed. "You don't have any excuse not to do it, right?"

"Of course I'll do it." Sarah said the words quickly enough, but he saw a faint flush in her cheeks and wondered how much she regretted being pushed into this project. Maybe he'd have done better to stay out of it.

"I can tell by the way Dad's looking at me that it's time we got to work," Nick said. He dropped a light kiss on Allison's cheek. "We can brainstorm some more at lunchtime, okay?"

"All right, I hear the message." Allison stuffed the notebook in her bag. "I get carried away—I admit it. I have things to do, too. See you later."

They went out of the workshop together, and with a quick wave, Allison headed for the rear entrance to Blackburn House. When Sarah moved to follow her, Aaron caught her wrist, holding her back. It felt small with his fingers encircling the fine bones, momentarily distracting him from what he intended to say.

"I'm sorry. I know you didn't want to be the one to go looking for a place to hold the festival. If I made it harder for you—"

"No, no," she said quickly. "It's fine. I don't mind doing it. Anything to help the firefighters, you know that."

"You looked as if you had some reservations about the whole thing."

She shook her head, and he suspected that if she did have qualms, she wouldn't share them with anyone.

A smile tugged at her lips. "I just thought maybe you were being railroaded into helping. If you don't have time to go with me, I can do it on my own. You're busy with the farm and with helping Ben Stoltzfus, as well."

"I'll make time," Aaron said. "Maybe we'll get lucky and find the right place the first time." That would probably cheer her up.

Sarah's lips curved, but he suspected she was still worried. "I hope it won't be difficult. Allison has her heart set on putting on this festival, and she definitely has a knack for getting other people excited, too."

"That's what we need, ain't so? Everyone pitching in to help."

She nodded, her smile becoming more natural. "I was glad to see Jonah taking his turn with the patrolling last night. Did he tell you we both had the same idea?"

"Jonah? No." Aaron's throat tightened. "When was this?" He tried to keep his voice casual.

"It must have been around nine-thirty, I think. It was already dark, anyway. Mamm and Grossmammi had gotten involved in plotting this festival, and we talked longer than we meant to." Sarah started walking, and he fell into step with her. "I was checking the outbuildings after Allison left, and when Jonah came out of the shadows by the barn, it scared me for a second. He's lucky I didn't scream."

"Ja, lucky." Jonah must have been on his way to whatever he'd been doing last night, then. It had been nearly two when Aaron caught him creeping into the house. "I didn't know he was going to check your place."

Aaron could feel Sarah's gaze on his face. She'd probably heard an intonation in his voice that he hadn't intended to let slip.

"He mentioned something that made me think he was trying to prove to your daad that he could take on the responsibility." She hesitated a moment. "Are there troubles between the two of them?" Sympathy warmed her voice.

Aaron shrugged, trying to loosen tight shoulder muscles. "Daad gets frustrated with him, that's certain sure."

"I always think rumspringa is hardest on the parents. And Jonah being the youngest—well, I'd guess my daad will worry more about Noah than Jonny and Thomas when the time comes."

"You're probably right." Aaron managed a smile. "It's hard to let go of the youngest one."

"Especially for Mamm and Daadi. They waited so long for another boppli after me that the boys are extra precious to them."

"Not more than you," he corrected.

Silence lay between them for a moment. He tilted the angle of his straw hat to keep the glare of the summer sun from his eyes, and wondered how Sarah managed to look so cool in her green dress and matching apron.

"Your daad fretting over Jonah's rumspringa behavior doesn't explain why you're worried, though." She gave him an apologetic smile. "I can see that you are."

"Ja." He frowned, staring for a moment at the row of maples that lined the quiet street. "I haven't said anything to Daad, but I don't think much of some of the boys he's running with. I hope he's not headed for trouble."

"Drinking?" Sarah knew as well as Aaron did how much grief could come from the beer parties the wilder teens managed to have.

"That, ja." The longing to unburden himself was overwhelming. He let out a long breath. "Last night I heard him sneaking in—not that he managed to be very quiet about it. He was stumbling around, more than half-drunk. I quieted him down so he wouldn't rouse the whole house, and got him to bed."

"And now you don't know if you did the right thing." She said the words he'd been thinking.

"Ja. Maybe it would have been better for him to face Daad. But . . . the thing was, his clothes smelled of smoke." There, it was out.

Sarah didn't speak for a moment, absorbing it, weighing the significance of what he'd said. Then she brushed his arm lightly. "You're worried. I guess I would be, too. But think about it, Aaron. There was no barn fire last night. Isn't it more likely that the kids were partying someplace and built a bonfire? That's just what they'd do, ain't so?"

The common sense of her words seemed to make some of his burden slip away. "Ja, that's true."

"Besides, I can't believe Jonah would think of setting a fire. He's been a volunteer firefighter for over a year. He knows what a barn fire would do. He'd never endanger the animals. Or the other firefighters."

Aaron let out a long breath, remembering his brother's face when he'd realized they hadn't been able to get all the animals out of Ben's barn. "You're right. I don't know what I'm doing, thinking that way about my own kinder."

"We're all on edge. Goodness knows what we'll be like if the fires get any worse." Sarah's expression tightened. "If only the police investigator can find the truth . . ."

Her words trailed off. Was she thinking, as he was, that it might be painful to know the truth?

But it was senseless to worry about the results. Truth was always best.

"Denke, Sarah. Your common sense was

just what I needed today." He glanced around, realizing how far they'd walked. "Where are we going?"

Sarah chuckled. "I'm going to visit Julia Everly. I don't know where you're going."

He laughed, clasping her hand for an instant. "Where is my head? I've been that ferhoodled with worrying about Jonah. I'd best get on my way home." He turned back the way they'd come.

SARAH WAS STILL thinking about that conversation with Aaron as she turned onto the quiet residential street where Julia Everly lived—not that any street in town was ever very busy, except during a special event like the annual spring fair. The ridge that gave the town its name rose sharply where the street ended, dark green now in midsummer, seeming to guard the town below, keeping its people safe.

Surely Jonah couldn't be involved in setting fires. Impossible. Aaron had seen that as soon as she'd pointed it out to him. Still, she could understand the nightmare fears that sometimes overtook one in the wee hours of the morning.

Aaron always seemed to feel responsible for the younger ones. She could understand his attitude. She felt the same about her young brothers. Most likely the age gap between him and Jonah made it difficult for Jonah to confide in him, especially about something as sensitive as the boy's rumspringa activities. Well, maybe the fact that Aaron hadn't given him away to their father last night would help matters between them.

Things had changed so much in her life in just the past few days—since she'd spotted the smoke announcing the fire at Julia's barn, in fact. Normally, despite the fact that they lived so close, she wouldn't see much of Aaron except at worship on alternate Sundays, or when everyone pitched in to help with the haying. She'd seen him more often this week than she had in the previous month.

It should become easier with repetition, shouldn't it? Well, it didn't. She couldn't see him without feeling the jump in her pulse and the longing in her heart.

And now to be committed to working closely with him on the festival project—how had she gotten into this predicament? He'd been trying to help her, most likely. And it was just as likely that Allison, who knew her secret, thought it a great idea to throw the two of them together. Sarah had to admit that just the thought of being with him that much sent her nerves singing.

Julia's house was just ahead, and she gave herself a mental shake. It was time to stop fretting about her own wayward heart and concentrate on something else.

When Julia had phoned the shop earlier, she'd

sounded triumphant. She'd gotten rid of Donna for the morning, she'd said, and she wanted Sarah to come over and search for her stored quilts without, apparently, having to argue with her cousin about it.

The woman had sounded like her usual feisty self, and Sarah thought again that Donna must be wrong about Julia failing mentally. Donna was one of those people who always saw the worst in every situation, and she was probably just taking an unduly pessimistic view of things.

The flower borders along Julia's front porch were crowded with marigolds, snapdragons and dahlias. They were all drooping, looking as if they could do with a drink of water. Sarah would offer to water them before she left.

She pushed the doorbell and then opened the unlocked front door, not wanting the elderly woman to struggle from her chair. "Julia?"

"In here. Come on in." Julia sounded stronger today, probably delighting in having outwitted the cousin she considered interfering.

Sarah found her in the usual chair, her walker on one side and a tray table in front of her with a laptop computer on it.

"Well, come on, come on. I found something I want to show you." She swung the small computer around. "Here, look at this."

"How are you feeling, Julia?" Sarah crossed the room to her. Julia's wiry hair stood out from her head, and her eyes glinted with enthusiasm.

"Fine, fine. I want you to see this article I found."

The lightweight laptop was Julia's latest toy. With her boundless curiosity and energy, she'd always been quick to adopt the latest technology, and she loved to show off her knowledge.

Sarah bent obediently to stare at the laptop screen and found she was looking at a display of quilts. "What is it?"

"An article about a big quilt festival they put on out in Indiana. Just look at the people they pulled in."

Julia clicked through a series of pictures, showing crowds browsing between rows of quilts, each displayed completely on a long rack. There were close-ups of individual quilts and another series showing what appeared to be classes in quilting.

"It says they made thousands of dollars in just three days. Imagine that. There's no reason why we can't do just as well."

We? Sarah asked herself silently. Clearly Julia had adopted the quilt festival idea as if it had been her own. Still, it was probably good for her to have an interest other than staring at the television.

"I don't think we can start out too ambitiously. Allison feels it's the sort of thing that will build over time," Sarah said, trying to be diplomatic.

"Even so, it will raise the money needed for the fire company. Not that people shouldn't make individual donations. I intend to. But some people have to have a little excitement to make them loosen the purse strings."

"I guess so." Sara studied a Sunshine and Shadows pattern done in brilliant, unconventional colors. "That's lovely. Startling, though, and I'm not sure I'd want to sleep under it."

Julia gave a snort of laughter. "It'd give you nightmares." She clicked through more screens impatiently. "There's another one—drat, I can't find it. Anyway, it's an antique postage-stamp quilt done in a Double Wedding Ring pattern, and you wouldn't believe what it sold for. Thousands! And I've got one that's every bit as good in a trunk up in my attic."

Clearly the treasure-hunting bug had bitten Julia in a big way. "I'll be glad to search for your quilts if you want. Is Donna still fussing about them?"

"She claims I got rid of them years ago. Silly hen. I might be getting old, but I know better than to dispose of something that valuable. You go on up to the attic. You'll find them."

"I'll try, but you have to stay put." Sarah gave Julia a stern look. "I don't want you trying to lug that cast up to the attic."

"I'm not that foolish," she said. She glared at the cast. "I'll be glad to get rid of this thing. It's

107

cramping my style. Well, go on. You know where the stairs are, don't you?"

Sarah nodded, suppressing a smile at her comments. "Yes, I remember." She'd hauled down some things that Julia donated to the Amish auction for Haiti relief last year.

"All right, then. I'm pretty sure I put all the quilts together in a trunk, but it might have been a storage box. You'll just have to check anything that's a likely container. And don't bother to tell me I should have labeled things. I don't have the time or patience for it."

That certainly didn't narrow down the search. Sarah would probably be at it for hours. Resigning herself, she went to the back hall and the door that opened onto the narrow attic stairs. At least it wasn't a trapdoor and ladder.

Sarah went up the steps, expecting to be met by a blast of hot air. But Julia's attic was as modern as the rest of her house, and was well ventilated, brightly lit and clean despite the stacks of boxes and pieces of furniture that filled most of the space. Obviously when she'd moved, Julia hadn't been able to bring herself to get rid of all the mementoes of her old life, no matter how loudly she'd talked about the folly of hanging on to things.

"Well?" The woman's shout was loud enough to penetrate to the attic. "Did you find anything yet?"

Sarah sighed, fearing it was going to be a long day. "Not yet. I'm just getting started."

With no clear idea where to search, she decided to begin with the trunks. Maybe Julia's initial thought had been right, before she'd started second-guessing herself.

There was an unfortunately large number of them—some flat-topped like a dower chest and others with a rounded lid. Sarah moved boxes from atop the first one to begin searching.

She soon decided that the only way she'd get through this was to ignore the temptation to look at everything she unearthed. Julia had saved things she could never possibly use again. One trunk was filled with long dresses—elegant things wrapped carefully in tissue paper. Relics of a more formal era in the woman's life, she supposed.

"Anything yet?" Julia sounded closer.

"Some pretty gowns," Sarah replied. "You're sitting down, aren't you?"

There was the scrape of a chair. "Of course," she said.

Sarah grinned. Julia was about as subtle as the average six-year-old, to say nothing of being as single-minded.

"I wore those gowns when I was first married." She sounded nostalgic. "My husband's company used to have formal dinners to celebrate their accomplishments. Not that I ever looked that good in a dinner gown. When you're built like a fireplug, the priciest gown doesn't help."

"You're not," Sarah said, although to tell the truth, it was probably an apt description of Julia's short, compact body.

"Try the other trunks. The quilts have to be up there somewhere. I know perfectly well I—"

The words cut off, followed by a thud and a cry. Sarah's heart stopped. She jumped to her feet and bolted for the attic stairs.

By the time she reached the bottom, she'd imagined finding Julia's lifeless body stretched out on the floor. Instead she found her struggling up with the aid of the walker and using language not fit for a lady.

"Are you all right? Where are you hurt?" Sarah grasped her arms and tried to ease her back to a sitting position. "Can you just sit here while I call the paramedics?"

"I don't need paramedics!" Julia snapped, her normally ruddy face nearly mahogany with rage. "I'm perfectly fine, no thanks to that idiot of a cousin of mine. Look what she's done. There's no pad underneath that throw rug."

Sarah spared a quick glance for the rucked-up rug. "Let's make sure you're okay before we worry about what caused you to fall. Do you hurt anywhere?"

"No." Julia managed a slight grin. "Lucky I came down on my bottom. It's well padded."

"Does your leg hurt?" Sarah looked uncertainly at the cast, not sure what she expected to see.

"It's fine," Julia muttered. "Nothing wrong with me except my pride. No thanks to Donna. Here, help me up."

Bracing herself, Sarah got one arm around Julia, clasped her firmly and helped her to rise. Her worry abated as she realized that Julia was able to manage a lot of the process. Once she was up and leaning on the walker, she paused, breathing heavily.

"Just give me a minute to catch my breath."

Sarah obeyed, using the time to survey the scene of the fall. There was nothing Julia could have tripped over, and the rug sliding on the polished wood floor did seem the most likely culprit. "Do you usually have a slip-proof mat under the rug?"

"Of course I do. I'm not an idiot." Julia thumped the walker and started to make her way back to the living room. Sarah hurried to assist her.

Once she was settled in the chair, Sarah surveyed her uncertainly. "It's not possible—I mean, you aren't thinking Donna would do that deliberately."

"Deliberate? Donna? She's never carried out a deliberate action in her life. She drifts. You know that. It's amazing she remembers to take her insulin shot every day. Anyway, she's not malicious. She probably took the mats to wash and forgot to tell me. It's just like her. Just you wait until I see her."

As far as Sarah was concerned, she'd just as soon not be present for that meeting. "Suppose I bring you a cup of tea? Or something cold, if you'd rather."

"Cup of tea would be nice." Julia cocked an eyebrow. "But if you're thinking it will soothe me, you're wrong. Of all the crack-brained ideas, Donna—"

Sarah escaped to the kitchen before she could hear the rest of that complaint. Poor Donna. She was in for a rough time when she showed up. If this spat followed past performances, the two of them would be on the outs for days.

Just when she carried the tea in, Sarah heard the front door rattle. "Cousin Julia? Are you here?"

"Of course I'm here," Julia shouted, her face darkening. "Get in here."

A few seconds passed—no doubt Donna making it known that she didn't like being addressed that way. Then she appeared in the doorway. "Hello, Sarah. I didn't know you were here again." She brandished a quart jar. "I brought you some soup from the café," she told her cousin.

"Is that your way of making up for half killing me?" Julia said.

"What are you talking about? I wasn't even here. How could I do something to you? I've been out. Anyway, what happened?" Donna flung out the stream of questions, gesturing wildly with the container.

Sarah rescued the soup. "I'll take this to the kitchen."

Unfortunately, even from the other room she could hear the resulting argument, with Julia accusing and Donna protesting that she'd taken the mats to wash them, but had told her cousin she was doing it.

"If you got hurt, it's your own fault. You didn't remember what I told you, any more than you remember what you did with those precious quilts of yours."

When Sarah returned to the living room, Donna was looking sulky and defiant, her arms wrapped around her thin body. "I'm trying to take care of you, and that's all the thanks I get. Well, you can just take care of yourself for all I care."

"Good!" Julia exclaimed, and Donna flounced out, the door slamming behind her.

"Idiot," Julia said again. She leaned back in her chair, looking refreshed by the quarrel. "Even so, there's no denying I could have been hurt. And I know I never got rid of those quilts. You won't let me down, will you, Sarah?"

"No, of course not." She glanced at the shelf clock atop the bookcase. "But I really have to get back to the shop now." She didn't, but Julia would probably calm down more quickly if she left. "I'll come back another day and look some more for the quilts. Do you want me to heat up some soup for your lunch?"

Julia shook her head. "My cleaning woman will be in before long. She'll take care of my lunch. You go on back to the shop. But you won't forget, will you? I'm counting on you."

"I won't forget. I promise. I'll just go and set things right in the attic before I leave."

This seemed to be a day of agreeing to things Sarah really wasn't eager to do. But she didn't have a choice, did she? She'd help Julia, despite all the other claims on her time, because Julia needed her.

And she'd work with Aaron on the quilt festival because she was needed there, as well, despite the risk of further bruising to her already wounded heart.

CHAPTER SIX

AARON WALKED TOWARD the house, yawning a little, after cleaning stalls in the barn. The nights spent watching for any sign of fire were beginning to tell on him. Jonah claimed it didn't bother him, but Aaron noticed it was harder and harder to get him out of bed at five thirty for the morning milking.

Movement across the road caught his eye, and he watched as a pickup pulled into the drive leading to Matt Gibson's place. Two men got out and began setting up something. It took a moment to recognize what it was. Surveyor's equipment. They were surveying the property lines.

Frowning, Aaron watched them for a moment and then began walking out the lane toward the men. Harvey Preston, the real estate agent, had been vague about the intentions of the buyers. Maybe the surveyors would be a little more forthcoming.

The July sun beat down with oven-like intensity. The younger of the two reached into the cab of the pickup and came out with a baseball cap. Slanting it down to shade his eyes, he picked up a tripod and began walking along the berm of the road, apparently following the gestures of the older man.

Aaron crossed the road, heading for the fellow who seemed to be in charge. He'd be the one more likely to know the answer to the question that pricked at the back of Aaron's mind.

What was going to happen to the property? There were plenty of potential uses that would constitute an annoyance to neighboring farmers.

When he neared the surveyor, the man was frowning at a clipboard. He looked up at Aaron's approach.

"Morning." He glanced from Aaron to the King farm. "You the neighbor?"

"Ja, that's right. Aaron King. My family owns the land across the road."

"I don't suppose you know anything about the property lines over here, do you?" The man's face was flushed from the heat, and he adjusted the hat he wore to shield his bald head, looking as if he'd rather be doing something else.

"A little, I guess. Matt Gibson was our neighbor for fifty years or so."

The surveyor seemed to assess Aaron for a moment before giving a nod. "Maybe you can interpret this for me." He held out the clipboard.

The document was apparently a photocopy of deed records. Aaron stared at it for a moment, trying to orient the words to the reality. Typical of old deeds, it didn't give any precise markers.

"The line runs from a mark on a willow tree

to the center of the bridge over the stream." The surveyor sounded exasperated. "I can see the bridge, but where the heck is the willow tree?"

Aaron tried to keep his lips from twitching. "That would be the big old willow that overhung the power lines down a ways." He pointed east along the road. "Trouble is, it came down in a windstorm ten years ago or so."

The man shook his head. "I might have known. We'll have to measure from the bridge, then."

He'd have to give the man more bad news. "I'm afraid that's not a good marker, either. That bridge washed out in the flood of '89. The flood changed the course of the creek bed, so the bridge isn't even in the same spot."

The surveyor groaned. "I might have known this wouldn't be straightforward. The lines never are when you're dealing with anything out in the country, especially around here. Out in the western states, even the property lines are set in a grid, most places." He nodded toward the clipboard Aaron still held. "Are *any* of those markers still there, do you know?"

Aaron studied the description. "I think this stone marker in the woods is still there. I walked up that way with Mr. Gibson once a few years ago, and he pointed it out. And you can probably get a good corner where Gibson's farm adjoins the land the Amish school is on. We had a surveyor when we built the school."

"Thanks for the help." Shaking his head, he gestured to the younger man to come back. "Just what I wanted to do on a blazing hot July day—take a hike up into the woods."

Grinning in sympathy, Aaron pointed to the lane behind the barn that headed up to the woods, eventually degenerating into a path. "If you go up that way, the path will take you to an abandoned railroad bed. Walk to the left along that, and you should come to the marker. It was on the uphill side, as I remember."

"Appreciate it." The surveyor gestured again to his helper. "Come on, move it. We're going for a hike."

The younger man's groan was audible.

This was probably the best chance Aaron would have to ask. "Do you know what the new owners are planning to do with the property?"

The man shrugged. "It's just a job to me. I'm not in their confidence. Still, if I were guessing from the orders we have, I'd think the owners were intending to divide it up for building lots of some sort."

"Home building lots, you mean?" Aaron found that hard to believe. "Why would anyone want to put in houses this far away from town?"

"Who knows? Seems kind of strange to me, too." The man mopped his face with a handkerchief. "I don't suppose you'd much like having a bunch of suburban neighbors, either."

"Complaining about the smell of manure and blaring their horns at the buggy horses? No, not much." Aaron could just imagine what it would be like.

The surveyor chuckled. "Funny how people think they want to move out to the country, and then as soon as they get there, they start changing it to make it more like the town they came from."

"True." Aaron frowned. "This land is supposed to be zoned agricultural, though."

"Yeah, it is." He winked. "Funny how planning commissions change their minds when it means a bunch of new taxpayers moving in, isn't it?"

Aaron's jaw tightened. What he said was true. Farmers had been dealing with that sort of thing for years. In fact, it was pushing more and more Amish out of areas where they'd had family farms for generations. He'd just thought it would never happen here.

"Do you know anything about the new owners?" he asked abruptly.

The surveyor ruffled through his papers. "Evergreen Corporation, it says. Headquartered in Delaware. Afraid I've never heard of them before."

Neither had Aaron. Did Matt Gibson know what the buyers planned for his property? Maybe, maybe not. But there was one person who ought to know. It looked as if he'd be paying a repeat visit to Preston's Real Estate.

• • •

SARAH HAD HOPED to have an opportunity to talk to Allison about Julia when she reached the shop, but Allison rushed off immediately to pick up a permit application for the quilt festival, and it wasn't until afternoon that they had a quiet moment together.

"Sorry I've been on the run." Allison stowed her bag under the counter and smoothed her ruffled hair. "It turns out we have to have a permit to hold the festival at a location other than our shop, so I decided I'd better go down to Town Hall to get the application."

"And you happened to run into the mayor while you were there, ain't so?" Sarah teased, enjoying the way her sophisticated friend sparkled like a teenager at the mention of Nick.

"We had to talk business," Allison said firmly, but her lips softened. "Nick says that the fire company's pumper is in worse shape than they'd realized. It's a good thing there hasn't been another fire in the past few days. It gave them time to get some repairs done, but it's still just a makeshift business. He's going to talk to the newspaper editor about running some articles."

Nodding, Sarah paused in the process of hanging a new baby quilt over a rack. "That will help, especially with folks in town. They have to be aware that the problem affects them, too, and not just the farmers." She smoothed her palm over the delicate yellow and green design of bunnies and daffodils, loving the joyful effect of the pattern. If she'd ever had need of a baby quilt, she'd have wanted one like this.

"And speaking of the festival, have you and Aaron made any headway in checking out the possible sites?" Allison sounded perfectly innocent, but her expression gave her away.

"Stop pushing. I'm certain sure you manipulated that deliberately to throw Aaron and me together."

"Not manipulated, exactly," Allison protested. "I couldn't be sure Aaron would volunteer. I just believe in taking advantage of opportunity when it presents itself. So, have you? Made plans to check out sites, I mean."

"I know what you mean." Sarah should be annoyed, but it was hard to manage it when she knew her friend meant nothing but the best for her, and Allison's own happiness with Nick made her want the same for everyone around her. "I'll set something up with Aaron the next time I talk to him, I promise."

Possibly she'd be able to tick a few places off the list on her own before that happened, she added silently.

"Well, when you do, try and act more like an available single woman and less like a childhood buddy."

Sarah just shook her head, knowing that

explaining all over again wouldn't deter Allison from her determination to see Sarah happy. "Now, enough about that. We need to talk about Julia."

"Julia?" Alarm showed in Allison's green eyes. "Why? What's wrong?"

"She's all right," Sarah said hastily. "But she had a fall this morning, and it worries me."

"You're sure she didn't hurt herself? At her age, a fall can be serious."

"As sure as I can be. She wouldn't let me call the rescue squad, and she did seem to be moving all right when I helped her back to her chair. I thought I'd stop by on my way home."

Allison was already shaking her head. "I know that makes you late getting home, and your mother will worry. I'll go. Maybe I can take a meal over and eat with her. That'll give me more time to assess the situation." She dived in with her usual efficiency. "But how did it happen?"

"That's . . . worrisome." Sarah hesitated, trying to decide just what she thought about that odd incident. "Julia's walker slid on a throw rug, and she went down."

"The last time I was there, she was having a spirited argument with the visiting therapist. He told her she should put all of those rugs away, but you know how Julia is. All she needed was someone telling her that to make her stubbornly insist on leaving them where they were."

"I'm sure. But it wasn't as simple as that. The rugs do have nonskid pads under them, but the pad wasn't there." She caught the sharpened look of attention on Allison's face and shook her head. "Donna came in about then, and she claimed that she'd taken them up to wash, and told Julia to be careful. But Julia insisted she'd never mentioned it."

"Why on earth didn't Donna just pick up the rugs, if so? It sounds odd to me."

"I know, but everyone isn't as efficient as you. It's just the sort of thing Donna would do. Start something and not carry it through." Now that she'd voiced her concern, Sarah had a sense of release. "I can just see her doing it without thinking."

"You're more trusting than I am," Allison said. "I don't like it."

Sarah blinked at the idea. "But Donna wouldn't want to see Julia hurt. Surely it was just a mix-up. She might have thought she'd mentioned it to Julia but hadn't. Or Julia might not have remembered, I suppose. Donna keeps saying that she's forgetting things, but I haven't seen it myself."

"It sounds to me as if dear cousin Donna has some explaining to do." Allison's expression was grim. "She's always saying she's Julia's only relative. And I'd guess that Julia is fairly well-off."

Sarah was already shaking her head. "No, no, that's impossible. People just don't behave that way. And anyway, tripping on a throw rug wouldn't kill Julia. Hurt her, maybe, but why would that benefit anyone?"

Allison shrugged. "Given the way Donna complains about everything she does for Julia, she might be happy to see her in a nursing facility. Then she wouldn't have to be bothered with her."

"I can't believe—"

The shop phone rang just then. Relieved to be distracted, Sarah scooped it up, only to hear Julia's voice.

"Julia?" She signaled to Allison. "Are you all right? Do you need anything?"

"Fine, fine." Julia sounded testy, and Allison was holding out a demanding hand for the phone. "I want you to do something for me."

"Of course. What is it?" She held up a palm to Allison, trying to stave her off. "And Allison wants to talk with you when we're done," she said, more for Allison's benefit than Julia's.

"Just stop by the cottage on your way home and tell Gus I want to see him here tomorrow morning at nine sharp. He's supposed to be doing the yard work here, and apparently he thinks because it hasn't rained there's nothing to do. Be sure he understands. If he wants to keep living rent-free, it's time he earned it, and you can tell him so."

Sarah mentally translated the demand into more tactful phrasing. "Yes, I'll see to it. Here's Allison." She handed the receiver off, listening with a fraction of her attention to Allison's efforts to persuade Julia that she was coming over with supper. Given the strong wills both of them had, an argument was inevitable.

As for her—well, it was not in her nature to argue with anyone, and she'd naturally agreed to Julia's request. But a little shiver snaked down her skin at the thought of another encounter with Gus after seeing his attitude about his privacy the last time she'd spoken with him.

SARAH HAD MANAGED to dismiss her qualms about Gus for the rest of the afternoon, but they came back in force as she approached the turnoff to the Everly property. Funny that she'd never realized before how isolated it was. Julia's husband had never farmed the land, so what had once been pastures had given way to scrub growth of pines and sumacs. He'd wanted the land for the woods, but the result was unfortunate. The trees and the bends in the road cut the cottage and what had been the barn off from view in both directions.

Molly shook her head, setting the harness jingling, when Sarah signaled the turn. Obviously the mare hadn't forgotten what had happened here. She probably never would. Animals seemed to have longer memories than humans for some things.

The cottage belongs to Julia, Sarah reminded herself as Molly trotted sedately up the lane. She was bringing a message from the owner. No matter how zealously Gus guarded his privacy, he had to respect that fact.

Sarah's gaze was inevitably drawn to the remains of the barn. With no rain to settle the ashes, they clung to a few skeletal timbers, and the charred odor wafted to her nose. There were a few orange markers around scene, left either by the police or the arson investigator.

The cottage door was closed, the windows dark. It looked deserted, but that didn't mean anything. Gus could still be holed up inside, ignoring anything as disturbing as a visitor.

Bolstering her courage with the reminder that she was here at the owner's request, Sarah mounted the steps and knocked. Nothing. She rapped again, louder this time.

"Gus! Are you here? Come to the door."

Still no response. "I have a message from Mrs. Everly. She wants to see you."

Either Gus wasn't there or he'd decided not to respond even to Julia's name. Or he was passed out.

Sarah's hand hovered over the doorknob. She'd opened it before, but then she'd had the excuse that he could be in danger. Delivering a message didn't constitute an emergency. Besides, if Gus was drinking, she didn't really want to encounter him.

Returning to the buggy, she fished out a notepad and pencil. She'd leave a note for him, and if he didn't respond to it, he'd have to explain why to Julia.

It was while she was scribbling the brief note that the feeling began to overcome her—a prickly sensation on the back of her neck, a sensation as if ants crawled on her skin. She stiffened. She was being watched. She knew it as surely as if she could see the watcher.

Trying not to give herself away by her body language, Sarah returned to the cottage door, using the opportunity to scan the windows. Nothing moved. No one stood at the windows watching. But the feeling increased, and she couldn't shake it off.

With no means of fastening the paper to the door, she picked up a fist-sized rock from beside the steps. It felt oddly reassuring in her hand. She stooped, propping the note against the door and putting the rock over the bottom of the sheet to keep the breeze from blowing it away.

Something rustled in the dense growth of rhododendrons that ran along the side of the cottage. Sarah froze for an instant, willing her fingers to let go of the stone. As she stood, the rustle came again, the branches moving as if someone was forcing his way through them.

Her courage fleeing, Sarah bolted down the steps, yanking the lines free of the post where she'd looped them. She scrambled to the relative safety of the buggy seat. Molly, seeming infected by her fear, needed no urging to step away from the porch and circle back to the lane.

Not daring to look around, Sarah snapped the lines, sending Molly down the lane at a sharp pace. Foolish, she was being foolish, the rational side of her mind told her, but apparently her native caution was stronger. She had to get away from the cottage.

A few yards farther on she came to a halt, checking Molly with an abrupt movement, as a car came toward her down the narrow lane. It pulled to a stop scant feet from the mare's nose. Trembling a little, Sarah drew on the lines. If she backed clear, she could send Molly onto the grassy verge and get around the vehicle.

But the driver was already getting out, and Sarah recognized him. Norman Fielding, the arson investigator from the state police.

Relief combined with a sinking feeling. She wasn't afraid of the watcher, not with a state policeman here. But she didn't relish another discussion with the man. Obviously she wasn't going to avoid it. He came toward her, making a cautious circle around the mare as if he half expected the placid creature to attack him. "Ms.

Bitler. What are you doing at the investigation site?"

Of course that was what it would be to him. Somehow that alleviated a little of her apprehension. "The caretaker still lives in the cottage. The owner asked me to drop off a message for him on my way home."

His scanty eyebrows lifted. "Really? Why didn't Mrs. Everly call him?"

"I don't know if there's a phone. She asked me to deliver a message, and I was glad to help her. If you're going to the cottage, you'll see my note on the porch."

"This caretaker, Gus Hill—he wasn't there?" The man seemed to study her face intently.

"He didn't answer when I knocked," she said carefully. "He's a bit of a hermit in some ways. He doesn't like visitors."

She considered telling him about her feeling of being watched and rejected the notion. He was looking at her suspiciously enough as it was.

"Seems a strange situation to me." Fielding's eyes narrowed. "What's Mrs. Everly doing with a caretaker who behaves that way?"

"You would have to ask her that question." Sarah raised the lines. "If you don't mind, I must be getting home. My family will be concerned at the delay."

It was an invitation for him to back off. He didn't. Instead, he put one hand on the buggy seat. "Not so fast. Since you're here, I'd like to take you over your evidence again. You can show me where you were when you saw the smoke and exactly where the fire started."

Sarah's stomach revolted at the thought of going back to the cottage. Would she have that sense of being watched again? She didn't care to find out.

"I'm sorry, but I'm already late. I must go."

He had a firm grip on the side of the buggy seat now. "It won't take long. I'll follow you to the barn."

Her natural deference to authority argued with her need to get away from the place. The fear won, giving her the ability to speak firmly.

"Not now. If you wish, you can stop at our house later. It's just down the road, and the name is on the mailbox."

"Just a few minutes," he said. "Taking care of this now—"

Sarah's fingers tightened on the lines. Molly, alert to the tiniest hint, began to back up, tail swishing, hooves coming down close to the man's feet.

He sprang back, paling. He really was afraid of the mare. If he'd only known it, Molly would dislike stepping on his foot even more than he would.

"It would not be appropriate," Sarah said. "You may talk to me at home, with my father there."

Her heart was in her throat at the temerity of defying him, but Fielding didn't look as if he intended to argue.

He stepped back, well away from horse and buggy, as she backed, swung in an arc around his vehicle and headed toward the road home, letting out a long breath as Fielding said no more.

How had she dared? She found she was irrationally pleased with herself for actually standing up to the man. Did that mean she was lacking in humility? Or obedience to the law?

Still, what she'd said was true, although it probably wouldn't weigh with Fielding. It was inappropriate for her to be alone in such an isolated spot with a strange man, especially an Englischer.

And if he came to the farm . . . well, she'd cooperate with the investigation. She certain sure wanted the arsonist caught before he caused any more damage. But she doubted that anything she could say or do would help.

CHAPTER SEVEN

SARAH HOPED SHE'D heard the last from the arson investigator, and her stomach clenched that evening when Jonny called out that someone was coming. A second later she heard the unmistakable sound of hoofbeats and relaxed. The thought of Fielding coming by horse to question her was enough to make her smile.

Aaron's deep voice sounded from the backyard, where he was teasing the boys as they vied to tend his horse. Daad looked up from the church newspaper, setting it aside, and Mamm took the remains of a blueberry pie from the cabinet and set it on the table just as Aaron tapped on the screen and came in.

Sarah pushed aside a little spurt of pleasure at the sight of him, reminding herself of her promise. She'd assured Allison she'd speak to Aaron about finding a venue for the quilt festival the next time she saw him. She just hadn't expected it to be so soon.

"Aaron, komm, sit." Mamm bustled over to pull out a chair for him. "You'll have some pie, ja? Sarah, bring a cup of coffee for Aaron."

Exchanging a smile with him, Sarah did as she was bid. She and Aaron both knew that neither of their mothers could be content unless they were feeding someone, and Aaron would have pie whether he was hungry or not.

"Denke, Hannah. I need some information, so I thought I'd stop by on my way home from the mill. You don't have to feed me, too."

"Ach, as hard as you work, there's always room for a little piece of pie." Mamm beamed, putting a slice in front of him. "Coffee or lemonade?"

"Coffee is fine." He accepted the cup Sarah handed him.

"Information?" Daad asked. "What can we help you with? Sarah usually knows everything that's going on in town, what with being so busy at the shop every day."

Daad, like her mother, had probably once longed to see Sarah settled with a family of her own, but he'd never said a word to imply that her shop was second best, and she was thankful.

"My mamm says that she thinks you have the address where Matthew Gibson went in Florida. I need to get in touch with him, so I hope you do."

"Ja, I'm certain sure I put it in my address book," Mamm said. She started to move, but Sarah forestalled her.

"I'll fetch it, Mamm." She crossed to the big cabinet against the far wall to pull open the drawer where Mamm kept all her correspondence.

Most Amish were great letter writers, and Mamm had always considered it her respon-sibility to keep in touch with distant relatives and friends. The address book was on top of a stack of round-robin letters from Mamm's cousins in Ohio.

Sarah brought it back to the table, handed it to her mother and fetched a notepad and pencil from the counter. When she slid into her chair, she tried not to look at Aaron sitting diagonally from her, but she couldn't help being aware of him. His strong hands held the coffee mug with what seemed an unusually tense grip.

Daad seemed to study Aaron's face while Mamm wrote down the address. "Greet Matthew for us if you're writing to him. Is there some special reason you need to get hold of him?"

Aaron frowned down at his coffee, as if trying to decide how to frame his answer. "Did you happen to notice the surveyors over at the Gibson place today?"

"No." Daad looked surprised. "It wonders me what they'd find to do, if the property's already sold."

"Since nobody around here knows what's going to become of the place, I figured I'd wander over and talk to them. It seemed at first they were just confirming the property lines." Aaron glanced up, a smile in his eyes. "A nice job they were having of it, too, with most of the old landmarks gone. Last I saw of them, they were trudging up through the woods to try and find the stone pillar that marks one corner."

Daad grinned. "I can't imagine they liked that. But what's the fuss about? If the place is going to be farmed . . ."

"That's just it. Apparently it's not. At least, not from what the surveyor said. He told me the owners hadn't confided in him, but judging by the job, he'd guess they intended to cut it up into building lots."

The three Bitlers stared blankly at Aaron for a moment before Daad spoke for all of them. "Building lots? But that doesn't make sense. Who would want to be building houses way out here?"

"There's not much demand for new houses even in town," Sarah said, puzzling over it. "Besides, this area is zoned for agricultural use, isn't it?"

Aaron nodded. "Well, it might not be housing lots. The surveyor couldn't really tell that from the job. But it wouldn't be the first time someone managed to get the zoning board to change the classification of land. Look what's happened elsewhere in the county."

"Ja, but over east they have more pressure from the suburbs for land." Daad's face was set in grave lines. "Making land so valuable for building that farmers can't afford to buy it. No wonder so many Amish have moved out west or up north looking for farmland they can afford."

"We thought it couldn't happen here, but . . ." Aaron shrugged, letting the words trail off.

Sarah's mind spun with possibilities. None of them would be eager to have a housing development across the road, changing the patterns of rural life. But where would all those people come from? It seemed so unlikely.

"When you talked to Harvey Preston about the sale, did he say anything about what the buyer intended? Surely he would know, ain't so?" she asked.

Aaron's lips set in a firm line for an instant. "He just said it was a company, not an individual. The surveyor said it was the Evergreen Corporation from Delaware, but that doesn't mean anything to me. I guess I'll be talking to Preston about it again. It seems like the neighbors have a right to know."

The way Aaron said it made Sarah uneasy. "I'm sure Harvey would tell you anything he could. He seemed very concerned over the whole situation."

"I hope so." Aaron shrugged, as if to try to shake off his concern. "Daad wanted me to contact Matt Gibson as soon as we found out about the sale, but I said no. Now . . . well, I'd like to hear his side of the story. If this Evergreen Corporation is really going to build something over there, you'd think Matt would give his neighbors some warning."

Daad was already nodding. "I'd have been certain sure he'd have told us, but looks as if I was wrong. Well, you'll write to him and find out. That's only right."

"I'll let you know what I hear from him," Aaron said, rising. "I'd best get home to tuck my girls in."

Sarah stood, as well. She still hadn't spoken to him, and Allison would give her a hard time about it if she failed now. "I'll walk out with you. I need to ask you something about the festival."

Aaron held the screen door, and they went out together. "I've been falling down on the job I agreed to, ain't so? We must get looking for a place where you can hold it. Do you have the list?"

"I do." She held it up. "But I was thinking that you're so busy I should just go ahead and do it myself. I'll be fine, really."

"Are you trying to keep me from helping?" He snatched the list from her, grinning, before she could pull it away. "You should know that won't work." He scanned the list quickly. "Mamm and Becky are planning to come to the shop tomorrow afternoon to work on some of the quilts for the festival that need repair. Suppose I bring them in when they come? Then you and I can get going on this list while they're working. All right?"

Sarah didn't seem to have a choice, and despite her concern, the idea of spending time with him elated her. "That will be fine. We should be able to check out a couple of places, at least."

He gave her a boyish grin. "Your partner's been bugging you about it, ain't so? That's the Englisch for you. Hurry, hurry, hurry."

"True, but if Allison weren't so energetic, we wouldn't have this chance of making the extra money for the fire company. We make good partners, because we each like different sides of the business."

"Is that what makes a good partnership?" Aaron looked down at her, his eyes seeming to smile in a way that made her heart turn over. "It's kind of like a marriage, then."

"I don't know much about that," she said quickly, afraid he'd see her blushing.

Aaron was silent for a moment, the laughter leaving his face. Suddenly his hand brushed hers, and she forgot to breathe. "You should be married with a husband and kinder of your own, Sarah. Why aren't you?"

Panic seized her, and she fought it off. He could never know the truthful answer to that question. "Just meant to be an old maid, I think." She was proud of the light tone she managed to achieve. "It's too late to change now." She took a step back, groping behind her for the porch railing. "I'll see you tomorrow then, Aaron."

He stood for another moment, frowning a little. Then he nodded and turned away. "Good night, Sarah." The words floated back to her on the warm air.

$\bullet \quad \bullet \quad \bullet$

THE HEAT FROM the burning building came at Aaron in fierce waves. He helped to steady the fire hose as the crew sent a stream of water over the flames. Sweat poured down his body under his turnout gear, and he fought to stay in unison with the others.

He suspected they, like him, had started to relax after several days and nights without incident, feeling the firebug had taken his last shot, or that he'd decided to fade into the background since the fire inspector was on his track. Obviously they'd been wrong.

"At least it's not a barn," Nick, next to him, yelled over the noise.

Aaron nodded. Something to be thankful for. This time the fire was at a detached garage in a residential area on the edge of town. Different—a break in the pattern, if there was a pattern. What would Fielding think of that?

The man was in attendance. Aaron had already spotted him pulling up not far behind the fire trucks. He'd been taking photos, making notes. Aaron frowned. Some of the photos seemed to be of the bystanders and even the firefighters. Was it considered suspicious to come out and watch when a neighbor's garage was on fire? Surely not.

Another firefighter moved forward and took over Aaron's position on point. He eased back, seizing a moment to look around. Where was Jonah? The boy should be here.

The alarm had sounded soon after midnight, apparently, and the pager the chief insisted upon even the Amish using now had gone off, startling Aaron. He hadn't even realized his brother was out, but when he'd gone to wake him, the bed hadn't been slept in.

Worry churned his stomach and gnawed at his nerves. How many nights had Jonah gone out that they hadn't known about? Well, Daad knew now, and he'd be having a serious talk with the boy come morning.

A shower of sparks flared out, going dangerously close to the neighboring house. A man wielding a garden hose was on it in an instant— probably the neighbor. Dry as the grass was, the flames could spread only too easily.

Aaron spotted a slight figure running forward through the crowd, pulling on turnout gear. Jonah. There he was at last. Exasperation mingled with worry. What were they going to do about him?

Jonah checked in with the chief and then ran toward them. He grabbed the hose where Aaron held it. "Chief says for you to come help with the pumper. I'm to take over here."

Aaron nodded. Now wasn't the time to say anything he might later regret. He relinquished his spot and jogged back to the truck.

"She's wheezing like an old lady." The fire

chief peered anxiously into the pumper's innards. "See if you can get the pressure stabilized."

This was the constant worry, and all the tinkering in the world hadn't seemed to help. The fact was they needed a new pumper, and sometimes Aaron thought it would take a tragedy to wake people up enough to see that they got it.

He tried to keep an eye on Jonah from his position on the far side of the truck. His brother had moved up now, taking the spot at the front end of the hose. The flames seemed to be dying down a little, or maybe just spreading out, ready to burst through somewhere else. Fire could behave like a wild animal, striking just when you thought it was under control.

But the pumper had steadied, and the men advanced slowly, obviously convinced they had the fire in retreat. Apprehension grabbed hold of Aaron's throat. Jonah was close to the flames now. Too close? He'd have moved in more slowly, but—

"Kerosene!" somebody yelled, and a man came running from a car that had just pulled up next to the house. "Get them back. I have kerosene stored in there."

The chief was already signaling, but the boys in the front of the line didn't react. Jonah—

Aaron leaped from the pumper, racing forward. Jonah hadn't heard the call, engrossed in the excitement of fighting the fire. "Jonah! Pull back, pull back!" The fire roared, blanketing whatever sound he made. Once it hit the kerosene, there could be a flashover, a sudden burst of flame igniting everything around it. Jonah . . .

Save your breath, use it for running. He seemed to be moving in slow motion, had to get to his brother . . .

Aaron reached, grabbed, connected, Jonah's startled face turned toward him. "Kerosene!" he shouted. "Run!"

The others, already warned, were racing back. Aaron clutched his brother's arm, pulling him along as they ran toward safety. A roar, deafening, and Aaron felt himself ripped away, flying through the air, descending into blackness.

It seemed only a second before he opened his eyes, struggling with hands gripping him. "Hold still," someone demanded. "Here. Take a couple breaths of oxygen. You'll feel better."

His head cleared, and he recognized Mike Callahan, paramedic with the rescue squad. Mike clapped an oxygen mask on his face before he could protest.

Aaron yanked it free. "Jonah—"

"Jonah's fine. He's right here." Mike sounded exasperated. "You're both okay, so just take it easy."

It seemed a chore to turn his head. Jonah was on the grass next to him, sitting up, head between his knees, looking young and vulnerable.

"You all right?" Aaron put his hand on his brother's shoulder, feeling the skinny strength of a boy turning into a man.

Jonah nodded. "Sorry," he muttered.

"Nothing to be sorry for," Mike interrupted. "You both did a good job, now relax and let the others finish up. They're not going to save anything of the garage, but any idiot who decides it's a good idea to store a couple of containers of kerosene in his garage deserves what he gets." Mike snorted. "Said he was buying up now for his kerosene heater while the price was low. Turned out to be a pretty expensive savings."

Aaron coughed and cleared his throat. "I don't suppose he planned on a firebug."

"We don't know for sure it was set," Mike said. "Though judging by the way that state police guy is snapping pictures, he must think so."

Someone called to Mike just then, and he moved away.

"You sure you're okay?" Aaron said, patting his brother's shoulder. "Mamm won't let me hear the end of it if you got hurt."

Jonah nodded, turning to look at him, his eyes red rimmed and his face sooty. "I meant it. I'm sorry."

"For what?" If he was talking about sneaking out, he'd best save that for Daad.

"When you grabbed me, I was mad at you.

143

I thought you were just being . . . well, you know. Like you didn't trust me to do anything right."

The words struck at Aaron's heart. Had he really been acting that way? Maybe so. Jonah hadn't been especially trustworthy lately, but dealing with that wasn't his job, as Jonah's big brother.

"Forget it," he said. "Guess I've been a little too bossy lately. I'm sorry, too."

Jonah ducked his head as if in agreement, grinning. Aaron cuffed him lightly on the shoulder, smiling back, and his spirit lightened. All of a sudden he felt closer to his brother than he had in a long time.

SARAH DIDN'T EXPECT Aaron to show up the next afternoon—not after she'd heard about the fire and the danger he and Jonah had been in. Nick had tried to downplay the situation, but she'd already heard a lurid account of the fire from Emily, the bookstore owner, whose home was just a few doors away.

Common sense told Sarah not to put too much stock in Emily's story, since the least thing was apt to become dramatic in the woman's mind, but even allowing for that, it sounded as if it had been serious.

They're all right, Sarah repeated to herself throughout the morning. If they weren't, she'd have heard by now. The Amish grapevine flourished, especially when it came to spreading bad news or calling for assistance.

Even so, she found herself jerking to attention each time the bell over the shop door jingled, and soon after lunch it announced the arrival of Esther and Becky King. Anna and Lena were behind them, each holding one of their father's hands. Sarah's breath went out with such force she felt as if she'd been holding it all morning.

"Wilkom." She smiled even as she searched Aaron's face for any sign of injury or pain. But he looked fine, nudging his daughters to respond to her greeting.

"You don't mind that we brought our two little helpers, do you, Sarah?" Esther removed her bonnet, patting the brown hair that was just beginning to turn gray.

"I'm sehr glad they came." Sarah bent to greet each of the girls personally. "Anna, you are looking more like your aunt every day. And, Lena, how did you get so tall?"

Anna darted a glance at her aunt Becky and smiled, as if deciding it was a good thing to look like her.

"Grossmammi says I'm growing right out of my dresses," Lena announced proudly. "Oh, look at the kitty."

Allison's cat, a fixture at the shop, approached cautiously and then allowed Anna to pat him, purring when she stroked his orange back. Lena squatted down, holding out her fingers, and giggled when he sniffed at them.

"I hope you don't mind them being here," Aaron murmured under cover of collecting bonnets and bags to stow away in the back room. "They wanted to come."

"You don't need to ask that, do you? They are always wilkom here. But I didn't expect to see you today. I heard you were injured at last night's fire." She tried to keep the anxiety from her voice and didn't entirely succeed.

"Ach, it was nothing. Jonah and I got knocked off our feet for a minute, that's all. I've had worse dealing with a bad-tempered bull."

"Was there an explosion? The arsonist . . ."

Aaron shrugged. "It looked like arson, but I don't know that the investigator has said for sure. Anyway, the arsonist probably couldn't have known that the homeowner had decided to stock up on kerosene for his heater. That was what caused the trouble."

Shivering a little despite the warmth of the day, Sarah kept her voice low. "They have to catch this person before there's a real tragedy."

"Daadi, I thought the kitty liked me," Lena said, coming to tug on Aaron's hand. "But then he jumped up in the window instead of playing."

"That's his favorite spot," Sarah told her. "He likes to watch what's going on outside from there.

146

Why don't you girls come to the back room and we'll find something for you to work on?"

"I like to make things," Anna said, tucking her hand in Sarah's. "Lena does, too, but sometimes she gets impatient."

At eight, she had a look of Aaron about her, Sarah thought, especially in the eyes, though she was more like Becky. Odd that neither of the girls looked more like Mary Ann.

Anna had a sweet smile and a responsible air, as if conscious that she was the big sister. Lena, skipping beside her, was the image of Becky with her pert, lively expression.

Sarah drew out the box of quilt squares she kept for just this purpose. "You can take this out front if you want and pick out some pieces you'd like to use for a quilt. Have you started a nine-patch yet?" It was a safe question, since just about every Amish girl from a quilting family started with that pattern.

"I made one for my doll," Anna said, taking the box. "I could start another one for my bear, ain't so?"

"A fine idea." Sarah turned to Lena, who was surveying the shelves of boxes and bolts of fabric. "What about you, Lena? Do you like to quilt?"

The girl screwed up her nose. "Can't I help you some other way?"

"For sure. I have a big tin of buttons that need

to be sorted into jars according to their colors, and I never get time to do that. Could you take on that job?"

She nodded. "Easy. Can I carry them?"

Sarah pulled the button tin from the shelf. "You take that, and I'll bring the jars."

When she turned to the door, she discovered that Aaron was standing there, watching his daughters, his brown eyes serious. "They're fine," she assured him. "You don't have to worry."

"Sure I do. That's my job." He said the words lightly, but there was an underlying gravity that she couldn't help noticing. Was he missing Mary Ann? Probably. Even with the help of his mother and sister, it couldn't be easy to raise two girls on his own.

Back in the main shop area, Allison had already set up a table and spread out the first of the quilts that needed work. Sarah paused to be sure Esther and Becky had everything they needed.

"The owner asked us to put new binding on, but I think we'd better do a careful cleaning first and check for any other weak spots."

"Ja, I can already see some that need stitching." Esther bent over the quilt, tilting her glasses a little as if that would help her focus. "We'll brush it first to get out any loose dirt."

Sarah nodded. A soft brushing was usually the best way to approach any old quilt. "We have a small hand vacuum you can use after the brushing, if you think the stitching will stand it." She smiled, glancing from Esther to Becky. "Ach, I don't need to tell two such wonderful fine quilters as you what to do."

Becky flushed at being categorized with her mother, ducking her head a bit. "We'll enjoy it, ain't so, Mamm?"

"If you're finished with your consultations, maybe Sarah and I had best get on our way." Aaron tapped his summer straw hat against his leg, a sure masculine sign of impatience with female chitchat.

"I'm ready."

Sarah grabbed the bag containing her notebook, pen and a folder of notes about what they'd need to house the festival. She was definitely ready in that respect. Whether she was ready to spend so much time alone with Aaron—well, that was another question, stirring up a mix of trepidation and excitement.

She glanced back at the shop as they went out. Esther and Becky were bent over the quilt, absorbed, while the little girls sat at the small table kept especially for young visitors to the shop. Allison, standing behind the counter, met her gaze with a mischievous smile and a thumbs-up that made Sarah turn her head away quickly, not sure whether to laugh or be annoyed at her friend's matchmaking.

She and Aaron had nearly reached the outer door when they had to step back for someone entering. Harvey Preston swung the door wide, holding it for them.

"Here you go. Aaron, nice to see you're all right. I heard about the fire last night." He shook his head, his jovial face sobering. "Terrible business. Terrible."

"It is that. At least no one was seriously hurt."

"Yes, we have to be glad at least that this madman hasn't been targeting houses instead of barns and garages. Even so, it has to be stopped. I'd think with all the expertise the state police have, the investigator would have gotten somewhere by now. But maybe they have?"

He gave Aaron an inquiring look, apparently assuming a member of the fire company would know more than the average citizen.

"Not that I know of." Aaron touched Sarah's elbow, detaining her when she'd have gone on out the door. "I'm glad we ran into each other today. It gives me a chance to ask you something."

Harvey's eyebrows lifted. "About the fires?"

"No. About what the buyer of the Gibson farm has planned for the property."

"Ah, that. Well, I couldn't say, actually. As far as I know, the company was looking to invest in land in Pennsylvania and thought this would be a good buy. Which it was, with the increasing pressure on available farmland in Lancaster County, as I pointed out to them when they inquired."

"So you didn't know they're surveying the property, apparently with a view to dividing it into some sort of building lots?"

"Really?" Harvey's eyebrows lifted further still. "No, I had no idea. How did you find this out?"

"The surveyor was on-site yesterday, and I talked with him."

Harvey shook his head. "Sounds like a mix-up to me. The people I dealt with didn't give me any indication of development. And I pointed out to them that the land is zoned for agricultural use."

"Ja, it is. Now," Aaron added.

But Harvey's expression had cleared, and he didn't seem to hear the implication. "Count on it, that's what's happened. The surveyor probably didn't understand their intent. Being that far away, the owners just want to make sure they have good boundary markers, since they're not around to see to the property themselves." He clapped Aaron on the shoulder. "Glad I could be of help. You just let me know if I can do anything else." He headed on toward the stairs without waiting for a response.

Sarah waited until they were outside before she spoke. "Did that explanation reassure you?"

"No." Aaron's flat tone was uncompromising. "Harvey probably thinks that's the answer, but I'm not so sure he's right. I just wish I knew how we can find out what's going on."

CHAPTER EIGHT

AARON, WORKING ALONG the second story of Ben Stoltzfus's new barn, found himself wondering whether the rapid rebuilding might be tempting fate—or in this case, the firebug. Might his twisted mind find it amusing to destroy the replacement? It was an ugly thought—one that would keep him awake nights if it were his place.

He sent a wary glance toward his father, who was working beside him. Daad would never admit that he couldn't keep up, but on such a hot day, he ought to take breaks. Convincing him of that might be difficult, though.

Pushing his hat back, Aaron mopped his forehead with his sleeve. Hot, dry days, one after another—this was prime weather for the arsonist to strike.

"Your mamm liked working on that old quilt yesterday." Daad's hammer didn't stop its steady tapping when he spoke. "Don't quite see it myself. Wouldn't brand-new quilts be what would bring folks out to spend money?"

"From what Sarah told me yesterday, they'll expect to sell a lot of new quilts at this festival of theirs, too. But she says showing the olden quilts will bring in Englisch visitors from out of town."

"She should know, that's certain sure, making

153

such a success of that quilt shop of hers." He paused. "Sarah's a gut girl. It's a shame she never married."

Aaron made a noncommittal noise. Was Daad matchmaking? He wasn't sure. And he couldn't argue with Daad's comment, since he'd been thinking the same thing himself just yesterday.

Their search for a proper site hadn't been too productive so far, but they had hopes the old movie theater building might work out, so they'd look at it next. He'd heard the owner had begun remodeling in hopes of renting it, removing the old seats and redoing the floors.

Sarah and Allison were impatient to get the location settled, but with the barn raising today and worship tomorrow, they couldn't get on with it until Monday. He'd told Sarah he'd let Mamm drive his buggy home when she and Becky finished at the shop that day, and he could ride home with Sarah when she went. That way they'd have more time.

He'd seen a moment's hesitation in Sarah's face before she agreed, and it puzzled him. It was a reasonable suggestion, wasn't it? And surely no one would start gossiping because two old friends were together.

It had been gut, spending time with Sarah that way. As often as he'd seen her in recent years, they'd seldom actually had a private conversation. It was as if he was just now getting to know the woman she'd become, and she intrigued him. Funny, how you thought you knew someone and then found greater depths than you'd imagined.

He'd seen Sarah's dedication to the project in her determination not to take any shortcuts. She wasn't likely to accept second best.

Was that why she'd never married? She had so much warmth and love in her heart that it seemed a shame she didn't have children to pour it on. But maybe she'd never found the right someone to love.

The thought drifted away when the youngest of Ben's boys came sidling along the rafter toting a thermos of water. Obviously proud of being entrusted with the task, he held it out to Aaron's father first, who drank and passed it to Aaron.

"We're keeping you busy with the water, hot as it is today, ain't so?" Aaron handed the thermos back.

The boy grinned. "Daad said if I do gut with the water maybe that means I'm big enough to help with the finishing work."

"Before you know it you'll be working up top with the rest of us," Aaron told him.

Ducking his head, the boy scurried on to the next set of thirsty workers—Jonah and one of his rumspringa buddies.

"Jonah's been working hard today," Aaron ventured.

Daad nodded, and Aaron thought he'd seen a little softening of his attitude toward Jonah since Aaron had told him about the incident at the fire scene. Nothing wrong with Jonah that a little time wouldn't cure, he suspected.

"A fine turnout today," Daad said, stretching his back as he surveyed the raw skeleton of the new barn, with men clambering over it looking like so many ants at work. Boys ran about fetching and carrying, while on the ground, the women and girls were starting to put out food on tables and benches brought in on the church wagon.

"Every family from our church district is here," Aaron said, "and a gut crew from as far away as Ephrata. We'll get it done today, that's certain sure."

"Ja." Daad patted the raw new timber that stretched upward. "Just hope the firebug isn't tempted by it."

Hearing his own notion echoed by his father seemed to reinforce it.

"I'll mention it to Ben, though probably he's thought of that risk already. Some extra watchers the next few nights might be best."

Daad picked up his hammer. "There's a lot of Englisch here today. Might be as well to keep an eye on them."

His father seemed unusually suspicious, but that was what fear of a firebug did to people.

Aaron had heard of one farmer letting off with his shotgun when he'd heard a noise, and peppering his neighbor's stray goat.

"Probably just here to help," he said, keeping his tone mild even as he looked from one to another of the non-Amish figures.

Most of them were people he knew well, like the Whiting family, who were all here today, the men working alongside their Amish friends, while Ellen and Allison helped with the food and young Jamie scampered around looking for a job.

Aaron's hand tightened on a two-by-four when he spotted one less-familiar figure—it was Fielding, the investigator. What was he doing here? The man seemed to be everywhere lately, but what progress he was making, no one knew.

Sarah had told him about her encounter with the man at Gus Hill's cottage, and Aaron had been bothered both by the idea of her going alone to see Gus at the isolated cottage and by the investigator's attitude. Aaron had to admit that Sarah seemed to have handled it well, but she shouldn't have been put in that situation to begin with.

His attempts to make her see that had been futile, as he might have known they would be. Julia Everly had needed something, so of course Sarah had jumped to fill the gap, never thinking of herself. Maybe sometimes she ought to put herself first, odd as that idea would sound to her.

The bell on the farmhouse porch clanged its announcement of lunchtime. All over the structure, men began scrambling down the ladders. They'd started at sunup, and after a long morning's work, they'd be ready for the spread the women had put out.

Aaron followed his father down the ladder, but hung back when he went to the table.

"Not hungry?" Sarah, a pitcher of lemonade in each hand, paused to speak to him. She looked as bright and cheerful as a new penny, despite having been up since well before dawn. Her blue eyes sparkled, and there was a light blush on cheeks that were as smooth as silk.

Sarah looked younger than most Amish women her age, he realized. Maybe it was because she wasn't chasing young children and managing a household. She seemed very little older than the girl he'd known so well before his marriage had seemed to put a barrier between them. Well, that had been natural, he told himself quickly. Mary Ann had wanted them to be friends with other young marrieds, not single girls. That was usual enough, he supposed, since in most Amish households, the wife was the one who managed their social life. But Mary Ann had seemed to exclude Sarah. He hadn't even realized how much he'd missed their friendship.

"I'm hungry, all right, but I'm curious, too. What do you suppose Fielding is doing here?"

"He's here?" There was an edge in Sarah's voice. "Where is he?"

Aaron tipped his head toward where the man stood on the edge of the crowd, looking and probably feeling out of place. He was talking to Ben Stoltzfus, making Aaron wonder what questions he had left to ask.

"He acts like he's watching animals in the zoo when he looks at us," Sarah said softly. "I wonder if he's actually going to find out anything."

Aaron shrugged, trying to suppress his own doubts. "Mac says Fielding's one of their top men."

"But he doesn't know anything about our ways or the people here," Sarah protested. "I'd think Mac would stand a better chance of learning the truth."

"I know. But Mac says he has the technical expertise they need. I think he'd expected the man would work more closely with him, though."

Aaron supposed that knowledge was important when it came to analyzing the fires, but Sarah was right. Didn't they also need someone who understood the community?

Mac had just shrugged helplessly when asked that question. Probably he didn't have a choice about who the state police sent.

"I'd better deliver this lemonade before they

start shouting for it," Sarah said. She turned toward the drinks table. "Mind you get something to eat, now."

He nodded, feeling reluctant to let her go and knowing that was foolish. They both had things to do. What was wrong with him?

Apparently the investigator had been looking for Gus Hill when he'd encountered Sarah at the Everly place. Had he found him? Gus seemed to be aware of everything that went on in the township, including some things people would probably rather he didn't know. He might easily have seen something suspicious and be squirreling the knowledge away, not trusting authorities in any shape.

His mind made up, Aaron headed for Fielding, nodding to Ben as he escaped the man's questions. "Taking a look at a real barn raising, Mr. Fielding?" Aaron asked.

Fielding stared at him for a moment, as if attempting to place him. "You're the firefighter who was hurt the other night. King, is it?"

"Aaron King."

"That's right. Your brother was involved, too. You're both okay?"

"No damage," Aaron said easily. "Jonah's at the lunch table. There's plenty for everyone, if you're hungry."

"No, no, thanks," the man said quickly.

Would that be too much like eating with a

suspect? The investigator was a mystery to Aaron, hiding whatever he thought behind an official mask.

"I understand you were looking for Gus Hill," Aaron said. "He's not much for strangers."

Fielding grunted. "So I've heard. I'll catch up with him." He was looking over the crowd of men settling at tables with their food. "Which one is your brother?"

Aaron gave him a sharp glance, wondering what was behind the question. "Jonah's on the end of the first bench."

"Hard to pick somebody out when they're all dressed alike." The man said it as if it was an attempt to make his job more difficult. "He's young to be a volunteer firefighter, isn't he?"

"Almost seventeen. We don't have so many volunteers that we can be choosy. Anyone underage has to have a parent's permission."

"Likes fighting fires, does he?"

The question might have been innocent, but it set off alarms in Aaron. What was the investigator implying?

"He likes doing his duty. The Amish benefit from the fire company, and we serve, too."

"Convenient, I suppose, the two of you responding together."

Aaron nodded. "We're usually picked up by one of the Englisch volunteers."

Fielding zeroed in on his face. "I understand

Jonah was late in arriving at two of the recent fires."

A warning stirred in Aaron, and he pushed it away to answer calmly. "Jonah is at rumspringa age." Seeing the man's blank expression, he knew he'd have to explain further.

"When Amish young people are in their late teens, they are allowed to experience freedom to do things with their friends—parties and such. It's a time to have a bit of freedom before making a lifetime commitment to live Amish. Time for young folks to start pairing off, too. So Jonah was out with some friends when the alarm went. He got to the scene on his own."

Why was Fielding asking so many questions about the boy? Jonah hadn't done anything to make him suspicious, had he?

"This partying that goes on—I suppose kids get in a certain amount of trouble, don't they? Drinking, vandalism and the like?"

"Beer parties, sometimes, I guess. Maybe some practical jokes, but they'd get in trouble with the church for any outright vandalism. If you're suggesting that a gang of rumspringa kids would set fires, you're wrong."

Fielding gave him a cold look. "I'm investigating every option. Frankly, young fire volunteers are always worth a second look in an arson investigation. They get caught up in the excitement of fighting a fire. Sometimes they set one, just for the pleasure of fighting it. Excitement, feeling like a man—that can be tempting to a kid."

"That's nonsense. I know all of our young volunteers." Aaron's hands curled into fists with the effort of keeping his temper when he wanted to rage at the man.

Fielding shrugged. "Sometimes I have to investigate a lot of nonsense to find the truth. But I always find it in the end." He turned and walked toward his car.

Aaron watched him go, torn between anger and fear. It was a bunch of foolishness, just as he'd said. Jonah would never put animals in danger, never burn down a neighbor's livelihood.

But in the back of his mind an image rose— of Jonah, his face filled with excitement as he battled the fire. And Aaron was suddenly apprehensive.

SARAH LEANED BACK in the buggy seat with a sense of satisfaction late Monday. The day had been a busy one, what with working in the shop and then getting through the remaining possibilities for the quilt festival site with Aaron. But it had gone well, and now they were nearly home without having even one awkward moment between them—just a wholehearted enjoyment of doing something with an old friend. This was how it should be between them, she assured herself, trying not to think of the way her heart thudded each time he touched her to help her up and down from the buggy.

Aaron, driving, checked Molly as they approached the lane to the Bitler farm, no doubt intending to insist on unharnessing the mare for her.

"Just drive on to your place," she said quickly, before he could make the turn. "I'll drop you and come back."

"No need." He slowed the mare and turned in. "I'll walk home across the field after I unhitch." Before she could get in a word of protest, he continued, "Now, did anyone save some supper for us? We deserve it, ain't so?"

"Your mamm has never let anyone go hungry in her house, and mine is the same, so I think we're safe." There was no point in arguing, and Sarah would enjoy a few more moments with him. "I'm wonderful glad you helped with getting a place for the festival. There's a lot more to do, but Allison keeps saying we couldn't move ahead until that was settled."

Laugh lines crinkled the corners of Aaron's blue eyes. "Sarah Bitler, you didn't need any help at all. I'd never have thought you'd be such a good bargainer. Another five minutes and you'd have had the man giving it to us free."

"That wouldn't be fair." She kept the words

serious, but a smile tugged at her lips, and her heart seemed to swell at his praise. "The owner should have enough to cover his costs, but not the ridiculous amount he asked for at first. After all, the money raised is for the fire department. He'd be the first one to yell for the firemen if something happened at his building."

Aaron grinned at her. "I'm glad you didn't tell him so. Everyone knows Henry Morrison is an old skinflint." He passed the house, continuing on to the barn.

"Ja, but he's a businessman, too." Sarah slid down when he stopped, not waiting for his help. She headed for the buckles on one side of the mare while Aaron took the other side. "If he wants to have a chance at selling or leasing the building, the best thing he can do is get a lot of people inside to see the renovations he's made. All I had to do was point out that hosting the quilt festival would work to his advantage."

"It's you who's the businessperson, Sarah." Together they slid the harness off. Molly shook her head vigorously at being free of it and stepped forward when Aaron patted her. "I never dreamed that shy little Sarah could have turned into such a businesswoman."

She really had to stop letting her heart flutter whenever he said something nice to her. "To be honest, I never dreamed it possible, either. When

Allison's grandmother offered me the chance at the quilt shop, I was scared out of my mind at the thought, taking on such a challenge when I was only eighteen."

She led the mare clear of the shafts while Aaron ran the buggy backward to its usual parking spot.

When he turned to face her, he studied her with unusual gravity. "Was that why you didn't marry? Because you had the shop?"

The question, coming out of the blue, rendered Sarah speechless for a moment. If he only knew . . .

"I think Mrs. Standish offered me the shop because she thought I wouldn't marry. She was a kind woman, and she wanted me to have something." Sarah kept her tone even with an effort.

"Eighteen was young to decide you weren't going to marry."

She shrugged, glancing away from him. "When you're that age, maybe you don't realize all the implications of the choices you make. Besides, we do some growing up in our twenties, ain't so?"

It wasn't really an answer to the question he'd asked, but he'd have to be satisfied with that much of the truth, because she wouldn't say more.

Aaron nodded, and there was an expression in his eyes that she couldn't interpret. "That's true."

He seemed to shake himself free of whatever he was thinking. He stepped closer, patting the mare affectionately, his gaze fixed on Sarah's face. "Anyway, you should be happy with the person you've turned into."

They stood for a moment, looking at each other across the mare's back. Aaron's expression was that of someone gazing at a sight he'd never seen before, his lips curving tentatively, something of a question in his eyes. His hand moved, his fingers touching hers.

Sarah's breath caught. Could he actually admire the woman she was now? She'd never thought, never imagined—

Molly shook her head impatiently, jerking Sarah back to reality.

Aaron stepped back, blinking as if to reorient himself to where he was and what he was doing. "There's your brother coming to help you." He cleared his throat. "I'd best get home. Jonah and I are trying to get Daad to let us do the patrolling, and we've had a struggle with him every evening."

He moved off before Sarah could even get her wits about her again. Turning the mare over to Jonny, she went to the house, still a bit bemused, her fingers tingling where Aaron's had touched them.

Sarah managed to shake off her feelings to get through what was left of the evening. Mamm had, of course, saved a generous helping of chicken pot pie for her, and wanted to hear all about using the old theater for the quilt festival. She was almost as enthusiastic as Allison was about the project, and came up with one idea after another for the festival.

Sarah shouldn't be surprised at her mother's reaction. After all, it was Mamm who'd talked her into going along with Allison's idea of having a website for the quilt shop, and that had turned out wonderful gut.

It was already dark by the time Sarah put down the mending she'd been doing and rose to glance out the window, stifling a yawn. After such a busy day, an early bedtime seemed appealing.

"I'll check the outbuildings before I go up, Daadi."

Daad laid aside his newspaper and glanced at the window. "Might as well let the dogs out before you come in."

"I will." She lifted down a flashlight from the row of hooks by the back door and stepped outside, standing for a moment to let her eyes get used to the darkness.

People like Allison talked about how dark it was in the country at night, but that was only because Allison had spent her life in the city. Here, a person got used to moving about in the moonlight.

The moon was nearly full, but fitful clouds

covered it momentarily and then moved away, letting the moonlight paint the scene in silver and black. Objects were just dark shadows, but since Sarah knew the location of everything on the farm, she could easily identify them. She walked toward the toolshed steadily, the flashlight swinging at her side, unlit. The night was so still she could hear the faintest rustle made by some nocturnal creature moving through the dry grass.

She wasn't sure when the uneasiness began—maybe while she was looking around the toolshed. Somehow the shadows began to seem darker, their shapes more ominous.

Nonsense, she lectured herself. *There is nothing here in the dark that's not here in the light.*

In any event, there certainly wasn't anything unusual in the toolshed or behind it. She moved on, trying to shake off the prickly feeling on the back of her neck.

One by one she checked the outbuildings, trying to deny that the sensation was growing. *There, nothing, you see? You can't be so foolish as to get panicky at your own home just because it's night. And you certain sure can't prove the men right when they say this is their job.*

She neared the barn, her steps moving more slowly despite her best efforts to speed up. Something rustled in the shadows cast by her buggy, and she froze, heart pounding, ears straining to identify the sound. Nothing for a moment, and then it came again. Her fingers were cold and awkward as she fumbled for the switch on the flashlight. It seemed to take forever to turn it on, and then the beam swung out, illuminating the shafts, body and wheels of the buggy. And a field mouse, startled into mobility, by one of the wheels.

Sarah let out a shaky laugh. How ridiculous she was being! She might have known it was something like that. An arsonist would make more noise than a gentle rustle. Switching off the torch again, she turned toward the barn door. She'd go inside and check, even though the animals would certain sure react if a stranger were in there. Molly would welcome a good-night pat.

The shadows lay deep on either side of the barn door, but Sarah's encounter with the field mouse seemed to have laid her fears to rest. She strode forward, but stopped once more when something moved to the right of the door.

Her heart thumped again. No doubt it was Jonah, making the rounds of the farms before bed, just as it had been before.

She switched the flashlight on and began to raise it. "Jonah? Is that you?"

Before she could complete the motion, before she could even think, a dark, man-sized shadow hurtled toward her out of the shadows. A blow sent the torch flying. She gathered breath to scream. Rough hands shoved her. She stumbled, fell, hitting the ground so hard it knocked the breath out of her. For an instant the dark figure loomed above her, seeming incredibly huge. She struggled for breath. She had to scream, had to call for help—

But she couldn't. Her chest seemed paralyzed, unable to draw in air. He leaned closer, hands reaching toward her. With an explosive gasp, Sarah drew in air and let it out in a piercing cry.

AARON WAS HALFWAY across the cornfield on his nightly round when he heard the scream. He bolted toward the sound, his heart pumping, his feet thudding on the dry ground between the rows. He tried to tell himself it was an animal, but he knew better. It had been a woman's voice, and whose would it be but Sarah's? If she had encountered the arsonist . . .

He burst into the open and spurted across the cleared ground toward the barn, sure that was where the cry had come from. Even as he ran, he saw lights coming on in the house, heard voices calling, and knew others had heard it, too.

Running full tilt, he nearly stepped on her. He dropped to his knees. "Sarah? Are you all right?"

To his relief, she was struggling to sit up, her breath coming in shaky gasps. Her fingers tightened on his arm. "Aaron. Someone—in the shadows—"

"Are you hurt?" He put his arm around her, supporting her. "Don't try to move."

For an instant she leaned her head against his shoulder and he cradled her in his arms. Then she straightened. "I . . . I'm all right. Just a little shaken."

The beam of a flashlight pierced the darkness, showing Sarah's pale face and wide eyes. Her heart-shaped kapp was askew, and there was a patch of dirt on her forehead. She gripped his arm as if unable to let go.

Another figure moved into the circle of light. "Was ist letz?" Eli Bitler knelt on the other side of his daughter, putting out a comforting hand. "What has happened?"

He looked at Aaron, but all Aaron could do was shake his head. "I was coming to check the buildings when I heard Sarah cry out. I didn't see anything."

Sarah's mother reached them. Brushing past them, she put her arms around Sarah. "Ach, my Sarah." She sent a quick glare toward the men. "Let me see if she is hurt first. Time enough later to hear what happened."

Aaron moved back reluctantly so that Hannah would have more room, and Sarah let go of his arm.

"I'm fine, Mamm. Really." She sounded more like herself now, probably determined to reassure her mother. "Someone was there, in the shadows by the barn door. He knocked the torch out of my hand and knocked me down." Her voice shook, and a wave of protective anger surged through Aaron.

"Could you tell where he went?" Eli asked.

"Toward the woods." She tried to gesture, and winced, as the movement must have hurt.

"You're safe now, my girl," Hannah crooned. "Komm, I'll help you into the house."

"I'll carry her," Eli said, bending, but Sarah managed a shaky laugh.

"Ach, I don't need carrying." She stood, swaying a little. Aaron had to repress the urge to pick her up himself.

Eli took one arm and Hannah the other as they started toward the house. Eli looked back over his shoulder at Aaron. "Will you wait? We should talk."

Aaron nodded. They should talk, that was certain sure. But first, he wanted to take a look around. He found his own flashlight and switched it on. The one Sarah had had, which the intruder had knocked from her hand, was lying a few feet away. He picked it up and shook it. Glass tinkled, and it refused to come on.

Well, his would be enough to enable him to take a good look. He swung it in a slow arc. The ground was so dry that it told him nothing. He aimed the beam in the direction Sarah said the man had fled. There was no sign of anyone, but trampled long grass and broken branches showed where he had forced his way through the blackberry brambles. Aaron marked the place mentally. He'd come back and have a better look in the daylight.

He turned slowly, letting the light probe the shadows. Nothing there. Maybe the man had been approaching the barn when he'd heard Sarah coming, and had hidden there. Or maybe he'd already been in the barn and was trying to get away from the scene before she saw him.

Aaron's nerves grew taut at the idea. The light showed him the barn door, open a few inches. He grasped it and pulled it back, dreading what he might find.

The animals moved slightly in their stalls, and Molly whickered. He flashed the beam around, and they stared solemnly back at him, all apparently safe in their stalls. But as the beam dropped, he saw something that made his heart stop. On either side of the door, rags and dry wood had been propped against the frame. He bent for a closer look, not touching, and the scent of oil turned his stomach.

"Aaron?" Eli appeared in the doorway. "What is it?"

"Wait—don't come in." He stepped out carefully himself, mastering the urge to kick the inflammatory materials away from the barn.

"Why not?" Eli craned his neck, alarm lacing his voice.

"The firebug was here. He must have been setting up to torch the barn when Sarah interrupted him." Aaron's voice sounded strangled, even to himself. Sarah, breaking in on an arsonist. Who knew what a man like that was capable of?

Eli muttered under his breath for a moment. Then he moved as if to go into the barn. "I should get the animals out."

Aaron caught his arm. "Don't. It's best not to disturb anything. The police will want to examine it."

"Police?" Reluctance was plain in Eli's voice. "I don't know . . ."

"You are going to say we don't call on the police—that we forgive and accept. But this isn't just you, Eli. The arsonist is like a wild beast setting fires, and he won't stop until he's caught. What if someone dies? What if one of the firefighters is hurt or killed the next time?"

Eli let out a long breath. "You're right. We must forgive, but we must also keep him from doing more evil if we can. Will you call? I must tell Sarah and Hannah what is happening."

"I'll call Mac," Aaron said. "He'll know what to do." Quickly, before Eli could have second thoughts, he strode to the phone shanty near the barn.

CHAPTER NINE

AARON WAITED IN the kitchen with the Bitler family for the police to arrive. The boys, lured by the noise, had dressed hurriedly and reappeared, managing to evade their mother's eye as best they could. They wouldn't want to be sent back to bed with all the excitement going on.

Sarah was sitting at the table, being fussed over by her mother. He studied her face. Her color was better now, but a red lump had come up on her forehead. Hannah produced cold compresses, and Sarah's grossmammi brewed a pot of chamomile tea, insisting it would calm her nerves.

Sarah's gaze met his for a moment of shared amusement. They both knew it was better to let them fuss over her. It was their way of dealing with their own worry and fear.

"Shouldn't we go outside and keep watch, Daadi?" Jonny, the oldest boy, suggested. "He might come back."

"I don't think there's anything that would bring him back to our place in a hurry," Eli said. "He'll know that the police will be coming soon, and he certain sure doesn't want to get caught."

Sarah patted her brother's arm. "That's right. That's why he knocked the flashlight out of my hand. He didn't want me to see him. I'm sure he's long gone by now."

Maybe Aaron was the only one who saw the faint shadow in Sarah's eyes when she spoke. It looked as if she needed reassurance on that subject, as well. He wanted to touch her, to promise nothing would happen to her, but he couldn't. All he could do was join her efforts to ease the children's fears.

"He wouldn't stop running until he knew he was safe. He's not dumb enough to hang around here and risk being caught," Aaron added for emphasis.

"If only you'd let the dogs out first," Eli said, looking harassed. "They might have smelled the man before you spotted him."

"You're right, Daad." Sarah seemed to think agreeing was the shortest way out of the conversation. "I should have done that."

"Ach, I'm not meaning to scold." Eli patted her hand. "You did just the right thing, yelling for help the way you did. As soon as you yelled, he'd know there was nothing for it but to run away."

"The police are here," Thomas announced, peering out the window. Jonny and Noah rushed to join him. "Two—no, three cars of them." He sounded a little awed by the importance of the event.

"You wait here," Eli told his family. "Aaron and I will deal with them, and if they need Sarah to answer any questions, they can come inside."

The boys' faces fell, but Sarah looked relieved. Aaron didn't blame her. She probably didn't want to relive the experience again when she was just starting to get back to her usual self.

As soon as the two of them were outside, Eli voiced Aaron's thought. "I hope they don't have to talk to Sarah. She's been upset enough for one night."

"You're right, but the police probably won't see it that way." It was only fair to prepare Eli for what he expected would happen. "They're sure to want to hear her account, even though she didn't get a look at him."

"I suppose, but . . ." Eli let that trail off as Mac Whiting came toward them.

Aaron stiffened when he saw who had accompanied Mac. It was Fielding, the arson investigator. The memory of their conversation at the barn raising still rankled.

Aaron forced the feeling aside and focused on Mac, and it was to his old friend that he told what had happened from his point of view. Then Eli had to tell it from his. And then the questions began.

Aaron would say one thing about Fielding— he was thorough. Not the tiniest detail escaped him.

Finally he nodded as if satisfied. "Now if we can see Ms. Bitler, we'll get her account."

Eli seemed ready to object, but Mac beat him to it. "Suppose we have a look at the barn first. We have to do it anyway, and it will give Sarah a little time to compose herself. I'm sure she's upset."

"Ja, that would be gut," Eli agreed. "This way."

For a moment, Aaron thought Fielding would object, but then he nodded. He went to his car and returned in a moment with a case.

"We're going to need a lot more light on the scene. Can't they turn on the outside lights?"

"No electricity," Mac said briefly. "We'll bring the vehicles up close enough to use their headlights."

A few minutes later the farmyard was lit bizarrely by the headlamps of the vehicles, probing into the shadows and turning the grass a ghostly white. Mac produced several strong torches from the police cars, and they began working their way over the whole area.

Fielding gestured to Aaron. "Show me where the fires are laid."

Aaron led the way to the barn. His family would be wondering what had happened to him. They'd see all the lights and be concerned. He wouldn't be surprised to see Jonah show up to find out what was going on. Then he thought of Fielding's attitude toward Jonah, and said a silent prayer that his brother would stay clear of the place tonight.

Fielding seemed irrationally pleased with the preparations for starting a fire. "This bird is learning as he goes along," he said.

"You mean setting the fire in the doorway?" Aaron had already thought of that. "It's like he's trying to make it difficult to get the animals out." The words left a bad taste in his mouth.

Fielding shot a sharp glance at him. "You realize that?"

"Anybody who's ever tried to get animals out of a burning barn would see it." He tried not to snap the words. Did the man think he was stupid because he was Amish? Probably.

"I don't need you any longer," Fielding said. "Send that younger patrolman in to help me."

"Mr. Bitler would like to take the animals out of here," Aaron pointed out.

"Well, he can't," Fielding snapped. "Not yet, anyway. I can't have a bunch of animals trampling over the clues." He waved his hand in a dismissing gesture.

Aaron was glad enough to get away from the odor of the oily rags. The smell was noxious enough, but the reminder of what had been intended made him sick to his stomach.

If the arsonist had had a chance to light the rags, what would have happened? Sarah might still have been the first to discover it, and Aaron had no doubt she'd have tried to rush through the flames to get the animals out.

Did the arsonist realize that? Was he trying to get someone injured or killed?

Aaron gave the message to Johnny Foster, grinning at the face the young policeman made over being told to work with Fielding. Then Aaron walked to where Mac stood, surveying the weeds between the farmyard and the woods at the back of the barn.

"Little hard to see anything in the dark, ain't so?" he commented.

Mac shrugged. "I wanted to mark off the place. We'll come back and have a better search in the morning. Is Fielding done with you?"

"He has Johnny working now. Fielding seemed very pleased to be looking at the fires the firebug laid. What he finds to be happy about, I don't know. It's not as if I caught the man." Aaron's fingers curled into fists.

"Careful," Mac said. "You believe in non-violence, remember? What would you do if you did catch him?"

The rage that coursed through Aaron was a warning of its own. Anger had to be combatted or it would control a man. Mac shouldn't have to remind him that an Amish person did not resort to returning evil for evil. But while he could turn the other cheek for himself, he was struggling with the idea where Sarah was concerned. "If I'd seen him, you'd have known who you're looking for."

Mac handed the end of a roll of plastic tape and a few thumbtacks to Aaron. "Here. Take this and attach it to the end of the toolshed."

He obeyed, playing the tape out as Mac released it. "Does Fielding have to question Sarah tonight?"

"He'll insist on it. The best I could do was delay him." Mac stretched the tape out to a handy tree and fastened it there, cutting it off with a pocket knife. "I'm afraid he doesn't think very highly of small-town cops."

"He's not so smart himself, then," Aaron said. "You know the area and the people in a way he never could. If anyone can catch this man, it's you."

Mac grinned. "Thanks for the vote of confidence."

"I'm right. You'll see." He hoped he was right, because Mac knew them all too well to be led astray. Who could tell what idea Fielding might get?

Too soon, the investigator came out of the barn, moving briskly. "All right. I've done all I can in there. I've given your man samples to take in for testing. See that he doesn't lose them on the way. Now I need to question Ms. Bitler."

He marched off toward the house, and Mac followed him with a rueful look at Aaron. After a moment's hesitation, Aaron went, as well. There was probably nothing he could do to help, but Sarah and her family might appreciate his presence.

Fielding gave him a look when Aaron edged into the crowded kitchen, but he didn't say anything, probably because Hannah was busy trying to persuade him to have a cup of coffee and a wedge of apple crumb pie.

Mac grinned, nodding his acceptance. "Never turn down a piece of your apple crumb pie, Hannah."

Fielding shook his head firmly, with the air of a man trying to hold on to a situation that was sliding out of control. Aaron sat kitty-corner from Sarah, giving her a reassuring smile when she glanced at him.

"Now, Ms. Bitler, if you can tell us what you saw, it may be of great help in catching the perpetrator. If you—"

"But I didn't really see anyone," Sarah said, pressing her fingers against her forehead. It was a measure of how stressed she was that she'd actually interrupted the man.

"Suppose you tell us the whole thing, just the way it happened," Mac said, his voice friendly. She could hardly be intimidated by Mac, sitting at the kitchen table eating pie as if he were still the little boy she'd played with.

Sarah visibly relaxed when she focused on Mac. "I went out to give a last look around before I went to bed. I took a flashlight, but I didn't turn it on right away because the moon was bright enough to see by."

Mac nodded, encouraging her.

"Well, I checked the toolshed first, and then the other buildings. The dog pen is by the barn, and I was going to let the dogs out when I got there." She paused, and Aaron, sitting so close to her, could sense her tension rising. "I started feeling nervous, like someone was there, over by the buggy. But when I turned the torch on, it was just a field mouse." She smiled, but it was just a nervous twitch of the lips.

Fielding moved, as if to speak, but Mac seemed to silence him with a look.

"You were going to the barn then?"

"That's right. I didn't hear anything from the animals, but it seemed to me that there was something outside, to the right of the barn door."

"Your right?" Mac asked quietly.

Sarah nodded. "It startled me, and then I thought it might be Jonah again."

"Jonah again?" Fielding broke in sharply. "What do you mean? Is this Jonah King you're talking about?"

Aaron's heart sank at the look in the man's eyes. If only Sarah hadn't mentioned his name . . . But how could she know what the investigator might make of it? She nodded. "Jonah King, that's right. You see, I'd run into him out by the barn a few nights ago, so I just jumped to the conclusion it was him again."

"Jonah and Aaron have been helping us patrol the outbuildings at night, along with Nick and Jim Whiting," Eli said. "You know that, Mac."

He nodded. "That's right. Most of the farmers in the township are doing something similar. They all help their neighbors at a time like this."

Fielding didn't look convinced. "Was there any other reason you thought it might be Jonah King? The shape, the smell, something you heard?"

"No." Sarah seemed warned by the tenor of his questions. "I've already said I didn't see anyone. I started to turn my flashlight on, and someone just burst out of the shadows at me. He knocked the flashlight away and pushed me so that I fell. He was nothing but a dark shadow."

"Couldn't you tell anything? His height? Size? You said 'he.' Are you sure it was a man?"

Sarah pressed her fingers against her temples again. "Nothing. I just said he because it seems likely the firebug is a man. It was dark. The moon was hidden by a cloud."

"You must have noticed something," Fielding pressed. "Think hard."

"I didn't." Sarah's voice shook. "I tell you I don't know anything more."

"I think that is enough questioning for now," Eli said, standing. "If we think of anything else, we will send a message to the police station."

"Thanks, Eli." Mac stood, as well. "We won't trespass on your hospitality any further."

Fielding wilted a bit before his firm expression. "Thank you," he said stiffly.

Sarah's tension eased, but Aaron suspected she was on the verge of tears. She wouldn't want anyone to see her cry—she never had, even as a child, and this grownup Sarah would feel the same. He got up, too, murmuring his good-nights, and held the door for Mac and Fielding to go out before following them.

That hadn't been as bad as it might have been, thanks to Mac. But still, Aaron couldn't help wishing Sarah had never mentioned Jonah's name.

"I HONESTLY COULDN'T even guess who it was." Sarah was in the middle of telling Allison about it at the shop the next day. She couldn't seem to help it when her voice shook a little as she did.

Allison gave a wordless murmur of distress and came around the counter to give her a hug. For just a moment, Sarah clung to her, hating to admit how much she needed the support right now. She'd managed to maintain a fairly calm exterior with her family, but each time she thought of those moments when the dark figure had loomed above her, she could feel herself shake inside.

But she didn't want to show her weakness, not even to a dear friend. She drew back, attempting a smile. "It's ferhoodled to be still upset. After all, no harm was done."

Allison squeezed her hand before stepping away. "It's not ferhoodled at all, whatever that means," she said. "The arsonist is a dangerous person, and you came too close to him. You shouldn't have—"

"Don't say I shouldn't have gone out by myself. If I hadn't . . . ." Her throat grew tight. "Well, the fire was laid, ready to be lit. Maybe even five minutes would have been too late. And with it set right in the doorway, we'd have lost time getting around to the back and trying to take the animals out the small door."

Allison rubbed her arms, as if chilled. "That's really nasty. It's as if the arsonist wanted to cause the most damage he could, even if someone got hurt."

"I guess that's the whole idea." Sarah's fingers, restless, toyed with a spool of ribbon on the counter. "Someone has to be crazy, I think, to do this."

"Maybe so. I've heard of people torching their own buildings for the insurance money, but this guy is setting fires that have no benefit at all to him. To me, that spells crazy." Allison frowned a little. "I suppose you had to talk to that man Fielding again."

Sarah nodded. "He seemed convinced I could remember something helpful no matter how many times I told him I didn't see anything. I can't even be positive it was a man, although I think so."

"Well, let's hope he at least found some physical evidence that will help. There may be some way of telling where the rags or oil came from."

"I hope so." But she doubted it. In a farming community, there were too many possible sources for a bit of oil or kerosene or whatever it had been. And who could keep track of rags? They might even have been taken from someone's clothesline.

She glanced at Allison, but her partner had gone back to her computer. Just as well. Sarah didn't want to confide the other thing that had bothered her about that encounter with the fire investigator.

Those moments when he'd zeroed in on her mention of Jonah—what had that meant? It meant something; she was certain sure of that. She had felt Aaron's tension even though he'd given no outward sign of anything wrong. Was it just that he didn't like her drawing the attention of the man to his brother, even though it had been perfectly innocent?

She couldn't help feeling there was more to it than that. Well, if Aaron wanted to tell her, he would. If not, she'd try to forget. But she still wished she hadn't babbled on the way she had.

"Look at this." Allison's excitement drew Sarah out of her fruitless thoughts. "There's a detailed account here about a quilt festival out in Oregon that even includes the schedule and the various workshops they held. We can get some ideas for things that work from what they did."

Sarah went to stand behind her and peered at the screen. As used to Allison's reliance on the computer as she was, she was still sometimes surprised at the amount of information one could find with the click of a button. And it was purely a pleasure to focus on the excitement of the quilt festival after the horrors of last night.

"That really is a good resource." She leaned a little closer to study the screen. "Can you print out a couple of copies of the schedule? We can look them over with Mamm and also with Esther and Becky. They'd love to help with the planning."

Allison nodded, clicking the buttons that set the printer in the back room humming.

A thought flitted into Sarah's mind, maybe because she'd just been worrying about Aaron and his brother. "With the computer, would it be possible to find out something about the company that bought Matthew Gibson's farm?"

"I don't see why not. Every company has a web presence of some sort now. Why?"

"It might give us an idea of what they plan to do with the land. Aaron says Harvey Preston was told it was an investment, but they wouldn't be doing a survey for that, would they?"

Allison shrugged, her fingers busy on the keys. "I have no idea, but I can certainly see what's available on them. What did you say the name of the company was?"

"Evergreen Corporation. Harvey said they were located in Delaware."

"Evergreen. Sounds like something to do with conservation, doesn't it? And it's common for companies to have headquarters in Delaware. There must be tax advantages to it. But let's see what shows up."

Sarah wanted to stand behind Allison and watch the information pop up, but the shop phone rang, so she went to answer it. It was Julia, sounding impatient as always.

"Julia, slow down. This is Sarah. What did you say?"

Allison glanced up from the computer at the mention of Julia's name, smiling.

"I said I found the pictures I took of some of my quilts. The oldest one is from my grandmother's family. It belonged to my great-grandmother, or maybe even great-great-grandmother. Isn't there something called an album quilt?"

Sarah's interest perked up at the words. "Album quilts can be very special. Does it have a different image in every block?"

"Yes, that's the one."

Sarah did some mental calculating, based on Julia's age. If the piece was an album quilt that had belonged to her great-grandmother, it might be quite valuable.

"It certainly sounds special. If you—"

"You need to come over right now and look for it." Julia's voice had its imperious note. "I'm not waiting for that lazy cousin of mine to get around to it."

Sarah sent a harassed look toward Allison. "I'd love to come over now, Julia, but we are so busy—" She stopped, because her partner was making shooing gestures with her hands.

"Go," she said. "You know she won't be content until you do."

Sarah covered the receiver with her palm. "I don't want to leave you alone in the shop again, but I'm afraid she might try to get up those attic stairs herself."

"It's fine," Allison said. "Go. If your mother or Esther and Becky come in before you get back, they know what to work on."

Sarah spoke into the phone again. "I'll be over soon, Julia."

"Good. Don't dillydally." She hung up without a goodbye, but then, Julia never had been as particular about etiquette as her dear friend, Allison's grandmother.

Allison was looking at her with raised brows. "Don't tell me she really has a great antique quilt. I thought it was a wild-goose chase."

"If what she's describing is accurate, and if it's as old as she says, and if it's in decent shape," Sarah said. "I can't tell anything until I actually see it."

"You'd better get going, then. I'll hold the fort."

Sarah reached down to retrieve her bonnet from under the counter. "I'll try not to be too long. Before I go, did you find out anything about the Evergreen Corporation?"

"No. Not a whisper." Allison was frowning, maybe because she hated to admit defeat.

"Well, you tried. I guess that's a dead end."

Her friend shook her head. "You don't understand. It shouldn't be a dead end. If such a corporation exists, there has to be a record of it somewhere. Given time, I'll find it. But it's very odd that a company wouldn't have a web presence. Very odd," she repeated.

"You're sure? I mean, the quilt shop didn't have one until you insisted."

Allison smiled. "Trust me on this one. I'll keep looking. We'll find something. Now go, before Julia calls again."

Nodding, Sarah hurried out. There was a lot to be said for their church district's ban on having telephones actually in the homes. The ringing seemed to demand an answer, no matter what else a person might be doing. At least with the phone shanty, they didn't hear that insistent ring.

As she turned away from the door, a movement at the rear of the hallway caught Sarah's eye. Now, what was Gus Hill doing here? Surely Julia hadn't sent him with a message when they had just spoken on the telephone.

No, that couldn't be it. Gus must have seen her come out of the quilt shop, but he turned away immediately, staring into the window of the bookstore.

Had Fielding ever caught up with Gus in his rounds of interviewing? Sarah hadn't heard. Knowing Gus, it was just as likely he'd stay out of the investigator's way, probably assuming he'd get blamed for anything that was going on. Certainly people were inclined to suspect him of petty thieving, even though he'd never been caught at it.

Maybe she should tell him Fielding was looking for him. But even as she started in that direction, Gus scuttled into the bookshop.

Shrugging, Sarah headed for the front door. She might mention it to Julia. If Gus hadn't spoken to Fielding yet, he probably should, if only to keep the man from suspecting him. Julia could convince him of that if anyone could.

CHAPTER TEN

JONAH LEANED ON his shovel and mopped his forehead. "Nothing worse than shoveling stalls on a stinking hot summer day," he muttered.

"Watch your language." Daad glared at him. "It has to be done, so get to it."

"I said it was stinking and it is," Jonah said, flaring up in an instant the way he always seemed to do lately.

Aaron sighed. Next Daad would respond, and then they'd be angry at each other again. There never seemed to be a good moment to bring up the danger of the fire investigator's suspicions, and yet he had to warn Jonah.

"Well, I don't know if it's the worst," Aaron said, trying to intercede before they got going. "It seems to be that baling hay might be more miserable when it's hot and humid and the hay sticks to you and gets in your hair."

That diverted Daad, at least. "You young ones don't know what it used to be like. Before we had a baler, we piled the hay on the wagon and forked it up to the loft. I thought we'd never get all the hay off us."

"We'd have to hose each other down if we did that," Aaron said, smiling with relief at having avoided a fight.

Daad shook his head. "We'd run down to the creek, strip off our clothes and jump in. The cold water never felt so good."

Even Jonah smiled at that image of their father skinny-dipping, and Aaron felt encouraged. Now if he could get a few minutes alone with Jonah, maybe he could clear the air.

It wasn't that he didn't trust his brother, he reminded himself. Jonah would never lose himself so much that he'd set a fire, whatever Fielding might say about excitement. But the boy had to be warned.

Aaron glanced down the row of stalls. "We're nearly done, Daad. Why don't you go get a cool drink? Jonah and I will finish in no time."

For a second he thought his father would flare up, like Jonah, and insist he could do as much work as either of them. But then he nodded, straightening slowly. "Maybe I will. Denke, boys."

Once Daad was gone, Aaron half expected Jonah to complain about being volunteered to finish the work, but aside from a sigh, he didn't comment. Aaron studied his brother's averted face. He and Jonah had been on better terms since that night at the last fire. He'd think that boded well for an honest discussion of the problem. On the other hand, he didn't want to ruin the fragile understanding, either.

"Daad was looking awful tired," he said finally.

"I don't think he's up to as much work as he thinks he is, especially in this hot weather."

Jonah didn't speak, but he seemed to be thinking over the words. "I guess," he said finally. Then his face clouded. "But he doesn't need to act like I'm not doing my fair share. Even if I'm out late, I still do my work."

Jonah's late outing the previous night had been the subject of this morning's heated debate with Daad, especially since Jonah's only explanation of where he'd been was that he was out with friends.

"Daad knows you're doing your share. He just worries about you."

"He shouldn't. I'm old enough to take care of myself."

Aaron's thoughts went to his own small daughters. "Maybe so. But I don't think Anna and Lena will ever be too old for me to worry about them. Not even when they have kinder of their own."

That surprised a smile out of Jonah. "Seems funny to think of them all grown up."

"Seems even stranger to me, but it happens." He was relieved enough at Jonah's attitude to bring up the previous night. "You missed all the excitement at the Bitlers' last night."

"Wish it had happened when I was looking around the place," his brother said. "Maybe I'd have caught him."

"And maybe you'd have been hurt trying. He was rough enough with Sarah."

Jonah's expression said he was tougher than any female. "Is Sarah sure she didn't see enough to recognize the guy? Seems like she must have noticed something."

"You sound like that arson investigator," Aaron said. "He was determined to get her to say she'd seen something, but she hadn't. And you know Sarah wouldn't lie." He hesitated, but there was something more that should be said. "We'll have to be cautious what we say about it. If the firebug thought Sarah could identify him, she might be in danger."

The idea seemed to scare Jonah nearly as much as it upset Aaron. "Is Sarah okay?"

Aaron nodded. "More shaken up than anything, but it was pretty frightening."

Sarah must start being more careful about where she went and what she did. The difficult thing would be to convince this new, independent Sarah of that fact. He admired her independence, but found he still wanted to protect her. Irrational—that was what it was.

"Ja, I guess it would be scary for her."

He was glad to see the boy taking it so seriously. Maybe it was safe to ask a direct question. "So where were you last night when all this was going on?"

He'd guessed wrong. He could see that in the sudden change of Jonah's expression.

"I was out with friends. Why are you asking? So you can tell Daad?"

"No, that's not it. Listen, Jonah, that arson investigator—Fielding—he's been asking questions about you. He's got this idea that a young firefighter might be looking for the excitement—"

Jonah threw down his shovel. "So that's what you think? You think I'm going around setting fires? You're even worse than Daad!"

"Jonah, no, I don't." But he was talking to an empty stall. Jonah had run out of the barn.

Aaron felt like banging his head against the stall door. He'd managed that badly, despite his good intentions. He'd probably created an even bigger chasm between himself and his brother. How was he going to protect Jonah now?

"WELL, WHAT DO you think?" Julia demanded an answer the moment she'd put the quilt photograph in Sarah's hands. "What is it? Is it valuable?"

Sarah tried to control her rising excitement. "I haven't had time to look at it yet, ain't so?" She carried the photo over to the window, where the light was better.

The image was in color, which helped, but it was faded, some of the detail lost. Still, she could see enough to know that it was indeed an album quilt, with each block done in a different design of flowers, leaves, trees and animals on a white background. With a magnifying glass, maybe she'd be able to see more.

She returned to Julia, who was leaning forward in her chair, fingers drumming on her cast.

"It looks like a lovely example of an album quilt. Its value will depend on how old it is and what condition it's in." She'd best be cautious if she didn't want Julia charging headfirst into finding it herself. "Do you know anything about the history?"

The elderly woman shrugged impatiently, making a face. "History! That's for that bunch of ancestor worshippers who talk about how their people came over on the *Mayflower*. I say it's what you do with your life that counts, not what you came from."

Sarah had heard Julia on the subject in the past. She and Allison's grandmother had had some lively arguments about it. If Sarah didn't head Julia off, she'd be in for a repeat.

"Ja, I'm sure you're right. But if we can establish who made the quilt and when, it will affect its value. And think of the draw it could be at the quilt festival." She didn't want Julia to forget the reason they'd embarked on this search to begin with.

"I don't care about the value," Julia said, still impatient. "I told you it was my great-grandmother's. What more could I know?"

"Well, sometimes folks talk about quilts to their family, so the kinder will know about their meaning. My mamm made a quilt for me that has a piece from every dress I ever had, back to when I was not much more than a baby." Sarah smiled at the thought. "She can even say how old I was with each one. It's a nice memory to have."

Julia actually seemed to be listening, instead of just waiting for her chance to argue. "I suppose I did hear a few things about that . . . what did you call it? An album quilt? My mother got it from her grandmother, I think. I believe there was some story about it being made for her wedding."

Sarah nodded. "That's pretty common for an album quilt. A group of girls will each contribute a patch to a quilt for the bride. Sometimes they put their names on their patch, sometimes not. Were they from around here?"

"No, no, that's the Herrington side of the family. They were from Baltimore. My mother moved here when she married my father."

"Baltimore." Sarah repeated the name, her mind calculating how old the quilt must be if it had belonged to Julia's great-grandmother. "That could be important. Album quilts became very popular in Baltimore in the mid-1800s, and a quilt in good condition from that period would be a wonderful good find."

"I suppose it would be . . ." Julia seemed to lose

track of her thoughts. She leaned her head on her hand, frowning a little as if trying to focus. "What was I saying?"

Sarah pulled a footstool closer and sat down next to the older woman, feeling concerned. This sudden fuzziness wasn't like the Julia she knew. "You were thinking about how old the quilt might be."

"Oh, right. My grandmother's quilt." She frowned again. "No, my great-grandmother. I just can't seem to think how long ago that was. Let's see. I was born in 1938, so my mother . . ."

"It doesn't matter," Sarah said quickly. "Maybe you have something in writing that would help?"

"Wait a minute." A bit of the usual spark came back into Julia's eyes. "I did keep my mother's Bible, and I think I remember that there was a family tree in the front. I'll look for it. It's here someplace." The wave of her hand seemed to take in the whole house.

"That's fine, but don't tire yourself out with hunting for it." Sarah watched her with some concern, Donna's words about Julia's forgetfulness coming back to her.

"I am tired," she admitted. "Don't know why, when all I do is sit here." Julia seemed to rouse herself with an effort. "Anyway, let's find the quilt first, so you and Allison can see it. I'm sure it's in an old trunk along with some other quilts and a few odd things. A silver chafing dish." She snorted. "I ask you, what does anybody need with that? Should have gotten rid of it years ago. Some other useless stuff in there, too. Just bring it all down, and we'll sort it."

Knowing how many trunks she'd seen in the attic, Sarah suspected that wasn't going to narrow the search much. Though Julia claimed to have no use for such sentiment, it had seemed to Sarah that the attic was crammed with things she'd kept.

"Do you remember what the trunk looks like?"

"Of course I do," Julia snapped. "It's one of those big, rounded-top traveling trunks. Shouldn't be that hard to find. Let's get at it."

Sarah had her doubts, but at least this time Julia had focused in on a particular type of trunk. With any luck, she'd be right.

Sarah obediently headed for the attic steps. A moment later, she stood at the top, staring rather helplessly at the assortment of crates, bins and trunks. At least there weren't too many of the rounded-top variety, assuming Julia was right about that.

Starting at one end, Sarah began working her way methodically through the contents of the attic, smiling when she remembered Julia's comments about those fancy dresses she'd found the last time.

But her thoughts were on Julia, who periodically shouted questions and instructions up to her. Had those moments of seeming confusion signaled a serious condition? Should Sarah talk to Donna about it? The woman often claimed to be Julia's only relative, but Sarah had no idea if that were true.

Somehow the idea of talking to Donna behind Julia's back left a bad taste in her mouth. She really didn't think she could do that, especially since the two women were so often on the outs.

She could talk to Allison, though. Allison was trustworthy, and her grandmother had been Julia's closest friend. The thought cheered Sarah. Even if Julia knew, she wouldn't feel betrayed at the thought of Sarah and Allison worrying about her. And if there really was something wrong with her, they could figure it out together.

The search seemed endless. Sarah unearthed more clothes from several decades, old linens and one trunk completely filled with yellowing photograph albums and newspaper clippings that were turning to dust. There were old badminton sets and what seemed a truckload of books.

Julia's questions had stopped, and when Sarah slipped down to check on her, she found her asleep in her chair. Well, that was certainly better than champing at the bit and threatening to come up the attic steps herself, cast and all. Sarah headed back up, hoping she'd find the quilts before Julia woke.

Finally, when she thought she'd checked

everything, Sarah found it. Pushed back under the eaves, the round-topped trunk must have been one of the first things put in the attic. Other objects had been piled in front of it until it was completely hidden.

Sarah's energy returned, and she dragged the trunk out under the light and opened the lid. The dragging sound must have roused Julia.

"What's happening? Did you find it?" she shouted.

"Ja, I think I did. Quilts, anyway, and some other things. I'll have to see—"

"Don't bother," Julia said. "Just bring all of it down and we'll look at it together."

Easier said than done, Sarah decided. She certainly couldn't haul the heavy trunk down. But she found a plastic trash bin and transferred the contents to it. She pulled the bin across the floor and bumped it down the stairs to where Julia was waiting.

"Dump it out. Hurry." Julia leaned forward in her chair. "Don't waste time."

"I won't ruin anything by haste," Sarah said firmly. She began taking the items out one at a time. Several quilts, each wrapped in a sheet, thank goodness. One pattern after another was exposed to view—a Lancaster Rose, the Double Wedding Ring Julia had mentioned, even a Drunkard's Path design. But no album quilt.

There were other things, too, including the

remnants of a flowered tea set. But no silver pieces such as the chafing dish Julia had mentioned.

Julia frowned at the contents, spread out around her. "Are you sure that's everything?"

"I'm certain sure. The trunk is empty now." Sympathy surged in her at the older woman's expression. "There are still some lovely old quilts here. We can clean them up for you if you'd be willing to display them."

"Fine, fine. Take them with you. But there should be more. I know it." Julia looked belligerent, but Sarah could see she was tiring by the way she kept rubbing her head.

"Maybe you got rid of the other things when you moved," she suggested, rewrapping the quilts.

"Now you sound like Donna. I didn't. I'm sure of it." But she didn't sound sure, and there was a bereft expression in her eyes that Sarah suspected had to do with more than a quilt and a silver chafing dish.

"Maybe—" she began, but Julia interrupted her by slapping her palms on the arms of the chair.

"Robbed. Someone must have stolen them. You said the quilt was valuable, and so was the silver. Go and call the police. I want to see Mac right now."

Sarah hesitated, trying to find a tactful way to urge caution.

"You're like Donna," Julia said, her temper flaring. "You think I'm senile, too."

"No, no, I don't think that at all."

Julia's temper left as quickly as it had come. She leaned back in the chair, resting her head on her hand. "Maybe Donna's right. I am forgetting things. But I'd rather be dead than senile."

Alarmed, Sarah put her arm around Julia's shoulders in a warm hug. "Please don't say that. It's normal to forget things, especially when you've been cooped up inside for so long."

Julia didn't seem to be listening. "I want to know what happened to that album quilt. If I'd sold it, you'd think I'd remember, wouldn't you? I don't know what to do."

The hopelessness of the final words struck at Sarah's heart. "Please don't worry. Let me take the photo and talk to Allison about it, all right?"

"You think you can find out what happened to it?" The woman's eyes lit with something of her usual spark. Sarah had no idea how to trace a quilt that might have been sold years ago. But she couldn't bear to disappoint Julia.

"If it can be done, Allison and I will find it," she said firmly. "I promise."

And what Allison was going to say about that promise, she couldn't imagine.

SARAH DECIDED SHE should have known Allison would see tracking down the album quilt as another challenge, and Allison loved challenges. Nick was going to have his hands full with her, Sarah thought with an inward smile.

"So we don't know for sure if it was sold, and Julia doesn't remember doing it." Allison summed up the situation.

"That's about it." Sarah frowned, trying to pin down the exact source of her concern about Julia. "She seemed more confused than I've ever seen her. You know how sharp she usually is."

"And how outspoken," Allison added. "I'm surprised you were able to keep her from calling the police. Are you sure that was the right thing to do?"

"I'm not sure of anything. But if Julia is getting forgetful, I wouldn't want that exposed by her starting a police investigation over something that wasn't stolen at all."

"We have the photo, at least." Allison propped it up next to her computer. "I'll scan it to see if I can bring up any of the details. And I can do a computer search among dealers as soon as I get a little time."

Sarah smiled. "I figured you and your computer could put us on the right track. I guess if anyone can trace the quilt, it's the two of us."

Allison grinned back. "Maybe we can set ourselves up as quilt detectives. But right now I have to get some letters out about the festival.

If you can handle things here, I'll go up to my office and deal with that."

Sarah nodded. "Esther and Becky should be here soon. I can't wait to show them Julia's quilts. You go on."

Allison would follow through, but the missing quilt—if it was missing—might have to wait a bit while they dealt with more immediate concerns.

Once Allison had gone upstairs, Sarah spread one of the quilts she'd brought from Julia's on the worktable. The Lancaster Rose design was beautifully executed. Sarah marveled over the tiny stitches that formed a feathery pattern in the quilting. The soft pink and rose colors looked faded, but that might just be surface dust.

She was bending over the quilt with a soft brush when the bell jangled.

"Are you taking over my job?" Becky questioned, shedding the bonnet that hid her blond hair the instant she came in the shop.

"Just getting it ready for you. Hi, Anna. Hi, Lena. I'm glad you came today."

Anna scurried over to Sarah, her younger sister following. "I'm working on a nine-patch doll quilt," she said proudly. "Do you want to see it?"

"For sure," Sarah said. "What about you, Lena?"

"I don't want to make any old nine-patch," she said, her young voice firm.

"But that's what Amish girls always start out on."

"Not me," Lena declared. "I want to be different." She looked at the quilt, her small body leaning trustingly against Sarah. "What's this one called?" One small finger prodded the quilt.

"That's a Lancaster Rose quilt. Can you guess why it's called Lancaster?"

" 'Cause we live in Lancaster County. I know that, even if I'm not in school yet."

"Right you are." She smiled at the little girl and turned, surprised to see that the children were followed by Becky and Aaron but not their grandmother. Sarah's heart gave a little bump when she saw Aaron watching his children with such tenderness in his face.

"Where's Esther today? I hope she's not sick?"

"Mamm's fine." Becky put her bonnet and the children's under the counter. "She has a dentist appointment this afternoon, though."

"I brought them on my way to the lumberyard," Aaron said. "Would you be willing to drop Becky and the kinder at home when you leave here?"

"Of course I will. It'll be a pleasure." Sarah would probably indulge in the dangerous daydream in which Anna and Lena were her own little ones, and they were all going home to Aaron.

"Good." Lena slipped her hand into Sarah's. "Tell us more about this quilt."

"Well, it came from an elderly friend of mine, and it was made by her mother or grandmother, so it's pretty old."

"Is that why it looks so faded?" Anna asked.

Becky joined them. "It might just be dirty. Maybe you can help me brush the dust out, if you promise to be very, very gentle."

"I can do that," the girl said.

"Me, too," Lena insisted. "Let me help, too, Aunt Becky."

"I think there are enough brushes to go around," Sarah said, smiling at them. "We'll all work."

Aaron touched her sleeve. "Before you start, maybe you could walk out to the buggy with me, all right?"

Sarah nodded, feeling suddenly shy. Aaron wanted to talk with her privately, for some reason.

The two of them walked to the back of the building, where a door led out to the paved parking area. Sarah reached for the latch and gave an annoyed exclamation. "This door has been left unlocked."

"It's not supposed to be?" Aaron tried it himself, as men so often seemed to need to do.

"The custodian is only supposed to leave it open if we're expecting someone to need it.

Otherwise, folks are meant to ring the buzzer by the door, and he comes and lets them in."

"He probably decided to save himself a trip," Aaron said, holding the door for her. He looked distracted, as if the failures of their custodian were of little importance.

"Is something troubling you?" She stepped outside to the parking lot, where Aaron's horse and wagon waited.

Across the paved area was the cabinetry shop, and next to it the fenced paddock for her mare, with a lean-to for Molly to shelter under on wet days. Sarah's own buggy was pushed back under the maple tree to leave as much space as possible for customers to park.

They'd reached Aaron's buggy before he answered, but his lowered eyebrows had already told her she was right.

"I had an odd message left on the answering machine at the phone shanty." He patted his horse absently. "You remember when I told you I was writing to Matt Gibson about the property sale?"

"Did you get an answer from him so soon?" But an answer, one way or the other, surely wouldn't worry him.

"Not exactly. I think he must have gotten my letter, or why the message? But he sounded upset, even angry. I certain sure didn't mean to question his judgment. He had a right to sell to anybody he wanted."

It seemed clear that Aaron was having second thoughts about having written. "What did he say?" Sarah asked.

"It was very short, but I remember Matt never liked to talk to machines, so maybe that was why. He'd probably started speaking before the recording began, so it picked up in the middle. He was saying something about a letter, and I think he meant he was writing to me. But then he said he'd be coming back to Pennsylvania soon. He said, 'We have to talk.' And then he hung up."

"But I thought the whole reason he sold the property the way he did was that he was feeling too poorly to travel." Now it was Sarah's turn to frown. "I'm sure he said in a Christmas card that his doctor told him he couldn't fly because of his bad heart."

"Ja, that's what I understood, too. So now I'm wondering if my letter upset him so much that he's risking his health to come back here. I didn't mean for him to do that. I thought he'd write me a note, that's all."

"You feel responsible for him making the trip, ain't so? But you should know by now that Matt Gibson makes up his own mind about things." She tried for a tone of calm common sense, even as her mind worried over what this might mean.

"Ja, that's true." Aaron's expression eased a little. "But still, I wrote the letter."

Aaron had always had a sensitive conscience,

212

quick to take responsibility even for things that weren't really his fault. He'd never outgrown that, it seemed.

"If he had a right to sell, you also had a right to know why he didn't honor his promise to you. The decision to come was his," she pointed out. "Did he say when he's arriving?"

Aaron shook his head. "Just that we have to talk."

Sarah touched his arm lightly and as quickly took her hand away. "Matthew is as stubborn as Julia Everly is. I hope I'm not that bad when I'm old."

Aaron's lips quirked. "I think there's no danger of that, Sarah. What has Julia upset now?"

Maybe talking about something else would ease his worries about Matt Gibson. "I wasn't able to find a special quilt she thought was in her attic, and she's bound and determined someone stole it from her. She wanted me to call Mac then and there."

Aaron didn't give her the expected smile in return. "Was it a valuable quilt?"

"If it really is a mid-1800s Baltimore album quilt, and if it's in good condition, it would be worth thousands. But that's a lot of ifs."

"Do you think she might be right about it being stolen? I've heard stories of people preying on the elderly, thinking them alone and helpless."

Sarah had heard the stories, too, and it saddened

her to think of those who were alone. Still . . . "How would anyone know she had a valuable quilt stored in her attic?"

Aaron didn't answer for a moment, studying her face. "You're trying to convince yourself, Sarah. I know that look. And you're determined to help her, ain't so?"

The warmth of his tone shook her. "You don't need to say it as if it's a fault to want to help others."

"Ach, I don't mean that." Now he clasped her wrist in a firm, reassuring grip. "I know it's useless to expect you to think first of yourself. You're a generous woman. Look how gut you are with my girls. All they can talk about is how much fun they have when they come to the shop."

If he kept on holding her wrist, he might detect the way her heart was racing at his touch. But she couldn't bring herself to pull away.

"Anna and Lena are such sweet girls. Who could help wanting to have fun with them? You are doing a wonderful fine job of raising them on your own."

"Denke." His expression seemed to darken, and his fingers moved against the skin on the inside of her wrist, his touch shimmering across her skin. "I'm glad you think so. Some people seem to think I should marry again as fast as possible, as if I can't raise them without a wife."

His tone seemed to say that remarrying was out

of the question. Her heart twisted. Did he still love his late wife so much that he couldn't bear to think of another woman in her place?

Sarah managed to force words through dry lips. "You have plenty of time. The girls are happy and healthy as things are, and they have your mamm and Becky." She took a breath. "I'm sorry the grief is still so painful."

Aaron's gaze met hers, met and held. She couldn't tell what thoughts moved behind that dark expression, but she felt as if she were drowning in his eyes. Slowly he lifted her hand, and for an instant she thought he intended to press his lips against her wrist.

Heat flooded her at the thought. Could he tell what she was thinking?

With a sudden movement Aaron swung away from her. He grasped the side of the buggy, his knuckles white.

"I must go." His voice rasped painfully.

He grabbed the lines. Released, she stepped away, dazed, unsure whether what she felt was grief or shame.

CHAPTER ELEVEN

SARAH WAS STILL trying to figure out what had happened between them when she went back into the shop. All she'd been trying to do was reassure Aaron, but that sudden surge of emotion . . .

Maybe she should have found a reason to stay out of the shop a bit longer. She wasn't sure she could keep her face composed.

No one seemed to notice anything, though. Becky had the children helping her to brush the Lancaster Rose quilt.

"Look, Sarah." Becky's enthusiasm bubbled over. "See how bright this little square is where we've brushed it."

Sure enough, the colors had emerged from the seemingly faded surface, as if they were real roses cleaned by a summer shower.

"It's beautiful, isn't it? The quilting stitches are as delicate as a bird's feathers. Julia's grandmother must have been a master quilter."

"Like our grossmammi," Anna said loyally.

"Like your grossmammi," Sarah agreed. "And Aunt Becky, too. You are wonderful fortunate to have two such fine quilters in the family."

A wash of color, as delicate as that of the rose on the quilt, tinted Becky's cheeks at the praise. "I don't remember that Mrs. Everly is interested in quilts at all," she said. "You'd think her gross-mammi would have taught her."

"I think they lived far apart, so maybe that was why she didn't have an interest," Sarah said.

"Ach, that is a shame." Becky's tone grew sad. "Nothing is more important than family."

Sarah nodded, glancing at the little girls. To the Amish, the Englisch pattern of moving far away from kin for new jobs and new lives seemed so strange. A birthday celebration for each of Aaron's children would mean a gathering of aunts, uncles, cousins, grandparents, all living within a short distance and part of their everyday life. Even without a mother, they didn't lack for relatives to love and care for them.

"At least Mrs. Everly kept the quilts. Although . . ." Sarah stopped, thinking of the album quilt.

Becky was looking at her, eyebrows lifted. "What? Does she want to sell them?"

"No, at least I don't believe so. But she had what I think was a very old album quilt that we weren't able to find."

"Maybe it will turn up," Becky said comfortingly. She turned back to the patient brushing. "I'm supposed to do a patch for my cousin Ella's wedding quilt, and I haven't decided yet what design to use. Maybe I could look through some of the books you have about quilts?"

Sarah hadn't realized Becky had noticed her small quilting library. "For sure. Anytime. You can take one home with you tonight, if you want."

"Denke, Sarah. Ach, Lena, not so fast with the brush," she said, turning her attention to her niece.

Lena put the brush down. "It's too hard to stand in one place so long. Can't I do something else?"

Lena's energy always amused Sarah. She could never be content with an activity that required being still.

"Sure thing. Why don't you help me with rearranging some of the fabric? I have to make room for some new fall prints that just came in."

"I can do that." Lena scurried around the table to her. "I'm strong enough to carry things."

"I'm sure you are. Let's start by unpacking the boxes in the back room."

Lena, it seemed, liked to chatter while she worked. After she'd exclaimed over the various bolts emerging from the boxes, she went on to tell Sarah about her favorite calf, the cow that had tangled its tail in the fence, the field mouse she'd seen in the barn, and the new kittens she was sure the barn cat had hidden somewhere.

"I wish she'd let us see the babies," Lena said wistfully. "Onkel Jonah says she doesn't want us touching them while they're so little, but I'd be careful."

"I'm sure you would, but Onkel Jonah is right. Mother cats are like that. Sometime soon she'll probably bring them out."

"That's what Onkel Jonah says."

It sounded as if Onkel Jonah had a devoted little follower in Lena. "You have a gut onkel, ain't so?"

The girl nodded, but a frown disturbed her usually merry face. "I wish he wouldn't get mad at Grossdaadi. And now he's mad at Daadi, too. I don't see how anybody could be mad at Daadi."

Obviously Daadi had first place, and Sarah was touched that such a small child could be sensitive to the currents among her elders. No doubt there were still issues over Jonah's rumspringa behavior, but it surprised her that Aaron had become involved. He seemed to try so hard to bridge the gap between himself and his young brother.

"I'm sure they'll make it up soon." Should she mention Lena's concern to Aaron? He probably would want to know, but given what had happened during their last conversation, she found herself shy of bringing it up.

By the time she and Lena carried the new bolts to the main room, Allison had returned, and she and Becky were having a lively conversation about plans for the quilt festival while they worked. Becky's enthusiasm for all things quilting-related were obviously overcoming her usual reserve with strangers.

"It's going to be a big success," Sarah said when there was an opening in the chatter. "With what we raise, we can see to it that the firefighters have what they need."

Becky grinned. "And besides, it'll be fun."

"Lots of work," Allison reminded her.

"That's what we call a work frolic," Sarah pointed out. "We work and have fun doing it because we do it together."

Almost before she knew it, the afternoon had slipped away. Everyone helped in closing down the shop for the night, the kinder as enthusiastic about that as they were about everything else. They were fine girls, and she thought again of what Aaron had said about folks thinking he ought to marry. Whatever anyone else might believe, he seemed to be coping very well in raising them without their mother.

When they'd finished harnessing Molly for the trip home, Sarah lifted the children into the buggy first. "Do you want to be behind the seat or squished onto the seat between me and Aunt Becky?" Her buggy wasn't the family carriage, suitable for more than two or three.

Lena started to climb into the small space behind almost before she had the words out. "I'll go back here." She scrambled over the seat, heedless of her skirt flipping around her.

"I'll sit between." Anna settled snugly in the middle. "I like it here."

Sarah exchanged an amused glance with Becky as they climbed up. The two girls were certain sure predictable. "Everyone ready? We're off." She set Molly moving with a soft click.

"I don't like driving in town when there's so much traffic," Becky said as they trundled down the main street. "It makes me nervous."

"Me, too," Sarah confided. "When I first started coming into town to work every day, Daad drove me. But I knew it wasn't right to take him away from his own chores, so I pushed myself to do it. Still, we turn off here on the back road, and then it's not so bad."

Sure enough, once they'd gotten a mile or two from town on the narrow blacktop that wound between farms, there was little enough traffic.

Becky relaxed the tense grip she'd had on the side rail. "Allison was telling me about searching for that album quilt that belongs to Mrs. Everly. Do you really think she can find it that way?"

"If anyone can locate it using a computer, I'd guess it would be Allison. That's if it's advertised online. We wouldn't have a website if it weren't for Allison's insistence."

"Lots of Amish businesses have them now," Becky pointed out. "Daad doesn't like them, or cell phones, either, but Aaron says folks can't run a business without them these days."

Sarah shot her an amused glance. "I suppose you have a cell phone?"

Becky nodded. "All the girls in my rumspringa groups do. I don't call much, but we text each other about our plans."

"Like what you're going to wear to the next singing?" Sarah remembered the chatter she'd get into with her friends when the every-other-Sunday-evening event for teens was approaching.

"For sure." Becky grinned.

"When I'm old enough for rumspringa, I'll have a cell phone," Anna said. "Won't I, Aunt Becky?"

"Probably, but you have a while to wait for that."

"It's a long time." Anna began counting on her fingers, presumably figuring out when she'd start her rumspringa.

"Just enjoy being the age you are," Sarah said. "I remember how much fun I had then, playing with your daadi and the other neighbors. I'll bet you do, too."

"Especially our cousins." Lena piped up from behind them. She wiggled, and Sarah felt her pressing against the back of the seat. "Look, that's where the first fire was." She pointed as the Everly property came into view.

No doubt Aaron was trying to protect his girls from fearing the arsonist, but children seemed to find out everything, no matter how careful the grown-ups were.

"That's where it was, all right." Sarah kept Molly moving at a sharp pace. The mare still showed some reluctance when they passed the property.

"Why doesn't anyone farm there?" Anna asked, turning to glance in the direction of the remains of the barn.

"Well, it belongs to an Englisch lady who lives in town, and I guess—"

Sarah lost the train of thought when Molly tossed her head, setting the harness jingling.

"Komm, now," Sarah chided the mare. "You go this way every morning and afternoon, ja?"

But Molly didn't settle. Her pace slowed. Just as Sarah lifted the lines to snap them, there was a loud cracking noise. The buggy lurched. Before Sarah could do more than drop the lines to grab a child in each arm, it tilted, flinging them out.

Sarah hit the ground, breath knocked out of her, struggling to make sense . . . But the buggy was overturning, coming at them; they'd be crushed . . . She threw herself over the children just as the seat struck her back, knocking her senseless.

AARON SENT HIS buggy rocketing down the road at a reckless pace. This once, he'd like to have a car to whisk him to the scene. Ben Stoltzfus had assured him that everyone was all right, but he wouldn't be satisfied until he held his two girls in his arms again.

He shouldn't have left them, shouldn't have relied on someone else to bring them home—

Stoppe, he ordered himself. This was foolishness. Sarah was a careful driver, and no one could control an accident. He must not blame her, but they were his kinder . . .

Thank the gut Lord he'd been where he could hear the phone ringing in the shanty. Ordinarily he might not have checked it until later. But that was foolish, as well. Ben said if he hadn't reached him right away he'd have sent one of his boys riding bareback to fetch him. The children were fine, Becky was fine and Sarah was fine. They were all just shaken and upset, with some bumps and bruises.

He turned into the lane at the Stoltzfus farm, where the new barn stood as a testament to Amish resilience. Even before the buggy came to a complete stop he'd jumped out, raced to the kitchen door and bolted inside without knocking.

"Daadi!" Lena flung herself into his arms, closely followed by Anna.

He held them tight against him, his heart still pounding. "You're all right? Do you hurt anyplace?"

Anna clung, her face pressed against his neck, but Lena wiggled free. "I scraped my knee, look." She pulled up her dirtied dress to show him.

He looked at it gravely. It had already been cleaned up, and someone, probably Miriam Stoltzfus, had spread ointment over it. "I see. I bet you were a brave girl when it was cleaned up."

"I was," she said, nodding firmly. "But I got my dress dirty when Sarah squished me."

"Sarah squished you to protect you from the buggy falling on you," Becky said, her voice shaking. "You should be grateful, not worrying about a dirty dress."

"But I am," Lena protested. "And I was just saying, that's all."

"Sarah and Aunt Becky took care of us when the buggy tipped over." Anna emerged from his neck, wiping away tears. "And I helped Sarah lead Molly out of the shafts."

"You were both very good and very sensible," Sarah said.

For the first time he had eyes for someone beside his kinder. Becky looked pale and a little disheveled, but she managed a smile.

"I'm fine," she said. "I fell down into the ditch. It was Sarah who had the worst of it. The buggy hit her."

He set Anna and Lena gently away from him and went to kneel next to the chair where Sarah sat. "Is that true? You should see a doctor. We should call the paramedics."

"I already told her that, but it was no use,"

Miriam said, handing what was probably a cold compress to Sarah.

"I don't need a doctor." Sarah's voice was firm, belying her pallor. "It wasn't that bad."

His gaze sought out Miriam's questioningly, and she smiled slightly, nodding. "She'll have a nasty bruise on her back where the railing hit her, and a headache, that's certain sure. But otherwise, they all came out of it well. Ben says the buggy is going to take some fixing. He's out there now with the boys."

"How did it happen?" He looked from Sarah to his sister, but it was Sarah who answered.

"The wheel came off. I've never had such a thing happen in my life." For an instant her voice wavered. "But Molly was very sensible. She must have figured out something was wrong, and she was nearly stopped before it fell clear off."

A good thing, he thought, but didn't say. If the wheel had come off at full speed, it could have been far, far worse. He frowned.

"I don't understand. What would make the wheel come off? Did you see anything? Notice anything wrong at all?"

Sarah's lips trembled at the questions, and he wished them unsaid. What was he doing, bombarding her with questions when she had just come through such an ordeal?

"Sarah can't tell you anything else," Miriam

said briskly. "Now, I just made hot chocolate for the little ones and some good sweet tea for Sarah and Becky. If you want to be useful, you can go join Ben and see for yourself."

Miriam had a habit of telling folks what to do, not unusual in the mother of a large family. And at the moment he deserved the implied scolding.

"You're right," he said, standing. "You girls sit down and have your treat. I'll be back in a few minutes, ain't so? Then we'll go home."

He gave Sarah what he hoped was a reassuring glance, and headed out.

It wasn't hard to find the wreckage. It was just around the next bend in the road, in front of the Everly property. Ben stood surveying the overturned buggy, while two of his sons held the mare on a lead line in the tall grass. She was munching away normally enough, seeming unaffected by the experience.

Ben nodded to him when he jumped down. "Nasty to see, ain't so?"

True enough. He'd seen buggies that had been involved in accidents before, and it always turned his stomach. Still, those had been encounters with cars.

"It is. How's the mare?"

"I checked her over pretty thoroughly, and she seems fine. Might be a little stiff tomorrow. It was the passengers who got the worst of this deal."

Ben was a good man with livestock. If he said Molly was fine, she was.

"She deserves an extra handful of oats tonight, that's certain sure," Aaron said. "According to Sarah, she sensed something was wrong and stopped. Probably saved them from being hurt a lot worse."

"Animals have a lot of sense sometimes," Ben said. "But look at this buggy. The wheel was clear over across the road. My boys brought it back. It must have really gone spinning. Wouldn't have expected it to go that far."

Aaron nodded, squatting next to the axle that dug into the ground. "Especially with the buggy nearly stopped when it came free."

Ben squatted next to him. "I'd be suspicious the buggy hadn't been maintained right if it didn't belong to Eli Bitler. But Eli's right handy with his equipment, and he's particular. He wouldn't let Sarah be driving a buggy that he wasn't sure was safe."

Running his hand along the axle, Aaron puzzled over it. There weren't that many things that could cause a wheel to come off. A buggy was a pretty straightforward vehicle, when you came right down to it. Not like a car, where a thousand and one things could go wrong.

"Have you taken a look at the wheel?" he asked.

Ben shook his head, getting up. "Best do that

now. It's over here." He led the way to the grassy bank where the wheel rested.

Aaron started to reach for the wheel and stopped, noticing a bit farther on the scuffed earth where the passengers had probably landed, with the buggy tilting over them. His stomach twisted. If Anna and Lena had been hit by it . . . But they hadn't. Apparently Sarah had thrown herself over them, bearing the brunt of the blow herself.

"Nothing here that I can see." Ben was examining the wheel. "Seems perfectly . . ." He stopped, running his fingers around the inside of the center, where it fit onto the axle. He drew them out and stared at them.

"Grease," he said. He rubbed his fingers together. "Or oil, maybe. Not enough to tell." He paused, frowning. "I guess Eli might have oiled it if it was squeaking." Ben's tone was doubtful.

"Maybe. It's easy enough to ask him." But Aaron had a sinking feeling that he knew what Eli's answer would be. "Do you think we can lift the buggy up enough to have a look at the axle?"

"Sure. Boys! Come over here. Just drop the line. That mare's not going anywhere with all that grass to eat."

With the aid of the two boys and a stout tree branch to use as a lever, they managed to tilt the axle end free of the dirt. Ben and Aaron squatted on either side, studying it.

Finally Ben grunted. "If it wasn't so unlikely, I'd say that someone loosened this wheel. But who would do a thing like that? It's impossible, surely."

"Maybe so." But he wasn't convinced. This was Sarah's buggy, and everyone knew she drove it back and forth to town every day.

If the arsonist believed Sarah had seen something that night she'd encountered him, might he try to silence her? Or warn her to silence? But would someone other than an Amish person even think of the buggy, let alone know what would make it dangerous?

Aaron didn't know, and he cringed at the thought of bringing the police down on them. But if Sarah was in danger . . . His heart seemed to miss a beat. He couldn't ignore that, either.

SARAH PATTED MOLLY reassuringly as she tied a lead rope to the back of Aaron's carriage. "You'll soon be home, my girl. I'll have a special treat for you tonight."

She hadn't expected to be making this trip to pick up the mare with Aaron, but he'd shown up after supper to let them know he'd go after Molly. She'd tried to insist he didn't need to do that, but in the end she'd given in and ridden along with him.

"She deserves it." Aaron ran his hand along the mare's flank. "From what you said, she might well have saved you from serious injury by stopping when she did."

"And the kinder, as well." Sarah hesitated, but there was something she needed to say. "I can't tell you how sorry I am that they were hurt when they were with me." Her throat tightened as she remembered too vividly the terror that had overwhelmed her at the sight of the buggy toppling toward those two innocent children.

"Don't say that. Don't even think it." Aaron rounded the buggy with her. "You risked yourself to protect them. I'm the one to be sorry that you were hurt."

"I'm fine. Just a little sore, that's all." She pressed her hand to her back, feeling the bruise.

"It was bad enough. I'm thanking God it was no worse." Instead of giving her a hand to help her to the buggy seat, Aaron startled her by lifting her bodily. He set her gently on the cushioned bench and climbed up next to her.

Brief as it had been, the pressure of his hands against her waist had snatched her breath away. Not wanting him to see her expression, she watched his strong hands on the lines as they started slowly down the road toward home.

"You really didn't need to come with me to pick up Molly," she said, once she thought she could control her voice. "Jonny was going to drive me."

"Your brother's a fine boy, but I don't think you

should be going down any lonely roads with only him for company just now." Aaron's tone and his face were grim.

"What . . . what do you mean?"

"Maybe I shouldn't be saying this to you, but it's best you're warned. I'm not convinced what happened today was an accident."

It took her a moment to absorb the import of the words. "You think someone did something to my buggy? But how could they? And why?"

"Why do I think it, or why would anyone do it?" Aaron frowned at the road ahead. The sun had nearly reached the top of the ridge while they were at the Stoltzfus place fetching the mare. The slanting rays seemed to touch the fields with gold.

"Both," she said. "I don't understand."

"You said it yourself. You'd never had such a thing happen before in your life. Neither have I. A carriage wheel doesn't come off that easily. So why did yours today?"

"Well, I . . . I don't know." Her rational mind rejected the idea, but fear came creeping along her nerves. "Daad had the buggy taken to the shop, but he didn't say anything about it not being an accident."

"Most likely he didn't want to worry you, and here I am doing it anyway." Aaron smiled slightly. "But I haven't forgotten that you came too close to the firebug. What if he thinks you can identify him? This might be a way of silencing you."

"But I can't say who it was," she protested, appalled at the thought he'd put into her mind. "I didn't see anything, and I told Mac and that investigator."

"The firebug might not believe it. I'm not saying this to frighten you, but just so you'll take precautions. Please, Sarah, promise me you won't go anywhere alone."

"My work, the shop . . . I have to go to town. I can't hide." She told herself he was imagining things, but that didn't seem to chase the fear away.

"Your daad and I already talked about that. Someone will drive you back and forth. They'd have to anyway, until your buggy is fixed."

"You talked to my father." She wasn't sure whether she was more offended or touched.

"I know I'm butting in, but I was afraid he didn't realize the possible danger. So I did, even if it makes you angry." Aaron darted a sideways look at her, as if assessing her reaction.

She let out a long breath before responding. "I'm not angry."

"Hold on to that thought, because I'm going to do something else you might not like. I have to tell Mac about it."

"Go to the police? But, Aaron—"

"I know, we don't go running to the police with everything that happens. If it was a chance act of vandalism, that would be one thing. But if it's related to the arsonist, Mac has to know."

The wheels rotated a few more times before she was ready to answer. Funny how aware she was of the buggy wheels now, when she usually barely heard them.

"I understand. I'm not sure you're right, but it's best if Mac knows. Anything to help him catch this person."

"Good." Aaron pressed his hand over hers where it lay on the seat between them.

She was still enjoying the sensation when she felt him stiffen.

"Look." He gestured toward the Gibson farm, coming into view along the road. "There's a car pulled up in the lane. Maybe Matt Gibson is there."

Sarah made out the glint of something silvery between the trees, hardly visible. "Could he have gotten here this soon?"

Aaron shrugged. "I guess. A plane to Philadelphia and a rental car the rest of the way wouldn't take long. I'll drop you off and then go and see."

"I'll go with you. If it is Matthew, there may be things he needs. In fact, since the house doesn't belong to him any longer, where will he sleep?

I'm sure Mamm and Daad would invite him to stay with us, if need be. Or at least to come over and have something to eat."

Aaron's lips tightened. "If he's upset with me, it might be better not to have you with me."

"If he's upset, having me there might be the best thing you could do," she pointed out. "He certainly shouldn't be getting himself excited with his bad heart."

"I don't think it's a good idea." Aaron was being unusually stubborn.

Well, she could be stubborn, as well. "If you drop me at home, I'll just walk over. Isn't it more sensible to go together?"

Aaron cast her an exasperated look, but then nodded. They rode in silence to the driveway and turned toward the house.

"How strange it must seem to Matthew, to come back to a place that was home for so many years, now that it no longer belongs to him." Sarah tried to put herself in that position, but she couldn't.

Nodding agreement, Aaron guided the horse around the car parked in the drive. With Molly plodding patiently behind, the buggy moved into position at the hitching rail Matt had put up years ago for the convenience of his Amish neighbors.

Aaron climbed down, coming around quickly to lift her down, just as he had lifted her up. When he set her on her feet they were very close, and he lingered for a moment, his hands on her waist.

"I hope we're doing the right thing," he murmured, almost to himself. Then he strode to the front door, with Sarah following.

He knocked once, then knocked again. There was no answer, but a faint glow came from inside—a light in the kitchen, Sarah thought.

"Someone must be there," she said. "The car, the light . . ."

Aaron knocked again, loudly, and added a shout. "Matt? Matt Gibson? Are you there? It's Aaron King and Sarah Bitler."

Still no response, and the silence began to seem eerie to Sarah. A slight breeze touched her arms, and she shivered involuntarily.

"This isn't right. He might be ill . . ." She let the words trail off as Aaron tried the door. It swung open.

He moved inside. "Matt?" he called. "Matt—" The sound choked off as if someone had grabbed his throat.

"Aaron, what is it?" His tall, broad body blocked her view. Impatient, Sarah stepped around him.

And then wished she hadn't. Matthew Gibson sprawled full-length on the living room floor, his head turned to the side, his eyes open and staring sightlessly at them.

CHAPTER TWELVE

AARON FELT AS if he'd been sitting in Matthew Gibson's old kitchen for hours answering questions, but since it was only now getting dark, it couldn't have been that long. Fortunately, the old Formica table and chairs had been left in place, or they'd have been sitting on the floor.

Mac studied the small notebook he'd been writing in. "So you're not sure exactly what time it was when you arrived at the house?"

"No." He clamped his lips shut on the word. Mac knew as well as anyone that farmers didn't consult watches and cell phones constantly. Aaron didn't have one, for one thing, and he didn't need it. Work on the land wasn't done by the clock.

"Sorry." Mac managed a slightly more human look. "I'll let you go soon, honest. How long had the car been sitting by the house?"

"No idea," he said tersely, and then regretted it. Mac was just doing his job, and Aaron had no reason to make it more difficult.

"Wouldn't you have seen it earlier, like when you left your lane?"

"Probably not." He frowned, trying to visualize the view of the Gibson property from their farm.

"The tree line hides that section of the drive from sight."

"But you saw it tonight?"

Aaron nodded. "Sarah and I happened to be coming up the road from the Stoltzfus place as the sun was setting. I guess the angle was just right for it to glint on the metal. I noticed it and pointed it out to Sarah."

He heard the sound of heavy footsteps in the other room, and someone shoved the front door open with a squeak. They must be taking poor Matthew away.

"Sarah isn't still out there waiting, is she?" Aaron asked. "She doesn't need to see Matthew's body again."

"No worries. I sent her home a half hour ago. Eli came over when he saw the police cars, so he took her. He said something about an accident she was in today?" Mac made it a question.

Aaron rubbed the back of his neck, trying to focus. "It's odd. I had just been saying to Sarah that we should tell you about it when this happened."

"An accident with a car?" His friend's tone was sharp. He was no doubt wondering why he hadn't been called at the time.

"No, nothing like that. She was driving home with my sister Becky and my two girls in the buggy when a wheel came off, down by the

238

Everly place. They were fortunate not to be hurt worse."

"I'm sorry. Your little ones are all right?"

"Fine." His thoughts flickered to Sarah shielding them. "Ben Stoltzfus and I both looked at the wheel and the axle. It seemed to have grease on it, or maybe oil. And Eli takes too good a care of his property to let his daughter drive a buggy that isn't safe."

"You think it was done deliberately." Mac filled in the blanks quickly. "Why?"

"I'm wondering if the firebug might fear Sarah could identify him in some way." Aaron shook his head, wishing he could shake off his worry as easily. "That buggy sits out behind the quilt shop all day long. It's more or less hidden by the building in front, that big maple tree Sarah puts it under, and your dad's shop. Someone could tamper with it easily enough."

Mac considered. "It would be a risk." He held up his hand when it seemed Aaron would interrupt. "I'm not dismissing it. It would be a nasty coincidence. I'll look into it. Is the buggy at the farm?"

"Eli had it picked up by John Shuman right away." Mac would know Shuman, the buggy maker.

"I'll stop by there and have a look at it. See what John thinks about it, too. Now, about your visit tonight—"

239

"I told you. We thought Matthew Gibson had come back. Sarah wanted to invite him to their house, and I knew he wanted to have a word with me."

Mac's attention sharpened. "How did you know that? Were you expecting him?"

"I didn't expect him to come here. I wrote to him, and I figured he'd answer with a letter or a phone call." Aaron hesitated, but there was no point in trying to keep back any part of the story. He had nothing to hide except the sense of responsibility that he'd prompted a sick old man to make a trip he probably shouldn't have. "He left a message on our machine, saying something I couldn't make out about a letter. Then he said he was coming up and that we'd talk. He didn't say when he was coming, but when I saw the car, I assumed it was Matthew."

"It sounds as if you wrote to him about something in particular. Must have been important, to bring him all the way back here from Florida."

"Not important enough for him to risk his health." Aaron sighed, feeling the weight of respon-sibility. "You see, he had promised me some time ago that when he was ready to sell the farm, he'd give me the first chance to buy it. I wrote to him because I couldn't understand why he'd go back on his word."

"So he didn't tell you it was up for sale?"

"No one here knew anything about it except

240

for Harvey Preston. He handled the sale, and he says Matthew never even mentioned me to him. I guess he might have forgotten, but I wanted to know why. And what the new owners are going to do with the place, too."

"You must have been pretty upset to find out he'd sold the property without even letting you know it was on the market."

"Disappointed, that's certain sure. I could have farmed this place and still been close enough that my mother and sister could take care of the children." His voice slowed when he realized Mac was writing down what he said. Wariness crept over him.

"You're asking a lot of questions that don't have much to do with poor Matthew having a heart attack," he said. "That is what happened, isn't it?"

"Too soon to tell." Mac didn't meet his eyes.

Aaron felt his muscles tighten. "It must have been. He had a bad heart, and his doctor had told him not to fly."

"How do you know?" Mac shot the question at him. It suddenly seemed he was a stranger instead of someone Aaron had known since they were children.

"He told us that in a Christmas card. Told the Bitler family, too."

"If that's the case, the medical examiner will figure it out." Mac hesitated. "There's just one thing that doesn't fit with that theory—there's been some sort of blow to the back of his head. It might have happened when he fell, of course. It probably did."

He sounded as if he'd like to believe that. Aaron could only stare at him, revolving the words in his mind until they made sense. Mac actually thought Gibson might have been murdered. And it sounded as if he thought Aaron had a motive to do it.

SARAH SAT ON the side of her bed, too tired even to take her clothes off. This had been a day that overwhelmed both mind and body. All she wanted was to topple over on the bed and escape into sleep, but the habits of a lifetime wouldn't allow her to do so without washing and changing into her nightgown.

Even as she tried to muster some energy, she heard voices from the kitchen below her bedroom. Daad was greeting someone, and the responding voice made her breath catch. Aaron. Why was he here so late? Had something else happened?

Drawing in a deep breath and straightening her spine, Sarah rose. Obviously she had to go down. Just as obviously she should keep this conversation brief, or she might treat Aaron to the spectacle of her dissolving in a puddle of tears. And the thought of what she might expose about her feelings in that moment frightened her.

"I think Sarah has gone to bed already," Daad was saying as she reached the bottom of the stairs. "Can it wait until tomorrow?"

"I'm still up, Daadi." Sarah went quickly into the kitchen, trying not to wince when the sudden movement sent a spasm of pain across her back.

"Sorry to bother you this late." Aaron's lips smiled, but his eyes were serious and furrows had formed between his brows. "It won't take long."

Daad looked from one to the other of them and cleared his throat. "I'll just take my newspaper into the living room."

They waited awkwardly until he'd gone, but even then Sarah could clearly hear the rustle of his paper in the quiet house. She nodded to the screen door. "Let's go out on the back porch to talk."

Aaron held the door, then closed it softly and followed her to the porch swing. When he sat, the weight of his body set the swing moving, and she was aware of every inch of him.

Aaron didn't speak, and she let the silence grow, unable to think of anything to say. The summer night seemed to press against her skin, and above the willow tree she could see the bright stars that made up Orion's belt. Lightning bugs flickered on and off in the lower field, leaving trails of light over the dry grass.

"I wish it would rain." Aaron's thoughts seemed to follow her own. "The corn is drier every day."

She nodded, not sure he could see the movement in the dark. "At least there haven't been any fires since last week. Maybe the firebug has been scared off."

"Maybe." Aaron turned slightly toward her, setting the swing vibrating. "Sorry. I was trying to think of some easy way to say this, but there isn't one. Before you talk to Mac again, you must know. He isn't convinced Matthew Gibson's death was natural."

It took a moment to grasp his meaning. "But . . . what would make Mac think that? We all knew how bad Matthew's heart was. He overexerted himself, and maybe just the stress of being back in the house where he'd lived so long . . ."

"I know. That's what I thought, too. And that would be bad enough. But Mac said there had been a blow to the back of his head." Aaron hesitated. "I'm afraid, from the questions he was asking, that he doesn't think it was an accident."

Sarah felt herself trembling. "It doesn't make sense. Surely Matthew could have struck his head on something when he fell. The idea that someone would—would attack him. That's crazy, isn't it?"

"Crazy things have been happening lately, ain't so?" Aaron's hand brushed hers, setting up a wave of heat that startled and dismayed her.

It was as if his slightest touch had the ability to shatter the self-control she prized.

"Who would do a thing like that?" She struggled to focus. "Who even knew he would be there? Maybe . . . well, maybe someone broke in, thinking the house was empty, and—"

"With the car sitting outside?"

That silenced her. Her mind seemed incapable of coming up with any other solutions.

"You asked who knew he would be there. I knew. At least, I knew he was coming. And from Mac's viewpoint, I had a reason to be angry with him."

"But that's nonsense! You knew he was coming, but you didn't know he was there already. Or even when he'd get here. I should think Mac had better sense than that."

"He's a police officer. He has to think that way." Aaron's fingers curled around her hand. "He'll probably want to ask you more questions about how we came to the house to begin with."

"Well, I'll tell him." She struggled to think, past the feelings his touch generated. "We were together for probably a good hour before we went to the house, so you couldn't have been there attacking Matthew. And you certain sure wouldn't have taken me to the house if you'd known Matthew was dead. Anyone would know that."

She felt Aaron's tension slip away at her words. "You're right. I hadn't thought of it that way." He blew out a breath. "Denke, Sarah. You are always sensible, ain't so?"

Sensible Sarah. Good friend Sarah. He'd probably meant the words as praise, but they seemed to strike at her already shaky control. How sensible was it to love a man who'd never think of you as more than a friend?

He clasped her hand briefly as if to thank her. "It will all straighten out. And it's in God's hands, as always."

Words pressed against Sarah's lips, but they were words that must never be said, and her eyes prickled with tears he mustn't see. She rose abruptly, fighting the impulse to run into the house.

"I'll talk to Mac. He'll see sense. Don't worry."

Aaron stood, maybe taken aback by her abrupt action. "I won't. Denke, Sarah. I'm sorry I disturbed you so late. Good night."

He stepped quickly off the porch and a moment later the darkness had swallowed him up. Sarah stood where she was, clutching the railing. If only she could make it up to the privacy of her room before Daad wanted to know what Aaron had had to say . . .

She closed her eyes, but could still see Aaron's face, could still feel his presence. What was she doing? What kind of a person was she?

Her common sense told her that she ought to be steering clear of him as much as possible. Nothing good could come of exposing herself to so much temptation.

But that was impossible. Aaron was her friend, if nothing else. He was in trouble, and she had to help him. Even if that meant running the risk of ruining everything by letting him see her true feelings.

"LOOK AT THIS!" Allison was excited enough to carry her laptop to the table where Sarah and her mother were looking over a quilt to be repaired the next afternoon. "Is it or is it not the same as the quilt in Julia's photo?"

Sarah was glad to have something to focus on other than the talk she'd had earlier with Mac, who'd been very much the police official this morning. She studied the image on the computer screen, comparing it with the photo Allison held up.

"It's certainly similar," she said, feeling some-one needed to remain cautious. "The detail isn't really good enough on that old picture to be positive. What do you think, Mamm?"

Her mother adjusted her glasses to peer at the image. "Close, that's certain sure. You can see the arrangement of this block with the lilac on it next to the one with the rose appliqué."

"Where did you find it?" Sarah tried to

make out the name of the website, but Allison had enlarged the image to take up the full screen.

"It's for sale at a shop in Lititz. If it is the same one, the dealer certainly ought to be able to tell us where he got it and from whom. That would settle matters." Allison looked ready to go and do battle with any number of dealers.

"If," Sarah repeated. "Album quilts are often signed and dated. Sometimes every block has the name of the person who made it, especially if it was for a wedding gift. So knowing the name of the person who made Julia's quilt would help. And the date, of course."

"Didn't you tell me Julia was going to look for more information?" Mamm asked. "She might could give you more to go on, ain't so?"

Allison nodded, seizing the laptop back. "And even if she hasn't, we should show her this image. It might jog her memory. Let's stop by and see. If she can help at all, we might just run over to Lititz and talk to the dealer."

Sarah hadn't yet gotten used to the way Allison darted from place to place. "We could call him," she suggested.

"It's always better to tackle a difficult subject in person. If we call, he might think we're accusing him of some illegality, and refuse to help."

She could plead that her back was aching, which it was, but then Mamm would insist she go home and lie down, and Sarah would rather be busy. And Allison's enthusiasm was infectious. Wouldn't it be wonderful if they could find Julia's quilt?

"What if Mac wants to talk to me again?"

"Then he can just talk to you later. There's really nothing more you can tell him, anyway. Hannah, you don't mind watching the shop for a bit, do you?"

Mamm shook her head. "As long as I know Sarah is with you and not off on her own."

"I'll stick to her like glue," Allison said. She nudged Sarah. "Come on. Let's go."

Allison hustled her out to the car and in a few minutes they were approaching Julia's front door.

"I suppose it's useless to hope Donna isn't here, since that's her car." Allison rang the doorbell. "She and Julia are bound to disagree about the quilt, and I—"

The door opened, cutting short whatever Allison had intended to say. It was indeed Donna, looking disapproving at the sight of them.

"I don't think—" she began, but Allison was already in the door and past her.

"Julia will want to see us," she said, perfectly assured. "You can go back to whatever you were doing. We don't want to interrupt."

That seemed to leave Donna speechless, and Sarah followed Allison into the living room.

Maybe she ought to adopt Allison's confident way of dealing with Donna. It certainly seemed to work.

Julia was trying to stand up from her chair. "Drat the woman. I told her I'd bop her with my walker if she turned away any more visitors."

The rattle of pans declared that Donna had retired to the kitchen, and Sarah urged Julia back into the recliner. "I'm sure she was just trying to help."

The older woman snorted, but Allison distracted her by plopping the computer on the tray table that sat next to her chair. "Look what I found. Is it the same quilt?"

Sarah shook her head slightly, but Allison wasn't fazed. She didn't seem to realize that her enthusiasm could easily sway Julia's opinion.

But Julia took her time, peering at the computer image. "It looks like the same one to me. Yes, I'm sure it is." She minimized the image, obviously more familiar with computers than Sarah, and studied the shop's main page. "So what is this Antiques and Collectibles store doing with my quilt?"

"That's what we hope to find out. We're going over there to talk to the owner."

"But it would help if we had some way of identifying the quilt for certain," Sarah said, giving her partner a warning glance. "If your quilt had a signature—that would make it certain sure. Were you able to find any information that might help?"

The swinging door to the kitchen opened, letting Donna through. She was carrying a tray with glasses of lemonade. Four glasses, Sarah saw. Obviously she meant to join the party.

"I thought you could do with a cold drink on such a hot day." She'd recovered her gracious manner. "Did I hear you say you found my cousin's quilt?"

"We may have," Sarah said. "There's an image on the computer of a quilt for sale that may be the one."

Donna swung the computer screen around so that she could see it. After a moment she shook her head. "I thought that quilt of yours had more pink and rose color in it."

"It did not." Julia joined battle instantly. "I think I know my own great-grandmother's quilt when I see it." She gave a satisfied smile. "What's more, here's the proof." From the depths of the cushions behind her, she pulled out a book. "My mother's family Bible. There's a family tree that shows the names and dates they all lived."

"Where did you find that?" Donna asked. "I've never seen it before."

"You don't know everything I have," Julia replied.

Allison was already perusing the family tree printed in fading ink inside the cover. Sarah

251

leaned closer to see for herself as Allison traced back through generations of the Herrington family.

"Would this be her?" She planted her finger on a name. "Margaret Herrington, born 1860, died 1895, Baltimore."

"She wasn't very old when she died," Sarah commented, but Allison didn't answer, obviously intent on the family tree.

"That's right. If I took much stock in such things, I could brag about the Herringtons of Baltimore." Julia's mischievous grin made her resemble an elderly monkey. "I'm pretty sure the quilt was embroidered with her name or some such thing."

Allison pulled out her cell phone. "Let's see if I can get a photo of the page. Then if the dealer is inclined to argue, we'll have proof." She carried it over to the window and snapped several photos, then brought the Bible back to Julia.

"Take good care of it," she said. "You may need it to prove ownership if the quilt was stolen."

"Stolen, indeed," Donna exclaimed. "How could anyone get into the attic to steal anything? Anyway, I'm sure you sold it yourself, years ago. All this fuss, and you're going to be embarrassed when the dealer proves it."

"I can stand a little embarrassment at my age," Julia said drily.

Allison was already putting away the phone

and gathering up the computer. She obviously intended to head straight to Lititz to confront the dealer.

"Just a minute before you go." Julia put out a hand to detain them. "What's this I hear about Matthew Gibson being dead?"

Sarah's stomach lurched. She didn't want to go over it again, but obviously she'd have to.

"That's right. Aaron King and I found him last night. We happened to see a car in the driveway and went to see if he'd arrived. . . ."

Julia patted her hand. "So sorry you were the one to find him. But don't feel too bad. He'd had a long life, and he was probably ready to go, don't you think? The heart went out of him when he lost his wife. He came back to see the old place one more time, I suppose."

"Something like that." She evaded a direct answer.

"Did you know he was coming?" Donna asked the question Sarah had hoped to avoid.

"I'd heard. He called Aaron to let him know he was coming."

"Aaron? Why Aaron? I'd think he'd have gotten in touch with your mother. She was the one always taking in meals to him." Julia's sharp eyes zeroed in on Sarah.

"He and Aaron had been in contact. You see, Aaron had hoped to buy the farm. He's eager to get a place close to his parents."

"And Gibson sold to some out-of-state company instead, I hear." Julia shook her head. "Maybe I'm old fashioned, but I don't like seeing the land going off to strangers from outside. Who knows what they might do? I had one of them bothering me to sell that property of mine, you know."

"No, I didn't know. Did it happen to be Evergreen Corporation?" If that company was buying up more land, it had to mean something.

Julia frowned. "I don't remember. I didn't bother much about listening to the details, to tell the truth. I just told them it wasn't for sale."

Donna put glasses back on the tray. "About time you got rid of it. It's just one more thing to pay taxes on, and it's not like you have any use for it." She carried the tray toward the kitchen. "Not that you'll listen to common sense." She swished through the swing door.

"None of her business," Julia muttered. "You'd think the property belonged to her, the way she tells me what to do."

"I'm sure she doesn't mean any harm," Sarah said, hoping to calm Julia down before they left. Sarah glanced at Allison. "If you really are set on getting to Lititz today, I suppose we should go."

They'd nearly reached the door when Julia called Sarah's name. She turned, to find the woman looking at her with an impish grin. "Tell you what. You have Aaron King come to see me one of these days. If I do end up selling that property, I'd a lot rather it went to someone like him who would farm it."

The clatter of dishes from the kitchen seemed to punctuate the words. "That . . . I'm sure he'd be wonderful happy to talk to you about it," Sarah said.

She shouldn't get too excited. After all, that land hadn't been farmed in years, and it was a little farther from the King place than Aaron probably wanted. Still, it was something good that might come of all the troubles that had beset the community lately. "I'll tell him the next time I see him."

CHAPTER THIRTEEN

ALLISON GLANCED AT her once they were on the road to Lititz. "I'm sure Julia meant that about the property. Will Aaron be interested in it?"

"I don't know. The land hasn't been farmed for years, so it might take a lot to get it in shape again, besides all the building he'd have to do. He'd need a house, a barn and some other outbuildings. But I'll tell him."

"It would still be reasonably close to his family's farm. And to yours," she added.

Allison had almost managed to make it sound as if Sarah would be living at Aaron's new place.

"Being close to his family is what matters to Aaron."

Allison's lips twitched. "Maybe so. But you two seem to be spending a lot of time together lately."

"Because you pushed him into helping me with finding a place for the festival," Sarah reminded her.

"You finished that days ago, remember? Come on, tell me. Hasn't he shown any signs that he looks at you as something other than an old friend?"

"Not . . . not exactly."

"I knew there was something!" Allison said triumphantly. "Give. What did he say?"

Sarah should have known better than to give anything away to Allison. Her persistence was unbounded. "He didn't really *say* anything." She seemed to feel Aaron's fingers moving warmly on her wrist.

"What did he do, then?"

"Maybe I'm imagining it meant something. I can't—"

Allison braked, slowing the car. "Am I going to have to pull off the road to get you to talk?"

"For goodness' sake, don't do that." Sarah cast a nervous glance behind them, but nothing seemed to be bearing down on them. "He's been very . . . well, worried about me. About my safety, I mean, with everything that's happened. But that's only natural."

"There's more, right? Meaningful glances, holding your hand a little longer than he needs to? Touching you?"

She couldn't seem to deny it. "I guess. But maybe I'm imagining it," she added quickly. "And he as good as told me that he doesn't plan on marrying again."

Allison dismissed that with a wave of her hand. "I'd guess that a few million men have declared they weren't going to marry. Right up until the time love hit them between the eyes." She grinned. "Look at Nick."

"That's different," Sarah protested, although to tell the truth, it wasn't, not really. "Anyway, there's nothing I can do about it."

"Would it be against the rules to let him see, just a little, how you feel?"

"I don't know." Sarah looked down at her hands, clasped in her lap. "I . . . I guess I'm afraid to risk it. If I let him see how I feel, and he doesn't feel the same, then what? How could we go on from there?"

Allison was silent for a few moments, and when she spoke, the laughter had gone out of her voice. "I know. I'm sorry. I shouldn't push you. It's just . . . well, you have to take a risk once in a while. If you don't, you'll never know how it might have turned out."

Sarah let the words sink in. To never know what might have been between her and Aaron—how could she bear that? But how could she make the first move?

When the silence stretched between them, Allison sighed. "I should change the subject, I suppose."

Sarah nodded. "That would be best, if you don't want to reach the shop with me crying, I guess."

"Okay. I give up. For the moment, anyway. Did you know that they still haven't finally determined the cause of Mr. Gibson's death?"

Sarah blinked, trying to adjust to the change

of subject as well as the news. "So they can't be sure anyone else was involved."

That was encouraging. Allison had undoubtedly picked up the latest from Nick. Mac didn't seem to keep things from his brother.

"Nope. Not yet, anyway."

"I still feel it must have been a natural death," Sarah said firmly. "It just seems odd, because it was so unexpected to find Matthew in his old house when we thought he was in Florida."

"Nick says Mac is in touch with the police where Gibson lived in Florida. They're trying to trace any friends or neighbors who might have known why he came back so suddenly."

Sarah turned that over in her mind. "We've been thinking it had something to do with the letter Aaron wrote to him, but maybe it wasn't that at all."

"With any luck, Mac will hit upon someone who knows all about it. Still, it's odd, finding Gibson there in a house he'd already sold."

"I don't know," Sarah said slowly, trying to put herself in Matt Gibson's mind. "He'd lived there for most of his life. Probably all his memories of his late wife are tied up in that house. He might have wanted to visit it one more time."

"Especially if the new owners plan to tear the house down." Allison took the turn that led into Lititz. "It's frustrating not to be able to find anything about that company. I spent a lot of time looking last night and didn't come up with a thing. I'm beginning to think Evergreen Corporation is a figment of somebody's imagination."

"Since they paid Matthew for his land, they must be real," Sarah pointed out. "You need to turn right here to go down the main street of town."

"This is charming," Allison exclaimed, as they passed small shops and historic buildings, with flowers blooming in pots and window boxes everywhere they looked. "Why haven't I ever been here?"

"You must tell Nick to show you around," Sarah teased. "He should take you to Sturgis Pretzels, at least, and let you make your own pretzel."

Allison leaned over the steering wheel, watching the signs. "Is Lititz mainly Amish?"

"Moravian," Sarah said. "They settled in the county about the same time as the Amish arrived, also looking for religious liberty."

"I can see I'll have to get Nick out of his comfortable rut to do some touristy things with me." Allison's gaze sharpened, and she pointed. "There it is."

Lititz was busy on a summer day, with visitors wandering up and down the narrow streets and admiring the serene lines of the Moravian Girls School in its green setting. Allison finally found a parking space, and they got out.

Sarah's back complained when she stood up

after even that short ride in the car. Maybe lying down would be a good idea, but it would have to wait until she got home.

They were walking toward the tiny shop before it occurred to Sarah to wonder exactly what they were going to do. She glanced at Allison, who was striding confidently to the door.

"Will you tell the owner why we're interested in the album quilt?"

"I think we'll let him assume we're interested in buying first. Time enough to get into that once we know what he volunteers about it. And we need to get a close enough look to see if the name is there."

"You'd better be the buyer, then," Sarah said as Allison reached for the handle. "He wouldn't believe an Amish woman was shopping for a quilt."

"Good point," Allison said, pulling the door open. "Just follow my lead."

Sarah could only hope that didn't involve her saying much. Or anything at all. She wasn't sure she was cut out for detective work, even about Julia's quilt.

The shop was crowded with all sorts of items— mostly old, some of them fabric goods, arranged in what seemed a haphazard manner. It was the sort of place that would lure buyers in, each of them convinced that he or she was going to discover a hidden treasure.

"Good afternoon, ladies." A man, probably the owner, emerged from the back and came toward them, rubbing his hands together briskly. Smallish, sixtyish, slightly graying, he wore a vague air that contrasted oddly with the sharp look in his faded eyes. "What are you looking for today? Samplers? Needlepoint?"

"Quilts," Allison said, her tone brisk. "I'm interested in an album quilt, and I found one you had displayed on your web page."

"Yes, of course." He seemed to be measuring the worth of Allison's linen slacks, silk shirt and designer leather bag. His gaze veered toward Sarah, and his expression became questioning.

"My friend is here to advise me on the quality of the work," Allison said smoothly.

Sarah could see that Allison's poise and confidence were making an impression on the man. She was so used to seeing Allison as her friend that she sometimes forgot the impact her sleek coppery hair, jade-green eyes and air of quiet elegance had on others.

"Certainly, certainly. The album quilt. Just one moment, and I'll bring it out for you to see."

It didn't take long. The quilt, encased in plastic, lay on a shelf nearby.

"You'll understand if I don't take it out of the bag," he murmured. "Such a valuable piece merits careful handling."

If they couldn't get a closer look, they wouldn't

be able to check for the signature. Sarah glanced at Allison, to find her fixing the man with an icy stare that reminded Sarah of Allison's late grandmother.

"You'll understand that I can't consider investing in such an expensive quilt unless I examine it closely," she said.

They gazed at each other, and then the man's eyes dropped. Wordlessly, he opened the encasing plastic and removed the quilt.

Sarah found she couldn't keep quiet, after all. "A quilt of that age should have been wrapped in acid-free paper before storage in plastic."

He looked a bit irritated. "Yes, well, of course I know that. I don't expect the quilt will be in the shop that long. Such a unique item," he murmured. "Several people are interested in it."

Together, Sarah and Allison spread the quilt out. The individual blocks seemed to jump out at them—each one unique, but blending together in a pageant of birds, animals, flowers and trees.

"No figures of people," Sarah said softly. "And none of buildings. I wonder if they agreed ahead of time on the design each would do."

"What about the stitching?" Allison deferred to her knowledge.

"Very sound. A little variation here and there, but you have to expect that when a different person makes each block." She bent to look more closely. "There's a little repair needed in a few places, but that wouldn't necessarily affect the value."

"Extraordinary condition," the shop owner said. "I don't know when I've handled a finer quilt."

Allison glanced around the shop. "You don't seem to specialize in quilts."

"No." He looked a bit discomfited. "But I know what to look for in a quality piece."

"Let's turn it over to examine the back," Allison said.

Sarah held her breath as they reversed the quilt. The stitches were easier to see on the plain backing, an intricate design that looked like the weaving tendrils of a vine reaching for the sun. And there, on the bottom right edge, were the embroidered words they longed to see. *Margaret Herrington, for her wedding, April 4, 1875.*

Excitement flooded through Sarah—to find the missing quilt so easily, and all because of Allison's expertise with the computer.

"You can see how fine it is." The man's voice gained energy, probably because they couldn't entirely hide their enthusiasm. "It's worth every penny of the asking price, and I couldn't possibly take any less."

He turned over the ticket attached to the quilt, and Sarah's breath caught at the price. It seemed astronomical, but Allison was nodding as if it was expected.

"Now, about the provenance of the quilt," her

friend said crisply. "You have documentation of its history, of course."

He seemed to draw back a little. "Unfortunately, I haven't been able to trace the history. I'm sure, given the name and date, it would be possible to learn more, but—"

"How did you come to have it in your possession without any documentation?" Allison's eyes snapped.

"There's nothing illegal about it." He was beginning to get sulky. "I purchased the quilt at a country auction, and the auctioneer wasn't able to tell me anything about the owner. Still, I could see the obvious quality."

How much did he pay for it? Sarah found herself wondering. Probably nothing near the value.

"Where was the auction?" Allison seemed intent on keeping the pressure on him.

His face seemed too close. "My sources are part of my business. I really don't feel inclined to give those to a stranger. Now, if you decide to buy—"

"Would you be surprised to learn that this quilt has been reported stolen?" She shot the words at him.

His lips moved several times before words came out. "It can't be. I bought it from a reputable auctioneer. He wouldn't deal in stolen goods."

"I don't know anything about the auctioneer,"

Allison pointed out. "I just know that you're in possession of stolen property."

The shop owner paled. "The police . . ."

"Fortunately for you, we represent the owner, not the police. If you cooperate with us, it may not be necessary to bring in the police at all."

"Of course, of course." He drew a ledger from under the counter and began leafing through it.

Allison exchanged glances with Sarah, and Sarah knew they were thinking the same thing— that the man wouldn't be giving in so quickly unless he'd suspected from the beginning that there was something fishy about his find.

He shoved the ledger over to Allison, pointing to a line item. "There it is. Those are all the things I bought at an auction house over near New Holland. It's just a small place—the guy who runs it collects stuff all week and runs an auction every Saturday. That phone number is the only contact I have for him. But you talk to him. He'll confirm I purchased the quilt in good faith."

Copying the information, Allison made a non-committal sound. "We'll be checking with him. In the meantime, I'd suggest that you take great care of this quilt until you hear from us. If it should disappear before this is straightened out, we'll have to call in the authorities."

Leaving the owner still mouthing his promises of cooperation, they left the shop. Once they were in the car, Allison looked at her, frowning. "Did you see the date on that sale?"

Sarah nodded. "Less than two months ago."

"So if it disappeared during Julia's move to her house, where has it been in the meantime? And if it disappeared two months ago . . . well, there aren't that many people who could have access to Julia's attic, are there?"

AARON FOUND IT took all the strength he could muster to trudge over to Ben Stoltzfus's place in the early dawn. How did you comfort a man who'd had such a blow again?

Not the new barn this time, thank the gut Lord. That would have been even worse, he guessed. Probably the arsonist had thought the raw new wood wouldn't catch fast enough. Instead, he'd struck at the tie stall barn where the cows were brought for milking. The building could be easily replaced, and at least no stock had been lost.

But the milk tank, the cooler, all the machinery needed to run a successful dairy operation— that was gone. How Ben was to cope with that financial loss, Aaron didn't know.

Ben was momentarily alone, leaning against a fence post, a glazed look on his face. Aaron stopped beside him and put a hand on his shoulder.

"Sorry. If only we could have saved something—"

"Not your fault," Ben said, seeming to make an effort. "You folks did all you could. The building was old, so the wood was dry as tinder. All the firebug had to do was splash some kerosene around and toss a match."

"Ja." What was there to say? "We can take a dozen of your cows at our place to milk with ours. I'll get people lined up to take the rest, for as long as you need. It's no trouble. Until you can get the equipment replaced."

Ben sagged, wiping his forehead and spreading a fresh layer of soot. Aaron knew he looked as bad.

"Don't know if it's worth it," Ben muttered.

His expression wrung Aaron's heart, but he had to find something encouraging to say.

"You're down now. Things will look better after you get some rest. You know the church will help with the costs."

Everyone would pitch in, giving as much as they could afford and maybe more. Ben and his family were part of them, and without insurance . . . well, that was part of being Amish. You accepted what the Lord sent and relied on your brothers and sisters.

"It's not just that." Ben's voice was ragged. "You know as well as I do how hard it is to make a living farming, with land prices going up by the minute, it seems like, and taxes, too."

True enough. Sometimes Aaron thought the

Philadelphia suburbs and the Lancaster ones would spread out so much they'd merge, with no room left for any farms.

"We're farmers. That's what we do, ain't so?" He tried to sound heartening.

"Might be easier to sell out. Pack up and go west to Ohio, or even south to Kentucky. Plenty of Amish have already done it."

He couldn't deny it, so he just patted Ben's shoulder. "Get some rest. We'll make arrangements about the cows quick as we can." No matter what else happened, the cows had to be milked on time.

Spotting the bishop heading toward them, Aaron slipped away. He'd best find Jonah and Nick and go home. Daad would be trying to get their milking done by the time they got there, and no doubt by the afternoon milking, they'd have some of Ben's herd to handle, as well.

He scanned the crowd—weary firefighters, neighbors flooding in to help with the stock, women pressing coffee and food on everyone. Where was his brother? Jonah had been out when the call came, but he'd made it to the scene by the time they had the hoses set up.

Then he saw his brother, standing a little apart from the rest. Mac and Fielding were there, as well, Mac looking stoic and expressionless and Fielding aggressive.

Heart thudding, throat tightening, Aaron strode to the trio, sloughing off his fatigue. He got there in time to hear Fielding shooting a question at his brother.

". . . answer me. Where were you before the firefighters arrived?"

A glance at Jonah's face told him that his brother was being sullen and uncooperative. To Jonah, all adults were the enemy just now.

"Can this wait?" Aaron said, dropping a hand on his brother's shoulder and feeling the tension there. "We've been fighting a fire all night."

Fielding transferred the antagonistic glare to him. "No, it can't. You'd better advise your brother to answer my questions if he doesn't want to land in serious trouble."

"Jonah?" He met his brother's eyes, willing him to listen. "Just answer the man's questions so we can get home. You must be as tired as I am, ain't so?"

But Jonah shrugged off his hand. "I didn't do anything wrong. Why is he picking on me?"

"You arrived late at the fire scene." Fielding interrupted him. "You've arrived late at the last few fires. Why didn't you come with your brother?"

Please answer. Don't make this worse than it is.

"I wasn't home." Jonah stared at the ground. "I was out."

"Out where?"

"Out with friends."

"Where? What friends? Where did you go?"

Jonah shot a resentful look at the man. "Couple of Englisch guys. They had a car. We were just riding around. We were gonna go get something to eat when I heard about the fire on their scanner. So they dropped me here."

"Names?" Fielding's pen was poised over a pad.

"Eric Conner," Jonah muttered. "Joey Marino."

The last two boys Aaron would have picked for his brother to hang out with. Older than he was, with a reputation for skating close to trouble.

"Been drinking?"

Jonah shrugged. "A couple cans of beer, that's all."

"You say they brought you here."

"Ja. Well, they didn't come up to the house. They dropped me off on the road, and I ran up here and got my gear on."

Aaron couldn't keep himself from speaking. "Eric and Joey—will they confirm what you say?"

"Sure." He looked at Fielding, then at Mac. "You ask them. They'll tell you."

From Fielding's expression, he didn't think highly of two possibly drunk teenagers as an alibi, Aaron could tell. He clasped Jonah's arm. "My brother has told you all he knows. I'm taking him home now."

For a moment it hung in the balance, but then Fielding gave a curt nod. "Don't take any trips." He stared at Aaron. "You're responsible for him. Make sure he shows up whenever we need to talk to him."

Aaron nodded. "Komm, Jonah. Let's go home."

They walked toward the spot where Nick had parked the car. Aaron could see his friend leaning against it, waiting for them.

Something had to be said before they reached him. "Jonah." He touched the boy's shoulder. "Don't worry. I know you didn't do it. Soon everyone else will know, as well."

Jonah resumed his study of the ground. But some of the misery had gone out of his face.

"I'LL SEE YOU LATER, Jonny."

Sarah raised her hand to wave to her younger brother, who was looking very pleased with himself at being permitted to drive her to work the morning after the fire. Everyone had been up most of the night with the trouble at the Stoltzfus place, and she'd insisted that Mamm not attempt to come in early today.

Jonny drove off, handling the lines intently, not that the mare couldn't have taken the trip herself, most likely. Stifling a yawn, Sarah headed for the back door of Blackburn House.

As if the fire hadn't been bad enough, devastating Ben and Miriam so quickly after the loss of the barn, the news that Jonah King was under suspicion had spread like wildfire through the Amish community.

It was impossible, wasn't it? She couldn't believe that the boy she'd known since the day he was born could do such a thing. But those Englisch boys he'd been running with . . .

Sarah let that thought die off as she entered the building. She had no right to make judgments about boys she didn't even know except by reputation. When she reached the deserted hallway she paused, waiting as Allison came down the steps.

"I heard about the fire," her partner said immediately. "And about Jonah. How is he?"

"I don't know. I haven't seen any of the King family since then. I did hear that the fire chief said it would be best if Jonah took some time off until the whole thing was settled."

"Poor Jonah. That must make him feel as if everyone is against him."

Sarah loosened her bonnet strings and removed it, frowning a little. Worry over the situation had kept her awake for what was left of the night, and none of her thoughts made sense anymore. It was time to think of something else for a bit.

"Have you reached the auctioneer yet?"

"No." Allison gave her a sharp glance, and then seemed to accept her need to switch to a different worry. "I did finally get someone to answer the phone. Apparently he's off on one of his collecting trips, and the person I spoke with said he might not check in for a couple of days. I stressed that he should call me the minute he got in touch." She looked frustrated, no doubt wanting to jump into action in tracking down the history of the album quilt.

"I just hope he'll be able to tell us where the quilt came from. And when he got it. If it's fairly recent—"

"That narrows things down." Allison finished for her. "Who would have access to Julia's attic other than Donna and possibly Gus Hill?"

"I wish I knew. Maybe someone else has a key to the house, like the cleaning woman. Or there might be one hidden outside. We never thought to ask Julia." Sarah was grasping at straws, and she knew it.

Allison's expressive face showed her doubt. "But whoever it was would have to know the quilt and those other things were stored in the attic. And the person who best fits that description is Donna."

The sound of something hitting the floor had them both spinning around. Harvey Preston stood at the foot of the stairs, looking shocked. His briefcase lay on the floor, papers spilling out of it.

"Harvey, let me help you." Sarah knelt to scoop papers back into the case even as he grasped it up himself.

"I'll get it." He straightened, his face flushed. "Sorry. I wasn't intentionally listening, but I couldn't help hearing what you said. Are you saying that Donna Edwards, of all people, has taken something from Julia Everly?"

Sarah exchanged looks with Allison, feeling her own face redden. They never should have talked about such a thing out here in the hallway, whether they thought they were alone or not.

"We're not accusing anyone," Allison said quickly. "It's just that a valuable antique quilt of Julia's has turned up missing, and we're trying to find out what happened to it for Julia."

"There might be some perfectly innocent explanation," Sarah said. "It could have been mislaid when she moved into the house, or . . ."

"I wouldn't put it past some of those itinerant dealers to steal something," Harvey declared, seeming to recover his poise. "You'd be surprised if you'd heard the stories I have from some of the elderly people I deal with who are selling up."

"Really?" Allison looked interested. Or maybe she was just encouraging Harvey to come up with an alternate theory to satisfy him. "I had no idea that went on."

Harvey nodded, his usually cheerful face solemn. "It's especially a problem with elderly people who live alone. I had one client on an isolated farm who let someone in to evaluate her antiques, or so she thought. A few days later, she discovered that an entire collection of antique silver had disappeared."

"That's terrible." They'd been walking as they talked, and had nearly reached the shop. With any luck, they'd been able to allay Harvey's suspicions. "We'll try and find out if anyone like that has been in Julia's house. Thank you for the suggestion."

"My pleasure. I just hope Julia doesn't have to deal with the police. I understand she's not in such good shape, either physically or, well . . . mentally. It might be time for her to make a move to assisted living."

And who had told Harvey that about Julia's mental state? Donna was the most likely culprit.

"I don't think she's considering calling in the police at this point." Allison unlocked the shop door and swung it open. "I know we can trust you to keep what we've said in confidence, Harvey."

"Of course, of course. It just enrages me when I see people taking advantage of the elderly. It's reprehensible." He seemed to realize they were waiting to enter the shop until he'd finished. "I'll say goodbye. I have a prospective client waiting for me. And don't worry. You can trust me to keep quiet." Shaking his head, he walked toward the front door.

"I wish that hadn't happened." Sarah switched on the lights. "I should have been more careful."

"I'm the one who brought it up," Allison said.

"But I don't think there's any harm done. A real estate agent like Harvey can't afford to give away secrets."

Sarah nodded, a little comforted. In any event, there was no point in worrying about something that probably wouldn't happen. She had enough to consume her with the difficult things that already existed.

CHAPTER FOURTEEN

DESPITE THE FAMILY'S fears for his brother, they ought to behave as normally as possible. So Aaron drove his mother, sister and the girls into town to the quilt shop the next day. While they were occupied, maybe he'd find a way to have a private talk with Mac Whiting. Surely Mac knew that Jonah couldn't be guilty of setting the fires. It had to be that man Fielding who was driving the suspicion.

Becky was in the backseat of the carriage with his girls, and they were playing some silly game that resulted in lots of giggles. Bless her for distracting the kinder and keeping them happy. His little sister was growing more mature by the day, it seemed. Maybe working at the quilt shop and getting closer to Sarah accounted for it.

Just thinking about Sarah seemed to create an odd feeling in Aaron's chest. He had been going along perfectly content, he'd thought, until circumstances had thrown him and Sarah together. And now—well, now he was no longer so sure of himself. At first he'd been able to reason away the sudden feelings he'd experienced—the need to protect her, the longing to touch her, maybe even kiss her . . .

He shouldn't even be thinking about it. Maybe not ever, but certainly not now. Until they were clear of the trouble they were in, he didn't dare.

Aaron glanced at his mother. She'd been silent throughout the ride to town, her lips pressed together, her face strained. He reached across to clasp her hand.

"Don't worry so. This will all be cleared up soon."

"Ja. That's what I'm praying. But that man from the state police—he seems to have convinced everyone he's right."

"I don't think so." Aaron didn't want to raise her hopes, but maybe it was best to say something about his plans. "I'll try to talk to Mac while you're at the shop. He must know that Jonah couldn't do such a thing. He's known him since he was a baby, after all."

Her face relaxed just a little. "You're right. We can trust Mac."

"That's so." Aaron patted her hand.

If his mother took comfort in the thought, that was the best he could do. But he wondered who held the power in the relationship between Fielding and the local police. If the man from the state was in charge, what would Mac be able to do?

He turned into the driveway that led back along Blackburn House, and stopped when he reached the hitching rail. Nick, just heading into the cabinetry shop, paused to raise his hand and then vanished inside.

Aaron reached up to help his mother descend. The girls were already jumping down, eager to hurry into the shop.

"Are you coming inside?" Mamm asked.

"Just for a minute or two." There was really no reason for him to go in. Still, he enjoyed walking into the cozy atmosphere and seeing what Sarah had created with her own hard work.

When they reached the shop, he noticed a dark green trash bag leaning against the exterior wall. Odd. Sarah wouldn't put trash out in the hallway. He picked it up and carried it in with him. He'd ask Sarah what she wanted done with it.

Anna and Lena were already hanging on Sarah, and she laughed as she tried to pay attention to both girls at the same time. Warmth unfolded within him. Sarah's serene face seemed to become beautiful when the love shone in it so clearly.

She hugged the kinder against her, saying something to them, and his heart stirred. If things had been different, maybe he and Sarah would have married. If he'd been a little older, he'd have known that there was a difference between the infatuation folks called first love and the real thing.

His imagination provided him with a picture of

Sarah, her hair loose on a pillow, looking up at him with that shining expression of love.

His breath caught. He couldn't go around thinking that way. It wasn't right.

Sarah was coming toward him, and he tried to compose his expression. "What do you have in the trash bag?" she asked.

"It's not mine. It's yours." He was surprised he sounded so normal. "I found it propped against the outside wall. Didn't you put it there?"

"No." She reached for the bag. "What could it be?" She opened the top, letting out the dank scent of must.

"Ugh," he said. "Whatever it is, it doesn't smell very good."

Sarah held her nose while she peered into the bag. "Ugh is right. It looks like quilts, but they smell as if they've been stored in a damp basement. Who would drop off a bag of old quilts like that?"

Allison swung around at the words. "Is that what it is? It must be that woman who called. She said she had some antique quilts she wanted to put on display and would bring them in. A Mrs. Burkholder, she said."

The other adults in the room grinned, making Allison look from one to the other. "Okay, what's going on? I can see the joke's on me. Who's Mrs. Burkholder?"

"Oh, dear." Sarah shook her head, smiling.

"She lives out on Foster Road in that big old ramshackle house. I'm afraid she's a little . . . eccentric."

"Odd," Aaron said. "She has a houseful of old junk she insists is a collection of valuable antiques. She once sold a pitcher and bowl to a dealer for fifty dollars, and that made her determined to find a hidden treasure in all the stuff she's collected, much of it from the landfill."

"So you're telling me she brought us a bunch of smelly old rags?" Allison advanced on the bag, as if to seize it and trundle it into the trash.

"No, no, they're actually quilts," Sarah said, closing the bag and tying the top. "We'll have to look through them and see if there's anything worth showing. But not until they're aired out."

"Take them home and hang them on the clothesline for a few hours," Aaron's mother suggested. "That should get the worst of it out so you can look at the quilts."

Sarah nodded. "That'll be best. I'll take them home with me."

"In the meantime, you'll have to get them out of the shop." Allison sniffed. "I can still smell them."

Aaron took the offending bag. "Shall I put it out back?"

Sarah chuckled. "Then it'll get picked up for garbage, and we'll never hear the end of it from Mrs. Burkholder. She'd probably sue us for some astronomical figure. I'll put it in the storeroom until I go home."

She reached for the bag, but Aaron shook his head. "I'll carry it. Show me where it goes."

"Denke, Aaron." Sarah led the way out of the shop, stopping to pick up a ring of keys from behind the counter. "I think Allison is just imagining she can smell it with the top tied, but it'll keep in the storeroom. This way."

She led him to the storeroom at the rear, stopping to unlock the door and switch on lights. "Let's put it back here on the floor. That way it won't be touching anything else, just in case."

They went past sets of metal shelves loaded with boxes and plastic bins, many of which seemed to hold books. Clearly Emily, from the bookshop, liked to accumulate even more than she could sell. Or maybe they were still left from the former owner, who'd never been able to get rid of anything.

Aaron stopped where Sarah did, at the back wall, setting the bag where she indicated.

"I'm glad we had a chance to be alone." Sarah looked up at him, her blue eyes darkened and serious. "I wanted to ask how Jonah is doing."

Aaron's throat tightened. "All this suspicion is hard for him. He imagines everyone is talking about him. And he's at such a rebellious age, wanting to be independent but needing reassurance."

"I'm so sorry for all of this. I know he's not as grown-up as he thinks he is. He's fortunate to have you to rely on."

Aaron clenched his fists. "I should have made more effort to get close to him. He's my little brother, and I should be looking out for him."

"Aaron, you're doing your best, I know you are. You can't blame yourself."

"I know he wouldn't do anything like this. Maybe some vandalism, if he got caught up in it when he'd been drinking. But he'd never put animals at risk." Aaron knew it, but felt helpless to convince anyone.

"I know." She touched his hand lightly. "I'm sure of that. The truth will come out. It has to."

Sarah cared so much. Her caring seemed to flow out from her in warm, healing waves, comforting him, easing the burden he carried.

"Sarah." He said her name softly. He seemed to be drowning in the deep blue of her eyes, sinking into the comfort of her caring.

Before he could think what he was doing, he lowered his head and captured her lips with his. For an instant she was still with surprise, and then she seemed to lean into him, her mouth softening under his, her hands grasping his arms.

He couldn't think. He could only feel. He'd been starved of a woman's love for so long, and Sarah . . . The feelings that had been growing inside him suddenly seemed to burst into bloom.

Sarah, his friend. Sarah, innocent Sarah, who trusted him. What was he doing? He'd just told himself he couldn't possibly do anything about Sarah while they were under such a cloud.

But it felt so good. They felt as if they belonged together.

The rattle of the door warned him, and they sprang apart. Sarah averted her face, her breath coming quickly. He had to say something to reassure her, but there was no time.

Allison erupted into the storeroom, waving a sheet of paper. "Sarah, I've found it!"

"Found what?" He didn't care, but he could at least give Sarah another moment to recover.

"The auctioneer got my message. He called." She hurried toward them. "What are we doing in this dark storeroom? Come on, there are things to be done."

"You're always in such a rush." Sarah turned to her, actually looking like her usual self.

How could she do that, when he must surely look as if he'd been hit with an ax?

"You don't understand." Allison waved the paper again. "He actually has records of the acquisition of Julia's quilt. He faxed it to me. He bought it five months ago from a woman who claimed to represent the owner, an elderly woman who was, she said, disposing of some of her household goods."

Aaron was struggling to follow the conversation. He'd known they were trying to track down a quilt that had belonged, or did belong, to Julia Everly. It sounded as if they'd found the answer.

"Does he have the name?" Excitement filled Sarah's voice, as if she'd forgotten their kiss as soon as it was over. "Who was it?"

Allison handed her the paper. "Just who we thought. Donna Edwards."

"Is the man sure?" Aaron didn't want to see Sarah getting involved in something that sounded like trouble with the Englisch law.

"He copies the driver's license for identification when he buys an item. It's Donna, all right." Allison looked at Sarah, her exuberance fading. "We're going to have to tell Julia what we know."

"I suppose so." Sarah's clear blue eyes clouded. "She's going to be upset. Angry, maybe, but mostly upset. After all, Donna is her own kin."

"And she's stealing from her." Allison shook her head at her friend's expression. "There's no use soft-pedaling it, Sarah. What other explanation could there be? We can't let the woman get away with stealing from her."

"I suppose not." Sarah sounded apprehensive.

Aaron thought he knew why. Warmhearted Sarah had set out to help someone she thought needed her, as she always did. Now she was faced with becoming enmeshed in what might be an ugly scene.

"You don't have to be involved." He touched her arm, as if to draw her back to him. "It's not your concern. I mean, you don't have to be the one to interfere. Julia might not thank you for it."

Sarah stepped out of reach of his hand. "It is my concern. Julia Everly might be Englisch, but she's also my friend. She asked for my help, and I won't let her down."

"You'd best talk it over with your daad first." Aaron knew as soon as he said it that Sarah would resent the words. All the sympathy was gone from her face now when she looked at him.

"It is a matter for my conscience, not my father's." She spoke with a firmness he hadn't known she possessed. "Excuse me." She spun and walked out of the storeroom.

SARAH SAT DOWN opposite Julia in her cozy living room, trying to decide how to lead up to the information they'd found. She and Allison had decided that only one of them should come on such delicate family business, and since she'd known Julia for years, it made sense that Sarah did it.

She'd felt awkward just walking in, but when she'd called to say she was coming, Julia had insisted upon it, saying she didn't want Donna butting in on their conversation. She'd obviously guessed that this was no ordinary visit.

But Sarah was only too relieved to get away from the shop and try to concentrate on something other than that kiss she'd shared with Aaron. She was glad Allison had interrupted them, even glad Aaron had so immediately made her annoyed. She had to focus on Julia's troubles right now, not her own.

"Well?" Julia thumped the arm of the chair with her fist. "You know something, don't you? Out with it. And tell me quickly. The physical therapist is due in a few minutes."

This was obviously bad timing. Julia would be upset by her news, and in no mood to cooperate with her therapist, if she ever was.

"Maybe we should postpone this until later. I can come back after the therapist has finished."

"No, you don't." Julia grabbed her wrist, as if to prevent her physically. "Now that I know you've found something, I can't sit around and wait. Don't treat me like a feeble old lady."

"I don't," Sarah said, smiling at the thought. "And you're not."

"Well, then, out with it. You and Allison traced what happened to my album quilt."

Sarah glanced around cautiously. "Is Donna here now?"

"Afraid of eavesdroppers? Well, I wouldn't

put it past her, but she's in the back bedroom, supposedly changing the beds, and she's got the radio playing. She won't hear anything we say, so you can talk."

Julia was determined, and Sarah could hear the faint sounds of music from the hallway that led to the bedroom section of the house. She took a deep breath, knowing she couldn't delay. "We found the dealer in Lititz who was trying to sell the quilt, and from him, we traced it to a small auction house near New Holland." Julia nodded, her wrinkled face showing no emotion. "And then?"

"Allison left messages for the auctioneer, and he called back just a bit ago. He was cooperative. He'd bought the quilt about five months ago." Sarah's voice started to drag. How would it feel to think that your own kin stole from you?

"Five months." Julia seemed to absorb that fact. "Then it didn't disappear when I moved."

"I guess not. He told Allison the buyer said she was selling it for an elderly woman who was getting rid of some of her household goods." Sarah sucked in a breath and watched Julia's face anxiously. "It was Donna."

For a moment there was no change in her expression. "Is he certain?" She rapped out the question. "If it was someone using Donna's name . . ."

"Allison says he copied the driver's license

for identification. He actually faxed it to her, so we're sure."

"That's it, then." Julia stared at the cast she was surely tired of after all this time. "Well, I'll have to deal with her." She looked up. "You understand, there's no question of going to the police, not when it's family. I'll deal with Donna myself."

"I understand." Julia was calmer than she would have expected, but Sarah suspected the calm wouldn't last when she confronted her cousin. "Allison said to ask if you want her to negotiate getting the quilt back. It seems unfair to ask you to pay to get it back, but I guess . . ."

"No, no, I don't want to haggle. Tell Allison to go ahead. I'll pay that dealer whatever it cost him, but I'm not rewarding anyone for buying something that was stolen. In the meantime . . ." Her face hardened. "Go and get Donna for me, please."

"Julia, you said the physical therapist would be here any minute. You can't start a conversation like that when someone else is due to walk in the door."

The woman seemed to grit her teeth for a moment, probably trying to hang on to her temper. "All right. But go tell her to see me after the therapist leaves. And tell Allison I'm grateful to both of you."

Sarah went toward the hallway reluctantly.

She had no desire to face Donna with this secret weighing on her, but she'd have to.

When she reached the bedroom area, the sound of the radio led her to the master suite. The door was open a few inches, giving her a partial view of Donna's back. But she wasn't changing the bed. She was talking on the phone.

Sarah stood where she was, uncertain. Should she call out to her? Then she heard Donna's voice, soft and coy in a way she'd never heard it before.

"But, darling, I simply have to see you. I can't stand it when we're not together . . ."

Sarah backed away noiselessly, her mind reeling. Donna? How could . . .

She shook the thought off, trying to close her mind to it, and went back to the living room.

"Did you tell her?" Julia demanded.

"No, I . . . I could hear that she was on the phone, and I didn't like to interrupt."

Shrewd eyes studied her face. "There's something more. What is it?"

Somehow Sarah had a feeling Julia would see through any evasion. "She seemed to be talking to . . . a sweetheart."

"Donna? That's ridiculous." Julia stared at her. "You're serious."

Sarah nodded. "You didn't know she has a boyfriend?"

"She doesn't. Not that anyone knows about, and goodness knows she'd be shouting it to the rooftops if she'd actually snared a man." Her color deepened. "He must be married. That's the only reason she'd keep it a secret."

"She wouldn't do that, would she?" The words Harvey had said earlier about people trying to cheat the elderly flitted into Sarah's mind. "Or maybe . . . what if it's someone who wanted to steal from you? He might be using Donna to do it. She'd have to hide her relationship in that case."

"Maybe so." Julia considered. "Either way, she's a silly, deluded spinster without an ounce of appeal. I know that's unkind, but it's the truth. Well, it doesn't change things. I still have to have it out with her. Though if there is a man involved, I'd like to see him in jail."

Something . . . some instinct . . . shivered inside Sarah. "Julia, will you wait just a bit? Let me talk to Allison about it first. She'd know better than I would how to deal with this situation." She could hear footsteps on the porch, lending urgency to her voice. "Please. Promise me you won't tackle this alone. At least let Allison or me be here with you. Promise me."

The doorbell rang, and Donna came clattering from the bedrooms. Sarah watched Julia's face.

"All right," she said finally, speaking under the noise of Donna admitting the therapist. "Maybe someone should be here as a witness when I confront her. But it has to be done soon."

SARAH'S MAMM TURNED from the stove to survey the kitchen table while Grossmammi set a bowl of freshly made applesauce in place. "Looks like everything's ready for supper. Ring the bell, please, Sarah."

Sarah slipped out the screen door to the back porch. Like most farm families in this area, they had a large bell hanging from the porch roof, used for summoning the family to meals as well as getting the attention of anyone working outside. She reached up to grab the rope and give a few loud clangs.

Daad and Jonny emerged from the barn. The two younger ones, in the paddock with the pony, bolted for the fence and hopped over, racing each other toward the house.

"Don't run into the quilts," she called, and Noah veered to avoid the clotheslines filled with the ones that had been in the garbage bag.

They probably weren't airing out as much as she'd hoped. The day was still and heavy, and it almost felt like rain, though it had been so long since they'd had a good downpour that she'd almost forgotten the sensation.

"They're coming. Feels like rain out," she added, taking the milk pitcher from her grandmother and finishing the task of filling glasses.

"Let's hope." Mamm peered out the window over the sink. "The boys have spent half the day hauling water to the garden. We're fortunate to have a spring that never fails."

"I hear some folks' wells are running low." Grossmammi took her seat at the table.

"Esther King says their well is getting low." Mamm's expression clouded. "I talked to her a bit today. She's taking it hard, this suspicion of their Jonah."

"It's a trial for them to bear, that's certain sure," Grossmammi said. Her gaze sought out Sarah's. "Have you talked to Aaron about it? Assured him of our caring?"

Sarah fought to keep her face expressionless. "I did tell him, when I saw him today."

The clatter of Daad and the boys coming in to supper diverted her grandmother's attention, relieving Sarah. Grossmammi, maybe because she looked on so much, always seemed to see more than the younger people might want her to.

But Sarah wasn't trying to hide a bit of mischief, was she? The memory of that kiss seemed to flood over her. She turned away from the table, busying herself with putting the milk in the gas refrigerator, and tried to rationalize it away.

It had been the impulse of the moment, hadn't it? Aaron had told her that he didn't think of remarrying, so it couldn't have been serious.

Still, even though teenagers might steal kisses

with little thought, people her and Aaron's age didn't treat a romance so lightly. She couldn't seem to forget the stunned look on his face when he'd pulled away.

What would he do now? He could feel he had to avoid her. That might be the safest thing. But then she'd lose the renewed closeness they'd had for the past few weeks, and the thought of that hurt more than she'd have believed possible.

The scrape of chairs recalled her to the present, and she hurried to take her seat. Daad bowed his head for the silent prayer before meals, and she obediently closed her eyes. But all she could see against her dark lids was Aaron's face.

Fortunately the boys more than made up for any silence on her part during the meal, and Daad made his own contribution, talking about the meeting he'd be attending tonight to organize the needed support for the Stoltzfus family. The dairy herd had already been dispersed to various farms close at hand, but the expense of trying to replace the lost milking equipment would be huge. Sometimes she thought the Englisch, with their insurance protecting them from the financial aspects of disaster, might have an advantage, but being Amish, they accepted what happened as God's will.

Could it really be God's will that a madman was torching barns and buildings throughout the community? She pushed the question away. The difficulty of understanding evil was always with them in this world.

With the usual bustle of after-supper work, Sarah was able to keep troubling thoughts at bay for a time, at least. But the house grew quiet once the boys were in bed, Daad out to his meeting and Mamm and Grossmammi settled in the living room with the mending.

Sarah sat down with them to help. "I heard today that they will be releasing Matthew Gibson's body for burial this week. Apparently he has a plot next to where his wife and his son are buried at the cemetery on the other side of town."

"That's a relief," Mamm said. "It troubled me, thinking of the poor man with no one to make his final arrangements for him. Have the police said anything yet about . . . ?"

She let that die out, but Sarah knew what she meant. About how he died. "I don't think there's been any announcement, but I don't see how it can be anything but a heart attack."

It would be such a relief to know for certain. Still, at least Mac hadn't been asking any more questions about it. Maybe that meant he was satisfied.

She took a pair of Noah's pants from the basket and glanced at the knees. Or rather, at the holes where the knees used to be.

"What was Noah doing in these pants?" She held them up. "Crawling down the gravel lane on his knees?"

Mamm chuckled. "Women have been asking that question for as long as there have been little boys. You'd think so, wouldn't you?"

"Ach, his daadi was just the same at his age. Boys are wonderful hard on clothes, but we'd rather see them wearing out their knees than their bedsheets, ain't so?"

Sarah smiled at her grandmother's words. Grossmammi always seemed to have a bit of wisdom to impart, and her stories of "when Daadi was a little boy" were very popular with the boys.

"You're right, and I'll put patches on both of them without complaining. Maybe we could find some extra strong fabric for the patches, and then—" Sarah stopped, listening. Had she heard what she thought? "Was that thunder?"

In a moment they were all sure. The rolling noise came from the west, and before they'd had a chance to speak, it grew louder.

"Sounds like a storm coming, for sure." Mamm bundled her mending into the basket. "And every window open in the house. Sarah, you'd best get those quilts off the line."

Sarah jumped to her feet. She'd nearly forgotten them. "Mrs. Burkholder would have something to say if I let them get soaked in a storm, not that it would be better than the way she treated them herself." She hurried to the back door, scurrying out.

The rain hadn't reached them yet, but the

western sky flickered with lightning, coming faster as she watched and streaking from sky to ridge. If only the storm brought a decent rain! It seemed they'd been yearning for rain for years instead of weeks.

Grabbing a basket from the porch, she plunged out into the yard. She hadn't thought to bring a flashlight, but with the way the lightning was coming near, she didn't need one. She'd almost reached the clotheslines when the wind hit, rustling the thirsty grass and setting the quilts billowing.

Well, she'd hoped for a breeze to air out the musty quilts. She just hadn't been looking for a gale. The wind swept across the valley, so strong it nearly took her breath away as she struggled toward the clotheslines.

It was going to be a job for more hands than she had to get the quilts down before the storm was right over her. She reached the first row. They snapped at her as if daring her to grab the clothespins and free them.

Struggling to capture the fabric in her arms, Sarah reached for the line. Lightning flashed again, flooding the lawn with garish light for an instant and leaving an imprint on her eyes even as it passed.

An imprint of the pale quilt she grappled with and behind it a dark silhouette—of a man, his hands like claws reaching for her.

CHAPTER FIFTEEN

SARAH DODGED AN instant before the man could grab her, the billowing quilt providing the smallest of protection. She felt a hand, covered by the quilt, graze her arm. She spun away from it, instinct screaming at her to escape, run, hide like a rabbit stalked by a hawk.

Her heart pounded so loudly it deafened her. *Think.* She had to think, and quickly, before he caught her.

She'd gone the wrong direction—away from the house. She had to get back there, slam the door to keep him out. But he was between her and the porch.

She stumbled along the line of quilts, batting her way past them, trying to focus. Lightning flashed again, followed in seconds by the boom of thunder, disorienting her.

Circle around, some rational part of her mind said. *Get on the other side of the second row of quilts, behind him. Quiet, don't make a sound.*

But her breath was coming in gasps. If she had enough air to scream . . .

She dared not scream. Mamm would come running if she did, and would run right into the man who was at least an arsonist and maybe worse.

Rounding the end of the first row of quilts, Sarah forced herself to stop. *Don't run mindlessly. Think.*

Where was he? Still between her and the house, at least. Moving? She listened with every fiber of her being. Nothing. Just the wind and the rumble of thunder. But he was still there. She could sense him. Waiting. Listening as she was.

If she ran to the phone shanty . . . But even the smallest sound of dialing 911 would alert him to her location. She couldn't possibly complete the call before he was on her.

She crept around the second row of quilts, her hand brushing one as it flapped in the wind. *Carefully, carefully. Move under cover of the thunder. Get to the house. Lock the door, turn up the gaslights.* He wouldn't want to be seen.

Lightning flashed, seeming to crack the sky. As the thunder boomed, she moved swiftly, silently, past one quilt and behind the next. The faintest sound of grass rustling came to her ears, and she made out the movement of other quilts. He was working his way along the row, checking behind each one. She couldn't just freeze and hope he'd miss her.

Another crash of lightning, followed immediately by the thunder, loud enough to deafen. It was right over them. He was coming nearer, and she had to risk moving.

One step, then another. Her eyes probed the

dark, trying to locate him. If she could only see him . . . but it wouldn't help to know who he was if she didn't live to tell anyone. Lightning again, dazzling her eyes, but against the fireworks she saw him—a dark shape at the end of the row.

He saw her, too. He lunged toward her. No more hide-and-seek in the dark. Just run, pray . . .

A few more feet and her foot struck the bottom step. Hope surged through her. Almost there. Almost—

Fingers grabbed her, grappling for her neck, jerking her back. One palm closed on her throat, nearly cutting off her breath. She struggled, trying to wriggle free, knowing if he got both hands around her neck she wouldn't have a chance . . .

But she was weakening. He was too strong, and she was failing . . .

Another strobe of lightning, crash of thunder, and the skies opened, not in a gentle rain but in a soaking torrent, as if someone had emptied a bucket of water over her head. She gasped, realizing it had startled her assailant, too, and for a precious second his grip loosened.

Sarah lunged forward, reaching out toward the door and safety. Her fingers brushed a rope . . . brushed and clung. The bell. Even as his hands tightened on her throat again, she yanked.

The bell clanged, startling him. He stumbled

backward but didn't loosen his grip. She pulled the rope again and again, hard as she could. The clamor of the bell seemed to drown out even the rumble of thunder as the storm moved on. The peals rang out across the valley; anyone who heard would know it was an alarm. Lights began to go up in the house. Dogs all along the valley took up the chorus. She heard her mother calling out from inside the house . . .

And then Sarah was thrown forward, crashing into the porch rocker, losing her grip on the bell rope. But the alarm was given. Voices—distant, calling from the Kings' house on one side and the Whitings' on the other. She sucked in a breath, trying to roll away from the blow she feared was coming.

But it didn't. When she looked up, he was gone.

AARON FELT HELPLESS, and he didn't like the feeling. He bent over Sarah, who was slumped on the top porch step, her mother's arm around her. Her grandmother hovered in the doorway, her hands clenching together. A raindrop fell from his hat onto Sarah's skirt.

"Shouldn't we get her inside? I can carry her." He spoke quietly to Hannah, not wanting to alarm the grandmother or the boys, who were in the kitchen behind her, struggling to see, their faces as white as their nightshirts.

"When she's ready," Hannah said. She stroked

Sarah's hair. "Komm now, my Sarah. You're safe now. It's all right."

Still Sarah curled into herself, wrapping her hands around her knees as if she wanted to make herself as small as possible. A shudder went through her, shaking her slim frame.

Aaron glanced helplessly at those behind him. Jonah, who had run over with him when they heard the bell clanging, was as white-faced as the little boys in the kitchen. The Whiting men had dashed from their place at the same time. Nick and Jim, his dad, looked as helpless as Aaron felt, standing there with the rain drenching their shirts.

Mac was already talking on a cell phone, calling for assistance and asking for paramedics. He clicked off, meeting Aaron's eyes.

"Medical help will be here in a few minutes. Maybe someone ought to check and see if he'd been setting a fire."

"We will," Jim said, nudging Nick. "Come on." Obviously Jim Whiting had thought to bring flashlights and he handed one to his other son as they headed for the barn.

"Sarah." Aaron leaned over her again. "Mac has sent for paramedics. They'll help you."

Surprisingly, that seemed to get through. She looked up at him, her wet hair hanging, loosened from her kapp. "I don't need them. I . . . I just need a minute."

"Gut." He held out his hand, and she grasped it. "That's gut. But just let them check you out, or how will Mac fill in all his reports?"

Her eyes were dark with shock, but she nodded.

"Gut," Hannah said briskly. "Now, Aaron will carry you inside. And all the questions and explanations can wait until you're dry and warm." She sent a warning look at Mac, and he nodded.

"I can walk." Sarah stood, a little shaky but determined, clinging to Aaron's hand until she was upright on the porch, her mother's and grandmother's arms around her waist. She let go of his hand with what seemed like reluctance, and a wave of tender protectiveness overwhelmed him.

Slowly they made their way inside, leaving him with Mac and Jonah. Aaron studied his brother's face, thinking the boy had had too many shocks of late.

"She's going to be all right." He tried to sound confident. "You go on home now and tell the folks what happened. They'll be worrying, and we don't want Daad walking over in the rain. I'll be along later."

Jonah, looking relieved, turned. He stopped at the sound of Mac's voice.

"Just a minute." Mac looked from him to Aaron. "Was Jonah with you when Sarah was attacked?"

The youth looked as if he'd burst out at that, but Aaron put a restraining hand on his arm. "Jonah was with the whole family." He could feel the stiffness in the words and reminded himself that Mac was doing his duty. "We were all on the back porch, watching the storm roll in, when we heard the bell. Jonah and I came running to see what was wrong."

"Good." Mac sounded relieved. "That's what I wanted to hear." He clapped Jonah on the shoulder. "You go along home now and get some dry clothes on."

Jonah swallowed whatever he wanted to say and went, trotting off toward home in the rain and dark.

"Jonah wasn't involved. Not in this, not in the fires." Aaron gritted his teeth, angry that he had to spell this out for someone he'd known all his life. "Or is it me who needs an alibi? If I'm a suspect in Matt Gibson's death, maybe you're thinking I would attack Sarah."

Mac ran a hand through his rain-wet hair. "Look, I'm just doing my job as best I can. I'm not saying I suspect either of you. But I figured you'd rather I asked the questions than someone else."

For a moment they glared at each other. Then Sarah's mother was calling to them from the kitchen. Well, it would wait. Sarah was most important at the moment, but then Aaron had to have it out with Mac. The lawman couldn't go on suspecting Jonah of being the arsonist when he had been right there with the family while Sarah was attacked. As for himself . . . well, Aaron had to believe the truth would come out.

Sarah sat at the kitchen table, a sweater wrapped around her over the fresh dress she'd already put on. Her hair, still damp, was back in its usual neat bun under a crisp kapp. Hannah put sugar liberally into a mug of steaming tea and set it in front of Sarah, who wrapped her fingers around the cup as if needing its warmth.

Mac took a quick glance around. "The boys safely out of earshot?"

Hannah nodded. "Their grossmammi took them upstairs." She drew a chair as close as possible to Sarah's and sat.

Mac took the seat across from Sarah, studying her face as if looking for a sign she wasn't going to fall apart on him. He didn't need to worry. Sarah was a strong person. After the initial shock, she'd cope. And Aaron would be here to see that Mac didn't push her too hard. He leaned against the counter, no more than an arm's length from her.

"The paramedics will be here quick, so let's just get a couple of questions out of the way first." Wearing jeans and a T-shirt, his damp hair in his face, Mac looked more like the boy he'd been than the police officer he was now.

Sarah nodded, her face pale but composed.

"Let me tell you what I understand, and then you can just fill in anything I missed, okay?" His tone was gentle. "When you heard the thunder, you ran out to get the quilts off the line. Your mamm says she went upstairs to close windows. Somewhere near the quilts, someone attacked you."

"I . . ." Sarah put her hand to her throat. Her voice was husky, not much more than a whisper. "I saw the outline of him when the lightning flashed."

"Not his face?"

She shook her head. "He was a shadow." Her soft words trembled, and then she went on, seeming to draw up strength. "He came at me, but I had enough warning to get away."

Aaron's own throat was tight. If not for that lightning, Sarah wouldn't have had any warning.

"You ran to the house?"

"He was between me and the door. I got behind the other line of quilts. Tried to keep him from seeing me. When I got close enough, I ran." Sarah stopped, taking a gulp of the hot tea. "He caught me at the steps."

She closed her eyes, and Aaron made an involuntary movement. She shouldn't have to relive it so soon—

Mac glanced at him and shook his head

warningly. "I understand. You struggled, you reached the bell rope and rang it."

"Ja," she whispered. "The dogs . . . the voices . . . he ran away."

"Who was it, Sarah? What did he look like?" The questions were suddenly urgent, and Aaron saw Mac's hands clench into fists for an instant before he flattened them.

"All I saw was a shadow." She sounded inexpressibly weary. "An impression."

"Big? Skinny? Any sense of his clothes?"

"Not Amish," she said suddenly, as if surprising herself. "No beard. Bigger than me." Her eyes lost that dazed look as her mind started to function. "Heavier, more . . . solid. A man, not a boy."

"Some boys are pretty big," he suggested.

Sarah seemed to grope for words. "He was older, I know. Just the way he moved, the set of his shoulders. A man, not a boy," she repeated firmly. Again she put her hand to her throat.

Aaron glared at Mac. Couldn't he see she'd had enough? The distant wail of a siren punctuated the thought.

"Just one more thing before they get here." Mac drew a cell phone from his pocket. "I'll have to take a photo of those bruises on your neck." Before anyone could protest, he went on. "We won't show your face. Your mother can hold a towel to shield you. But this is a police matter, and I need a photo for evidence."

Sarah and her mother exchanged glances. Wordlessly, Hannah took a tea towel from a drawer and unfolded it, holding it so that Sarah's face was hidden. Sarah's fingers fumbled to pull the sweater away from her neck.

Aaron's breath caught at the sight of the ugly marks on her pale skin, and a temper he'd never known he possessed made him want to smash something. He fought down the rage until he could speak.

"Just another minute now," he said gently. "Then you can rest."

Mac snapped several photos. His face was impassive, but the cords on his neck stood out like ropes, and Aaron could feel his anger boiling. Mac had known Sarah ever since he could remember, of course. He couldn't look at this like any other assault—that was certain sure.

Mac and Aaron went out onto the back porch together when the paramedics arrived—a man and a woman Aaron knew vaguely. Mac greeted them by name, murmuring a few words as they went into the kitchen, and then turned away to stand with Aaron staring out into the gently falling rain.

"We've been hoping for a break in the drought," Aaron said. In any other circumstances, he'd be elated, but not when Sarah was inside hurting.

Mac stared gloomily at the rain. "Washing away any signs this bird might have left. But as careful as he's been so far, he's not likely to have been that cooperative tonight."

The bobbing of flashlights announced that Jim and Nick were coming back from checking the outbuildings. Quickly, before they could reach the porch, Aaron spoke.

"Jonah isn't the arsonist. You must know it. Who but the arsonist would go after Sarah that way?"

"I know. And I'm glad to clear the boy out of the way. But as far as Fielding is concerned . . ." Mac let that trail off, shaking his head. "I'll do my best to make him see sense."

"Denke." No time to say more, as Jim and Nick were upon them, shaking themselves like wet dogs once they'd reached the shelter of the porch.

"We had a thorough look around." Jim Whiting had the same lean, rangy build as his sons, though his hair was graying. "Not a sign of any attempt at a fire."

"He was after Sarah," Aaron said. "This proves it. But she can't identify him. Why doesn't he see that by now?"

Mac shrugged. "A lot of people around here know the Amish are reluctant to go to the police. I'll start confiding in a few of the local gossips that she doesn't know anything. They'll spread the word."

Aaron didn't care for it as a solution, but likely Mac was right. The firebug would be more likely

310

to heed something his neighbors said than to take stock in any official statement from the police.

"No point in you hanging around." Mac glanced at his father and brother. "Go home and get dry."

"What do you plan to do?" Nick said. "Spend the night on the porch swing?"

Mac grinned. "Something like that. If the town council would give me another patrolman, I wouldn't have to."

Nick cuffed him lightly. "I'll bring you some dry clothes. And I'll be back to spell you after a few hours."

"I can stay," Aaron said.

Mac shook his head. "I can deputize Nick, if need be. But not you, unless you want to be in big trouble with your bishop. Sarah wouldn't like that, would she?"

No, she wouldn't. "All right. But I'll be by, patrolling for fires, anyway."

"Not likely, with this rain," Nick said.

Mac nodded. "I think he's done for tonight. He's going to lie low for a while, if he's smart."

"I hope you're right." Aaron swung around sharply as the paramedics came out. "How is she?"

The woman paramedic gave him a reassuring smile. Maybe she thought he had a right to be asking. "She'll be fine after a day or two of rest. She doesn't want to go to the hospital, and there's really no reason."

"We gave her something to help her sleep," the man added. "That's the best thing for her right now. That and knowing the guy who did this is behind bars." He looked at Mac.

"Nobody wants that more than I do." Mac bit off the words.

The paramedics left, and Jim and Nick headed toward their place. Mac settled in on the swing.

Aaron opened the door with a certain amount of hesitation. Sarah might not want to see him, but he couldn't go home without making sure she was all right.

She was getting up from the chair when he entered, and she froze, looking at him with an expression he didn't quite understand. Was she upset with him about that unexpected kiss? They'd have to talk, but not now.

"I just want to make sure everything's okay." He felt awkward saying it. He looked from her to Hannah. "Is there anything you need? Do you want me to stay with you until Eli gets home?"

Hannah's arm tightened around her daughter's waist. "That's wonderful kind of you, Aaron, but no. You go on home and get dry. We'll be fine."

"I know you will. Mac's going to spend the night on your back porch to make sure."

Hannah shook her head. "That boy. I can't get used to thinking of him as a grown-up policeman. As far as I'm concerned, he's still the little boy who showed up at the back door every time I made doughnuts. Well, I'll take him some coffee once I have Sarah settled."

"You can feel safe, anyway." Aaron longed to touch Sarah, just to be sure she was all right, but he'd better not. "Try to get some sleep. If you want, I'll take my sister in to the shop tomorrow to help Allison."

"That's sehr kind," Hannah said, before Sarah could speak. "We can trust Becky to help, and that will ease Sarah's mind. She's not going in tomorrow, if I have to sit on her."

Sarah almost managed a smile. "You two are talking about me as if I'm not here." Her voice was still husky but not quite as strained. "Denke, Aaron. I . . . I'm wonderful glad you were here."

He nodded, daring to clasp her hand for an instant. "Sleep well. I'll see you tomorrow."

He went out quickly before he could give away the tumult of emotions that were roiling inside him.

SARAH MADE A few protests at staying home the next morning, but the truth was she was just as glad not to face anyone. And when Mamm insisted she go back to bed for a bit, she realized that her legs were shaky enough to make that a good idea.

She slept for a while, but when she woke

313

again, she found that lying down encouraged the reliving of everything that had happened last night. She sat up abruptly. Even the protests of stiff muscles were better than lying there thinking of hands closing around her neck.

Getting out of bed slowly, Sarah moved to the chest of drawers to consult her mirror. The bruises, handshaped, were black against her skin, and something inside her started to shake.

Stoppe, she commanded. *It's over, and you are safe.*

The question of what to wear troubled her. Englisch women had a choice of styles, including no doubt some that would hide the marks. All Sarah's dresses were made to the same pattern, but the green one did fit a little higher on the neck. Moving as stiffly as if she were Grossmammi's age, she began to dress.

It took an effort and cost her some pain, but once she was done, her hair neat under her kapp, Sarah felt more like herself. There—that was the best she could do. Maybe by the time she returned to the shop the next day the bruising would have faded a bit.

When Sarah reached the kitchen, she discovered the boys at the table, consuming a little snack of shoofly pie under Grossmammi's indulgent eye. Mamm was putting a pitcher of milk in the refrigerator, but she turned at the sound of Sarah's entrance.

"Ach, you shouldn't be up. I was just going to bring you a cup of tea."

"I didn't want to stay in bed any longer," she said quickly. Her voice was no longer the whisper it had been last night, but talking was still an effort. "Tea sounds like a good idea."

"It will soothe your throat," Grossmammi said, urging her to the table. "Maybe with some honey in it. And a piece of shoofly pie will go down easily, ain't so?"

Sarah doubted it, but she took one to please her grandmother. Then she realized that her brothers were staring at her with varying expressions. Noah, the little one, looked almost afraid, and that hurt her heart.

She held out her hand to him. "Komm, Noah. It's all right." She drew him close beside her. "Don't worry. I'm fine, really I am." At her gentle voice he seemed to relax.

He touched her neck. "Does it hurt?"

"A bit, but it will soon pass away. No more than your bruises hurt that time you fell out of the apple tree, remember?"

He nodded, his smile returning. "Let me carry the tea for Sarah, Mamm." He scurried to the counter, to return holding the mug with both hands.

"Denke," she said gravely, and he smiled.

Thomas seemed relieved once his little brother

had been satisfied, but Jonny . . . Sarah hesitated, troubled. He looked angry.

"Jonny?"

He clenched his fists. At twelve he'd shot up recently, and his shirtsleeves showed bony wrists and tight hands. "I wish I'd been there. I'd have hit—"

"Jonny!" Mamm said, shocked.

"You're angry." Sarah understood his desire to protect her. But this was one of those moments when the older must teach the younger the Amish way. "I know."

"Aren't you?" He stared at her, his clear blue eyes clouding.

"No," she said, knowing that was honest. Maybe it was best he hadn't asked if she was scared. "I'm not angry. Whoever he was, I forgive him." She would keep saying that until she knew it was true.

"But . . . but I heard Mac say the man had to be caught. Isn't that right?"

Sarah nodded, exchanging glances with Mamm. Did she want to take over? But Mamm's look persuaded her to continue.

"There's a difference between forgiving and letting someone get away with wrong," she said. "If you do something wrong, Daad forgives you, ain't so? But you still have to take the consequences. If we don't, how will we ever learn what is right?"

Jonny considered that for a moment, and then he nodded. "I see. Like if I go and play ball instead of doing my chores, I have to do extra so I'll remember next time."

"Ja," she said, relieved.

"So Mac has to catch the man so he won't do it again."

Sarah nodded, deciding talking about jail wouldn't help matters.

"All right," Mamm said, brisk as she took control. "You boys get about your chores and let Sarah eat in peace."

The three of them departed noisily, and the kitchen fell quiet.

"That was well done, Sarah," Grossmammi said, giving an approving nod. "You would be a gut mammi yourself."

She escaped answering that with a gulp of tea. Usually her grandmother was the soul of tact, not mentioning Sarah's unmarried state or making comparisons. Had she been infected with Allison's matchmaking bug?

By the time she'd been moving around a bit, Sarah found the stiffness passing. She'd certain sure be able to get back to a regular routine by tomorrow, and that would be a relief. She wasn't used to being home during the day anymore, and time dragged when Mamm wouldn't let her pitch in.

All her wariness returned when she heard a car

coming down the lane. If it was Mac with more questions, she'd have to relive last night's assault again, just when she'd succeeded in dismissing it from her mind for at least a few minutes at a time.

She stepped out onto the back porch and was instantly distracted by the smell of the air. It was fresh and rich after last night's rain, reviving her just as it did the plants. Even the corn in the field stood up straighter and looked greener, as if it had grown overnight.

Maybe the drought was over. The thought cheered her, making the world seem a less dangerous place than it had recently.

Allison's car came to a stop by the porch and she got out, carrying a big bouquet. "I know, I know, you have plenty of flowers, but these are from the other businesses at Blackburn House. Emily organized it."

"That was wonderful kind of her. Of everyone." Sarah took the blooms, inhaling their rich aroma as she returned Allison's hug. "But what are you doing here? You should be looking after things at the shop."

"Don't be such a slave driver." Allison kept her arm around Sarah as they went into the kitchen. "Everything is fine at the shop."

"But you didn't close early—"

"Of course I didn't." Allison went to greet Mammi and Grossmammi, receiving hugs.

Allison was one of the few Englisch who'd gotten past Grossmammi's reserve with strangers, and the elderly woman grandmother now treated her like another one of her chicks, albeit a more brilliantly colored one.

"You'll have something to eat," Mammi announced. "Folks have been bringing food in all day to wish Sarah well."

"If I ate it all, I'd be the size of a tent," Sarah said. "Luckily the boys don't need any encouragement."

Allison nodded agreement to a piece of cinnamon walnut streusel cake and settled at the table. "People want to do something to show how sorry they are for what happened." She studied Sarah for a moment. "The bruises are nasty, but you look better than I expected after hearing Nick's account."

"Ach, I'm fine." Sarah put her hand to her neck self-consciously. Eager to change the subject, she returned to Allison's arrival during business hours. "But what about the store? Not that I'm not glad to see you," she added hastily.

"I told you the shop is fine," Allison said. "Don't you believe me? Aaron brought Becky in first thing this morning, and she's been great. I showed her how to work the register, and after an hour she was faster than I am. To say nothing of knowing a lot more about the fabrics."

"Takes after her mamm, she does," Sarah's

mother said, an approving note in her voice. "She's just the person to help out with the quilt shop."

Allison nodded. "In fact, she's so good that I was thinking maybe we ought to ask Becky if she'd like to work a few hours a week. It would free us up a little, and we could be training her to take on more responsibility, in case, say, either of us wanted to get married." She sent a sly glance toward Sarah.

"You'd better be talking about yourself," Sarah warned.

"If you'd only see what's right in front of your face . . ." Allison began.

Mamm nodded. "You're not past the age of marrying, not at all."

"And those girls of Aaron's couldn't ask for a better mammi," Grossmammi added.

Sarah stared at them, aghast. "Are you all conspiring against me?"

"Komm, Sarah." Mamm was sounding reasonable. "We three know your feelings for Aaron. There's nothing wrong with it, and you'd be a fine wife to him."

"To say nothing of the way he looks at you," Allison added. "Trust me, I've seen that look before."

Sarah grasped at her only defense against hope. "Aaron as much as told me he didn't think of marrying after losing Mary Ann. Surely that means he loved her too much to care for anyone else."

And even if Aaron was interested, as that kiss they'd shared had indicated, how could she marry a man who didn't love her?

"You are thinking you can't wed someone who doesn't love you," Grossmammi said with uncanny accuracy. "But there are other reasons than a broken heart for Aaron thinking he wouldn't marry after Mary Ann's death."

Sarah could only stare at her. "But . . . what else could it mean?"

"The heart is capable of all sorts of feelings, my Sarah. Regret, sorrow, guilt. And a person's first love isn't always his lasting love. It is wonderful fine if it is, but the love that comes from living together and suffering through troubles together can be a much deeper and richer thing." Grossmammi seemed to be looking back at her life with love and longing.

"Your grandmother is a very wise woman," Allison said after a moment's silence. "Listen to her."

Sarah nodded, not daring to disagree, but not daring to hope, either.

Seeming to sense that they'd given her enough to think about for now, her grandmother turned to Allison. "Did you have many folks in the shop today, then?"

"A ton," Allison said. "Asking about Sarah, of course. But the funny thing is that most of them ended up buying something, too. I think they wanted to show support. And a number of people offered to help with the festival." She grinned. "It was as if we were all closing ranks against the firebug. A great feeling."

Sarah's mother nodded. "Nothing like trouble to bring folks together, I guess. Is there any news about what the police are doing?"

"Mac was pretty frustrated that the guy got clean away without leaving a trace last night. But he and Fielding have been putting their heads together. He says the investigator now seems a bit readier to admit that Mac knows the area better than he does."

"I'm glad to hear it." Maybe that meant they'd start to make some progress, if Fielding admitted he didn't know everything.

Allison tilted her head to one side. "He told Nick that they'd realized something that might be important. All the fires, except for that one in town, have been in pretty much the same area."

Sarah considered a moment. "That's true. We've been saying that all along. They were on different roads, but if you just look at the properties, they were all quite close except that one fire. But what does it mean?"

"They're thinking likely it's someone who either lives or has lived or worked in this area," Allison said carefully. "Nick says he thinks Mac is starting to look suspiciously even at his nearest and dearest, he's so frustrated."

Sarah nodded slowly. It was a chilling thought that someone she knew, someone she saw often, was the face that belonged on the dark silhouette of her nightmares.

"Someone is coming," Mamm said, at nearly the same moment shoes sounded on the back porch. "Aaron."

Noting the change in her voice as she said the name, Sarah felt heat flood her cheeks. She didn't want to meet him here, under the gaze of the three people who knew so well what her feelings were.

"Komm in," Mamm said. "You're just in time to help us eat some of these desserts folks keep bringing in."

"Denke, Hannah, but I just came to see how Sarah was." He nodded to the others, and by the time his eyes met hers, she had managed to compose herself.

Allison stood. "Nice to see you, Aaron. But I must be getting back to work. Sarah, you take care." She bent for a quick hug, giving Sarah a conspiratorial smile.

"Ach, I need to . . . to pick some tomatoes for supper." Mamm grabbed a bowl from the counter.

"I'll help," Grossmammi said, and in an instant everyone had left, leaving her to face Aaron alone.

CHAPTER SIXTEEN

AARON STOOD INSIDE the kitchen door for a moment, unsettled by the flurry of people who seemed to think his arrival a signal to depart. Still, given what he'd come to say, he couldn't complain.

It was difficult to know what to say to Sarah when his own feelings were so confused, but he owed it to her to try. Otherwise she'd be blaming herself, most likely, for that kiss, which had seemed to catch both of them off guard.

He was so preoccupied with his own thoughts that it wasn't until he'd taken the chair kitty-corner to hers that he took a good look at her. Sarah seemed more herself, that was certain sure, but the bruises stood out starkly against her pale skin. Rage surged through him anew, and his breath caught with the effort to control it.

"Don't, Aaron." She managed a slight smile despite how she must be feeling. "You're angry. I understand. Jonny was the same way when he saw me."

"Jonny is beginning to turn into a man. He naturally wants to protect his sister."

"Protecting is one thing, but revenge is another." There was a decided note in her words, as if she'd considered this carefully already. "I'll tell you what I told Jonny. I forgive the man, but I want him caught. He has to be stopped before he hurts anyone else, and he must face the consequences of what he did. And we must forgive, because that is who we are."

Aaron's hands relaxed and he smiled a little ruefully. "You are in the right, Sarah. I'll try. But it's easier to forgive a wrong done to me than one done to someone I care for."

The faintest rose color came up in her face, and he wondered if he should have put that another way. But it was true—he did care for Sarah. He just didn't know where that could lead.

"You've been a close friend all my life, ain't so?" he added.

She nodded, but she still looked a bit unsettled.

Hoping to remove the wary expression from her eyes, he tried to change the subject. "I took Becky to the shop first thing this morning. She said to tell you she's wonderful glad to help out."

"I know." The sparkle came back to Sarah's gaze. "That's what Allison was just telling me. In fact, Allison felt so comfortable leaving Becky in charge that she drove out to check on me."

He nodded, pleased. "I'm certain sure she doesn't need to worry about Becky. She's a smart, responsible girl."

"She is that." Sarah hesitated. "Allison suggested we ought to hire Becky to help in the shop a few days a week. We can afford it now, and it would free us up a bit." The flush was back in her cheeks, and he didn't know why. "Would that bother you, to have Becky working for us? I know you count on her help with Anna and Lena, and we wouldn't ask her if it might cause a problem."

He didn't even have to think of his answer. "Ask her, for sure. I would never want to hold Becky back, and we can manage easily. Becky should follow her heart."

Maybe that wasn't the best way to put it. How had it come to be so difficult to talk to Sarah, when it had always been the easiest thing in the world? Glancing around for some way to ease the moment, he noted the lineup of baked goods on the counter.

"I see the sisters have been outdoing themselves, expressing sympathy with food," he said.

"Ach, ja." Sarah looked relieved. "Most of the church has been by already. Even Miriam Stoltzfus came with a peanut butter cake, and she has so much on her hands these days that no one would expect it."

"It's like her, though. She'd likely say that helping someone else is a good distraction from your own troubles."

"That sounds like Miriam, all right." Sarah's expression grew more serious. "Have you talked to Ben lately? I hear this second blow hit him hard."

"It has. He was even talking about selling out

and heading someplace where there was more available land. It doesn't surprise me. Seems like there's less farmland in the county every year. I know that better than most." The thought of the farm he'd lost still rankled.

Sarah gave a little gasp. "How could I forget? I've wanted to talk to you, but . . ." She let that trail off. "Well, I didn't get time, but you must know, in case you're interested. Julia Everly asked me if you might want to buy that land of hers. She knows it hasn't been used for farming in a long time, but she thought maybe . . . anyway, she said you can let her know, and she'll give you first chance at it."

"It would take a lot of work," he said slowly, turning the prospect over in his mind. "Still, it wouldn't have to be done all at once. The kinder and I could stay on with my folks until things were up and running." He was thinking aloud, working it out, and gradually beginning to see advantages as well as disadvantages. "The land is good, and it wouldn't be hard to clear a little more if needed. Do you know how many acres there are?"

Sarah shook her head, looking pleased with the result of her news. "I've no idea, but quite a bit, I think. You ought to stop by and talk to Julia about it."

"Ja, I will. Denke, Sarah. That's the best news I've had in a while."

"I'm glad." But a cloud seemed to grow in her candid eyes. "I wonder . . ."

"What?" he asked when she didn't complete the sentence?

"Allison was saying that because almost all of the fires were on property in the same area, Mac thinks that means the arsonist is from out here. But I wonder if that's right. I mean, what if it's the location that's important, not the fires?"

He frowned, not sure he was following. "What could that have to do with it? Barn fires are usually started by people who just want to see something burn. That's what they always investigate first. Or maybe sometimes a fire might be started because the firebug has a grudge against someone."

"Maybe I'm being silly," Sarah said slowly. "But I was remembering Julia saying that someone had approached her to sell that property of hers. And then there was Matt Gibson, selling to a company nobody ever heard of."

Aaron wanted to dismiss the idea, but he couldn't. It seemed unlikely, but what if the two things hung together? The repeated fires at Ben's had him talking about selling up.

"Why would anyone go to that much trouble to try to buy up property around here? It's not as if it's valuable for much except farming."

"You're probably right," Sarah said quickly. "I said it was silly."

"Not silly at all. I think it's worth telling Mac about, anyway. But in the meantime, you mustn't worry about it."

"I'll try," she said, her voice husky, reminding him of her pain.

"Sarah . . ." The sudden serious tone in his voice must have warned her, because she looked at him warily. "I don't want to tire you, but there's something we must talk about. The day I kissed you."

"You don't need—"

He interrupted her. "You're trying to make it easy for me, ain't so? But you are my dear friend, and I want you to understand." His lips twisted. "As much as I understand, anyway."

She nodded, seeming cautiously resigned to listening.

"I told you I felt I could not marry again after Mary Ann's death." The words tasted acrid, like the aftertaste of a fire. "You thought that meant I'd loved her so much I couldn't love anyone else. But that's not so."

Sarah stared at him, her eyes wide, the blue seeming to darken. "But I thought . . ."

"You thought what everyone did. That ours was a real love match." He shrugged. "Maybe it was. I was the happiest man in the world when Mary Ann said she'd be my wife. But a few years later, I looked at her and felt as if we didn't really know each other at all." He stopped, trying to find the words to tell Sarah the rest of it.

"I'm sorry," she said softly. "But you don't have to say anything to me that you don't want to."

Oddly enough, that made it easier to go on. "We weren't much younger than most Amish when we got married. But I felt as if I'd been floating along on a cloud. Mary Ann was so pretty and popular. Everyone liked her." He shook his head, looking down at his clasped hands. "But when you're that young, you ought to keep on growing for a time, ain't so? Mary Ann didn't. She just still wanted to be the pretty girl who was the center of attention. That sounds mean, but that's how I was thinking when we got her cancer diagnosis. That changed everything, and I felt . . ." He groped for the right words.

"You felt guilty." Sarah supplied them.

"I did. I felt as if it was my fault for not loving her enough." He rubbed his face with his hands. "I wanted to help her, but everything I said just seemed to make matters worse. She expected me to save her, and I couldn't."

He stared bleakly at the past until Sarah put her hand over his.

"I understand," she said softly. "But there was nothing you could do. You know that."

"I do. But it doesn't make it easier. I felt . . ." He struggled for the words to describe it. "I felt as if I couldn't risk loving again. Failing again.

That was all right. I didn't want anything else— just to raise my girls the way I should and make it up to them. I didn't have any desire to find someone else. And then . . . and then I started having feelings for you. I kissed you." His gaze touched her face and then skittered away.

He waited for her to say something, but she didn't. She just sat, warmth and sympathy flowing from her as it always did. A person could count on that with Sarah. You knew what you were getting with her.

He backed away from that thought quickly. "It took me by surprise, Sarah. I knew I'd been feeling attracted to you, but I didn't know it was going to happen, and after it did . . . well, I didn't know what to say. I'm not sure I'm ready to feel this way about you."

He hated this indecisiveness. But at this point in his life, with his children to consider, he couldn't move forward with Sarah unless he meant marriage. Unless he meant forever. Was he ready to risk that again?

"It's all right. I know." She sounded as if her throat was too tight to say more, but she forced herself. "I care about you. You must know that. But I won't ask for something you can't give."

Her words seemed to strike him in the heart. He held her gaze, aware again of the feelings tumbling around inside him, longing to take the next step but afraid. Afraid to fail Sarah, of all people. But at least he knew this much. "I would do anything not to lose you as a friend."

"That's one thing you never need to worry about." Her fingers closed over his for an instant. "I will never stop being your friend."

SARAH WAS RELIEVED to be back at the shop the next day. It didn't free her from curious glances or anxious questions as to how she was, but at least she could stay busy. Keeping occupied was the only way to stop thinking about Aaron for more than a minute at a time.

Aaron—caught between his irrational guilt over Mary Ann and his longing to move on. To move on with her. Sarah held the thought against her for a moment, feeling its warmth.

But could he ever get past his feelings of responsibility? That was inherent in him, and she didn't want to see him without that part of his character. If only he could see that what went wrong with Mary Ann didn't mean he couldn't love again. If Sarah could help him see that . . .

And there she was, caught back in the endless circle of questions. It was better not to dwell on it. To trust that in this, as in everything, it was God's will.

Allison seemed to understand her need without explanations. She seized the box that held Mrs. Burkholder's quilts and began to spread one out on the table.

"At least these smell better now. You'd better have a look and separate the wheat from the chaff. They all look uniformly dismal to me."

"It's a good thing our business doesn't rely on your quilt expertise." Sarah managed a fairly credible light tone. "There's more here than that. Don't you agree, Becky?"

Becky traced the intricate design of a postage-stamp quilt done in a Sunshine and Shadows pattern. "That's certain sure."

"Good thing I have my sales and advertising skills to recommend me, then. Tell me what's special about this quilt, besides the fact that it looks as if Mrs. Burkholder stored it in a hayloft." Allison flicked at a wisp of straw with her fingertip.

Sarah nodded to Becky, curious as to what the girl would say.

"These tiny postage-stamp–sized pieces are difficult to work with at best," Becky said, touching a tiny square. "To use those in a design like Sunshine and Shadows, where the colors seem to move in a wave from light to dark to light again—ach, that's hard to arrange with the tiny pieces. It's like the woman who made this quilt could visualize the whole quilt top so well that she knew where each tiny square fit."

Allison smiled, obviously impressed by Becky's passion. "I bow to the superior knowledge of you two experts. How hard is it going to be to get it in shape to show?"

Sarah and Becky exchanged glances. "I'd be wonderful glad to do it," the girl stated. "It'll take time, but be worth it."

"Speaking of worth," Sarah said, "if I know Mrs. Burkholder, she won't part with a cent for the cleaning and repair. In fact, she'll probably try to charge us for exhibiting it at the festival."

"She won't succeed." Allison's tone was firm. "I'll see to that. If she wants to sell it at the festival, we'll take our usual commission. I'll be happy to confront the woman."

She would, too. When Allison took on her brisk businesswoman's attitude, Sarah was happy to leave things to her. "Speaking of confronting people . . ." she murmured.

Allison nodded. "I suggest we both plan to go to Julia's house later this afternoon. I agree with you that she shouldn't be alone when she does it."

"Good." In the back of Sarah's mind had lurked the worry that Julia would attempt to confront Donna on her own, and if there were indeed some man involved who was trying to take advantage of Julia, that wouldn't be safe.

Becky had watched this exchange with curiosity in her blue eyes, but she asked no questions. Allison had been right about hiring Becky. She seemed to have all the qualities the shop needed.

And while Sarah didn't think she'd be backing away from running the shop, it was certainly possible that Allison might want to spend less time here. Especially if she and Nick married, which Sarah felt confident they would.

Allison turned away from the table to consult the notes on her phone. "By the way, I talked to the newspaper editor about giving us some advance space to drum up local interest in the festival. He seems enthusiastic about it and wants some photos and a story about how we're turning the old theater into a venue for the event. The idea is that the paper will show the progress, so we need you and Aaron to make some final plans about the display racks and how to use the space. Do you think you can do that soon?"

If Becky weren't there, Sarah might be able to tell Allison just why she didn't want to do something that would result in her being alone with Aaron right now. But his sister was already nodding enthusiastically.

"Aaron will be happy to," she said. "I'll tell him to set it up with you, Sarah."

"Denke, Becky." It was all she could say.

"Oh, and I was supposed to tell you that Emily wanted to see you. She came in every hour yesterday, I think, asking about you."

"I'll run over to the bookshop and let her see that I'm back to normal." Emily was a sweet woman, but inclined to fuss over everything.

"Why don't you do that now," Allison suggested. "I think we can safely delegate decisions about the rest of Mrs. Burkholder's quilts to Becky. And I'm supposed to remind you not to do too much today." Her smile flashed. "Your mother's orders."

"She worries too much." And everything that had happened recently had just added to her worries. Mamm had always thought her kinder were safe when they were home on the farm, but now the outside world had struck at them there, as well. Mamm was struggling with it, trying to balance her trust in God's providence with her tendency to hover over her family.

"Maybe Emily can assure people I'm fine, and they'll stop asking me."

"You can try, but I doubt it," Allison said, grinning.

Leaving them to deal with the shop, Sarah started down the hallway to the bookshop. In that short distance she was stopped twice for anxious questioning, once by the young attorney whose office was upstairs and a second time by a customer leaving the bookshop. Sarah escaped into Emily's haven, breathing a sigh of relief when she saw that no other shoppers were in the store.

Emily came rushing toward her, her fluffy white curls bouncing. "Sarah, you're here. I'm so glad. When I heard, I was afraid you had been badly hurt." She threw her arms around her. "You've always been so kind and helpful to me, and I just felt helpless to do anything for you."

"It's kind of you, Emily." She disengaged herself gently. "I'm fine, as you see. Just a few bumps and bruises, that's all."

Emily surveyed her anxiously. "And they still haven't caught this person. It's terrible. I don't know what the police are about, letting someone run loose to set fires and attack young girls."

Sarah decided it was pointless to argue about whether she was a young girl or not. It wouldn't change Emily's alarmed attitude.

"I'm sure they're doing everything they can," she murmured. "It's not easy to find someone who uses the dark for cover." Aaron's belief that she was a target because the firebug thought she could identify him niggled in the back of her mind. "I've been close to him twice, and all I could say is that it was definitely a man."

"With all those modern methods of determining the guilty party, I'm sure they could do better. Still, I suppose in a small town we don't have access to all the DNA testing and that sort of thing." Emily sounded wistful, as if she'd like to encounter the characters from her favorite television show on the streets of Laurel Ridge.

"Mac knows everyone in the area," Sarah said firmly. "He'll find out who it is if anyone can."

Emily didn't look convinced. "Well, I'm glad you're all right, in any event. I'm sure you were wise to stay home a day to recover. You missed all the busybodies who kept coming into the shop for the latest news."

Sarah suppressed a smile when she thought of Becky's report. "It was good," she said solemnly.

"And I have a little gift for you." Emily bustled to the counter, leaving Sarah to follow her. "I was going to give it to Becky or Allison to give to you if you weren't back today."

"You don't need to do that . . ." Sarah began, but Emily was already pressing an illustrated history of quilting into her hands.

"I want to. I'm sure you know everything that's in this book already, but I was looking through the stock for something suitable, and I thought you'd like it."

"It's lovely," she said, leafing through the pages. "That's so kind of you."

Emily beamed. "You've done so much for me since I took over the bookstore. It's just a way of saying thank you."

Since giving the gift obviously meant much to her, Sarah decided not to argue. "It's always a pleasure to help out," she said. "Oh, and I'll be going over to Julia Everly's house this afternoon, so if you have anything for her, I'll be glad to take it."

"I don't believe anything has come in for her

lately." Emily turned away to check her records, handling the computer with an ease that belied her fluffy little-old-lady manner. "No, she hasn't ordered anything in over a month. But tell her I'd be happy to bring anything she wants. Poor soul, she must be getting bored, being stuck in the house so long."

"I'll tell her." But Sarah frowned, remembering the day she'd noticed Gus Hill in Blackburn House and seen him enter the bookstore. He seemed an unlikely patron for Emily's shop. "I saw Gus Hill coming in here not long ago, and I just assumed he was picking up something for Julia."

Emily appeared distressed. "Yes, he did come in, and it made me uneasy. Not that he doesn't have a perfect right to read, but he always looks so disreputable. I don't think my regular customers would like it. But he didn't speak to me. Or even glance at any books. He just sort of loitered for a few minutes, and then he left."

Maybe he'd lingered in the bookstore long enough for Sarah to go away. Had he been avoiding her? She hadn't heard if the fire investigator had tracked him down. Gus might not want to run into her or anyone who would urge him to talk to the man. Still, it was odd. If he had some real reason for avoiding questions . . .

But that wasn't rational. Gus couldn't be involved in the fire setting, because the destruction of the barn had led to Julia's thinking of selling the property. If that happened, he'd lose the only home he'd known for the past twenty years or so, along with whatever Julia might pay him for his nonexistent work. Sarah couldn't believe he'd willingly risk it.

Still, the fact that he'd been in the building for no apparent reason left her feeling uneasy. What was he doing here?

CHAPTER SEVENTEEN

ON THE RIDE to Julia's house in Allison's car that afternoon, Sarah seized the chance to talk with her friend about her sighting of Gus Hill loitering in Blackburn House. Allison didn't seem to be overly impressed.

"He's not a desirable character to have around, I agree, but I don't see what nefarious purpose he could have in hanging around. Even if he were the arsonist—"

Sarah shook her head. "I can't believe he'd risk losing the only home he has. He must know that no one else would treat him as well as Julia has."

"I agree with you, remember?" Allison glanced at her. "I can see it worries you, but really, what did he do? We can't prevent the public from coming into the building, even if sometimes we might want to."

"I know, I know. It just makes me uncomfortable. He ducked into the bookstore as if he was avoiding me, not that I especially wanted to run into him, anyway." Talking about it made it seem even less threatening, but it still troubled her.

"Maybe he was toying with the idea of talking to you and chickened out when he saw you. If so, it's more likely that he's afraid you've been bad-mouthing him to Julia." Allison smiled. "Which wouldn't be hard to do." That made more sense than anything else she'd thought of. "That could be, I guess. But I haven't said anything that other people haven't, and probably in stronger terms."

"I'd forget about him," her friend advised. "The arsonist is the one who's a threat to you."

"Still, the last I heard Gus was still avoiding Mac and the arson investigator." Sarah knew all the reasons why that was like him, but even so . . .

"I didn't mention it, because you were worried enough," Allison said slowly, not looking at her, "but Mac did catch up with Gus. They questioned him."

A shiver of alarm went through her. "But why didn't you tell me? What did he say?"

Allison hesitated, slowing as they approached Julia's drive. "Nick says Gus claimed he didn't know anything about the fires, of course. But he said he saw an Amish boy 'sneaking around' that garage where the fire was." She darted a look at Sarah. "He said it might have been Jonah."

"But—but it couldn't be. Anyway, Jonah wasn't the person who attacked me."

"I know. That's one reason I didn't mention it, since it doesn't really matter now. And there's no point in worrying about it," she added firmly. "So don't start."

Sarah managed a smile she didn't feel. Thank

the good Lord Jonah had witnesses to prove he couldn't have attacked her.

They were pulling into Julia's driveway by then, and they'd need to focus on the upcoming interview with Donna. Sarah's stomach felt queasy at the thought. At least she could count on Allison to do the talking, assuming she could wrest control from Julia. They were two strong-willed women.

Donna came to the door in answer to their ring. "Julia's waiting for you," she grumbled. "It seems the four of us are to have a conversation. I don't know what all the mystery is about, but she never tells me anything."

Sarah thought she detected a trace of nervousness behind the complaining tone. Donna might sense a slight change in Julia's attitude toward her, and a guilty conscience would do the rest.

"Come in and sit down." Julia sat up very straight, even her hair seeming to bristle. "You, too, Donna. This concerns you."

They'd no more than sat down when Julia launched the attack, giving no one else a chance to speak. "Donna, I asked Allison and Sarah to be here to witness this conversation. You've been stealing from me."

Her cousin flushed with what seemed righteous anger. "You have no right to say a thing like that to me. Talk about ingratitude. After all I've done to help you, sacrificing my time—"

"You may as well stop right there," Julia said, her voice sharp. "You're no fonder of me than I am of you, but I'd rather not have a relative of mine in jail."

Donna paled at that. Her mouth opened, but she didn't speak.

"Now, then," Julia said briskly. "Here's what I know you've taken—an antique album quilt, a silver chafing dish and a set of silver salt and pepper shakers. There may be other things, but I won't be able to confirm that until I can do a thorough search of the attic. I'm giving you the chance to confess here and now and save everyone a lot of trouble."

"That's ridiculous." Some of the strength came back into Donna's attitude. "I suppose this all comes about because Sarah couldn't find some old quilt that you probably got rid of years ago." She sent a look of active dislike toward Sarah.

"I found out because of the quilt festival, but I'd have discovered it eventually, anyway. How did you think you'd get away with it?" Julia's tone was grim. "Or did you think I'd die and no one would ever know?"

"Of course I didn't. I'm telling you I don't know anything at all about your quilt or the silver whatever-they-were. Sarah probably didn't look in the right place."

"I searched carefully." Sarah surprised herself by speaking up.

"We've traced the album quilt," Allison inter-
jected, her tone icy. "We know it was sold."

Donna transferred the glare to Allison. "Not
that it's any of your business, but if it was sold,
my cousin probably did it herself. She got rid of
a lot of things when she moved into this house.
That's the answer, and you've got a lot of nerve
fixing on me—"

"I traced the sales records," Allison said. "It
was sold in the past six months."

If that was a blow, Donna didn't let it show. "I
don't know anything about it. Julia probably sold
it herself and forgot all about it. You don't know
how she forgets things these days."

"The dealer identified you as the woman
who brought the quilt in." Allison seemed
unaffected.

That silenced Donna for a moment, and Sarah
could sense her mind working feverishly behind
that rather foolish face. "Oh, that old quilt," she
said. "Yes, I know the one you mean. Cousin
Julia asked me to sell it for her."

Julia gasped. "That's an out-and-out lie. I never
did anything of the kind."

"You've forgotten, that's all." Donna sounded a
bit smug, maybe satisfied that she'd hit upon the
perfect defense. "Everyone knows how you're
forgetting things."

Sarah couldn't let that pass. "Has Julia's doctor
confirmed that? Because as far as we can tell,

you're the only one who's been saying that, Donna."

"I'm the one who sees her every day. Not you. Not the doctor. If I were to tell you of all the things she's forgotten, like leaving the stove on and mixing up her medicines—"

"Liar!" Julia thundered. "I never thought to hear you being so malicious, Donna. You may as well admit it right off. That's the only way you're getting out of this without my calling in the police."

"You wouldn't. You said you didn't want a cousin of yours in jail."

"I'll do it if I have to." Julia was firm, brooking no argument. "Who was the man? How was he involved?"

That rocked Donna. Sarah could see it. The woman didn't speak for a long minute. Then . . .

"I suppose you've been eavesdropping. Yes, I have a man who is interested in me. He doesn't have anything to do with any stupid old album quilt."

"So you admit you took it."

Donna traded being indignant for a sullen face. "Well, what if I did? That old quilt wasn't worth all that much, but the dealer offered me five hundred for it. So I took it. I needed money, and I didn't want to hear another lecture from you about living within my means."

"So you turned to stealing."

Julia's tone expressed so much contempt that Sarah began to feel sorry for Donna. She'd hate to be spoken to that way.

"It's not really stealing," Donna protested. "After all, it will all come to me when . . ." She stopped, maybe realizing that wasn't a very good argument.

"When I die," Julia finished for her, her face grim. "Don't count your chickens before they're hatched, Donna. I might be better off leaving everything to charity rather than to a thief."

"You wouldn't! Julia, we're kin. I admit it, I've been foolish, but I never meant you any harm. You know that, don't you?"

"You'd better tell me the rest of it." Julia seemed to take advantage of Donna's dismay. "What about the silver?"

Donna hesitated for a moment. Wondering how much they knew? Finally she shook her head. "I don't know anything about it. Maybe it's in some other storage box." She seemed to gain assurance from their expressions. "All I ever took was the quilt."

Julia didn't press the matter, which was just as well as far as Sarah was concerned. She doubted that even Allison could figure out how to trace something like that.

"I repeat, how does the man fit into this? Did he suggest you might take something of mine?"

"No! He'd never do anything like that."

"If he turned your head with flattery and used you to get at my property, I might not blame you so severely." Julia held out the bait.

Did she mean it? Sarah forced herself not to fidget. This confrontation seemed to contain plenty of pitfalls.

Donna straightened, her head coming up. "You're wrong. You think no man could be interested in me, but he is, and he's a better catch than either of you two could get." She glared at Allison and Sarah with something near hatred. "You're jealous of me, but you'll never get me to say a word against him. Never!"

"That's enough." Julia's voice cracked like a whip. "I've heard enough from you to last me quite a while. Get out, and don't come back unless I send for you."

"Fine! Take care of yourself, then. See how far you get." Donna grabbed her purse, flounced to the door and went out, slamming it loudly behind her.

For a moment the bang seemed to echo in the sudden quiet. Julia sagged in her chair, all the fight going out of her. Sarah was at her side in a moment.

"That was so hard on you. Tell me what I can do for you. Do you want a cup of tea? Coffee?"

"A stiff drink would do me more good." Julia waved her away. "All right, stop hovering. I'm fine." She snorted. "Donna always was a fool.

I don't know why I'm surprised that hasn't changed."

"Still, she's right about one thing," Allison said, her tone practical. "You need help, at least until that cast comes off."

"I've already arranged it." It was Julia's turn to look smug. "I knew I wasn't going to want Donna around any longer, no matter how this turned out. I have a girl coming in a few hours a day to help me. I should have done that to begin with, but Donna was so insistent about taking care of me that I didn't."

"I'm sure she'll apologize and try to make amends." Sarah wanted to make things better, but suspected that wasn't possible. And Julia wasn't one to look for someone else to shoulder her burdens, anyway.

"She's trying to protect some man. She'll come to her senses when he dumps her." Julia was cynical about it, but it might well be true.

At least Julia didn't seem to mourn over people she couldn't change. Sarah could learn something from her.

AARON HAD BEEN a little surprised when Becky came home with the information that Sarah would like to go with him to the theater building to make plans. Somehow after their last conversation he'd had the feeling that she'd want him to keep his distance for a bit.

But if she felt able to get back to their usual friendly terms already, he certain sure wasn't going to argue. At least he'd have time to consider where his relationship with Sarah was going. She'd shown she cared, hadn't she?

When he reached Blackburn House, Sarah was waiting. She climbed into the buggy clutching a notebook and evading his glance.

"I have some possible arrangements for the festival that we've made up. Mostly based on things that other festivals posted online, according to Allison. She says there's no point in starting from scratch if someone else has already worked out the best way to do something."

So they weren't back to their usual friendship, after all. Sarah was talking too quickly, too intent on business to be anything near normal.

Well, it was his fault, wasn't it? He'd upset the balance of their friendship with that kiss, and he'd probably made matters even worse by telling her about what had happened with Mary Ann.

Why had he? He never talked to anyone else about it, not even to Daad and Mamm. Why had he burdened Sarah with his guilt and self-blame?

Because she would listen without blaming, he supposed. That was one of Sarah's gifts, and he'd taken advantage of it. He stole a glance at her, but her head was averted and the bonnet's brim cut off any view of her face. He had to try to return things to their usual friendship, and didn't know how. If he didn't manage to . . .

That didn't bear thinking about. Sarah was a valued friend, and he couldn't lose that. During the years of his marriage he'd felt separated from her in a way, but somehow that hadn't changed their easy friendship. A return to that was the best he could hope for, at least until life returned to normal. How could he think of other things until he was free of the shadow of Matt Gibson's death? Of the arsonist haunting their valley?

Aaron cleared his throat, trying to hit upon a subject that would not be personal but would show he still considered her his friend.

As often happened, she saved him the trouble. "How is Jonah doing now? Feeling better? The police don't suspect him of the arson now, do they?"

"As to that, Mac is satisfied. He says Fielding is still being stubborn, saying maybe the attack on you had some other cause entirely. As if you went around making enemies left and right."

Something flickered in her face at that. "But Jonah?"

"Jonah is better himself, I think." Aaron frowned a little, thinking of his brother. "He's been staying home instead of running around every night, for one thing. And he seems a lot more serious all of a sudden."

"Maybe the trouble has helped him mature,"

Sarah suggested. "It affects people that way. If so, it's good, isn't it?"

"For sure. Daad's happier, anyway, so they aren't arguing as much. Makes supper a more pleasant experience," Aaron added lightly, and looked for her answering smile.

But Sarah seemed distracted, frowning at some thought of her own.

He hesitated. "If you are worrying about what happened between us . . ."

"Ach, no." Sarah seemed so surprised at the idea that he was instantly reassured.

"I'm sehr glad of that. But what are you fretting about, then?"

She sighed. "It's nothing I can do any more about, I suppose. I told you a little about the problem with Julia Everly, ain't so?"

"That some things were missing from her house, ja," he said. "Is something more missing?"

"No, but we—Allison and I—were able to trace the quilt. It was exciting, in a way." A smile teased at Sarah's lips. "We felt like real detectives, following the trail."

"You had an adventure, ain't so?" It surprised him, in a way, that Sarah had undertaken such a thing. Maybe it was a measure of how much she'd grown and strengthened in the past few years.

"Ja, but then when we found out it had been stolen by Donna . . ." She hesitated, and the smile vanished. "That was painful. Julia wanted to confront her cousin about taking her album quilt and selling it, and Allison and I felt we should stay and support her. It wasn't pleasant, but Donna finally admitted it."

"That's gut, surely. But I'm not sure why you had to be there." He tried to keep the words from sounding as if he questioned her judgment. She'd jumped on him before for that mistake.

"We were concerned that Donna might have become involved with some man who was using her to cheat her cousin. Harvey Preston was telling me about some people . . . con men, I guess . . . who take advantage of elderly people, especially those who don't have family to protect them. We were afraid it might be that, and, well, we thought it would be safer for Julia to have witnesses."

"It was unpleasant for you. You shouldn't have had to be involved." He couldn't seem to help himself.

"I was the one who started it all, by looking for that album quilt of Julia's. How could I not be involved?" Sarah hesitated for a moment. "In a way, it was good to see that Julia is as strong willed as ever, even if it was difficult to witness."

Sliding his hand across the bench seat, Aaron clasped hers for a moment. "You feel responsible, and maybe a little bit guilty, ain't so? But much as I hate to admit it, you couldn't have done anything else." He suspected he sounded rueful. "So I hope you're not going to be mad at me again."

That surprised her into a soft laugh. "No, I won't be mad at you." She glanced at the theater, coming up on their right. "I think you can safely leave the horse and buggy along the side of the building."

He nodded, accepting that the subject was closed. Finding a shady spot for the horse, he sprang from the seat and was in time to offer Sarah a hand as she climbed down. She fished out a key as they approached the door.

"We're entrusted with a key, since we'll be going in and out with the quilt racks and so forth."

She opened the door, and they stepped into the lobby. Light flooded in the front glass doors, laying a pattern on the freshly tiled floor.

"Will you be using the lobby for the festival?" Aaron measured it mentally.

"We think it should be a welcome area, where people buy their tickets to the quilt show. We're undecided about having some food vendors in here. We wouldn't want careless people spilling drinks on the quilts."

"You could post a few signs, saying No Food or Drink Past This Point, but people might still try to bring things in."

"We'd have someone on each door to make

sure folks obey. In any event, if we allow vendors, they'll bring their own setup. Ellen Whiting says she'll borrow as many folding tables and chairs as we need from her church. But Allison thought we'd need something here in the center of the lobby to hold a big banner or a quilt."

He scanned the woodwork and ceiling. "Shouldn't be a problem. I can suspend a rod from the ceiling for that, making it as high or as low as you need."

"Good. We'll want it to be high enough that people can't brush against it." Sarah scribbled something in her notebook. "Most of the display racks will be in the main part of the theater." She led the way to the nearest swinging door and pushed it open. Darkness loomed beyond. "I hoped the custodian would have left the lights on for us."

Aaron moved next to her. "Do you know where the switches are?"

She nodded, and he felt the movement of her head, her kapp brushing his shoulder. "They're midway along the left-hand wall. Seems like an inconvenient place to put them, but that's where they are."

"We can prop this door open to give us enough light to find them." Aaron grabbed a folding chair that had been left leaning against the wall. Flipping it open, he wedged it into the doorway, double-checking to be sure it wouldn't slip away.

"Good." Sarah sounded a little breathless. Probably the dark contained bad memories of her struggle with her assailant. "This way."

She caught his hand, leading him to the wall and back along it, stretching out her other hand to feel her way as they moved farther from the light. His fingers tightened on hers, and a wave of unwelcome feelings surged through him. He had to stop this, or at least learn to ignore it for the time being.

"Here they are." Sarah sounded relieved, and he heard the swish of her hand against the wall. There was a click, but no welcoming light came on.

"Is there more than one switch?" he asked, feeling for the panel himself, his hand brushing hers.

"Several." She drew back as he flipped switches, to no avail.

He could hear her quickened breath and knew she was afraid. "There must be a circuit box somewhere around. You can wait in the lobby until I find it."

"I know where it is." Sarah seemed to force herself to speak normally. "There's a door opposite us but closer to the entrance. You can just make it out, see? The box is there. I'm sure I saw it when the custodian showed us where cleaning equipment was stored."

"Go back to the lobby," Aaron said, pressing her gently in that direction.

"I'll wait here," she replied, her tone firm and decided now. "You'll need me to tell you when you get the right switch."

"Sarah . . ." he began.

"Just go. I'm not going to start being afraid of the dark at my age."

He understood, but he didn't like it. Still, he did as she said. Sarah was usually the most gentle of creatures, but she could turn stubborn as a rock when it came to something she considered a duty.

He made his way across the room, moving surely until he bumped into a folding chair that clattered noisily to the floor.

"Aaron?" Sarah sounded alarmed.

"It's nothing," he said quickly. "I knocked a chair over." Feeling around, he set it up again. "The owner ought at least to have made sure the lights are working. What if you or Allison came here alone?"

"Better not let her hear you say that," Sarah said.

He had to smile, thinking of Allison's probable response to that. If there was something Allison Standish feared, he had yet to see it. Maybe her courage was helping Sarah to recognize her own.

"I'm at the door," he said, when he felt the handle. "It'll just be a minute now." Or possibly longer, since the inside of the closet was as dark as a cave. He felt along the wall until he touched the cool metal of the circuit box and fumbled for the handle. "Got it."

He groped for the top switch, holding the closet door open with his foot. "Let me know—"

The chair he'd set to hold the lobby door open clattered to the floor. The door swung closed, plunging them into complete darkness. He heard the sound of Sarah's gasp from across the empty theater.

His own breath caught. Empty? How was it then that he heard movement somewhere near the front? It couldn't be Sarah—she was farther back along the wall. And she couldn't have knocked the chair away.

Someone was in here with them.

Should he continue trying to find the light or go back to Sarah? A stifled sound from her decided him. He bolted back toward her, letting the closet door slam. In its echo, he heard stealthy movement toward the direction where Sarah must be.

"Who's there?" he demanded.

No answer, but he could sense the man heading inexorably toward Sarah and closer to her than he was.

"Sarah, be very still. I'm coming." Aaron lunged forward, forgetting the chair, and barreled into it again, sending it flying and losing his balance for an instant. Sarah, where was Sarah?

There was no sound but the harshness of his own breath as, groping wildly, he rushed toward the spot where he'd left her. If he caught the man, he'd—

Not strike, no. But he'd keep him away from Sarah, whatever the cost.

His outstretched hands hit the wall, then the row of switches. But no Sarah. Where—? A movement behind him alerted him. He shoved out, encountering grasping hands that fell away instantly when the man realized he'd caught Aaron instead of Sarah.

Aaron flung out his arm, hoping to grasp the intruder, hold him, but that quickly he was away, footsteps fleeing toward the front of the building. But Sarah . . .

"Sarah, where are you?" The lobby door swung open, letting in a shaft of light as a dark figure bolted through it.

"Is he gone?" Sarah's voice was small and breathless.

"Ja. Where are you? Are you hurt?"

"Down here." Her voice shook.

He followed the sound of it, groping until he connected with her head and shoulders. She was crouched against the wall in a small niche just past the switches. He drew her to her feet, supporting her as he pulled her close.

He shouldn't. But he had to. And Sarah came

willingly, closing her arms around him and hanging on tight.

"It's all right," he soothed, smoothing his hand down the sweet curve of her back. "You're safe now."

"He got away again." There was a catch in her breath.

"Not for long," Aaron said grimly. "I saw just enough to recognize him. It was Gus Hill."

CHAPTER EIGHTEEN

SARAH FELT AS if she was outwardly composed and hoped she was right about that, especially since most of Laurel Ridge's small police force milled around her. The fact that she was still shaky inside was no one's business.

Allison, sitting on a folding chair next to her in the now brightly lit theater, edged a little closer. "Sure you're okay?" she asked quietly.

Nodding, Sarah made an effort at a smile. "Just thankful I wasn't alone in this place." She glanced around and shivered despite her resolve. With all the lights full on, the theater was just a large, windowless room now, without much character. But half an hour ago, it had been a terrifying place.

"We could go out into the lobby," Allison suggested.

"Mac said people are gawking in the windows. That would be worse." She hated being looked at as if she were an object in a display, to be stared at. Strangers did that often enough when you were Amish.

Mac came over to her, dragging a chair behind him. He flipped it out and sat, giving her an encouraging smile. "Feel able to talk about it?"

"Ja . . . yes," she amended, aware of Fielding, the arson investigator, lurking a few feet away, as if he wasn't invited to be part of the inquiry, but intended to hear what was said nonetheless.

Aaron made no pretense of lurking. He moved behind her chair and stood there, his fingers resting lightly on her shoulders. Even without turning, she could feel his solid presence close to her.

Would Mac object? Apparently not, because he glanced briefly at Aaron and then at his notebook before focusing on her.

"I think we're doing this too much, right?" His serious expression relaxed in a quick smile. "Just tell me what happened in your own words. We'll get it down in an official report later."

She sucked in a breath and seemed to feel strength flowing into her through Aaron's hands. "You know, more or less. Aaron and I came over to decide on what quilt racks and display areas we'd need for the festival. I had the key, so we let ourselves in."

"Did anyone else know you were coming?"

She shrugged, spreading her hands. "Plenty of people, I guess. We talked about it in the store. Anyone might have heard."

Mac nodded. "And if they didn't hear, they might have guessed you'd be back to the building soon. Did you come straight in here?"

"We stood in the lobby for a few minutes,

talking about what we'd need out there. Then we started inside and found it was dark."

"Had you expected the lights to be on?" Mac looked up, alert.

"I'd called this morning and left a message on the answering machine for the custodian as to when we'd be here. But anyway, I knew where the switches are, back along that wall." She pointed. "Aaron blocked the door open with a chair so we'd be able to see our way a little."

Mac's gaze switched to Aaron. "You're sure the door couldn't have swung free?"

"I am certain sure. I checked it twice. The chair could not come out on its own." Aaron's voice seemed to rumble through her, he was so close, and she tried not to think of those moments when she'd clung to him.

"When we hit the switches, nothing happened. I knew the circuit breakers were in the closet opposite us, so Aaron went to find it while I stayed put. We were talking, you see, so I knew where he was the whole time. He had gone into the closet when suddenly the chair clattered and fell and the door swung shut, leaving us in the dark." Despite her efforts, her voice trembled a little.

"Just take it slow," Mac said. "Did you hear or see anything to make you think someone else was in here?"

She nodded. "I couldn't see, but I could hear

him. He was coming toward me from the door. And Aaron was coming, too, but was farther away. Aaron shouted at the man. He didn't answer, but I could tell he was getting close."

She stopped, swallowed, and Aaron's hands tightened on her shoulders as Allison gripped her hand. If they could do this instead of her, they would, she knew.

"So I slipped back along the wall a little. I knew there was a corner where the wall was set back a few inches. When I reached it, I crouched down."

Sarah's throat closed, and she couldn't go on. She was kneeling there in the dark again, feeling the rough plaster behind her back, trying to make herself so small no one could find her.

"That's enough." Aaron's tone was hard. "I already told you who it was. I saw him. It was Gus Hill."

"I know." Mac sounded as if he was trying to be patient. "I just need to know what Sarah saw."

"I didn't see him," she managed to say. "I had my head down when I heard him go out. But before that . . ." She stopped and cleared her tight throat. "When he was close, I could smell him. Aaron is right. It was Gus."

Fielding made a derisive sound at that, but Mac nodded. "Yeah, he could be pretty fragrant, couldn't he?"

"Why aren't you out looking for him?" Aaron interrupted. "He's getting away."

"He won't get far if he tries to run. I've put an alert out for that old rattletrap pickup he drives, and I've notified other local law enforcement. My guess is he'll leave the truck somewhere and take off into the woods. This time of year, it'll be a job to find him."

That was true enough. Julia said her husband had claimed that Gus knew the whole ridge like the back of his hand. If he wanted to disappear, they wouldn't locate him until cold or hunger drove him out.

Sarah rubbed her forehead, feeling the tension there, and wished this was over.

"I still don't see why Gus would do it," Allison said. "Set the first fire, I mean. He must have known that burning the barn on her property would make Julia more likely to sell, and he'd lose his home."

Mac nodded. "That's why I haven't seriously considered him up to now. But there might be something else involved we don't know about. Suppose someone wanted to buy the land. Gus might very well be glad to pocket the cash for making that happen."

"I was going to talk to you about that." Aaron's hands tightened a little on her shoulders. "Sarah began to wonder if the land might be behind these fires, since most of them have happened in the same area. If someone wanted to buy up the land, barn fires would be sure to make folks more likely to consider an offer."

Sarah nodded. "And Julia did say that someone had called her about selling her property not too long ago, but she turned them down."

"Did she say who it was?" Mac's tone had quickened.

"She said she didn't remember."

He nodded. "I'll talk to her about it, anyway. We hadn't really considered that kind of a motive for the fire, not when it looked so much like the rash of barn fires we had years ago. Of course Gus might easily have set one for a payoff, decided he liked the excitement, and gone on to set more."

Aaron moved slightly, and Sarah could almost sense his frown. "If it's bigger than that—well, some out-of-state company just bought up the Gibson place, don't forget. I can't think why someone would take such risks to buy property out our way, but it wants explaining."

Mac rose. "We won't ignore that possibility, believe me. The important thing now is to find Gus. Then we'll get some answers."

Aaron's hands tightened into fists. "If you need a search party, I'll help. He has to be made to pay for what he's done. Letting my brother be blamed for his actions, and hurting Sarah the way he did . . ."

Mac glanced from Aaron to Sarah. "I know what you mean. We'll get him. Meantime, Sarah, I'll send you home in a police car, so—"

"No," she said quickly. "Mac, it would scare my little brothers to death if they saw me coming home in a cruiser."

"I'll take Sarah," Aaron said.

"It will be faster and simpler if I run her home." Allison rose. "Aaron, if you could go back to the shop and ask your sister to close up, that would be a big help. She must have thought I was crazy when I went running out of there."

Aaron's hand lingered on Sarah's shoulder for another moment. "Ja, you're right. I'll tend to it. You get Sarah home safe."

"I will." Allison put her arm around her. "I parked in the alley. If we go out the side door, we can avoid the crowd."

"Denke. Thank you."

Aaron nodded briefly. "I'll come by tonight to be sure you're okay. Don't worry. Gus won't dare come near you again."

"I know." Sarah managed to smile at him, and she had to be content with that. If she'd hoped for a warmer goodbye . . . well, that would be foolish in front of all these people, even if he felt it.

SARAH PAUSED IN the act of shaking out the back doormat at the sound of tires on the gravel lane. The boys, on their way into the house, stopped and stared as if Mac was a stranger in his uniform, instead of someone they'd known all their lives. She forced a smile, hating that recent events had changed their perception of the world.

"Look, here's Mac come to visit."

They weren't taken in by her cheerful words, watching him warily as he got out of the police car.

Daadi came out to stand beside her. "What are you boys standing around for? Greet Mac and then head upstairs. Jonny, you play a board game in your room with your brothers until bedtime."

"Farm Race," Noah shouted, scrambling for the porch.

"No, Chinese checkers." Thomas was right behind him.

Jonny nodded to Mac, his gaze solemn, before he headed after his brothers. "Maybe we can do both," he said, playing peacemaker.

"Don't slam—" Sarah began, and paused as the screen door banged against the frame "—the door."

Daadi didn't even give Mac time to speak before he rushed into the question that was on everyone's mind. "Did you catch Gus Hill yet?"

Mac's jaw seemed to tighten. "Not yet. We'll get him, don't worry." His voice seemed to soften as he looked at Sarah. "He won't dare to try anything else."

"I'm sure you're right." But if she was certain, why were her nerves jumping as if they were on fire?

"Komm." Daad held the door. "You'd best have some coffee while you tell us about it."

Mac nodded. "Sorry," he muttered, looking for all the world the way he had as a boy when he'd confessed to breaking a branch on Daad's cherry tree.

Daad seemed satisfied, because his stern expression eased as they went into the kitchen. Mamm was already cutting wedges of the shoofly pie left from breakfast, while Grossmammi poured coffee.

"There'd be snitz pie to offer you if those greedy boys hadn't finished it up for dessert," Mamm said. She knew Mac especially loved her dried apple pie.

"Next time tell me before you let them at it." Mac grinned, taking a seat at the kitchen table as he'd been doing since he was a boy. He looked from Mammi to Grossmammi. "Sorry I don't have better news about Hill. We found that pickup of his run into the woods a mile or so from the cottage, but no sign of him yet."

"I still have trouble seeing what made Gus think I was a threat to him." Sarah tried to look at it calmly. "Even if you're sure he was the arsonist—"

"We're sure." Mac's face was grim. "We

searched the cottage and found the evidence. Kerosene cans, oily rags . . . The wonder is he didn't kill himself, careless as he was."

"It might be he thought Sarah had seen those things in the cottage when she looked for him the day of the first fire," Daad said slowly.

"But I didn't. And he must have known I'd have told Mac if I had." The frustration ate at her. Bad enough to think someone wished her harm, and it was even worse not knowing why.

"He's been pickling his brains with alcohol for so many years I'm not sure he thought anything through," Mac said. "Although he's been clever enough to escape us for weeks," he added, his tone wry. He bit into a wedge of Mamm's wet-bottom shoofly pie, eating it as if he hadn't stopped for supper.

"Cunning, maybe," Daad said. "Sarah, you spoke to him a time or two. Did you say anything he might take to mean you knew something?"

Her mind scrambled back over that encounter at the shop. "I don't know . . . I don't think so. I remember I mentioned saying something to Julia, but I was just trying to get him to leave, not threaten him."

Mac shrugged. "It might have been enough. And after you interrupted him when he was trying to set a fire, he could have figured you knew more than you were saying. Anyway, it was stupid of him to come after you at the theater today." The lawman paused then, shaking his head. "I wouldn't have thought he'd do that, not right in town and when Aaron was there. Hill must have been crazy to think he'd get away with it."

"It's hard for a righteous man to understand the ways of the wicked," Daad said. "We don't blame you. At least now young Jonah is cleared. And surely Gus wouldn't dare try anything else now that everyone in the valley is watching for him."

A little shiver crept down Sarah's spine. They all kept saying Gus wouldn't try anything more. Rationally she knew that was true, but some instinct inside seemed to tell her they hadn't finished with this trial yet.

Feet pounded on the stairs, and they all swung round to see Jonny racing toward them, his face white, the other two boys stumbling behind him in their haste. "Fire!" he shouted. "The Kings' barn is on fire."

Sarah gasped, her heart seeming to stop for an instant. Mac had already pulled out his cell phone, snapping instructions through it as he ran to the door, with Daad right behind him.

"Jonny, you come to help!" Daad shouted. "Thomas and Noah, ring the bell to alert the neighbors. Keep ringing until you're sure everyone has heard."

Mamm was saying something to Sarah, but

she couldn't seem to hear anything beyond the rushing urgency in her blood. She ran after the men, her thoughts tumbling.

They'd said Gus wouldn't dare try anything, but he had. He'd set another fire, and at Aaron's place this time.

When she reached the yard she could see what Jonny had spotted from the upstairs window. The back corner of the barn was blazing. Figures struggled in the distance—they'd be trying to get the animals out.

She ran, her breath coming sharp and painful. *Aaron.* Gus had started a fire in his barn, and had good reason to hold a grudge against Aaron after what had happened. Her mind filled with an image of Aaron lying helpless, unconscious, inside the burning building, maybe lying dead the way Matthew Gibson had—

Run, she ordered herself. *Just run. Don't think.*

Jonny and Daad got there first, Jonny running to help Becky as she wrestled sections of hose together, and Daad dashing into the barn behind Mac. Where was Aaron?

Sarah couldn't stand here worrying—there was work to be done. She ran over to grasp the halter of the buggy horse Jonah had just led out. "I'll take it."

He nodded, racing back inside. The animal tried to rear, and she jerked the halter. "Stoppe!" she commanded, and led it to the gate into the nearest field. When she released the halter the horse cantered, bucking once or twice, to the far end of the pasture.

Hurrying back, she met Jonah again, and again started to take the frightened animal, but he shook his head. "We can do this. Better you help my daad with the chickens."

"Where's Aaron?" She couldn't hold back the question, and Jonah grinned, his teeth white in a soot blackened face.

"He's okay. Trying to fight it from inside." Jonah ran back, and it seemed to her she could see him turning from a sulky teen to a man all in a minute.

Aaron's safe. The words echoed in her heart as she ran for the chicken coop. It was close to the barn—too close. At least the heavy rain would have helped.

Carrying an objecting hen under each arm, she ran back and forth. Too foolish to do anything sensible, they'd probably head into the fire if she didn't keep a firm grip. Becky ran up and grabbed a pair.

"Jonny's manning the hose. We got it to reach. If only the truck comes soon . . ."

"It will." Sarah looked toward the barn, longing to see Aaron's tall figure safely outside. She knew what he'd be doing—trying to wet the fire down, pulling away anything that would spread the flames. And Daadi would be right beside him.

If they stayed too long . . . If the fire roared out of control . . .

But it didn't. Even as she and Becky leaned against the brooder coop, breathless after shoving the last of the hens inside, she could see that the men seemed to be gaining control. Jim and Nick Whiting were there, and she hadn't even seen them come. A car screeched into the lane and stopped in a spray of gravel as a couple of the Englisch neighbors arrived.

Figures appeared in the barn doorway—Jonah, supporting Aaron, who doubled up, coughing. And then Mac and Daad, dragging something between them.

No, not something. Someone. But who . . . ? She glanced around. Everyone was accounted for.

"Who is it?" Becky's young voice was scared.

"I don't know. We'd best see if we can help." They hurried toward the small knot of men.

Daad turned and, seeing them, held them back. "No. Don't go. There's nothing you can do."

"Are you sure? The ambulance . . ." Sarah could hear the wailing of sirens coming down the road fast.

"It's too late. He's dead." Daad's voice sounded strained. "It's Gus Hill, and he's dead."

AARON WAS OVERCOME by another fit of coughing as he tried to process the words.

Through the smoke he'd glimpsed a pair of legs, grabbed them and tried to make it to the door. Thank the gut Lord the others had come in time. He might not have made it out by himself.

But they hadn't been in time. Gus was dead.

Aaron straightened, his arm still around his brother's shoulders, and Jonah moved quickly to support him.

"You should sit. Drink some water."

"In a minute." His voice sounded like gravel. He pulled Jonah close. "Denke, little brother. You saved me."

He could see Jonah's blush even under the soot.

"You'd have made it," he said.

Aaron shook his head. He might have, if he'd left the body behind, but he wouldn't. And still, Gus hadn't made it.

Aaron tried to focus his stinging eyes. The volunteers had set up the pumper quickly. It grumbled and complained, but sent out a steady stream of water. The flames were nearly under control already, and it looked as if they would save most of the barn.

Darkness was drawing in, seeming to make the glow from the fire brighter and burnishing the faces of the volunteers. He shuddered. It was a scene from a nightmare—the flames, the firefighters, the body . . .

Mac was kneeling over the body on the ground, his face grim. Surveying, not touching.

"He must have been setting the fire and been caught by it himself." Eli Bitler spoke gravely, staring down at the mute form. "Caught in his own trap."

"Maybe." Mac sat back on his heels and began speaking into his phone. When the ambulance crew approached, he waved them off. "There's nothing you can do. I don't want him touched until the medical examiner arrives."

The paramedics exchanged a startled glance and began moving through the crowd, checking people out for burns and smoke inhalation.

Aaron caught Sarah's horrified expression as she realized the import of Mac's words. She seemed to feel his gaze and came quickly to him.

"You should let the paramedics check you out." She glanced at Jonah, who nodded and headed for the nearest one.

"I'm not burned. Just swallowed a bit too much smoke is all." Aaron glanced toward Mac and instinctively lowered his voice. "He's going to investigate. Just when we thought the worst was over . . ."

"It will be all right." She clasped Aaron's hand, heedless of who might be watching. "Gus was caught in his own fire, like Daad said. What else could it be?"

Aaron shook his head, unable to accept the easy explanation. "Mac wouldn't look that way if it were that simple. The body isn't burned. If he made a mistake, maybe splashed kerosene on himself, he would be."

"He could have been overcome by smoke. Maybe trapped by the flames and passed out. It could be that." Sarah sounded as if she was trying to convince herself.

"It's like a nightmare. Jonah is cleared, but now we are entangled with the police again. And there are still no answers about Matt's death. It feels as if it will never be over."

Her grip tightened on Aaron's hand. "You don't mean that. Have faith that the truth will come out. It will, you know it."

His eyes met hers, and the love and caring he saw there struck him right in the heart in a wave so strong it nearly knocked him off his feet. He leaned toward her, longing to feel her arms around him again. Sarah's eyes darkened, and her breath caught in an audible gasp.

The noise and confusion around them seemed to recede, leaving the two of them enclosed in a tight little circle, untouched by the world.

A hand landed on his shoulder. "Let's have a look at you, Aaron. Your brother says you swallowed a mess of smoke in there."

It was Mike Callahan, one of the paramedics. Even as he longed to shove Mike away, Aaron knew it was just as well they'd been interrupted. Otherwise he and Sarah might have stood there, wrapped up in each other, until everyone noticed them.

"Go find somebody who needs you, Callahan," he rasped, and Mike grinned at him.

"Listen, you might know fires, but I know smoke inhalation. You march right over to the truck and get some oxygen, or I'll have Sarah make you."

"Go on," she said. "I'll help your mother get some drinks out."

In a few minutes Mike had him perched on the step of the EMT vehicle with an oxygen mask on his face. Much as he hated to admit it, Mike had been right. Aaron could almost feel the oxygen flooding through him, chasing out the constriction in his chest and returning the energy to his body.

From here he had a good view of the whole scene. He saw the medical examiner arrive, hurrying toward Mac to kneel next to the prone, still figure on the ground.

Why had Gus come back? Was he so crazy he thought he could get away with another fire when the whole valley was searching for him? Well, maybe so. He'd nearly done it. If it hadn't been for Jonny Bitler's sharp eyes spotting the flames so quickly, the whole barn could have gone.

Daad came to him, moving at a pace that showed his age. He shouldn't have been running around trying to save everything, but no one could have stopped him.

"You are all right, ain't so?" Daad's gaze assessed him. "The paramedic says you'll be fine."

Aaron took the mask away. Traci Elder, the young woman paramedic, looked for a moment as if she'd object, but then she let him do it. Maybe she'd dealt with enough stubborn patients to know when to quit.

"I'm all right." He forced a smile. "It's not as bad as it could have been, ain't so? We'll have to do a lot of repair work, but everyone will help."

Daad nodded, his red-rimmed eyes filling with tears before he blinked them back. "We saved all the animals. And no one was hurt except—" He stopped, casting a sidelong glance toward the body. "Anyway, the family is safe. We'll rebuild."

"We will." Aaron put a comforting hand on his shoulder. "Jonah and I will see that everything is done just the way you want it."

"Ja, I know you will." Daad's gaze seemed to follow Jonah, who was now working with the men wetting down the barn. "Our Jonah has done some growing up, I think."

Aaron agreed absently, his own gaze drawn inexorably to Sarah. She was setting cold drinks and coffee out on the picnic table near the back porch. She seemed to turn at a sound behind her, and he saw that Anna and Lena had come out onto the porch, barefoot, in their white nightgowns.

He started to move, but Sarah was already dealing with them. He watched as she knelt to talk to them, whatever she said chasing the scared look from their faces and making them smile. In another moment she had scooped Lena up in her arms. Anna grabbed her hand, and the three of them went inside.

How had he been a blind fool for so long? How had he not seen how perfect she was for him and for his daughters?

The feeling seemed to well up from deep within his being. This wasn't the flash and sparkle and excitement of the first love he'd had for Mary Ann. It was something far deeper, flowing smoothly and strongly. Quiet, and yet sweeping everything before it.

He loved her. He'd loved her since they were children, and that love had matured into something strong and enduring. If only they could get clear of this current trouble . . .

Mac was walking the doctor to his car. A snatch of conversation came to Aaron's ears.

". . . tell more after the autopsy. I'll let you have a report as soon as possible, but in the meantime, I'd say you should proceed as if it was murder."

Murder.

CHAPTER NINETEEN

SARAH THOUGHT SHE'D be relieved to get to the shop the next day to distract herself from the whirling thoughts that had kept her awake much of the night. Unfortunately, it didn't seem to be working. Every other person who came in the shop wanted to gossip about Gus Hill's death.

After Allison had taken over one especially persistent customer and finally seen her out the door, Sarah was ready to explode.

"I think some of them are making up excuses to come in here just so they can gossip," she fumed.

"Sure they are." Allison was resigned, but then, she wasn't the one most deeply concerned. "It's natural, I guess. They're not all as mean-spirited as that woman was, though. Just to spite her, I'm going to make sure she never gets another coupon to use here."

Sarah tried to smile. "Don't do that. We'll take her money, no matter what her motives are. But imagine saying that probably Matthew Gibson was murdered, just like Gus Hill!" And the police had questioned Aaron about Matthew, showing that they suspected him. How much more might they suspect him of Gus Hill's death?

"People like to exaggerate. Gossip is only fun for someone like her if she can add a little spice to it. It doesn't make sense. Besides, the police haven't even established that Gus was killed by someone else. He's just as likely to have killed himself, trying to set that fire."

"I hope that's true." Sarah hesitated, but she longed to talk to someone about her fear. "But I've heard that the medical examiner thought it could have been deliberate."

"Poor Aaron. It was bad enough for him to find his barn was on fire, and then to find a body . . ." Allison let that trail off. "I'm sorry. I'd forgotten that you were the one to find Matthew Gibson's body. It's stupid to remind you of that."

"Well, Matthew was an old man in poor health. Everyone knew with him it was just a matter of time, and I do think he was ready to go. He missed his wife, you see. They'd lost their only son in a motorcycle accident, and when she died, all the hope seemed to go out of him."

Sarah thought of Matthew the way he'd been the last time she'd seen him alive. He'd come to supper the night before he'd left for Florida, making an obvious effort to eat and talk and seem enthusiastic about his trip. She'd thought then how lonely he was, and how different his situation was to that of her grossmammi, living as part of a large family. Matthew, like Julia, hadn't had anyone of his own.

"From the things I've heard, no one is going to miss Gus Hill much," Allison said, taking advantage of the quiet in the shop to flip through her notes about the festival. "Except possibly Julia." She glanced at Sarah in consternation. "We probably ought to make sure she's all right."

"I'll go this afternoon." Somehow, whether it was wise or not, she'd begun to feel responsible for Julia. They'd been friends a long time. "If she has questions about his death, maybe I can reassure her."

Allison shuddered. "Probably the fewer details, the better, but I don't suppose Julia will let you get away with that. She's certainly someone who believes in facing the truth."

Sarah nodded. "Maybe that's better than hiding from it."

Her partner looked at her with lifted eyebrows. "In that case, why don't you tell me what really worries you. It's Aaron, isn't it?"

"It's that obvious, is it?" She tried to smile.

"Just to me," Allison said quickly. She dropped the file and came to stand by Sarah, touching her hand. "Why are you worried? Is it something he said?"

"Partly." She rubbed her forehead, trying to think it through. "He was telling me it feels as if we will never be free of this situation. Now that Jonah has been cleared, it should be so simple to get back to normal. To move on with our lives."

Allison studied her face. "And will your life include Aaron?"

Sarah's cheeks grew hot. "I'm not sure. Maybe I'm reading too much into it."

"Tell me." Allison's caring shone in her face. How much she had changed from the big-city businesswoman she'd been when she first came to Laurel Ridge.

"I . . . we were talking about this situation. About his feelings at finding Gus dead. I was trying to comfort him, I guess. We looked at each other, and . . . well, I don't know how to explain it. The feeling, as if we were connected . . ." She sought for words. "I know he felt it, too, and he even told me he's begun to care."

"Well, then." Allison's voice was very soft, and her smile said she was thinking of Nick. "If you felt it, and he felt it, that's reason to be happy, not worried."

"But this murder, if that's what it is. How can I not worry?"

Allison's eyes widened. "You don't suspect Aaron of killing Gus, do you?"

"Of course not! But I just fear that all this trouble will somehow keep us from happiness."

Allison gripped her hand. "You know what you need to do. I told you before. You have to talk to Aaron about all of this. That's the only way to resolve it."

"I know." But what was there to say? As long as Aaron feared committing himself to her, she was caught just as much as he was by that fear. "But it's not so easy, even to find a moment alone with him."

Allison glanced over her shoulder, and a smile teased her lips. "I don't think it's going to be so hard."

Sarah turned as the bell on the door jingled. Aaron was coming in, his face so grim it frightened her.

AARON HAD TOLD himself it would do no good to frighten Sarah by confiding in her. Unfortunately, his steps had taken him straight to the shop when he left the police station, regardless of what his practical side was saying.

Now, seeing Sarah and Allison both staring at him, he had no idea what to say.

Allison, it seemed, was never at a loss. "Take Aaron in the back room and give him a cup of coffee. He looks like he needs it."

Sarah hesitated, and Allison gave her a little push. "Go on, before someone else comes in to babble about the latest rumors."

Sarah nodded. Wordless, she led the way to the small room at the rear of the shop. Aaron followed her, thinking again that he shouldn't have come.

"Allison's right." Sarah turned to him once they were alone, looking more herself again, a gentle smile curving her lips. "We've had more people in this morning than we usually have all day, and most of them are just trading gossip."

"About us?" That came out more sharply than he intended.

"No, of course not." The smile vanished. Sarah's hand moved, as if she would touch him, but then she drew it back. "It's all about Gus Hill being the arsonist and dying in the fire he set that way."

"Sorry." Aaron shook his head, trying to clear it. "I'm acting ferhoodled for sure. I just wanted . . ." *I wanted to feel the comfort of being with you.* No, he couldn't say that. "Denke. You were wonderful kind to my girls last night. Mamm told me how you comforted them and made them smile with your stories."

"It was nothing. It's what I do with my little brothers when they have a bad dream." Her direct blue eyes seemed to be searching his face for any hint of what he was thinking.

"This is a bad dream, that's certain sure." He sat down on the edge of the table, feeling as if he could relax for the first time in hours. "I just came from the police station. From being questioned about Gus's death." They were out, the words he hadn't planned to say. He ran a hand across his forehead, as if he could wipe away the memory of that questioning.

Sarah gasped, but there wasn't even a shadow

of doubt in her face. She reached out and clasped his hand, drawing closer to him. "That is so foolish. Surely Mac doesn't think—"

"Not Mac. Anyway, I don't believe he thinks I had anything to do with it, but he's a police officer, and he has to go by the rules. It was the others—Fielding, and a man from the district attorney's office."

"But Gus died in the fire, ja? And they know he was the arsonist. Mac told me they found the evidence at the cottage."

"That's just it. They say he didn't die in the fire. He died of a blow to the head."

Aaron could almost see the thoughts spinning in Sarah's mind. He knew. He'd reacted the same when he'd heard it. To think that there had been two evildoers there in his barn, so close to his kinder—one with arson in his mind, the other with murder in his heart . . . It didn't bear thinking about.

Sarah took a deep, steadying breath, seeming to square her shoulders. It was a familiar gesture. She'd done that since childhood, whenever there was something challenging to be faced.

"What does it have to do with you? With us? They can't believe you had anything to do with it. Why would you?"

"The man from the district attorney's office suggested that maybe I found Gus setting the fire. That I fought with him and he died. He even said the law would understand that I killed him defending my property."

"He doesn't know anything about the Amish, if he thinks that. And he certain sure doesn't know anything about you."

Her staunch belief in him seemed to heal the ragged edges of Aaron's spirit, battered by the obvious suspicion in the man's questions.

"No, he doesn't understand Amish ways. Maybe with his head he knows we're nonviolent, but he doesn't understand with his heart." Aaron met her clear eyes, knowing he had to say the rest of it. "Fielding was even worse. He implied that I was angry because Hill had attacked you and tried to cast blame for the fires on my brother. He thought that a motive for murder."

Sarah shook her head slowly. "It is crazy. Just . . . crazy. I don't know how someone can think that way. But Mac believes in you, ain't so?"

"I think so. But like I said, he has to follow the rules. He couldn't keep them from questioning me. If they decide they have enough evidence against me, they could arrest me, and he wouldn't be able to stop it."

"Aaron . . ." Sudden tears filled her eyes. She clasped his hand in both of hers and drew it to her heart. "This can't be happening. We must find a way out. We . . ."

He couldn't stand it any longer. He pulled his hand away. "No." He couldn't help sounding harsh. He had to protect Sarah. She couldn't be touched by this ugliness. He couldn't fail her, not now. "Not you, Sarah. This is my problem, not yours."

She just stood there with tears moving down her cheeks. "I care about you, Aaron. I can't stand back and do nothing."

"I won't have you involved." He took two quick strides to the door. "The burden is mine, not yours. Stay out of it."

The pain in her face struck at his heart. He wanted to take her into his arms, hold her close against him and never let her go.

But he couldn't. He had already failed a woman he loved. He couldn't let Sarah be hurt just when they'd begun to come together.

"I'm sorry," he muttered, and went blindly out the door.

SARAH SAGGED AGAINST the nearest shelf, pressing her palms to her face and feeling the hot tears well against them. Aaron was gone from her, as surely as he had been the day he'd married Mary Ann. If he couldn't turn to her in this terrible situation, he never would.

She should have spoken. Should have made him listen. But she couldn't.

The door opened slowly, and Allison peeked in. When she saw Sarah's face, her own expression crumpled in empathy. "Oh, Sarah. I'm so sorry."

She came quickly to gather her into her arms. "Cry as much as you need to."

Somehow being given permission to weep dried up her tears. She sniffed a bit, wiping her face with her palms. "I'm acting like a baby."

"No, you're not. It's natural to cry when a man tramples on your heart. I was so sure Aaron cared."

Sarah shook her head, fighting for composure. "It's not . . ." She wasn't sure which was more painful. "Aaron said that the police think he killed Gus."

"Not Mac!" Her partner's voice was sharp.

"Maybe not Mac, but he said Mac isn't the only one involved. They actually questioned him—Fielding and some lawyer from the district attorney's office. He could see they suspected him."

Allison seemed to consider it carefully before shaking her head. "They don't know Aaron. But you do. If you're sure he couldn't have done such a thing, then I'm sure, as well. And if I know Mac, he won't rest until he knows the truth."

Sarah tried to find comfort in the words. "He has to. From the sounds of it, the others would be content to blame Aaron without looking any further." She pressed her fingers to her temples, trying to make her brain work. "I don't know where he'll even start. Who would have killed Gus that way? And why at Aaron's barn?"

Allison leaned back against the table, clearly turning it over in her mind. "We know Gus was the arsonist, right? But what if he wasn't alone in it? What if he really was working for someone else?"

"That's what I've started thinking. But if some company like that Evergreen Corporation does want the land, it's hard to imagine them resorting to murder."

"If they were willing to pay someone to burn barns, who knows what they might do."

"I guess." It seemed fanciful, but everything that had happened in the past month had been so unlikely that she was almost ready to believe anything.

Allison studied Sarah's face for a moment. "But that's not all that's going on. You wouldn't be crying because Aaron is a suspect. Angry or determined, maybe, but not tearful."

Sarah rubbed her temples again. "I wanted to help him. Or at least to comfort him. But he pushed me away. He insisted I have nothing to do with him. He won't let me be drawn into this because of him."

"He wanted to protect you."

"He wanted to push me away. And I let him." A tidal wave of shame swept through her. "I let him. Give in, let go. That's the Amish way, and I believe in it. But I think I use it to excuse my own timidity." She turned on Allison.

"You wouldn't have let him walk away, would you?"

"Maybe not, but I wasn't raised to give in to anything. And I don't know that I would have succeeded. Men can be stubborn, especially when they think they're doing something for your own good."

Something in Allison's tone caught her attention. "Are you talking about Nick?"

Her friend made a face. "I was trying to sympathize with you, but I guess I did veer into my own troubles for a minute. Sorry."

"No, I'm sorry. What has Nick done? Don't forget, I've known him since he was pulling my pigtails when I was three." Thinking about Allison's problem was a relief from dwelling on her own.

"He keeps saying I should take more time. That I shouldn't rush into a commitment to being a wife and a stepmother. But I don't want time. I know my own mind. Nick and Jamie are my life. I don't want anything else."

Sarah felt a moment of sympathy for Nick. He probably thought he was doing the right thing, knowing how different the life he could give her was from the life she'd known before she came here.

But he was wrong. Allison knew what she wanted.

"Don't give up," Sarah said firmly. "Nick can

be stubborn, but he always listens to reason in the end. Just don't you give up on him."

Allison's smile sparkled, and she squeezed Sarah's hand. "As long as you promise the same. Don't give up on Aaron. Don't let him shut you out, no matter what he says."

"At least you know . . ." She stopped as the bell over the shop door jingled.

"Customers always come at the worst time." Allison turned to go. "I'll deal with it. You don't have to come out."

"I'm fine." She brushed her fingertips over her eyelids, hoping they weren't too red. "I'll come."

They walked back into the shop to find Harvey Preston standing by the door, looking around with a rather helpless expression at the bolts of cloth.

"How can I help you, Harvey?" Allison went toward him with her usual assurance. "Don't tell me you're looking for some fabric?"

He gave his usual hearty chuckle at that, his face wreathed in smiles. "Afraid not, though I might have to do my Christmas shopping at this quilt festival you ladies are cooking up."

"You just let me know what you're looking for, and I'll put it aside for you," Allison responded, never one to let a sale slip away.

"I'll do that." He focused on Sarah. "I really stopped by to see how Sarah is. That fire last night was a terrible thing. I can't imagine how you felt, seeing your neighbor's barn on fire."

"It's good of you to be concerned." She managed a polite smile somehow. "Only the corner of the barn was destroyed, so they will be able to rebuild it soon. Everyone is pitching in to help."

"If there's anything I can do, please let me know." Harvey shook his head, looking for a moment like a mournful bulldog. "Terrible business, the whole thing. I've never had much respect for Gus Hill, but I couldn't imagine him being a firebug. And there was poor Julia Everly, trusting the good-for-nothing."

"I don't think she'll be too upset," Allison said, relieving Sarah of the necessity of continuing the conversation. "Julia's a realist. Takes people as she finds them, even if . . ."

Sarah shot her a sharp glance, afraid she was going to blurt out something about Donna.

Allison blinked. "Anyway, I don't expect her to be cut up about Gus Hill."

"Good, good." Harvey looked to be at a loss. "Well, people will be relieved that the arson has come to an end. It was bad for business. Who'd want to buy a property when it might be set on fire the next night?"

"I'm sure that's a relief to you." Allison's tone was dry.

Harvey seemed taken aback, maybe wondering if that was an insult.

"We've certainly had plenty of customers today," she said hurriedly. "I hope business picks up for you."

"Oh, things are going fine. Busy, actually. People who are planning a move want to get settled before school starts."

Sarah nodded in agreement. If he was so busy, why was he lingering here, talking about nothing?

Harvey cleared his throat. "I've heard some gossip that Aaron King was involved in Gus Hill's death. I'm sure it's nonsense, but—"

"It is," Sarah snapped. "Aaron had nothing to do with it. In fact, it was Aaron who pulled him out of the flames." Pressure built in her, so that she imagined it exploding out, searing everything in sight. She clamped her lips closed, holding on by a thread.

"That's what I thought." Harvey took a step back. Maybe he sensed danger. "And I'll say so to anyone who brings it up to me. Aaron's a fine young man. I still feel bad about that mix-up over the Gibson farm. If only Matt Gibson had told me about it, that could have been avoided entirely."

Sarah didn't trust herself to speak. Fortunately Allison seemed to sense it.

"We'll let you get back to business, Harvey. Thanks for stopping by."

"Right, yes." He nodded to them and headed for the door. "Don't forget to let me know if there's anything I can do to help the King family."

"Pompous," Allison muttered when the door closed behind him.

He was, Sarah supposed, but that wasn't what concerned her at the moment. If Harvey Preston was repeating the gossip linking Aaron to Gus Hill's death, it must be widespread. Aaron had been right about one thing—this was like being trapped in a nightmare, seeing something terrifying coming toward you and being unable to move.

CHAPTER TWENTY

LISTENING TO ALLISON on the telephone as she negotiated with the dealer in possession of Julia's album quilt, Sarah found her partner's crisp tones an antidote to her own depression. No one would know that Allison had a care for anything other than business. Surely Sarah could manage to emulate her for the rest of the afternoon, at least.

"That's ridiculous." Allison cut into the apparent complaints of the dealer. "You're in possession of a stolen article of value. If this business goes to the police, the quilt will be impounded, you'll get nothing and you might very well be charged with receiving stolen property." She grinned at Sarah as she said the final words, indicating she had no idea whether that was true or not.

Allison listened for a moment, and Sarah could hear a whining sound coming from the receiver.

"My client is willing to pay you exactly what you paid for the quilt and not a cent more." Her voice was crisp. "If it's delivered here tomorrow in good condition, we'll add on a consideration for your time and travel. Agreed?"

Apparently he succumbed to the force of her words—or maybe just her determination. After a few directions, Allison hung up the shop phone and smiled.

"All right! Tell Julia she'll have her quilt back tomorrow. You'll probably want to discuss with her any necessary cleaning and repair work, but if it's as good as you say, it'll definitely be a draw for quilt lovers at the festival."

"I'll tell her. At least it will be some good news for her." Sarah paused at the door. "Are you sure you can manage on your own?"

"Go." Allison waved her away. "I can deal with the gossips better than you can. What is the word your mother uses for them?"

"*Blabbermauls.*" She had a quick vision of sophisticated Allison accusing nosy visitors of being blabbermauls. "It means . . . well, *gossips,* I guess comes closest."

"Good. I like that word—very descriptive. Give Julia my love."

Sarah was relieved to get outside into the warm summer air. She'd begun to feel hemmed in at the shop, as if she were unable to escape the worries and fears that beset her, to say nothing of the curious who kept wandering in. At least once she reached Main Street she could keep moving away from any stares.

And there were a few, she realized as she passed the storefronts in the few larger buildings in Laurel Ridge, then a number of shops and services housed in what had once been private homes. No new buildings had gone up on Main Street in her memory, although businesses had moved in and out of the available storefronts.

She'd always enjoyed her time in town, but the number of curious glances she was receiving made her long for the security of the farm. Still, the brisk walk made it easier not to dwell on Aaron and what might have been.

When she turned onto Julia's street she quickened her pace. She should have come earlier, but she'd wanted to be sure she had control of her emotions before venturing out. Julia must be wondering why someone hadn't come to talk to her about Gus.

No one came in answer to her knock at the door, but Sarah could hear Julia's shouted, "Come in." The door was unlocked, so she followed orders.

"Is no one here with you?" She went quickly through the hall into the living room. "I thought you had someone to help you."

"She came this morning." Julia stifled a yawn. "Don't fuss. She'll be back again for a couple of hours this evening. That's really all I need for now. And next week I get this thing off." She tapped the cast with her knuckles.

"That's wonderful news. You'll feel like a new woman without that holding you down."

Julia nodded with something of her usual assurance. "The doctor keeps muttering about taking it slow and going to physical therapy, but at least I'll be able to get out of the house."

"That will cheer you up. And here's some more happy news. We should have your album quilt for you tomorrow. Allison flatly refused to pay the dealer anything more than he paid for it. You should have heard her."

"Great, great." Julia yawned again. "Sorry about yawning. What I really need is some fresh air."

"Would you like me to help you out onto the porch for a bit?" Sarah felt as if she were postponing the moment she had to talk about Gus Hill. Even thinking the name brought back the image of the men dragging a body from the burning barn.

"Not now." Julia gave her a stern look. "We'd better not put it off. Is it true? Was Gus the firebug?"

Sarah hitched her chair a bit closer. "I'm afraid so. Mac said they found all the things he used to start the fires hidden at the cottage. And he was starting a fire in Aaron's barn when . . ." She let that trail off.

"When he died. You don't need to find a way to soften it. I know he's dead."

"I'm sorry. I know you had a soft spot for Gus because of his friendship with your husband."

"You don't need to worry that I'm going to burst into tears." Julia's tone had regained its tartness. She ran a hand through her short gray hair, making it stand on end. "Wish I could think better. I've felt like my brain is stuffed with mush lately."

"That's surely natural enough after a bad accident. And most likely the doctor has given you some medication for pain that will make it worse." It was the first time Julia had given a hint that Donna's comments about her memory might be true, and Sarah's throat tightened as she stroked the woman's arm soothingly. "You'll feel much better once you can be out and about again."

Julia frowned, seeming to force herself to concentrate. "When you get to be my age, you've already lost a lot of people from your life. Maybe it doesn't come as hard. Anyway, I never had many illusions about Gus. I wouldn't put petty thievery out of the question for him, but to go around torching people's barns . . ." Her hands moved against the heavy cast. "It doesn't make sense, not if there was nothing in it for him." She shot a sudden sharp look at Sarah. "Is that it? Was someone paying him to do it?"

"I don't know." She was just as glad she didn't. If Gus had been up to something criminal, the police could surely explain it better than she could. "Mac is looking into it. I'm sure he'll let you know what he finds." Her thoughts slipped to Aaron. If Julia asked about Gus's death, she'd have to answer honestly, but she hoped she wouldn't ask.

Julia didn't speak, staring a bit vacantly at the cast, her eyes heavy-lidded. Probably a nap would do her good, but Sarah hadn't the heart to leave on such a sad note.

"Have you seen anything of Donna since you confronted her?" She posed the question with a bit of hesitation, not sure that was a good topic of conversation, either.

But a little of Julia's fire came back into her weathered face. "She actually came over here this morning, trying to pretend she was worried about me. The nerve of her!"

"Maybe she is worried," Sarah suggested. "After all, you are kin."

Julia snorted. "She should have thought of that before she stole from me. For that matter, she ought to have known that if she needed money that badly, I'd have given it to her. I have often enough before, Lord knows."

Sarah wasn't sure what to say to that. Her natural instinct was to want family to forgive, but there was something so distasteful about Donna sneaking a family treasure out of the house to sell it.

Julia yawned again, rubbing her eyes like a sleepy child. Sarah stood. "You're tired. I should let you get some rest. We'll come over tomorrow when we have the quilt."

"No, wait. That reminds me. I'm sure I have some photos in an old family album upstairs that show the quilt years ago. Maybe even a picture of the woman who made it. That would add to the interest when you put it on display, right?"

"It would, that's certain sure. But we don't have to do that now—"

"I'd rather find it while it's on my mind. You don't mind going up and looking for it, do you? I'm sure I put the albums in one of the old traveling trunks. You can find it easily."

Obviously it would be on Julia's mind until it was found. She was like a dog with a bone when she latched on to an idea.

"I'll have a look," Sarah said. "I think I remember seeing some albums when I was searching for the quilts. But I do need to get back to the shop before too long."

Julia grinned, satisfied that she'd gotten her way. "Better start, then."

Sarah climbed the narrow stairs to the attic once more, imagining the complaining the movers must have made at bringing all these heavy things up.

Reaching the top, she switched on the light. The attic was as depressingly crowded as she remembered, but she could at least eliminate everything that wasn't a trunk.

What would Julia do with all these things eventually? It seemed a shame that there was no family to cherish her heirlooms. Sarah's grossmammi had begun giving her belongings, sparse in comparison to this, to each of her grandchildren. The hand-painted dower chest in Sarah's bedroom had belonged to Grossmammi, and to her grossmammi before that. It was sad to think of Julia being so alone she didn't even have someone to cherish her things. Just Donna, whose only interest was in their monetary value.

Somewhat to Sarah's surprise, it didn't take all that long to locate the chest containing the photo albums. Of course it helped that she'd been through the attic's contents so recently. The older ones would be what Julia wanted, and they'd been wrapped in a sheet to protect them.

Sarah lifted them out, holding them carefully. Some of the pages were dry and loose, and an unwary movement might send them flying all over the attic. Best if she wrapped them in the sheet again for safety's sake. A moment later, carrying the bundle close to her body, she made her way down the stairs. Her sneakered feet made little sound on the steps.

Julia had seemed so tired. She might well have fallen asleep while Sarah was in the attic. If so, she could leave the albums close at hand and slip out.

She reached the door to the living room and looked inside. Her breath caught, and for an instant she was frozen in place. Julia *was* asleep, slumped sideways in the chair. But Donna stood over her, holding a hypodermic needle near her cousin's bared arm.

"Donna! What are you doing?" Sarah started forward, still clutching the sheet-wrapped bundle.

Donna jerked around at the sound, the needle wavering. Then her eyes narrowed, and she aimed the needle at the exposed veins in Julia's arm.

Even as she rushed forward, Sarah knew she wasn't going to be in time. The needle point would pierce the skin before she could reach them; Donna would drive it home . . . Sarah had to do something. Raising the bundle of albums, she threw it as hard as she could at the hand holding the needle.

All those hours spent playing ball with her brothers paid off. The bundle hit Donna's arm, the sheet loosening, albums spilling all over the place. Sarah barreled into the woman, knocking her back. Thoughts tumbled through Sarah's head, training battling instinct. She couldn't attack another person. But she had to protect Julia, who was helpless and vulnerable.

They fell together, but Donna still gripped the needle. Sarah grabbed at it. If she could smash it against the floor, break it—

Donna drove her knee into Sarah's stomach, knocking the breath out of her. She gasped, struggling for air, and felt the woman wrench the needle free. No! Forcing her muscles to work, Sarah grabbed for Donna, but she was already moving toward Julia. Scrambling to her feet, Sarah lunged forward, grabbing her arm. They struggled, swaying back and forth, Sarah hampered by her need not to strike.

Sound penetrated, freezing them both. The doorbell rang insistently.

"Help!" Sarah screamed the word. "Help us!"

She heard the door open, the rush of feet, saw Harvey Preston's bulky figure fill the doorway.

"Help me! She's trying to hurt Julia!"

Harvey came toward them, reached them, thank goodness. He would help. He . . .

Harvey drew his arm back and struck Sarah full in the face. She flew backward, heard the crack, felt the pain in the back of her head and slumped to the floor, trying to fight the blackness that overwhelmed her.

AARON PULLED UP in front of the police station and leaped down from the buggy. If he'd been able to drive a car, he'd have broken every speed limit getting here. He dashed inside, gripping the letter that had brought him here. Ignoring the receptionist, he burst into Mac's office. Thank the gut Lord his old friend was here and alone.

"Look at this." Aaron shoved the envelope into his face. "It just came in today's mail. It's from Matthew Gibson."

Mac, apparently infected by his urgency, yanked out the letter, letting the envelope drop to his desk. He spread it out, reading the short note Aaron had already committed to memory.

"It's in answer to my letter to him. He wrote it from Florida before he came. I knew I should have had a letter in answer. Look at it! He says Preston didn't follow his orders about the sale of the property. That he was supposed to offer it to me first. Instead, he sold it to that out-of-state company without a word to me."

Mac's eyes met his, blazing with anger. "He says he's coming back to confront Preston. Seems to me his death was mighty convenient for Harvey Preston. If this got out it would destroy him."

"I didn't think that far. I just wanted an explanation. I wanted to know that Matthew hadn't forgotten his promise. Are you saying he might have been involved in Matthew's death?"

"I'm saying Preston has some explaining to do." Mac glanced at the date on the letter. "I don't get it. Why did this take so long to reach you?"

"Look at the envelope."

Together they studied the address. Matt Gibson's hand must have trembled, the letters wavered so. And the zip code was wrong.

"Looks like it went to Ohio before someone caught the mistake in the zip code and forwarded it on here. We're lucky Matt didn't put his return address on it. Otherwise they might have returned it to Florida and we'd never have seen it."

Mac pulled a plastic sleeve from his desk drawer and slid letter and envelope inside. "Too bad we both touched this, but we might still be able to raise Matthew's fingerprints. And we can find something with his handwriting to compare."

"You're thinking of a trial?"

"I'm thinking it very likely will come to that. For fraud, or malfeasance, or some fancy term the lawyers will come up with, even if we can't prove anything against Preston in Gibson's death."

Mac put the sleeve into his desk drawer and turned to Aaron. "I'm going to find him now. Thanks, Aaron. This is going to open up a whole new case."

It was on the tip of his tongue to ask to go with him, but Aaron didn't want to put Mac into a position where he had to become official.

"Can you give me a lift to Blackburn House, then? I want to check on Sarah." That was a good reason to invite himself along, and despite his resolution to keep Sarah out of his troubles, she deserved to know about this development. She and her family had cared about Matt Gibson as much as anyone.

"Come on, then."

It only took a moment to climb into the police car, and little more than another to reach Blackburn House. They strode in the front door to find Allison standing in the entrance to the quilt shop. She seemed disappointed that they were the ones who'd come in.

"Where's Sarah?" Aaron didn't bother with greetings, an unexplained urgency pushing him forward. The need to see her built like pressure inside him. But she might not want to talk with him, not after the way he'd treated her the last time she saw him.

Allison frowned, her green eyes worried. "She went to Julia's to talk to her about Gus Hill, but that was ages ago. She should be back by now."

"Have you seen Harvey Preston? Is he in his office?" Mac cut in.

Allison blinked at his tone. "He went out about fifteen minutes ago."

"I'm going to check on Sarah." The need pushed at Aaron, demanding action.

"Wait." Mac was peremptory. "I'll drive you. I don't have a good feeling about this."

They hurried back to the police cruiser. "Keep an eye out for Preston or his car on the way," Mac muttered. "I'd like to find him before I put out any announcements. There's no reason to think he knows we're after him." His jaw tightened. "But he wanted Gibson to sell, and now Gibson's dead. Julia told me a couple of times that he'd urged her to sell the farm property, and then her barn burned."

"If someone was paying Gus to start the fires—"

"Supposition. But it makes me want to check on Julia Everly."

And Sarah is there. Aaron's hands clenched. *Sarah.*

CHAPTER TWENTY-ONE

SARAH CAME BACK to herself slowly, vaguely aware of voices murmuring, sounding like the lapping of a creek. Her eyes were closed, and it seemed too much of an effort to open them. The nap of the carpet brushed her cheek.

Pain crept in. Pain in her jaw, pain in the back of her head. The pain sharpened her wits, and now she kept her eyes shut in defense. Donna—Donna and the needle approaching Julia's arm, Julia helpless and unconscious in her chair. Sarah had struggled with Donna, trying to get the needle away from her.

Her forehead wrinkled as she struggled to think, but that seemed to increase the pain. Harvey Preston had come in. She'd thought they were saved. And then Harvey had hit her with his fist.

Clenching her jaw convinced her it was true. Harvey—genial, neighborly Harvey—had struck her.

The murmur of voices grew louder, more distinct. Sarah forced herself to focus. Harvey and Donna sounded angry—angry at each other, it seemed.

"I tried to do everything I could to help you."

Donna flung the words at him. It sounded as if the two of them were across the room, closer to the kitchen door. "The least you can do is help me now."

"You helped me?" Harvey's voice filled with scorn. "You were supposed to be convincing Julia to let me handle selling the farm. You told me you could do it. You claimed to have influence over her."

"I did. Until those two women put their noses where they didn't belong. They caused the trouble, not me."

"You did it yourself. Greedy. You couldn't be content to wait. You had to help yourself to that damn quilt. And then you said Gus Hill could help me get control of the property I wanted. He'd do anything for money."

"Well, he would. You should have kept better control of him."

They sounded far enough away that Sarah risked opening her eyes a slit. Engrossed in blaming each other, they didn't even glance her way. She mentally measured the distance between where she lay and the door, and then between where they stood and her. She might make it out, if she caught them unaware. If her legs supported her, which seemed doubtful.

And there was Julia, helpless, immobilized by her cast and whatever drug Donna had given her. Julia said her cousin had been here earlier.

She must have given her something to make her sleepy then.

Sarah couldn't run and leave Julia to their mercy. And most likely she couldn't make it to the door, anyway.

She dared open her eyes a little wider, risked turning her head slightly while they hurled insults at each other. She was only about five feet from the large window. If she threw something at it, would it break? Would anyone hear and come to investigate? She'd have only one chance. She had to make the most of it.

"Gus was never supposed to know I was involved at all. You must have let it slip. He started prowling around Blackburn House, spying on me."

"I didn't tell him." Donna's voice grew shrill. "He saw us out at that diner on the highway. I don't know why we had to keep our relationship a secret, anyway. You're divorced now. We can be together."

So here was Donna's mystery boyfriend. Harvey and his wife had divorced a year ago, and folks said she'd cleaned him out. Somehow he must have thought he'd recoup his losses with this scheme, whatever it was.

"Gus was worse than useless, setting fires I didn't tell him to. And attacking Sarah Bitler—how stupid was that?"

"He said she'd threatened him. Said she'd talk

413

to Julia. He said he had to scare her into keeping quiet. It wasn't my fault."

"No, nothing's your fault, is it?"

Between slitted eyelids Sarah watched Harvey's face.

It was as cold as his voice.

"It wasn't." Donna looked as if she wasn't sure of her ground. "Anyway, you have to help me. I did it for you. If Julia dies, I inherit. You can have the land, and we can go away together."

"Aren't you forgetting about Sarah? She's not likely to stand back and let you live happily ever after."

Sarah's breath caught. Julia's hand moved slightly. Her eyes, like Sarah's, were barely open, but she was conscious. If she moved, if she drew attention to herself . . .

"Sarah has to have an accident. Like Gus. Like Matthew Gibson. You didn't balk at that, did you?" Donna was taunting him, and that didn't seem like a very safe thing to do.

"I told you I didn't touch Gibson." Harvey's voice didn't get louder. It got quieter . . . deadly quiet, making Sarah's breath catch yet again. Who would have thought such evil lay behind the mask of the jovial, outgoing businessman?

Julia's hand moved again. She grasped the edge of the tray that sat on the table next to her. If Julia tried something, there would be no time left.

Maybe there wasn't, anyway.

"I suppose you're right." A decisive note sounded in Harvey's voice. "I'll have to make a clean sweep here. That's the only safe way."

He turned. He was coming toward them. Sarah had to act, now. She braced her hands against the floor. *Push yourself up. Try to protect Julia. Pray surprise gives you time to attract help—*

Harvey swore under his breath. He must have seen her movement. He came toward her fast—too fast. She tried to rise to her feet—

Julia slung the tray and its contents toward him as he passed her. It broke his stride and he stumbled, then turned toward Julia, anger distorting his face. *No time.* Sarah shoved herself against him, praying, pleading with God to send help. But Harvey's hands were around her throat, tightening—

The front window broke with a deafening crash. One of the porch chairs tumbled into the room, distracting him for a crucial second, long enough for Sarah to pull herself free. Mac threw himself through the window after the chair, tackling Harvey and sending him falling away from her.

And then Aaron was there, rushing toward her.

"Grab Donna," Mac ordered, his knee on Harvey's back, fastening handcuffs as the man writhed, trying to free himself. "Hurry."

With a quick, reassuring glance at Sarah, Aaron ran to the kitchen door, closing it and standing against it. Donna spun, took two steps toward the other door and then stopped, hearing the sirens wail in the street outside.

She dropped to her knees. "It wasn't my fault," she cried. "He made me do it."

The room was suddenly full of people. Sarah grasped the arm of Julia's chair and struggled to stand. "Are you all right?" She leaned over, putting her arm around the elderly woman.

"I stopped him," Julia said, satisfaction filling her voice. "Try to kill us, will they? We stopped them, the two of us."

Julia was obviously triumphant, but all Sarah could feel was pain . . . pain for the wasted lives. And then Aaron picked her up and carried her to the nearest armchair, and she stopped thinking entirely.

BY EVENING, AARON felt as if this day had been a week long. Sarah had been rushed off to the hospital as soon as an ambulance reached them, and the paramedics had insisted on taking Julia in to check her out, as well. Mac had kept Aaron tied up making a lengthy statement, and then Mac had gone to the hospital to take statements from Julia and Sarah. Aaron felt he had been pushed to the sidelines, not even able to ferry Sarah's parents back and forth, since Allison had taken over that job.

He'd been left to go over and over it in his mind. Sarah had nearly been killed. If he'd been faster, if he'd been smarter, if he'd understood what was going on . . .

Well, he still didn't really understand. He'd picked up bits and pieces, leaving him even more confused. A reporter for the local newspaper had actually turned up at the farm right at suppertime, to be sent away with no information, but a slice of Mamm's cherry pie. He'd seemed satisfied enough, come to think of it.

Aaron walked across the field to the Bitler house that evening, his eagerness to see Sarah mixed with his apprehension over what he would say to her. But Mac had sent a message that he'd meet Aaron there to wrap up details. Ready or not, he must face Sarah.

The sun was slipping behind the ridge as he approached the house, and the farm was settling down for the evening. The stalks of corn were soft to the touch, coming back after the recent rains. The wild raspberries along the bank had begun to turn a rich purple black. It felt as if nature, as well as humankind, was returning to normal.

Mac's police car came down the lane as he approached, so Aaron waited until Mac got out and joined him. The lawman looked tired but satisfied, his official face relaxed into that of a friend again.

"You okay?" He elbowed Aaron as they mounted the steps. "No repercussions from the bishop for getting involved in helping the police?"

"I'm not worried." True, the Leit generally steered clear of involvement with the authorities if possible, but they were expected to do their duty to what was right. It was sometimes a difficult balancing act, but he had no worries on that score.

No, his worries were much more personal, and they were centered on Sarah. He had come so close to failing her. A moment or two later, and she might have died. Aaron couldn't stop thinking about it.

As always seemed to happen, they gathered around the kitchen table. He suspected Mac would feel as odd about it as he would if they were ever ushered into the living room. The Bitler kitchen table had felt like home for a long time.

Aaron studied Sarah as her mother fussed around, trying to feed them as always. Sarah's face had regained much of the serenity that was such a part of her, though her blue eyes looked a little strained, as if she had a headache. It would be no wonder if she did. The bruise on her jaw where Harvey had struck her was turning purple, and from what her mother said, they'd had to put a couple stitches in her head. When he'd picked her up, she hadn't even seemed to be aware of the blood that stained her dress. All her attention had been on making sure Julia was all right.

Sarah seemed to feel his gaze on her, and she gave him a slow, sweet smile that stirred his heart. She would forgive him for his failure. Probably she already had. But he didn't think he could forgive himself.

"Well, you look like you've been through the wars, Sarah, but I'm glad you're going to be all right." Mac accepted the mug of coffee Hannah was handing him. "Julia's even better, as far as I can tell."

"Are you sure? They didn't let her go home alone, did they?" Concern filled Sarah's voice.

Mac grinned. "It was an interesting battle between her and the doctor, but she finally agreed to let them call the woman who's been helping out with the house. She's going to stay the night, just in case, but I doubt Julia will need her. She's a tough old bird."

Hannah gave him the kind of "mother look" that all mothers seemed to perfect, his own included.

"What?" Mac said innocently. "It's a compliment."

"I'm wonderful glad she's all right." Sarah shuddered a little. "When I saw Donna with that needle . . ."

Hannah patted her shoulder. "You don't need to think about it anymore. It's over."

"I know. But I must think about it, Mammi.

Mac will need me to read and sign my statement." She glanced at him, a question in her eyes. "Are they . . . are they both in jail?"

Mac nodded. "Locked up until and unless the judge decides to grant bail, which I'd say is unlikely. After all, you witnessed Donna attempt to kill Julia. We recovered the syringe. It was loaded with insulin. Apparently Donna's on insulin for diabetes, and she must have emptied every vial she had into that syringe."

Aaron hadn't known Donna Edwards was diabetic, but Sarah was nodding. "They won't let Harvey out of jail, will they?" She shivered, wrapping her arms around herself. Her mother moved a little closer, and Aaron had to suppress the urge to go and put his arms around her.

"I don't think so." Mac frowned. "He's lawyered up now, so we won't get anything else out of him, but Donna is willing to tell anyone and everyone how he was behind it all. And that he got rid of Gus because Gus knew. And I think it's telling that he locked the door after himself when he came in. He didn't want anyone walking in on him while he was mopping up witnesses."

"But what was it all about?" Eli had sat silent until now, but he obviously couldn't contain himself any longer. "I don't understand why they did it at all."

"Greed," Mac said succinctly. "Everybody

420

knows Harvey lost a lot in his divorce last year. According to Donna, Harvey found out that the medical center is thinking of building a medical research site in this area. He figured he could buy up the most desirable land, put it together in a package and sell it for a fancy payoff. But he couldn't let anyone know what was happening without messing up the whole deal."

"So the land he wanted ran from Julia's property to Ben Stoltzfus's to Matthew Gibson's." Eli's expression made it clear he didn't think much of that use of good agricultural land. "It seems chancy. They might have decided to build on another piece of land."

"I know. Harvey was desperate, I think. He wanted to make a big killing and get out of the area before anyone caught on."

"He got involved with Donna thinking she could influence Julia to sell," Sarah said. "I heard them say that. Paying Gus to set the fires was her job, and Gus wasn't supposed to know Harvey was behind it, but he found out."

Mac nodded. "Harvey's scheme started falling apart. Donna, not willing to wait for her money, took some things she thought Julia would never miss, but thanks to Sarah, she was found out. And Gus couldn't be relied on to follow orders. He set unnecessary fires and went after Sarah." Mac's face sobered. "He thought she knew something about him."

"The guilty flee where no man pursues," Eli said, his tone solemn.

Aaron stirred in his chair. "Was Harvey responsible for Matthew Gibson's death?"

"Good question." Mac's jaw tightened. "He's morally responsible, if not physically, but whether we can prove anything is another story. In any event, he'll be going to jail for a good long time. The DA seems inclined to go after him for Gus's death, feeling he can make a stronger argument there."

"It's up to the law now," Eli said. "You have done the best you can."

"Will the hospital still try to take over land here?" Hannah looked dismayed at the thought, and Aaron felt the same. Their lives would be forever changed if that happened.

Mac shrugged. "I'm no expert, but I'd guess the directors won't want to do anything that reminds people of this case once the whole thing is made public. They'll find some other site. But unfortunately the Gibson property will probably be locked up in litigation for years as the courts try to figure that one out."

Aaron wasn't as upset by that news as he might have been. Julia had spoken to him at the hospital while he was waiting for news of Sarah. She'd decided to sell the property, and she wanted him to have it. The price she had named was ridiculously low, but she'd insisted that it was fair since he'd have to spend a lot to get the place back into farming condition.

So that was one piece of his future settled. As for the rest . . . He looked at Sarah, unable to suppress the longing that welled up in him. Why had it taken so long for him to understand what he felt for her?

Now—well, now it was too late. He'd let her down. He'd promised himself he would never let another woman rely on his love to keep her safe, and he'd been right.

SARAH SIGNED HER name at the bottom of the typed statement of her words and prayed that she would not have to testify at a trial. Perhaps Harvey and Donna would repent, tell the truth and accept the consequences, but she couldn't bring herself to believe it. Well, if she had to testify, she would, and no doubt Aaron would do the same.

She looked across the table at him as he signed the bottom of his own statement. He looked so solemn. It was a serious thing, of course, but he hadn't smiled since he came in the door, it seemed to her. And he'd avoided her gaze.

Her heart hurt—an actual physical pain in her chest. Aaron was turning away from her. He would shut her out, and there was nothing she could do about it.

Nothing? Something inside her rebelled at the

thought. She'd believed that once before, and she'd ended up handing Aaron over to Mary Ann. Had she learned nothing since then?

If she planned to do something, she'd best do it soon. Mac and Aaron were already standing, saying their goodbyes as they moved to the door.

With an energy she thought had fled, Sarah shot to her feet and went after them. They were about to go down the steps as the screen door closed behind her.

"Aaron, wait." They both turned. "I'd like to talk to you, if you can stay a bit."

He didn't speak for a moment, and Mac gave him a nudge. "You heard her, Aaron. Sarah needs to talk." He grinned at her and went quickly to his car. "See you both later."

"You should rest." Aaron seemed to find his voice. "If it can wait—"

"No, it can't."

Her own boldness startled her, but she did wait until Mac was safely on his way. Behind her, she could hear Mamm hustling her father into the living room, with Daad objecting, not understanding. Finally their voices faded away, and Sarah was alone with Aaron.

She sucked in a breath, straightening her shoulders. She could do this. She had to, or be forever unhappy.

"Aaron, once before I failed to let you know

how I felt. I'm not going to do it again. You must know what I'm feeling. I love you. If you don't feel the same, I can accept it, but I can't pretend anymore. I'll always be your friend, but I want to be more."

Her courage faltered in the face of his failure to respond. She'd thought that if only she could say the words, surely he would answer. But he didn't, and she felt the blood drain from her face.

"Don't you care for me at all?" Her words came out as little more than a whisper. Her heart hurt so much that she put her hand against her chest, as if that would ease the pain.

Aaron's face twisted. "Sarah. My Sarah. I let you down. How can I say I love you when I let you down? You could have died."

My Sarah. The words seemed to sing in her ears, telling her all she needed to know.

"When will you stop being so foolish?" She grasped his arms, feeling she'd shake some sense into him if she had to. "You're not to blame for what happened. I stumbled into trouble by being in the wrong place at the wrong time, but God used it for good. I was there to save Julia. And you were there to save me."

His eyes were stormy, with hope seeming to battle with pain. "We almost weren't. Another couple of minutes—"

"You were in time. That's the important thing.

And even if you hadn't been . . ." She looked at him steadily. She loved him with all her heart, and it was important to get this right. "Even if you and Mac hadn't been in time, it wouldn't have been your fault. You are not God, Aaron. You couldn't save Mary Ann. If it had been my time, you couldn't have saved me. We can't work miracles for those we love. All we can do is love them."

She felt as if she'd forgotten to breathe. She watched the realization dawn in his eyes, saw hope and love replace the despair, and love flooded through her, exultant.

"Ach, Sarah. How did you get so wise?" His smile shook a little as he clasped her shoulders, drawing her toward him.

"Not wise. Just a little braver than I used to be." One day she'd tell him about that conversation she'd had with Mary Ann, but not now. Now belonged to them.

"I love you, Sarah." His voice was strong and sure. "When I was young and foolish I didn't even understand what love is. But now I do. I love you, and I want you to be my wife. I want us to be the family God intends for us to be."

She wrapped her arms around him. "We will be," she said, knowing she was at last where she belonged.

Aaron bent his face to hers, and she gave herself up to his kiss, holding him close, rejoicing in the solid feel of his arms around her, his body against hers.

Happiness flooded her, bubbling through every cell in her body, filling her with life and strength and hope. No more regretting the past. This time their lives had worked out the way they should.

EPILOGUE

SARAH STOOD IN the lobby of the old theater, watching with satisfaction as people passed through the door to the display area. It was hard to believe that just six weeks ago she'd been standing here, trying to decide where displays should go. Now the Laurel Ridge Quilt Festival was in full swing, and by any measure, it was a success.

She'd been glad they'd had the festival preparations to distract her in those days after the arrests. It had been a difficult time, and the curiosity of acquaintances and the questions of reporters had been hard to bear.

But the story had faded from the newspapers as the legal machinery began to grind slowly through the process. Other preoccupations replaced it in the public mind, and people stopped asking questions she couldn't or wouldn't answer.

Nodding to the volunteer who was manning the door, Sarah slipped into the main room. She'd felt apprehensive the first few times she'd come in, half expecting the lights to flicker off, but that fear had quickly vanished. She'd been too busy to pay attention to it. Now the room glowed with the bright and jewel-like colors of the quilts, displayed in rows, with a separate section holding those that were for display only, not for sale.

Julia's Baltimore album quilt had pride of place there, and it generated a lot of interest. Allison had put together a wonderful display, incorporating a family tree, with photos of the maker and a precious image of the woman whose bridal quilt it had been. Julia had spent most of the day lingering nearby, engaging people in conversation. Getting rid of the heavy cast had given her renewed energy, and her boundless enthusiasm was hard to keep up with.

Sarah's gaze searched the crowd until she saw Allison. Her partner was in her element, directing the proceedings with effortless grace.

The diamond ring on Allison's hand sparkled as she waved it, directing someone to the workshop area. She had succeeded in convincing Nick that she didn't need time, and they planned to be married at Christmas.

Becky hurried up to her, looking worried. "Sarah, are you sure you want me to do the workshop? I . . . I think I might be getting sick. My stomach feels all fluttery."

Sarah couldn't help smiling. "That's nerves, not sick. You're going to be fine. I'll come over when you're ready to start, and if you run into any trouble, I'll pitch in." She pressed her hand reassuringly. "Talking to strangers is a challenge, but I know you can do it."

Some of the tension slid from Becky's face.

"Denke, Sarah. I know I can count on you." She smiled. "Soon you'll be my new sister. I can't wait."

"I can't, either." She was filled with such happiness that she couldn't hide it. It just seemed to bubble out. For a moment they grinned at each other. Then, with a glance at the clock, Becky scurried away.

As if Sarah's appearance in the room was a signal, several other people came up to her. She fielded questions, gave explanations and soothed ruffled feelings. Finally everyone seemed satisfied, and she had a moment's respite.

Sarah felt someone stop behind her and knew without turning that it was Aaron. The link between them grew stronger each day, and she prayed it would continue to grow all their days.

"You aren't nervous about being here again, are you?" His breath stirred the hair at the nape of her neck.

She glanced briefly at the panel of switches on the side wall, where she'd cowered in such fear. "Not now. Just happy to see everything going so well. I think you're going to be amazed at the amount we'll donate to the fire company. This is beyond our hopes."

"And it's thanks to you and Allison. You make good partners, ain't so?"

"We do." Was he wondering how she felt about the changes that were coming? "Look at Becky, setting up for her workshop. She has so much more poise than I did at her age, and she loves the shop. She'll be able to take over whenever I need her to."

"You know I don't want you to give up something you love."

His tone was grave, and Sarah looked into his face, loving every line of it.

"I won't. But I'll want to spend more time at home with our girls after November."

That was the traditional wedding month for their church, and they would be wed the first Thursday in November. The happiness bubbled up again. Already her family and friends were engrossed in plans for the wedding, and the house and barn would be filled to bursting that day as their community celebrated with them.

"We have time to make up, the two of us," he said softly, his eyes glowing with the love and warmth she cherished.

She nodded, her hand pressing his for just an instant. "Things work out in God's own time," she said, needing to share the understanding that had been growing in her. "Because of Mary Ann, we have Anna and Lena to love. And because you married her, I had the shop, and I've grown so much from that experience. I think maybe our marriage will be all the stronger because of what we can bring to it now."

Aaron's fingers moved on her wrist, gently

caressing. "There are too many people around," he complained, his eyes laughing. "How am I supposed to kiss you now?"

"Later," she promised him, and her voice caught with longing on the word.

They had time, she reminded herself. With their community returned to normal and the promise of a future with Aaron, she had everything she could need or want.

Center Point Large Print
600 Brooks Road / PO Box 1
Thorndike, ME 04986-0001 USA

(207) 568-3717

US & Canada:
1 800 929-9108
www.centerpointlargeprint.com